WHEN THE WORLD STARTS TO FRAY

ANAGOVIA BOOK ONE

SAM PARRISH

SWAMP
SAGE
BOOKS

For everyone who dreams of adventure.

CONTENTS

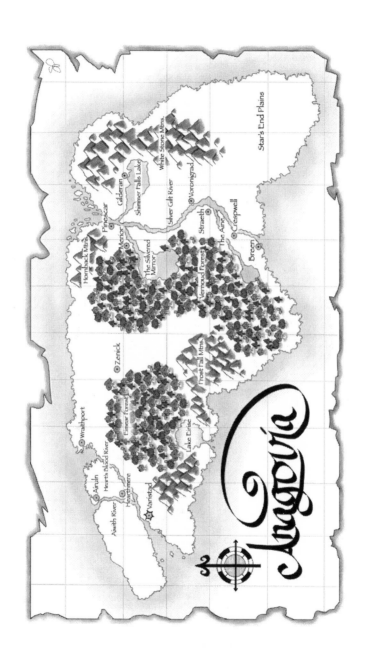

Prologue

41 years ago

The waters of the Rak-Shai Sea were a black so deep they seemed to swallow all light.

Ordelieus Thalken stood on the walls of Pinescar, gazing out at the great expanse of bay where the swamp met the ocean, shivering in the night air. Whether it was the void of the water or the hiss of the humid wind through the cypress trees, he couldn't shake off the feeling of being watched.

Resting his spear in the crook of his arm, he swiped his helmet off and ruffled his dark hair, mentally berating himself for his fatigue. He was on edge. Had been for weeks. War was looming on the horizon and every soldier in Pinescar was running on precious little sleep.

"Dreaming of your bed?" a familiar voice came from behind him.

Ordelieus started and spun around. His sergeant stood behind him, arms crossed over his barrel of a chest, an easy smile on his lips.

"No, sir. Of course not." He slapped his helmet back on and snapped into a crisp salute, right fist to his chest.

Sergeant Vernulf chuckled and came up to stand beside Ordelieus against the pine logs that made up the wall of the city.

"It's alright. You work too hard and I know you didn't volunteer for this watch because you enjoy it."

It was true. Ordelieus's wife, Milla, had just given birth to their third child and wasn't ready to return to work. Meanwhile, their other two children were outgrowing shoes and clothes at an alarming rate. They needed the money, so Ordelieus jumped at the opportunity to take on a second shift.

"That easy to read, eh?" he conceded, self-consciously brushing a few specks of dirt off his chain shirt.

"You are," Vernulf said with a laugh. "Don't fret, I completely understand. My own are likely to eat me out of house and home."

Ordelieus chuckled, but the spear in his grip wouldn't let him forget the other reason he was standing guard that night- the reason all the guards were being offered double shifts in the first place. "Has there been any news of the war?"

Vernulf pushed away from the wooden battlements with a sigh. "Nothing new since yesterday. The Rak-Shai are still moving in on Wraithport. But stay vigilant."

"Yes, sir."

Vernulf strolled along the wall towards the guard tower about fifty paces away, the light of the full moon reflecting off his armor. Ordelieus was once again alone with his growing sense of unease. He shifted his grip on his spear, adjusted his sword belt just to be sure, and looked back out towards the water.

A shadow pulled around one of the mangrove islands in the bay.

A ship. As it drew closer, Ordelieus could see the continual shifting of multiple triangular sails, could see how low the ship sat in the water as it cut through the pitch-black waves. And on its bow, a bright white serpent coiled, shining in the moonlight, its mouth opened towards the city. Muffled oars rose and fell along its sides, speeding it silently forward.

"Rak-Shai," he whispered.

He backed away from the wall, his heart leaping into his throat as a second and third ship slipped into the bay.

The war had finally found Pinescar.

"Rak-Shai!" he yelled as he bolted towards the guard station and the warning bell at the top of the tower.

Vernulf stopped dead in his tracks and spun toward the port. "*Shit*," he hissed as Ordelieus raced by. "Men! To arms!"

Fire sprang to life on the ships as he ran. Out of the corner of his eye he saw the bright points of light arc up and across the bay, thudding into the longships and brigantines lining the docks. The tar used to seal the hulls and sails burst into flame.

Ordelieus flew through the open doorway and into the guard tower. Four more guards sat around a battered table throwing dice.

"Rak-Shai in the harbor! Get your weapons!" Ordelieus yelled. He snagged spears and bows off a weapon rack and tossed them at the men, not even waiting to see if they were ready. If the idiots couldn't react fast enough for that, they were doomed anyway.

"The bell! Alert the Weavers!" he bellowed up the stairwell before dashing back out onto the wall.

Panic had wound its way between Ordelieus's ribs, but

his training took over and guided his feet to his station. He was back at the battlements, beside his fellow soldiers and stringing his bow as well, before the bell started ringing. It tolled a deep, hollow peal that echoed across Pinescar. In a matter of moments, signal bells all across the city answered.

By then, there were eight ships bearing down on the city and likely even more just out of sight. They were close enough that the flash of bared steel was visible on the deck of every ship. Soldiers, and lots of them. Sweat slicked Ordelieus's palms and ran into his dark eyes, but he widened his stance and took a steadying breath. He would be ready if the new regiment of Weavers fell.

He hated not knowing what to expect from the so-called blessed warriors of the Seamstress. The goddess had only made herself and her chosen soldiers known a few months ago. This contingent had arrived only two weeks prior, greeted with a celebration fit for visiting nobility. Ordelieus had only caught glimpses of the mysterious soldiers since then, and he hadn't seen anything particularly impressive. But he was prepared in case they should fail. He nocked an arrow and waited for the ships to come into range.

Movement on the docks pulled his attention away from the invaders. The Weavers had arrived and were filing out onto the longest dock in the harbor.

There were only twenty of them to face down the incoming army. All of them wore simple black leather in the place of useful armor with nothing denoting rank, just the silver star of the Anagovian crest on their backs. Ordelieus's eyes darted from one Weaver to another as he searched the group for any kind of weapon. There were none. They were completely unarmed and *completely* unprepared.

Then, as one, the soldiers reached their hands forward, drew back, and flicked their hands out like they were cracking a whip. Tiny flashes of light flared and died out over the bay, like fireflies. As the sparks faded, the water heaved.

A large wave rolled out towards the invading ships and their progress slowed to a crawl. The Weavers all reached to the right and their hands closed in white-knuckled fists, like they were trying to pry apart iron bars. The tiny lights crackled around them as they heaved back to the left. A towering wave rose up from the black water and crashed against the side of the lead ship. The water rolled over the deck, capsizing the vessel as it went. Faint screams echoed over the water, reaching all the way to where Ordelieus stood.

Impossible.

"Hold your places!" Sergeant Vernulf yelled. Before them, the Weavers created another wave and sunk a second ship, then a third, and a fourth. "Just look at that. Amazing, isn't it? We're just a redundancy tonight. No way they're getting past that."

"What exactly *is* that?" Ordelieus asked, but Vernulf didn't hear him over the crashing of the waves, the cries of the dying, the groan of breaking wood. He just kept walking.

Ordelieus stood with the rest of the guards and watched as the Weavers churned the water in the bay into froth. He scanned the shores and the piers, but none of the Rak-Shai made it out of the water. The animated waves threw them from the ships and dragged them straight to the bottom. They never stood a chance.

The Seamstress was a vicious goddess to give her chosen such terrible power.

"Corporal Thalken!" Vernulf's voice carried over the crashing of the waves.

Ordelieus was so engrossed in the one-sided carnage that he barely heard his commander. The words didn't click into place; it was just more noise joining in with the rest.

"Ordelieus!"

He flinched and turned, falling into another hasty salute. Vernulf's voice carried an edge in it that left no room for any other kind of response. Scores of soldiers and civilians had crowded onto the top of the wall- another thing he hadn't noticed- and his sergeant's face was lost in the crowd. A cheer went up as the last Rak-Shai warship toppled under the waves.

"Run an update to the general. Tell him the Weavers were successful. The Rak-Shai have been crushed."

"Yes, sir!"

Ordelieus left his bow and spear with the other defenders and squeezed through the crowd before making for the closest set of stairs leading back down into the city.

Compared to the crowded wall, the streets of Pinescar were strangely empty. Before the war, the trade city had been a bustling hub of commerce between Anagovia and Rak-Shai. After the first attack from their neighbor across the sea, Pinescar had become an important staging ground for the war, citizens and soldiers alike balancing on the edge of a blade, waiting for the day when they would be called into battle.

But now, Ordelieus's footsteps were the only ones echoing off the walls as he jogged towards the barracks where the general was waiting.

Gravel crunched behind him and Ordelieus whirled, reaching for his sword. But nothing was there, not even a flicker of movement. He kept his sword loose in the scabbard and turned back towards his destination.

The gravel crunched behind him again, this time in the unmistakable pattern of footsteps. Ordelieus spun to face whoever it was but found that his hand was frozen on his sword's hilt. He couldn't draw his weapon, his fingers as still and heavy as a statue's. A familiar tightness took hold of his lungs, restricting his breath, even as his heart broke into a gallop. He took deep, even breaths and fought to stay calm.

A cloaked figure stepped into the street in front of him, the cowl of the cloak drawn to conceal their face.

"Weapons won't be needed," an odd, androgynous voice rasped from under the cowl. "I'd much rather just talk."

"Show yourself." Ordelieus tried to walk towards them, but his feet refused to obey him. "What in the name of the gods?" he muttered.

"Trust me, soldier, the gods, the Seamstress, none of them have anything to do with this. They really don't have much to do with anything at all."

Ordelieus gritted his teeth and strained. His feet didn't budge, his hand didn't draw his sword. He needed help, but no one was likely to come. All the people in the city were distracted, probably even beginning to celebrate Anagovia's victory. He doubted he could ever be loud enough to get a guard's attention over that.

"No, no, no. I see what you're planning. We don't need others interfering," they said, chuckling.

Ordelieus's heart pounded against his ribs and he fought against his own body to draw breath. Did they really just read his mind?

Inhale for three counts, exhale for three counts, he told himself.

"You seem like a hard-working man and you'd make a

good leader- firm, with a fire in you. I was watching you on the wall. Those men respected you. I need someone like you for a... very special job."

"I feel like I'm going to have to refuse."

Ordelieus railed against whatever was holding him, but still he was locked in place. He hadn't shifted an inch.

There was no fighting his panic then. All he could think of was never getting home to his wife and children. Terrible images of what they might have to resort to flashed across his mind's eye and he threw all his weight against whatever was holding him. The force locked around his entire body like a vice and *squeezed*. He cringed, taking his eyes off the cloaked figure for a split second.

When he looked back up, he gasped. They were mere inches from Ordelieus's face.

A sharp smell, like the air after a lightning strike, rolled out from under the dark cowl as the stranger spoke.

"This isn't an offer you're capable of refusing, Ordelieus."

A crushing pain wrapped itself around Ordelieus's skull as a massive weight landed on his shoulders and forced him to the ground. The pressure on his head increased and he cried out, then utter darkness fell over him and he knew no more.

Chapter One

A Good Reputation

Now

For three days, storms had battered the twenty merchant wagons as they lumbered down the road from Crespwell to Breen. Three days of bogged-down wagons, horses with missing shoes, and no cook fires for warm meals. Li'or Halwyn- originally hired as lead guard for the trip- had quickly turned into lead farrier and primary mud-mover. The twenty-five silver stars she'd charged the merchant weren't nearly enough.

She still regretted her low price, even when the clouds finally parted. The wagons bumped along the road on squeaking wheels, drivers called back and forth to each other, and laughter rang out from up and down the line. There were nineteen other swords for hire that she'd been keeping organized during the short trip. Together they formed a loose circle around the wagons as they rattled along.

"Li'or! My dear! Up this way, if you would?" Yorren,

the owner of all the wagons in the caravan, called to her from the front of the line.

Li'or sighed, pushing her horse into an easy canter and riding to the front where Yorren rode with his nephew. He was an aging, round-bellied man with hardly a hair left on his head; it had all moved to his cheeks in a wild, snarled beard. He was a rarity, an honest and hardworking merchant. He was also one of Li'or's favorite men to work for, hence the reason she was on her fourth trip guarding his wagons.

"We should be seeing the gates of Breen before night-fall tomorrow, and it's about time! Didn't expect all that rain to catch us so early," he said with a cheerful chuckle. "Thank the gods I was able to find you again for this trip. The animals would all be barefoot and we'd be lucky to make it to Breen before the snows came if you hadn't been here to patch us all together! The gods of the sky really gave us a show, eh?"

Li'or paused, one of her eyebrows lifting.

"You keep to the old gods?"

"Eh, well, you know," he said with a shrug. "I'm an old man. I was already grown by the time the Seamstress showed up and started making people into Weavers. I'll stick to what I know."

Li'or nodded. It wasn't often she met people that kept to the old gods. The revelation only made her respect Yorren more. He hadn't flocked to the Seamstress crowd like so many others.

Now, if only he wasn't quite so loud...

But he was right, the gods of the sky had rained torment down on them. It hadn't taken long for the roads to turn to mush in the relentless downpour and many of Yorren's horses had their shoes simply sucked off in the deep mud. Li'or had been able to nail them back on, all the while thinking in the back of her mind how much more practical oxen were. Oxen were stronger and didn't wear shoes, but Yorren always pointed out that they didn't make as flashy of an entrance as a matching set of horses.

"Gods and goddesses aside, thank you again for riding with us," Yorren said earnestly. He reached into the pockets of his trousers and pulled out a small coin purse. "Humor an old man and accept a small bonus? I know you don't work for free and you've worked twice as hard as usual with all this rain."

Li'or grinned and reached down from her tall bay gelding's saddle and accepted the purse. It was polite to refuse a gift twice before accepting it, but she'd earned it. It had been a rough few days. "Thank you. I'm going to run a quick loop around the wagons. This mud could still pull a shoe." She didn't comment that a few of the guards needed more hands-on management and that she needed to make sure they weren't drinking. She'd tell Yorren not to hire them again once they got to town, when they'd all left to go their separate ways.

"Of course, of course. Let the others know we're riding all the way until dark! Make up for lost time! I swear I can already smell the sea." Yorren waved her off and immediately turned to his nephew, a soft-looking boy of about ten with fair hair and skin, and launched into a lecture on the differences between various types of silk. Li'or smiled at the boy as she turned around. He looked like he would rather have been walking than endure that particular speech.

Moving her gelding up into a canter again, Li'or headed against the flow of the wagons, her long braid trailing behind her. She stopped and got updates with each guard as she went, most of them inclining their heads and treating her with respect. She was nearing her one hundred and fiftieth year, the last thirty of which she'd spent building a reputation for herself among the sell-sword circles. She'd only had a few issues with insubordination along the way, but that was expected with any group of mercenaries.

She'd been lucky. Being an elf meant most people expected her to be mysterious and wise, whether that's how she really felt or not. So she had easily slipped into leadership positions and learned to fill those shoes along the way.

After making her rounds, she reported back to the front to Yorren, who had moved the subject of his lecture from silk trading to bartering strategy.

"Yorren… Yorren!"

"Li'or! All is well, I trust?" He was grinning ear to ear.

"The mud is still a hindrance, but there's not a lame horse, bandit, or zhu'dac to be seen," she replied, smiling as well. She had always tried to keep a professional distance from all her employers, but Yorren was so damned likable. Between that and how long she'd worked for him, he'd started to work his way under her skin. It saddened her, but this would have to be the last time she rode with him. She felt herself getting too attached.

"As I knew it would be with you along for the trip! My boy!" Yorren exclaimed as he slapped his nephew's back so hard the boy was almost thrown from his seat. He latched on to the armrest at the last moment. "If Mistress Li'or is still running with caravans when you take your first trip, you'd be a fool not to bring her along."

The boy glanced up at Li'or and a blush crept from the collar of his shirt, well up into his hairline, and he quickly looked the other way, causing Yorren and Li'or both to laugh. Yorren grabbed the boy up in a one-armed hug and dropped the reins to ruffle his hair.

Li'or looked away out over the plains and sighed as a

familiar twinge twisted in her chest. A breeze rolled over the grass, rippling the blades like water, blowing south right alongside the caravan. As she watched, the wind abruptly changed direction. The grass stilled and then bent to the north as the wind swept back towards the wagons. Only a few small clouds floated by, interrupting the perfect blue of the sky. It didn't look like they would be in store for another storm today, no more violent wind or rain.

Then a few tiny motes of light flared and died on the wind- a telltale sign of Altering.

She frowned, eyeing the clouds a little longer then looked back towards Yorren.

"Yorren, do we have a Weaver in the caravan?"

"Li'or, dear, you know I tell you about everyone and everything in my wagons. If we'd had a Weaver, it would have been the first thing I'd have told you."

Li'or nodded absently and went back to making her rounds.

For the rest of the day, Li'or stayed on patrol around the entirety of the caravan. The odd shifting of the grass and the flickers of light made her uneasy, so she sent out scouts as well. Normally, she would have expected complaints, but the hired swords grinned as they cantered off. That, of course, only made her frown. Hopefully, they'd do what she told them.

Li'or herself rode circles around the caravan, pausing here and there beside a wagon to take in the surroundings and check on the wagoners before moving on once again. Her main concern this close to Breen was bandits. The beast-like zhu'dac that ranged through the mountains weren't a threat in the Silver Gilt River basin. They didn't tend to go far from their caves and typically didn't move in large enough groups to threaten an entire caravan. They weren't smart enough.

True to his word, Yorren kept the wagon train going until the sun started to disappear behind the horizon. The sparse clouds glowed in shades of pink and gold as the light faded around them. All the wagon drivers moved with practiced efficiency to arrange the wagons end-to-end in a large circle, then herded all the oxen and horses into the center where they were hobbled for the night, brushed down, and fed. The merchant's wives and the hired cooks all came out of their wagons, bringing with them spits for roasting meat and pots for tea and stew. The lively mood that had come with the departure of the rain carried into the evening. One man even pulled a gudok and bow out from one of the wagons and played while a few people danced.

Li'or watched them all with a contented sense of detachment. Humans lived their fleeting lives with an enthusiasm and recklessness that she couldn't understand, even though their company was all she had ever known. It was as if they tried to fit as many life experiences into their short time as they could, even if some of those things were outright dangerous. But she wasn't sad. Keeping them all at arm's length was better in the long run. She'd experienced more than enough loss while watching her village grow old and die around her. Let them live their fast-paced, abbreviated lives without her. Eternity loomed over her shoulder. That they could never understand.

She watched for a time while she groomed and fed her horse, then ate her own dinner. As the revelry died down and people began retiring to their wagons and bed-rolls, she got up to take one last patrol for the night to ensure all the night's guards were set.

She ducked down and crawled under one of the wagons, coming out right near the feet of a guard. She glanced up as she rose and had to fight to keep the scowl off her face. Terric stood watching her, his arms crossed and a smug look on his face.

"You know what kinds of things crawl around on the ground?" he asked. "Poisonous snakes, carrion beetles, yo-"

"You forget yourself, Terric." Li'or said, brushing off the knees of her breeches.

"I forget nothing," he scoffed.

She frowned. Terric was notoriously difficult to work with. He had unwittingly built himself a reputation for insubordination, limiting the number of people who would hire him. It was unfortunate because he was good with a sword and had enough of an analytical mind that he would make a good leader. But he was just blighted mean.

"That is true. Meanwhile, I seem to have forgotten the watch schedule tonight. I thought I was stationed here." She crossed her arms and tried to look disappointed.

In the low light of the torch, it must have been convincing. Terric gave her a look halfway between a glare and a smirk. "I don't know how you keep getting hired as captain of these little jobs. Has to be for the novelty of a woman running about in men's clothing. You're not until the last shift, *Captain*. I have this one with Leif- that lad's Threads are all tangled- Bootstrap, Bodell, Clicks- he's too damned old for this- and Dathen. Right useless, that one. I had to give them all a swift kick in the arse, but they're in place." He put his hands on his hips and spit.

Li'or fought down a smirk. "Well, perfect. That's all I needed to know. I'll leave it in your capable hands."

Terric just scowled and turned away from her. She allowed herself a smile as she crawled under the wagon and back into the protective ring of the camp. No matter how many times she played him, it never got old.

She wandered back over to where the horses were

hobbled and spread her bedroll near a supply wagon. Lying down, she watched the stars until she drifted into sleep, lulled by the steady sound of the horses nibbling on grass.

*

THE CARAVAN GOT off to a late start the next day and it wasn't until after noon that the city finally came into view on the horizon. Breen was a large port city that shipped wares from all up and down the Silver Gilt River across the sea and south to foreign markets in Vaeshek. The walls of the city were tall and stark white with a heavy black gate facing the north. Li'or made her way up to the front of the caravan and rode alongside Yorren as they approached the entranceway.

When they were still about a quarter of a mile out from the city, a horn rang out over the top of the walls and the gates swung open with a loud groan. No less than fifty soldiers in black and white armor poured out of the city, Breen's black and white banner snapping behind them as they charged.

"What in the name of the gods..." Yorren muttered. He held up his hand and signaled for the caravan to come to a stop.

Li'or reined in beside him and watched the soldiers race across the field towards them. She'd heard the lord was eccentric, but surely this kind of greeting was unusual even for him. She shifted in her saddle, feeling anxious.

An odd noise drifted towards them from over a hill to their right. It swelled and morphed into a low howling. Li'or's heart leapt into her throat.

"Yorren, signal the guards!" She kicked her horse forward and swung around in between Yorren's wagon and whatever was coming. "And send the women and children into the wagons!"

"What is that noise?"

"The gods-damned signal, Yorren!" Li'or snapped. She stepped off her horse and quickly strung her bow and nocked an arrow.

The howling rose in pitch and a mob of zhu'dac flooded over the hill, more of the creatures than she'd ever seen in one place. The beasts never moved in such large numbers; they were too aggressive and fought too much amongst themselves. What she was seeing defied logic. But still they came, waving their rusted swords and make-shift clubs in their clawed hands, saliva and foam flying from their canine-like muzzles. They charged towards the caravan.

Li'or glanced back towards Breen's soldiers. They weren't going to get to them in time. A few of the zhu'dac pulled ahead of the pack, running on all fours like wolves.

Li'or gritted her teeth and loosed an arrow. It took one of the closest beasts in the chest and it fell with a yelp. She grabbed another arrow and repeated the process, scoring another kill, but there had to have been close to a hundred of them. Two wouldn't matter. A few of the other guards got themselves together and launched some arrows into the mob with questionable success. It still wouldn't be enough.

Before she could stop and think about her odds, she swung herself back into her saddle and drew her sword with a rasp. The soldiers from the city were in a full charge, but they still wouldn't make it in time. By the time they rammed into the flank of the zhu'dac horde, the creatures would already be ripping the wagons apart.

"Form up!" she screamed to the guards. "We're meeting them out there, away from the caravan!" She could at least buy them some time. "Yorren… when we charge, you get into the city."

She didn't even look towards him as she frantically tried to come up with a plan. She only had nineteen guards. It was going to be a massacre.

"Piss on this!" Terric yelled. "I'm not dying for some trader." He spurred his horse toward the city. A few others hesitated then peeled off after him. Li'or's heart caved in on itself. Fifteen.

There was no more time. Ten guards had gathered while the others tried to usher the people into their wagons. That would have to be enough. She set her heels into her horse and they leaped forward.

It was pandemonium. Her guards' battle cries cut off as they collided with the zhu'dac. Her horse leaped and swerved as he struck out with his hooves. Li'or clung tightly with her knees and swept her sword in great arcs, trying to catch as many of the beasts as she could. They fell around her and she surged forward only to meet with another wall of bodies. Her horse reared and darted to the side. He kicked out with his hind legs and nailed one square in the chest. The zhu'dac was shoved backward and into two of the others, but she was still forced to yield ground as more swarmed forward to take their place.

Li'or risked a glance towards the reinforcements and she nearly dropped her sword.

The soldiers had stopped and were lining up their archers, all the armored cavalry in the back. She scanned the contingent and found the commanding officer off to the side, flanked by guards and wearing a ridiculous plume on his helmet. He was going to let them die, possibly kill some of them with misplaced arrows.

She yelled in frustration and urged her horse forward with renewed purpose. Zhu'dac fell to either side of her horse as she lathed her sword back and forth in a rage. She pushed harder, claws raking her legs and catching in the leather of her saddle until she finally surged out of the horde. Her gelding stretched low over the ground and they barreled towards the officer.

"What in the five realms are you doing?" she demanded when she reached him, her horse sliding to a stop.

The bastard sneered at her through a bushy blond mustache. "We're about to kill zhu'dac, obviously."

"You're about to kill my men!"

"A few mercenaries is a small price to pay when Breen and her people are in danger."

The clamor of the battle and the fleeing wagons rang in Li'or's ears. She glanced down at her sword, coated with blood and matted with brindle zhu'dac fur. She hated the poor reputation that men like Terric gave swords for hire. She'd spent too long building a good reputation to be treated like a mangy stray, and she had good men and women working for her on this trip. Her resolve hardened and she whipped her blade up to the officer's throat. Metal sang as all his guards drew their swords.

"Call them off of me and send them in to fight. Now."

"What do you think you're doing?" he stammered.

"What's right. Now send them into the fight before I lose my patience. Your guards may get me, but not before I get you first." Blood dripped from her sword and landed on the officer's white breastplate.

"There will be repercussions for this, elf," he spat, face blazing red.

"I'll deal with that later." She met his eyes, unblinking.

"Men! A wedge formation! Charge the zhu'dac!"

Li'or waited until she heard the concussion of the calvary hitting the mass of creatures before she lowered her sword. A quick glance over her shoulder showed the zhu'dac mass shattering under the hammer that was the cavalry, many turning tail in full retreat.

"I wonder, has the punishment for blatantly disobeying your superiors changed since I was in Breen last, or are you still completely stripped of all rank?" she asked.

The officer's face deepened from red to purple, telling her all she needed to know. He'd made the decision to use only archers against his superior's orders.

"Who are you to question how I command my soldiers?"

"I'm just a mercenary. Anyway, I'll take my question to General Vidgar. It's been a while since we've shared a pint." She cast him a bitter smile over her shoulder and charged back into the fray, indignant stuttering following after her.

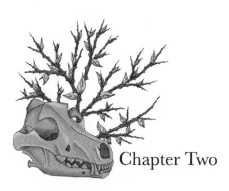

Chapter Two

Expected

*H*ashkan Clearont tried his best to read a scroll while swaying on the upper deck of the ship as it pulled towards the port in Breen. A large swell sprayed over the railing and plastered his dark hair to his forehead, nearly ruining his scroll. He jerked his arms up at the last second and barely kept the documents dry. His gray Weaver's robes didn't fare quite so well. He scowled and stood up, miffed. He had booked passage with the trader that owned this ship in order to get here quickly from Varistad and he was convinced it was the worst decision he had ever made in his twenty-four years.

It had taken the better part of the month to get around the Vernoud Forest Peninsula and he had been sick for about nine-tenths of the time. Here towards the end, he had finally found his "sea legs" and had been able to try and enjoy the remainder of the trip. Unfortunately, the activity of the crew had tripled as they prepared to make port, so it was either be jostled on deck or sit in his dark hole of a room. And so, he had sworn to himself that he would not travel by water again, no matter how quick and convenient it may seem.

But he was finally arriving. They were pulling into the bay and Hashkan could see the masses of black roofs and the bright white walls enclosing the city. All the noises of the port could be heard echoing off the walls and water. A sailor stepped up into his peripheral vision.

"Apologies Weaver, but I need to get to those ropes behind you." She gestured to the ropes attached to the main sail and averted her gaze.

Hashkan sighed and struggled to keep the patient demeanor expected from his position. *Seamstress*, he could not wait to get off that ship.

"Don't apologize, madam. I've got to finish gathering my things, anyway." He forced a smile and she bowed as he walked off.

Hashkan went below the deck to his room and collected his few belongings. He had five scrolls on Altering theory, three bound books of blank paper for taking notes, and a few changes of clothes. Even with the extra care he took while packing the scrolls, he was still finished long before they were at the docks. He was on deck waiting as the ship slid into its place in the harbor and his feet were the first to hit dry land.

All eyes were on the Weaver as he strolled down the gangplank. As hard as he'd fought to grow accustomed to the swaying of the ship, now he found himself fighting for balance on dry land. He clenched his jaw and struggled to keep his footing but held on to his cool exterior. His pride refused to let them see him struggle. He was a Weaver. A Weaver didn't struggle.

Everywhere around him, men and women scrambled around the pier carrying goods, loading and unloading ships and wagons. Here horse-drawn carts wheeled away, loaded down with fish, and across the way, pulleys on huge rotating arms lifted boxes and swung them onto the boats on creaking, straining ropes. It seemed every other person was trying to sell something they had just pulled off a ship or trying to get rid of things they didn't want to take with them. It reeked of fish and the salt of the ocean.

And it was so crowded! Hashkan had spent the last ten years of his life studying and serving at the Seamstress's Gathering in Harthmere, hardly ever leaving. The only crowds he saw were the ones that came to worship in the Sanctuary. Now he found himself having to walk sideways through what tiny gaps he could find in the crowd. He took his pack off his back and carried it across his chest, concerned about cut-purses in the thick mob. He hadn't been to Breen before, so he pushed through the crowd trying to get out onto the main road where he could find a guard and ask for directions to the Gathering.

He finally got out of the massive press of people around the docks and had walked only three steps into the main road before he was nearly run down by a carriage that was moving at a canter *into* the mob of people moving along the dockside road. He stared after it, incredulous, as people jumped out of its way, the coachman yelling warnings and profanities as he went.

"By the Seamstress…" he muttered. This city was nothing like sleepy Harthmere.

He moved out of the middle of the broad road and started walking close to the storefronts and away from the floods of people, squeezing his thin frame between the crowds and the walls of the buildings. He kept his eyes open and, fortunately, didn't have a hard time spotting a guard in their black and white uniform.

"Excuse me, can you direct me towards the Gathering?" he asked.

The guard took one look at Hashkan's Weaver's robes and silver eyes before snapping to attention. "Of course, Weaver. In fact, I'd be glad to escort you there myself." The guard bowed to him, also.

Hashkan fought down a smirk. He'd been expecting the escort offer, but it was still always pleasant to get the treatment his status deserved.

"That would be much appreciated, thank you."

"It's to the north in the city square. Right this way, along this road. The Land-and-Sea. It was named that since it connects the port to the northern gates."

"Of course."

The guard kept rambling as they walked, his nerves evidently compelling him to spew endless amounts of trivia. Hashkan nodded and made polite remarks when necessary.

The square at the center of town was itself impossible to miss. The entire thing was set with black and white mosaic tiles, making up the image of multiple massive waves at the crest of which sat the lord's palace. As he walked across the tiles, tiny details, like the swirls of currents and sea creatures, could be seen hiding within the bigger image. Hashkan tried not to look like he was gawking. Newcomers to the city were easy to spot as they ambled around the square, heads bowed and marveling at the details in the mosaic. A Weaver had to have more dignity than that.

The Gathering was easy to find. Like a small forest thrust into the center of the city, tall pines and oaks looked out at him from over the garden walls made out of the same white stone found in the rest of the city. The trees were so ancient and thick that they blocked the roofs of the

Weaver living quarters within from view. Black gates stood open into the square displaying a circular clearing edged with a multitude of tiny white flowers. Hashkan glanced at the gates as he passed through into a shaded clearing. They were carved into the likeness of the four elements, all woven together like the Fabric of existence itself.

The guard bowed again and left Hashkan to pass through the gates alone. Gravel crunched to his right and a young girl dressed in white apprentice robes came down a path between two wide evergreens. She looked to be about ten years old.

"Is there something that we can help you with?"

The voice came from behind her. Hashkan looked up and saw a tall, thin man looking down at him. He wore deep crimson robes and had a neatly trimmed beard, more white than black. His face was narrow and pale, made entirely of sharp angles. His silver eyes pierced through Hashkan and held him in place.

"Yes," Hashkan said as he drew himself up straight. "My name is Hashkan Clearont. I should be expected. I came here to assist the High Weaver with his studies."

"I see. Well, I didn't expect you to be so young after reading all the things you've mastered already. You had quite the list of accomplishments. And you were ranked in the second tier, correct?"

"Upper second tier…" Hashkan shifted his bags on his shoulder uncomfortably.

The thin man smirked down at him.

"Second tier. Exactly. All the same, right this way. Milling around in the gateway gives the impression that we don't have other work to be doing." He turned on his heel and strode deeper into the Gathering, the apprentice following in his wake.

Hashkan stood in the gateway for a split second longer,

gaping, before trailing behind them through the trees. "Excuse me, sir, but just for clarity's sake, are you High Weaver Skaen Liestenin?"

The man didn't even turn to look at Hashkan as he swept through the immaculately tended garden. "Of course I am. Who else do you think would be able to welcome you into my Gathering? The help? An apprentice? I should think not."

Hashkan nearly tripped over his own feet. Greeted at the gates by the High Weaver himself? And one with such a prestigious reputation! He tried not to let his excitement at his new assignment be tempered by the frigid welcome. He had heard the High Weaver was a tough but effective teacher, but he had not heard that he was as charming as the ocean in winter. He set his jaw and pushed a hand through his dark hair. He would not be warded off so easily.

"Your quarters are here off the east side of the Sanctuary," Liestenin said.

He gestured towards a group of small buildings to the left of the path. They had white walls and black roofs just like the city outside. Another Weaver stepped out of the front door of her room. When she noticed the small procession, she bowed, two right forefingers pressed to her temple. Hashkan paused to bow back while the High Weaver swept past the woman with hardly a nod.

Rude.

"You will have an apartment to yourself. The kitchen and dining building is to the north of the Sanctuary. My chefs typically serve breakfast at first light, lunch at noon, and dinner at twilight. They do not provide tea or snacks. I find people who take those to be slovenly…"

He continued on in this manner, laying out more rules for Hashkan's stay as they walked the whole of the property. The Gathering was very large and painstakingly land-scaped, right down to the tiniest of details. Weavers and apprentices flocked everywhere, weeding, watering, and trimming plants both native and exotic. Benches and tables were scattered under the trees and near the fountains and reflection pools, all painted black or white and carved with designs just as intricate as the ones on the front gates. All the statutes of the Seamstress and of Her Loom were even black and white and at least the height of two men. To Hashkan, it made Her look stark and uninviting, but he bit his tongue as he trailed behind the High Weaver like a duckling.

On either side of the Sanctuary were more clusters of apartments, similar to the one Hashkan would be staying in. Behind them was a small but impressive herb garden, which he learned he would be in charge of while he was there as payment for his stay.

Hashkan groaned inwardly. He hated chores. He had not been in charge of caring for a garden for years, not since he had first learned to Alter earth and stone. It grated that he would be expected to attend to things normally left to the apprentices- he was a full-fledged Weaver, after all. But Liestenin was rumored to be on the verge of an Altering breakthrough and Hashkan wanted in. If he had to garden to get there, then garden he would.

After a full tour of the Gathering, the High Weaver brought Hashkan back to his quarters.

"I will expect you at breakfast and once that has been finished, we've got to go through some testing. I need to be sure you're at the level you claim. Not everyone is what they say they are. I'll see you at dinner if you would like to attend." With that, the High Weaver turned on his heel and walked away, following the branch in the path that led back into the Sanctuary, the apprentice scurrying along at his heels.

Once they turned the corner, Hashkan let out the sigh he had been holding in. The High Weaver's abrupt greeting made him feel like he was still trudging through his apprenticeship. He rolled his shoulders, trying to shake it off, and opened the door to where he would be staying.

The black door swung forward without a sound into a small bedroom. A narrow bed with a thick mattress was tucked against one wall, while two plush chairs competed for space with a large bookcase on the other side of the room. A small chest sat at the foot of the bed for his clothing. Another door on the rear wall led to a private bathing room. True to the theme of the rest of the Gathering and the city itself, everything was clad in black and white. His rooms were exactly what he'd expected- and normal for a Weaver living in a Gathering- but with finer fabrics and more decorative details.

It felt like luxury compared to his closet of a room onboard the ship.

Hashkan put his small pack on the floor next to the chest and hurled himself onto the mattress. Despite his excitement, apprehension hovered in the back of his mind like a fly that was too quick to swat. What would tomorrow have in store?

THE NEXT MORNING, Hashkan rose, dressed, and was in the dining building just as the Gathering's volunteers began setting out breakfast. He took a seat at the far end, a couple seats down from the head of the table where he imagined the High Weaver would sit when he came in.

Hashkan waited, impatiently tapping his fingers against

the rosewood table, while the meal was set out before him. There were several pastry options, toasted bread, various sausages and sliced ham, freshly cooled milk, cheeses, pots of tea, fruits of every kind, and eggs- scrambled, poached, and boiled. It seemed the people of Breen were unusually generous with their donations to the Gathering.

It seemed so wasteful. Based on all the Weavers and apprentices he'd seen yesterday, there was too much food and too many seats at the table.

The High Weaver swept in, draped in red once again, just as the help finished setting down the last dish. The man sat down without a word, just a tight smile aimed at Hashkan and the others who had trickled in. Right after Liestenin took his place, all the servers took seats at the table and began helping themselves to the food.

Hashkan sat in stunned silence. It was one thing for the apprentices to eat with them, but the serving staff? The men and women were there to serve the community or as penance to the Gathering. As Weavers, they ranked higher on the social ladder than any of the nobles in Varistad. He hadn't shared a meal with common people since he was a child.

Eventually, he picked up his utensils and ate in silence, only the clinking of plates and silverware breaking the stillness. Hashkan could not think of a single thing to say and the longer the silence dragged on, the more uncomfortable he felt. When they finished eating, the volunteers rose and began to clear the table and the High Weaver left the building, gesturing for Hashkan to come with him. Hashkan found himself following along behind the apprentices, feeling like a duckling again, just like the ones his parents used to have on their farm. The thought made him roll his eyes and he quickened his pace to walk in front of the apprentices.

Better.

They followed the High Weaver to the two-story building that housed his private quarters and study, which took up the entire first floor. Liestenin sat down behind an extravagant desk made of some dark, gleaming wood that Hashkan couldn't name. The entire length of the eastern wall was made up of windows and the man pointed at one of the apprentices and then at the windows, sending the apprentice scurrying over to open the heavy crimson drapes. The bright light of morning flooded into the room and flickered across motes of dust in the air.

Hashkan scowled but followed the example of the students and sat in one of the chairs fanning out around the High Weaver's desk. They all waited in anticipation while he rustled through papers, disrupting the neat stacks in front of him. He appeared to find what he was looking for, set it aside, then steepled his fingers and regarded them all with eyes like chips of ice.

"It was brought to my attention last night that the city has nearly depleted my supply of sparrowthorn, which as you hopefully know, is a key ingredient in many salves for wounds. It helps fight infection and pain. Falian has assured me that he has not been able to find any in the market over the last week. Now, that brings us to the first order of business for your stay here, Clearont." Hashkan barely contained himself from jumping and he held his spine rigid and straight as Liestenin's gaze settled on him.

"Breen hasn't had a Grand Master Herbalist for several years, so I volunteered the services of the Gathering to fill the gap." Another small smile played on his lips. "It's been our tradition since then to have the newest Weaver go out and get herbs when we run low. So, that's you this time, Clearont."

Hashkan clenched his jaw in an effort to bite down his

retort. He hadn't made such a long trip just to run errands. The apprentices around him pointedly avoided looking at him and he could have sworn more than one pair of lips was quirked up in a smirk.

Liestenin picked up the piece of paper that he had set aside before and handed it to Hashkan. "Take this to the innkeeper at the Tilted Barge and he will provide you with one of my horses that he stables. You'll have to ride out to the edge of the Vernoud in the northwest, gather a few bags' worth, and ride back. Have you any questions?"

Hashkan hesitated just a moment as he struggled to keep his expression neutral. Sparrowthorn was a wood-like, dense plant completely covered in thorns. Harvesting and transporting it was an act of patience and care; it was often a test for new apprentices.

"No, not at all High Weaver. I'll prepare my things right now and be on my way before lunch."

"Excellent. The votaries are preparing you some rations for travel. It's roughly a day and a half each way so the trip should not take you any longer than a week, even if you have to go out a little further to find enough sparrowthorn. They will provide food for the full week just in case. I don't expect there to be any problems. I have it from an exemplary lieutenant that the area has recently been cleared of any hazards."

"Thank you, sir." Hashkan stiffly rose and excused himself from the study. It was a slight to the Grand Weaver to exit the room without leave, but he couldn't be bothered. It was a bigger offense to send a Weaver on an apprentice's errand.

He shuffled through his pack and removed his scrolls and books from the bags, lest they be damaged on the ride. He carefully tucked them in with the others on the bookshelf before stomping down the path to the kitchen to collect his rations.

The woman who packed them for him was dainty with chocolate brown hair, maybe a few years younger than Hashkan. She smiled when she handed his pack back to him.

"Isn't it generous of the High Weaver to volunteer the Gathering's resources to help the healing houses?"

Hashkan forced a smile and hoped it didn't look too brittle. He looked at her a little closer, noting the gentle curves hiding under her unflattering uniform.

"It's very philanthropic. I'm sorry, what was your name?" he asked.

"Eivette." She blushed adorably.

"Eivette. I'm Hashkan. Thank you for the food." He took a deep breath, "And wish me luck. I've never been out in the wilderness in these parts." *Or any parts, really.*

"Oh, I expect you won't need it. Things tend to be pretty tame near the city. There was some trouble a few days ago, but the guards handled it. I do hope you'll be back soon, though." She was still blushing a sweet pink.

Hashkan was suddenly acutely aware that his dark hair had become a bit unruly recently and that he was in need of a shave, but it did feel good to have a bit of female attention.

"I'll try not to disappoint you." He met her eyes with a smile and then went on his way.

The Tilted Barge, according to the paper the High Weaver had given him, was located a few streets away near the Market Square. Hashkan stepped out from under the Gathering's trees and into a bright day with just enough of a breeze to feel refreshing. He inhaled deeply and tried to focus on the good he'd be doing, instead of lingering on how overqualified he was to be running errands. With his chin held high, he forced his way into the crowded street, a calm smile fixed to his face despite the near-constant jostling.

The Titled Barge was almost half the size of the Gathering. The sign out front featured a large shipping barge, tilting to the side on a wave, with an over-sized bottle hanging out from the side, a mystery liquid pouring out into the waters.

Likely ale, Hashkan thought.

He let himself inside into a bright and open common room that was full of tables. There were also booths upholstered in tan and navy along the windows and against the walls. The long bar dominating the right wall had a mirror behind it and stairs rose up to the second floor against the wall across from the doors. Several patrons sat around the room and serving girls, all dressed in matching blue dresses with bright white aprons, scampered to and fro carrying trays of food and drink.

Hashkan walked up to the bar where a tall, dark-skinned man was filling drink orders. Hashkan perked up. He had never met anyone from the Gnürian Isles. Nearly everything they knew about herbs and medicine had been discovered by Gnürian scholars.

"Welcome, welcome," he said with a smile as Hashkan approached the bar. "What can I be helping you with today, my good man?" He spoke with a rolling accent that lingered over the vowels instead of the consonants like most Anagovians.

"I'm looking for the innkeeper."

"You've found him! Do you need a room?" He passed some drinks over to a waitress and set right into making the next round.

Hashkan pushed his paperwork across the bar. "I was actually sent by High Weaver Skaen Liestenin. He said you kept his horses here. I need one of them for an errand he's sending me on."

"Alrigh' then." He glanced down at Hashkan's documents with barely a pause. "I'll have one of his horses saddled and brought around. Should only be a few minutes. Want a drink?"

"Yes, please."

Hashkan sipped at his drink, once again working to keep the scowl off his face. Now that he was inside and sitting still, he forgot about the beautiful day and remembered being dismissed so easily after all the hard work he had put in to get a position in Breen. His mind wandered even further and he realized he was actually nervous. He had spent nights out in the wild before, but that had been over ten years ago now, and his family had been with him.

His thoughts continued to turn until a stable boy came in and led him back out into the street to where his horse was waiting. He was being lent a dappled-gray mare, built very well with a soft eye. Hashkan felt his spirits rise. This was the type of horse he'd dreamed about owning when he still lived on his parent's farm. He buckled his pack behind the saddle and swung up onto the mare's back.

He rode through the city, the mare easily pushing her way through the crowds. From where he sat, he could see over the masses of people and found himself admiring the layout of the city. There was none of the hasty building and poor planning here that he had seen on the outskirts of Harthmere and, briefly, in Varistad. He was admiring the architecture of the city so much that he was disappointed to see the northern gate coming into view.

Hashkan joined the crowd passing through the massive gates. The Silver Gilt River Basin spread out before him, a sea of plains speckled here and there with moss-covered rocks. The Silver Gilt River wound like a ribbon through the grass and disappeared off into the distance, a well-trod road running alongside it.

While the rest of the crowd followed the road to the north, Hashkan set his jaw and turned west onto what was little more than a game trail. The forest and the sparrowthorn were waiting.

Chapter Three

Good Soldiers

8 months ago

*O*rdelieus laid sprawled out on a filthy floor, dust motes dancing in the weak light that filtered through dirty windows. His head felt like it had been split open with an axe. Even the dim light stabbed like daggers into his eyes.

A few moments passed while he kept motionless and tried to figure out if he was injured. He ached everywhere and distinctly remembered a crushing weight collapsing on top of him just before he blacked out. All his fingers and toes were working. Somehow, other than the aches and the blighted headache, he was all in one piece.

Inch by inch, he peeled himself off the floor. Vertigo swirled around him as he got his feet underneath himself and he staggered to the side, barely saving himself from smacking back into the floor by catching hold of a dilapidated pile of wood against the wall. All the jarring exacerbated his headache and his vision blurred.

Just as quickly as it came, the pain faded until it was

just a dull throbbing between his eyes. His vision cleared and he was finally able to get a good look at the room. It looked like a barracks. The wood he was leaning on was the remains of a bed frame, one of many that lined the wall, and between each bed, dusty weapon racks dangled off the walls. There was one door at the far end of the room, sagging on its hinges as light seeped in between the wooden planks.

Ordelieus worked his way towards the door and by the time he reached it the stiffness was gone from his limbs and he was able to move easily again. He pushed the door open and the bright light of morning assaulted his eyes, forcing him back into the shade of the building and nearly blinding him. Once his eyes finally adjusted, he slowly crept back out into the light.

He was standing in the ruins of a city. The building he had left was a stone's throw from a wall that was crumbling much like the building itself. Entire sections of the once towering fortification had been blown inward and the pieces were scattered everywhere, littering the streets and, in some places, punching holes through nearby buildings. Everything in sight was damaged. To the northeast, the caps of mountains peeked over the wall.

Ordelieus turned in a circle as panic started to settle in like bricks, one block at a time. He had no idea where he was.

As soon as that thought occurred to him, his headache flared back up in a white-hot fury. It sent him straight back to the ground where he curled up and held his head as a scream built up in his throat.

And just like that, it was gone. He'd forgotten whatever it was he'd been worried about. It didn't matter. All that mattered was finding himself a base of operations.

Ordelieus picked his way through the streets of what

had once been a prosperous city. The buildings, now dilapidated and overgrown with vegetation, still showed signs of
expensive and decorative architecture. All the buildings
were made of the same white marble as the walls. He
passed through a town square where there had been a
permanent marketplace with stone merchant stalls instead
of the temporary wooden ones found in most trade cities.

As he walked, he came upon several other barracks,
evenly spaced throughout the city at crossroads that would
be easy to defend. The farther he went, the more the
layout of this place made him grin. This was how he would
have designed a city. The streets were organized to funnel
invading armies right into the perfect places for defenders
to set up ambushes. It was an ingenious design.

Closer to the center of the city, the buildings grew in
size and elaborate ornamentations peeked through the
vines and mold on the walls. Detailed filigree and chipped
gold foiling trimmed windows and doors while snarled and
overgrown gardens took over large lawns. Ordelieus craned
his neck back and could just make out the upper floors of a
keep looming over the other buildings in the very center of
the city. His feet turned towards it as if guided by instinct.

It was nearly noon by the time he reached the keep.
The gates were wide open and the portcullis raised as if
someone had been waiting for him. Only the generations
worth of cobwebs lacing the bottom of the gate and the
vines wrapping around it hinted at anything different. It
was shameful how neglected this place had become. He
marched through an overgrown yard to the front doors.
They were also open and waiting so he let himself in
without a moment's pause.

Directly in front of him was a grand staircase that
climbed to about three stories high. Halfway up, it ended
at a landing before splitting and curving to either side in

great, sweeping lines. Above it all hung a massive chandelier, the crystal covered in more disgusting cobwebs. He frowned at the filth and climbed the first flight of stairs, then chose the easternmost wing and continued to climb, searching for a path that would take him to the rooftop.

He passed several rooms that he didn't bother examining and wandered until he found the exit to the roof through a trap door in one of the towers. He pushed on the trap door only to discover that the hinges were rusted shut. Ordelieus stood on the ladder, wedged his shoulders against the door, and pressed against it with all his strength. The door opened with a scream that made him grit his teeth, but it swung free and fell back onto the floor above. He climbed the ladder and stood up in the open air of the rooftop.

The top of the keep was enclosed in crenelated battlements and offered an excellent view of the surrounding land from between the merlons. Ordelieus stood in the center and rotated in a full circle, quickly memorizing the details of the landscape.

The mountains he saw earlier rose to the north and east, the peaks softening and turning into rolling hills as they stretched to the south. Northwest of him were great oak and cypress trees, heavy with moss, and the wind blowing from that direction carried with it the scent of a bog. To the south, a long but narrow lake glinted in the sun.

Not only was the city built defensively inside the walls, nature would be its greatest defender. There were natural obstacles surrounding it on three sides that would force any invading army to a single approach. He looked curiously to the west, to the only entrance to the city, and wondered what kind of army could have bested these defenses. The natural barriers and the high walls would have forced most armies into a long, miserable siege.

He remained on the tower for a time, studying the landscape and the layout of the city, before climbing back down the ladder to continue exploring the keep. What he wanted now was a map. He thought he recognized the mountains, but he needed to double-check.

In the northwestern tower, he found a library. The bottom two floors of the tower made up the living quarters for scribes and the remaining five floors were dedicated solely to the books and scrolls. A black iron spiral staircase rose from the middle of the room, connecting to three landings. There were ladders on each floor to help would-be readers reach all the shelves where thousands of books lined the walls on the dusty wooden mantels. Ordelieus dragged a finger through the dust and revealed the glossy rosewood underneath. He scanned the bindings of the books and gently sifted through the scrolls that were tucked away in individual, diamond-shaped cubbies that reminded him of wine racks.

He climbed a ladder one careful, slow step at a time- it creaked and sagged under his weight, threatening to break at any moment- and searched through the top cubbies. All the scrolls on the top shelf were maps, labeled in a system of numbers he didn't understand. He picked one at random and pulled it from its slot. It was nearly as long as he was tall and he had to lean back precariously on the ladder to get it out of the cubby. He carried it to the heavy desk that sat in front of a window on the northern side of the tower, slowly unrolled it, and weighed the corners down with books that had been abandoned on the desk by their previous owners. Scribes were all sloppy to a fault.

The map was so detailed that it was obviously of elven make. His location was easy to find after his study of the area, nestled between the White Stone Mountains, Pinescar Marsh, and on the northern shore of Shimmer-falls Lake. Gilderan, known for its white marble quarry. The *ruins* of Gilderan.

The desk creaked as he leaned against it and he sighed in relief. He knew where he was and, even better, it wasn't too far from home.

As soon as the thought of home flitted across his mind, his headache returned with the explosive force of a war hammer. He stumbled to the side, flinging discarded books off the desk and onto the floor. He followed them down with a gasp.

The pain chased all other thoughts from his mind as he laid there panting, trying to control his body. Whatever this was would kill him this time, no doubt about it.

Relief washed over him as the pain died like a snuffed candle. Hesitantly, he stood back up and brushed himself off.

"Now, where was I?" he muttered.

The sun had passed its zenith and was shining in through the western windows but there was still so much that Ordelieus wanted to do before nightfall. His eyes started to drift in and out of focus as he rolled up the map and he shook his head. He was tired and hungry, but he wasn't *that* exhausted.

His eyes slipped out of focus again and his breath caught in his throat. He wasn't looking at scrolls and books anymore, but at the Threads that wove together to make them. He was seeing the Fabric, the intricate weavings of power and light that formed everything in existence. This is what the Weavers were said to see. He reached out with his mind and brushed against the Threads. The Fabric rippled like water and a few stray papers blew off the desk.

He looked closer and the tiny Threads that made up all

the dust and grime began to appear. He reached out again with his mind, his hand unconsciously mimicking the gesture, and took hold of the Threads for the dust. He drew the lines taunt, then flipped them like a whip and the dust and dirt of ages gave way in a rolling, growing cloud. The Threads rubbed against each other and tiny motes of light flared and died like fireflies dancing on a summer evening.

He continued to grab at Threads of dust and air, flipping them out in front of him to push the cloud around and out of the room. He followed it along the hall, towards the sweeping western stair, opening doors and pulling the filth out of the rooms that he passed, then adding it to the dust storm that he was creating in front of him. He whipped the cloud down the great stair, out the grand front doors, and allowed it to spread and dissipate on the ground just outside of the portcullis. He went inside and repeated the process through the entire building, removing the dust, mold, and cobwebs from each room, on every floor, until the keep was spotless.

The process took him longer than he would have liked. Commanding the countless Threads was exhausting, but he couldn't bring himself to quit until he was finished. By the time he was done, he was panting and sweating so he shrugged off his rusted chain shirt and discarded it just inside the front doors of the keep.

He turned his attention to the outside of his new fortress. He grabbed the Threads for the creeping vines and mold and ripped them from the stones. Underneath all the debris was broken mortar and rotten windows and door frames. He frowned; he was going to have to get some masons, carpenters, and other craftsmen out here if he was going to rebuild the city. That would delay his progress but it couldn't be avoided. What good would arming the walls be if the walls themselves were already broken?

He continued his work past nightfall, pulling filth from the walls all the way up to the tops of the towers. He worked well past the point of exhaustion, never stopping to eat or rest, only focusing on his goal. There was a strange, manic urge in him to keep pushing, driving him forward to get as much as possible done as quickly as he could. By the time he felt satisfied enough to stop for the night, he was sagging where he stood and his joints felt like mush.

Ordelieus turned to go back into the keep. He was too worn out to track down something to eat; it was sleep he needed the most. Before he could finish closing the front doors, however, he was interrupted.

A guttural howling echoed down the streets, the pitch too low to belong to a wolf. Ordelieus stood completely still in the doorway, too stunned to even react. He'd heard howls like that when he was younger and still worked in the hills as a shepherd. Zhu'dac.

Another cry invaded the courtyard, this time closer. Then one by one, the creatures trickled through the gates on their catawampus legs. The smell of carrion drifted in with them on the night air.

On and on they came, until roughly thirty of them were standing in the courtyard. They sniffed at the air and barked at each other, claws and fangs black in the darkness.

Ordelieus's entire body had gone cold. He took a step back, moving with agonizing slowness as he tried to retreat. He grabbed the doorknob again and started to pull the door closed. It moved with the faintest of sighs.

Every mangy head turned and buried him under yellow-eyed stares. Ordelieus's heart nearly burst. He reached frantically for his sword. It was gone. He couldn't remember the last time he'd seen it.

Then it was like he'd been shot with an arrow in the side of his head. He jerked to the side, colliding with the door frame. A cold sweat broke out on his forehead, but the pain started to gradually fade away almost as quickly as it'd come. He righted himself and looked back out at the zhu'dac.

Not a one of them had moved.

What good soldiers.

Chapter Four

Traveler's Camaraderie

Now

"I'm sorry, you want me to do what?"

Li'or was standing outside of the Tilted Barge, looking the chicken-shit officer from outside the gate square in the eyes yet again. She'd learned he went by Lieutenant Aighar and wondered who he'd paid off to rise that far in rank.

"Take care of the straggling survivor zhu'dac. They've been harassing hunters near the Vernoud Forest and some of the farmers as well. As much as I hate to… bother you, I can't spare the time to rearrange my men to handle such a small issue. I've been told it's only three or four of them. And I'm sure, given your profession, you've taken jobs like this in the past." He all but spat at her, his face twisted like he had just smelled something foul.

"You were told right, I have." She flicked her light brown braid over her shoulder. "And I always ask, 'How much?'"

Li'or didn't think it possible for the man to look more

disgusted, but his face crumpled in on itself and proved her wrong.

"Typical mercenary," and then he really did spit. "The lord has deemed this mission to be worthy of five silver stars, half now and half when you return with ears for proof."

She crossed her arms. Why was it acceptable for guards to expect a salary, but so disgraceful for her to expect payment? "I'll do it for a gold face."

"Fine. One face. Here's ten stars. You'll get the rest if you come back. I expect you to leave immediately. Preferably before you cause another scene. And, elf… keep it clean, for the Seamstress's sake. Don't cause a fuss." Then he spun around, nearly collided with a cart, and stormed off.

Li'or shook her head. "All I do is clean. Clean up after myself." She knew right after the incident at the gate that Aighar would find some way to get her out of the city. She sighed and tucked away the small coin purse.

Probably should have asked for more. He caved too easily.

She stepped back into the inn and walked up to the bar where the innkeeper, a man from the Gnürian Isles called Captain, was polishing the countertop. She sat down on the stool across from him and waited while he poured a few drinks for a waiting barmaid. She took the drinks over to a group of nobles who were trying and failing to look like commoners.

"They're still too clean, eh?" Captain asked, noticing where Li'or was looking.

She smirked. "I was just thinking the same thing. Those are commoners' clothes, but they're brand new. Those would be Gathering or festival outfits."

"I'll be sure to tell them that later on. What can I be getting for you, Li'or?"

"I'll actually need my horse brought around, please, Captain. I've been offered a job by the illustrious Captain Aighar."

"Oh yes, that blighter. He comes in here from time to time. Acts like his shit doesn't stink."

"That's the one."

"I hope he's paying you well. I'll tell the boy to bring your gelding and I won't charge you for the afternoon feeding. That picky eater of yours probably didn't eat it all yet anyway," he added with a wink.

"Thank you. I'll get my things." She put three copper crosses down on the bar anyway. It hadn't taken her long to learn that good tippers got better rooms and their horses got better stalls.

She climbed the stairs up to her room and gathered up her few belongings. She shrugged on her leather armor and scooped up her pack; she never really unpacked anything just in case she needed to leave quickly.

Once she had gathered her few things, she went around back to supervise as the young groom finished saddling her horse. The big bay didn't take well to being stalled, even for just a few days, and was dancing back and forth in the cross-ties, shoes ringing like bells on the stones, while the groom followed him with various pieces of tack. He got most of it on but was struggling to get the girth tightened. She could see his frustration starting to get the best of him so she walked over and stood at the horse's head, grabbing his halter and calming him down.

"Good job keeping a cool head. That's the most important thing for a horseman to have. I'll take it from here." She handed him a copper cross. "I know how anxious he can be when he's been kept up."

The boy dashed off across the yard and she finished attaching her saddlebags to the back of her saddle. She checked her horse's shoes just to be sure and then had him bridled and was headed off just a little past noon. She kept a brisk trot through the city, hardly sparing a glance for any of the traffic, and was at the city gate not long after. A few guards were standing at their posts, looking bored as foot traffic and the occasional wagon rolled past. Li'or turned her horse to the side and rode towards them. She needed to know where the zhu'dac had been spotted if she would stand a chance at finding them. She had a creeping feeling that Aighar was sending her on a wild goose chase.

She stopped and spoke with the guard who was standing just inside the polished black gate. He was of average height and build and slouched against his spear like it was the only thing holding him upright. "Excuse me, do you know what farms have been having issues with zhu'dac?"

The guard stood straighter, spine stiff and eyes wide, and glanced past her to the steady trickle of people being let out of the gates.

"How do you know about that?" he whispered. Li'or was barely able to hear him over the noise of the crowds, even with her heightened elven senses. He took a half step closer to Li'or and her horse pinned his ears back.

"Aighar hired me to go take care of the problem," she answered.

"Well, try to keep it to yourself. We aren't releasing that information to the public. If there's a panic in the farmlands, it would be disastrous. Can you imagine all those extra people in here?"

The corners of Li'or's mouth tugged down. "I see." Once again, the poor were left to defend themselves. It always shocked her how little nobility cared for the people that grew their food.

"Anyway," the guard continued in a hushed tone, "it

was the Millwright family that first complained of it. They live along the stream that's almost due north of here. They said it was their outermost fields, though. Then we had the farm next to them file a report about zhu'dac too. They saw them a bit closer to their homes... The Hartwick family."

"Thank you."

She nodded to the guard and nudged her horse forward to join the crowd passing out of the gates.

※ ⁎

SHE MADE it to the Millwright farm by mid-afternoon.

The Millwrights were rich by a farmer's standards. They had a large stone house and several barns competing for space near the banks of a quick running stream that joined up with the Silver Gilt River farther to the north. They also owned a modest mill that ran off the power of the stream and ground a large portion of the countryside's flour.

As Li'or crossed a field filled with sheep, two of the farmer's sons met up with her and after a few quick words walked her up to the house where she met Orston Millwright. He was a tall, bent man with far more wrinkles than his age should allow. He very politely avoided staring at her ears or anything other than the ground for that matter.

"I didn't see any zhu'dac, mind you," Orston explained. "But we had a calf ripped right to shreds. Looks like the work of those knotted beasts. Looked like they were dragging the body out towards the Hartwicks."

Li'or scowled as she rode off. A mangled corpse could have been caused by any number of things, some worse than zhu'dac.

She followed in the direction Orston had pointed her but didn't quite make it to the border of the Hartwick farm before the sun started to set. She found a suitable campsite tucked against the back of a larger hill and ringed by a few stray trees where she began to make camp. She unsaddled her gelding, hobbled him to graze, and was brushing him down when his ears flicked forward and he picked his head up to stare off into the deepening shadows. A few seconds later, she heard a large animal approaching through the brush.

Li'or had to squint for a moment but then picked out a man riding towards her on a dappled gray horse. He wore a deeply cowled cloak and rode with his hood up, hiding his face. The tack the horse wore was too fine to belong to a common man- likely a marauder that had gotten lucky with a caravan if the bulging bags hanging off the saddle were any indication.

She immediately drew and nocked an arrow. "Stop where you are and show yourself! Try anything stupid and you're dead."

She heard a gasp from under the hood and the rider raised his hands slowly then lowered his hood. He was a human man, probably in his mid-twenties, pale with dark hair and the beginnings of a beard dusting a strong jaw. His cloak parted to reveal stained and travel-worn robes as he started speaking with his hands as much as his words.

"I'm sorry. I didn't see you, but... traveler's camaraderie? Companionship on the road? I'm Weaver Hashkan Clearont. I've been sent on an important errand for the Gathering." He pushed a hand through his hair and paused, looking anxious, as if waiting for her to say something. "For the love of the Seamstress, can you point that thing somewhere else?"

Li'or lowered her bow. If he was putting on an act, he

was very good at it. She looked back at the horse. Was it one of the ones stabled at the Tilted Barge? She took a closer look at Hashkan and noted scrapes and scuffs on his arms. Had he been in a fight? She watched closely as he swung himself down off the horse, nearly falling when his feet hit the ground. He certainly didn't move like a fighter.

So he was either entirely harmless or incredibly dangerous. Maybe he had a bounty on him and she just hadn't heard about it yet. Well, there was one way to find out for sure.

"Get over here and let me look at your eyes," she said.

"Excuse me?"

"You heard me. If you want a 'traveler's camaraderie' then I have to know for sure that you are who you say you are. Now get over here."

"It's blasphemy to impersonate a Weaver! I would nev-"

"Yes, and I've seen it done before. But they can't fake the eyes. So, do you have something to hide?"

He scoffed but walked the last handful of steps into the small clearing. As soon as he stepped out from the nearest tree, the dying light flashed off his silver eyes, irrefutable proof that he was a Weaver.

Li'or sighed. He wasn't lying, but now she'd be expected to share her camp. Weavers got everything for free and were treated better than royalty. She didn't follow the Seamstress, but offend one Weaver and they all heard about it. The last thing she needed was more people watching her every move back in Breen.

"You can share the camp with me if you like. But I don't have any extra food."

"Oh. Well, that's fine. I have some of my own." He began unsaddling the mare and moved to put her next to Li'or's gelding.

"No. Not there. See how I'm using him as a barrier to my front like how the hill is to my back? Put her just to the side of him and we'll have a more protective ring."

He stopped and looked back and forth between her horse and the hill, brow creased. He reached some kind of conclusion, nodded to himself, and moved the mare over to where she had indicated. His movements with the animal reiterated that he was not used to horses. He had probably had formal training at some point but never grown accustomed to daily interaction with them.

As he continued unpacking, she put her bow and the arrow back in her quiver and swung the whole rig off her back, putting it down on the ground near her bedroll. She had already collected wood for a fire, as even during the summer months, the nights this far south could bring with them an uncomfortable chill. She had just arranged her kindling and begun working with her flint and steel when her new companion interrupted her again.

"If you can get a good spark, I can coax it to catch on the rest of the kindling," he said.

Li'or raised an eyebrow at him but kept striking the flint. She got a good spray of sparks on her third strike and Hashkan quickly reached out towards the sparks and made a fist. The number of sparks doubled, tiny white flares mixing in with the orange, and then they all clustered together onto her scrapes of tinder. The dry leaves crackled as the fire took hold in earnest.

Hashkan sat back with a self-satisfied grin on his face. He watched the flames for a moment then met her gaze in the light for the first time. "You're an elf! I was wondering how you spotted me so quickly in the dark. I had no idea you were here."

Li'or shrugged. "Yes, well, I guess it does give me an

advantage occasionally. My name is Li'or Halwyn by the way. Thank you for the fire," she added begrudgingly.

"You're welcome, and it's nice to meet you." He leaned forward, eyes wide. "I can count the number of times I've been in an elf's company on one hand. It's always a treat- so wise and you all see things so differently. It's refreshing. Tell me, have you read the latest works on weather Altering? What's your opinion on Skein Liestenin's work?"

Li'or smiled and shook her head. "This may come as a disappointment, but we aren't all scholars. I was raised by a trapper and a midwife in a tiny village with no other elves. I don't have anything to say about Altering theories."

Hashkan paused and picked a stick up off the ground then poked around in the fire, sending a shower of sparks into the air. "Well, I'm sure there are interesting things to say about those subjects as well..." he trailed off a bit but then renewed the conversation with vigor. "Is that what you're doing out here? Headed off to hunt?"

"Yes, hunting zhu'dac."

"Zhu'dac?"

"That's what I said."

"You act like it's as simple as going out for fox skins." He tossed another twig into the fire.

"It's three, maybe four of them. Not worth the guard's time, but it pays enough to be worth mine."

"So you're doing this alone?"

"Clearly," she replied gesturing to the empty land all around them.

"You should go back into Breen and hire a few more swords."

"Groups are hard to keep quiet. Trust me, for the small group that the farmers have described, I'll be just fine. Once I wound a couple, the rest will run away."

Silence fell over them. They ate and before turning in

for the night, Li'or gathered her weapons and ran a quick patrol. She didn't find anything and hustled back to camp. She estimated that she may have been gone half of an hour, but when she returned to the camp Hashkan was soundly asleep.

He may have been a Weaver, but he was also a fool. Had she been raised differently, she may have stolen his belongings just to teach him a lesson. Instead, she settled down in her bedroll with her sword in her hand and her knife at her side. She had every intention to stay awake through the night. Hashkan may indeed be a Weaver, but they weren't all as honest as their scriptures claimed.

※ ⁕

JUST BEFORE DAWN, Li'or jerked awake, snapping her dagger out of its sheath and cursing under her breath. She scrambled to her feet and looked around, fully expecting for all her things to be gone, or worse, for Hashkan to be standing over her with a knife.

But he wasn't. All her things were exactly where she had left them and Hashkan was fast asleep with his mouth hanging open. He hadn't so much as moved.

Li'or heaved a sigh and sheathed her dagger.

Thank the gods. He's as harmless as he looks.

She started to sit back down when it occurred to her that it would be a good time to leave. It was light enough that she could see, the predators of the night would have already made their way back to their beds, and Hashkan would never notice her packing.

She crept back to her feet and rolled her bedroll back up, inch by inch as quietly as she could as the sky turned from a deep violet to a pale lilac. She tied it back to her saddle and buckled her sword and dagger in place, moving slowly so the belt buckles didn't jingle.

There was a heavy inhale from behind her and she froze.

"Morning already?" Hashkan grumbled.

"Gods-damnit," she hissed under her breath.

He was quieter in the morning, at least. He squinted more and more as the light grew around them and fumbled around trying to get his breakfast together. It wasn't until he started packing his belongings that he started to talk again.

"So, I think it would be best if I went with you," he blurted out as he was cinching up his mare.

Li'or had already finished saddling and was strapping on her saddlebags. She paused and turned towards him. "We went over this. I'll be more efficient alone."

"I know, and I understand that. It just seems to me that the risks outweigh the benefits in this situation."

"They don't." Li'or turned from packing and leveled her gaze with the Weaver's, crossing her arms.

He raised his chin and set his jaw. Li'or hadn't thought it possible, but he looked even more pigheaded than before. They kept glaring at each other until he finally broke the silence.

"Fine! Even if you don't need my help, I still insist on going. In the interests of Breen and the Gathering of the Seamstress."

"What?" Li'or asked, narrowing her eyes.

"All of the information we have on zhu'dac is terribly dated. Nearly irrelevant. I'll go with you and get information to update our records."

"This isn't a scientific expedition," she started, slicing the air with the side of her hand.

"I won't hinder you. You can deal with them as you normally would."

Here she was again. She could refuse and leave him behind, risking the ire of the Gathering, or she could juggle a liability that she didn't want to deal with. As much as she hated to admit it, she shrank away from the thought of stirring up more trouble in Breen. She'd already have to lay low after the incident at the gates. Probably for years. It was best not to add to the tension.

"Fine," she huffed. "Just hurry up."

They both finished packing in silence and were on their way before the sun was fully over the horizon.

Li'or led the way, following the directions she'd gotten from the farmer. At about midday, they were riding up to the border of the Hartwick farm. It was a smaller operation and the family seemed to make most of their living off of sheep. If she looked closely enough, she could just make out the sharp eyes of the shepherd hounds living among the flock, watching them warily as they rode past.

The Hartwicks pointed them to the west and into the forest. The farm had lost a few sheep near the edges of their property but hadn't even seen the zhu'dac. They listed off all their issues to Hashkan while Li'or sat on her horse nearby and scowled. A couple missing sheep could have easily been wolves. She was more and more convinced that Aighar had made the zhu'dac up just to get her out of the city.

Once the farmers finished complaining and Hashkan had finished his impromptu ritual in honor of the Seamstress- complete with the strange, staccato speech pattern they used in their lectures- they set off. Li'or increased their pace to a trot. If there really were lingering zhu'dac, she wanted to try and catch them during the day. They were

mostly nocturnal and she was hoping to avoid a fight alto-
gether by catching them in their sleep.

They had been going at that pace for the better part of an
hour when she spotted tracks on the ground. She slipped out
of her saddle, hitting the ground at a jog. Her horse stopped
as soon as she started slipping down his side and he stayed
next to her, ready, as he had been trained. She patted the
horse's neck and then crouched down to look at the tracks.
Hashkan dismounted and crouched down next to her, peering
over her shoulder with an inquisitive gleam in his eyes.

"What do you see?" he asked her.

"Look here," she said. She parted the grass gently to
reveal more tracks. "Four claw-like toes in the front, one in
the back. That's a zhu'dac footprint. Look at this one. See
the odd creases across the center? And how its corre-
sponding print here is slightly deeper? This one was
limping and had some kind of bandage around its foot."

"I think I see it…"

Li'or stood up. "And here you can see where they
pushed through the grass on their way to wherever they've
holed up. They probably aren't too far ahead."

Hashkan stared where she was pointing, shaking his
head with a blank look on his face. "How do you know all
of this?"

Li'or grabbed her horse's reins out of habit and
continued forward on foot, keeping her eyes on the zhu'dac
trail.

"Raised by a trapper, remember?"

Li'or's foster father had started taking her out into the
woods with him as soon as she could walk. She didn't
remember a time he'd failed to invite her out into the forest
with him. He'd taught her everything he knew about
finding game and surviving in the wilderness.

She followed the trail as it curved off to the north slightly, going around a small pond.

"Well, I'm impressed. You've spotted things I would have never even noticed," Hashkan said.

Li'or bit back a sarcastic response. "It's all about practice and knowing what to look for. Look at that broken branch. That wasn't made by an animal; that was our little friends. We're on the right track."

They followed the trail a little farther, Hashkan fidgeting in his saddle the entire time. He broke their peaceful silence yet again.

"So is this your main occupation? Breen's lord sends you out to track down threats to his farmers?"

She found herself grinning at the irony. She was out here because Breen was trying to get rid of her, not hire her. "I mostly guard caravans. I do odd jobs like this when I'm between bigger jobs." She paused and crouched down to examine the trail again and then turned them slightly to the west.

"So you're a mercenary?"

Li'or turned back towards him, surprised by the tone of his voice. There was none of the disgust that nobles and their ilk usually sent her way. Only curiosity. "You could say that."

"That's fascinating! I've never met a mercenary."

Li'or didn't know what to say, so she turned back towards the trail. They rode in silence for a time until the trees started to grow closer together and blocked the sun. She could practically feel the questions bubbling out of Hashkan as they went, but, mercifully, he kept them to himself.

"We'll leave the horses here," Li'or told Hashkan as she turned off the trail. "They make too much noise and we're getting closer. The wounded one's limp has gotten worse and the others probably left him behind when he started to slow. We might be running into him soon. None of them will go too far into the forest if they've a brain between them. Too many elves."

"What if we don't find them? Won't they steal the horses?"

"No. The only use a zhu'dac has for a horse is for food. But we'll find them. They won't get anywhere near the horses."

They found a tighter clump of trees and tied the horses to a long and low branch on an ancient oak. Li'or strung her bow with well-practiced ease and made sure none of the fletchings on her arrows were burred. She double-checked all the buckles on her leather vest and then turned her attention to Hashkan.

"Now, let's make something clear. I won't be able to watch you and them at the same time, so do as I say. The idea is to sneak up to them in their sleep and not have to fight them at all. We're going to be moving slowly and quietly. Step where I step and don't say anything unless there's an emergency. If they're further in than I antici-pate and they're awake when we find them, we'll stop far enough back to make a new plan. And if they find us first, we go back-to-back and hit whatever is in front of us."

Hashkan looked slightly pale, but he nodded and rolled up his sleeves, nervous but ready. Hopefully. She turned and waved him forward.

The trail wound through the trees, sticking to the areas with the most shade as the zhu'dac sought shelter from the threat of daylight. Li'or walked carefully in the growing underbrush, bow in hand with an arrow nocked and ready to go. Hashkan lagged behind a little but followed her directions and carefully put each of his steps where hers had come before. They were moving more quietly than she'd hoped.

It wasn't long before the tracks revealed that the wounded zhu'dac was lagging farther and farther behind. She was honestly surprised he had managed to stay with the group as long as he had, and it was no surprise when she spotted him. His bandaged foot was sticking out from under a large bush to the left of the trail.

She stopped and pointed him out, Hashkan freezing behind her. Once he nodded to her that he had seen the zhu'dac's foot, she handed him her bow and placed a hand on his shoulder, stared pointedly at him, and took a few steps away while shaking her head. He nodded again, tense; he'd stay where he was.

Li'or stalked towards the bush. She placed her feet down a hair's breadth at a time, easing them down so carefully that even a dried leaf wouldn't have crunched. Once she had drawn even with the bush, she carefully parted the branches at the top with her right hand, moving ever so slowly.

The zhu'dac inside was still asleep, curled on its side, a piece of raw meat tucked between its arms. It had long pointed ears that curved backward away from its head, a large snout not unlike a wolf's, and its mouth hung open slightly, revealing jagged fangs. Its whole body was covered in coarse brindle fur. It had pieced together a pair of worn and ragged trousers out of odd bits of cloth and had somehow squeezed itself into a leather vest. The smell of carrion rolled off it like a fog.

She reached down and slowly drew her arming sword. She kept it well-oiled and it slid from its sheath silently. She spun it point-down in a reverse grip and, quick as a thought, thrust the blade into the creature's neck just at the back of its skull. Its eyes flew open and its mouth moved to scream, but it was dead before it could finish drawing a breath.

She jerked her blade free, grabbed the dead zhu'dac by the ankle, and dragged it out from under the bush. It made more noise than she wanted, but it couldn't be helped if she was going to collect the ears for the bounty. She heard Hashkan come up behind her as she cleaned her blade on the zhu'dac's pants.

"By the Seamstress, it's ugly. I've never seen one before. Wha-"

She turned and glared at him and he closed his mouth with a snap. She nodded, satisfied, and drew her dagger, making quick work of removing the dead zhu'dac's ears. She saw Hashkan pale again out of the corner of her eye and sighed as she put the ears in the pouch at her waist, then started off again. The other zhu'dac were likely only an hour or so ahead at most. She could tell from this one's poor shelter that he had likely chosen a place to sleep out of desperation after the sun had already come up.

Li'or looked towards the horizon where the sun was hanging low. The bottom of the sphere was starting to disappear behind the trees and the shadows of forest were getting longer, swallowing up the light. She was running out of time. She was likely to find the rest of them awake and alert. She took her bow back from Hashkan and held it at the ready.

It was full dark before they found their first sign of the remainder of the zhu'dac band. They could hear them bickering in their barking, course tongue. Li'or slowed her pace and crept forward until she could just make them out ahead.

They were in the center of a patch of ancient evergreens so tall that even their lower branches were above both Li'or and Hashkan's heads. The trees were so thick that no light was able to penetrate through the branches and only sparse plants grew up around their trunks. The zhu'dac lit no fire, but even in the dark, Li'or could make out bones from large and small animals alike strewn about the area, a few days' worth of food for the ravenous creatures. There were four of them left, standing in a circle, flinging their arms around and nipping at each other as they argued.

She waved Hashkan forward and, keeping her voice very low, explained the plan to him.

"If you can, Alter some kind of distraction when I get even with the trees. I'll rush in and take out as many as I can in the confusion. If things get out of control, just stay back here and throw what you can at them. Do not, for any reason, get into the melee. Do you understand?"

He nodded, lips pressed into a thin line.

She clasped his shoulder, gave him a quick shake and started off towards the zhu'dac.

Chapter Five

There's Danger

Hashkan watched as Li'or stalked away towards the zhu'dac, slipping through shadows like a cat. He started to inch forward after her. Despite what she said, it would be better for her if he was closer to the fight. As he crept along, he stepped on a twig and it snapped. He flinched reflexively and Li'or whipped around, her glare like ice.

Li'or made everything look so easy. She moved through the brush like it was second nature, tracked the zhu'dac using footprints he could barely even see, and killed the creature without a moment's hesitation. Now here he was, unable to take three steps without making a mistake.

It didn't take Li'or long to reach the edge of the trees. She paused for just a moment then sprang forward into the clearing.

Hashkan's heart leapt into his throat. He thought he'd have more time to prepare; instinct, honed from years of training, took over.

His eyes shifted focus and he stopped seeing each individual entity before him. Instead, he saw a vast tapestry. A multitude of different Threads weaving through one another and intertwined to create the world around him.

He focused his gaze on the zhu'dacs' Threads. They flowed over the dense Threads of the ground as the zhu'dac turned to meet Li'or's charge. Hashkan reached out with his mind, visualizing it as his hand, and grabbed the soil just under the zhu'dac's feet. He jerked it towards himself as hard as he could, like snatching a rope.

Tiny white sparks flared as a thin layer of soil under the closest two zhu'dac shifted with a rasping hiss, moving about an arm's span towards Hashkan. The creatures stumbled to the side as they were knocked off balance.

Before they could regain their footing, Hashkan grabbed hold of the Threads again. He flicked the Threads like a whip, putting as much force as he could behind it. The earth under the zhu'dac rolled and skidded back into place, pitching them back the other way. They barked in alarm, then screeched and ran toward the others. They all flew into a panic and ran around the clearing crying to one another and looking in every direction.

Then Li'or reached them. She carried her sword in her left hand and her dagger in the right. With cold efficiency, she dashed up to the closest of the group and slashed his throat from behind with the dagger. The zhu'dac went down, spouting blood like a red fountain and clutching at his throat. She spun, following the momentum of her slash and moved to the next one. As her turn finished, she brought her sword arm around, taking the next zhu'dac in the neck. There was another flash of red and that one went down beside the other.

The last two stopped scrambling and went on the

offensive. One grabbed a crude club off the ground and the other drew a rusted scimitar. They yipped and slobbered as they slowly closed in on Li'or. They split and moved to her left and right, trying to flank her.

Still as stone, Li'or held her ground with her blades raised and watched as they stalked towards her. Hashkan's thoughts tumbled through his head as he tried to think of something to do. If he didn't act fast, her back would be exposed no matter what she did. Why wouldn't she *move?*

Desperate, Hashkan reached back out to grab the Threads. At the same time, Li'or shifted towards the zhu'dac on her right, blade rising to strike. The zhu'dac on her left leaped towards her with his blade held high over his head, screaming.

Hashkan froze, hand extended while he watched their individual patterns converge. He was too appalled to move.

At the last second, Li'or reversed her grip on her sword and thrust it behind her, impaling her attacker in the gut. The zhu'dac staggered backward off her blade then fell as his legs collapsed. The feeling returned to Hashkan's hands. She'd planned it out and pulled a feint to bait one of them in. Brilliant.

The last zhu'dac threw his club down and turned, howling as he tried to flee the clearing. Li'or flipped her dagger and prepared to throw it while Hashkan pieced himself together and grabbed hold of the Threads that made up the zhu'dac's ragged clothing. The creature lurched to a stop and Li'or threw the dagger. It spun end over end and sunk into the zhu'dac's back. The impact sent it sprawling forward, staggering before it fell flat on its stomach.

Hashkan drew in a long, steadying breath. The only combat he had ever seen was the wrestling matches they used to hold near Harthmere during the solstice festivals.

This was something else entirely. It was chaos. Li'or had run through the zhu'dac like a whirlwind.

He brushed imaginary dirt off the front of his robe and started walking up to where Li'or was collecting her dagger. The dying light reflected off puddles of blood and entrails. His stomach turned, forcing him to look away. He quickened his pace over to Li'or.

She stood back up and met his eyes with a steady, inscrutable gaze. It was so unnerving that Hashkan stumbled over a discarded club and barely got his feet under himself in time to avoid landing face-first in the dirt. She was so *elegant*, even standing amid all the corpses. It was baffling.

He cleared his throat and pushed a hand through his hair. "So, are you going to cut the ears off of these as well?" He walked slowly and had to force the words out around the lump that had risen in his throat.

"Of course," she stated, voice smooth as if it should be obvious, as if this was normal. "How else would I prove I got them all?" She then set to work cutting off the ears of all four zhu'dac, dropping them all into the same pouch where she'd stowed the others.

"Seems like a rather barbaric practice, honestly…"

"Do you have any better ideas?"

"Well, not right at this moment, but I'm sure given time I could think of a better solution."

"You do that. In the meantime, I think it's about time for camp. Let's go back to the horses."

He followed her back through the forest. Even though they weren't trying to be stealthy this time, it was still just as hard to keep up in the growing darkness. Once they made it back to the edge of the forest, they found the horses exactly where they had left them.

"That was a nice trick you pulled with the Altering

back there," Li'or said once they'd gathered fire wood and gotten a small blaze going. "So where does it come from? The Altering I mean."

Hashkan creased his brows together. "Don't all elves know some small bit of Altering? That's what I'd heard."

Li'or scoffed. "You forget, I was raised by humans. If there are extraordinary abilities in me, I don't know about them."

"Oh. I'd forgotten, I apologize. But surely you've spent some time with other elves, haven't you?"

The bit of a smile she had been wearing a moment before slipped from her face. "No."

Hashkan waited, expecting her to elaborate. The silence stretched on as they broke into their rations, Hashkan feeling more and more awkward with each minute that passed. Finally, he just started spurting out the story of the Gifting. "Well, it came from the Seamstress-"

"I've heard that story, Hashkan," she said and waved her hand dismissively. "I'm older than the cult of the Seamstress. What do you think really happened? Why do you think we just discovered Altering forty-something years ago?"

Hashkan exhaled heavily. "We aren't a cult. Anyway, we know that Weavers' brains are different. They're woven together differently. That's what the tests are for, when children are selected for Weaver training. The differences in our brains allow us to see the Threads that make up everything and allow us to pull and Alter the Threads to an extent... I guess no one was desperate enough before the Rak-Shai War to really see them, to really take hold."

"There have been wars before."

"Maybe we didn't need it before. Maybe the Seamstress saw our need-"

Li'or chuckled. "A new gift, just when you need it, without danger or limits. It seems too convenient."

"There's danger!" Hashkan leaned forward, ardor rising as the debate continued. "When I had just started my training under High Weaver Ioron, there was an older boy studying with him who had just started to Alter earth and move small rocks around on the ground. We're always started with earth because it's heavy so it's difficult to grab more than you can safely handle.

"But the other boy… he was ambitious and felt like he could do more. He thought he was a prodigy. One night, he brought all of the other children in the town out behind the stables and tried to Alter fire. He succeeded, but you can only hold on to fire for so long. It will burn your mind just like it'll burn your body. He caught the paddocks on fire and he, essentially, burned his brain. He made himself a simpleton. He couldn't speak anymore, let alone study Altering."

Li'or stared him for a moment through the glow of the fire. The light danced in her bright green eyes and it was easy to see why people said all elves were Weavers. He could have sworn she was looking through him, to his Threads, and then analyzing them and rearranging them as if she had power over them like the Seamstress herself.

"I suppose I owe Weavers more respect than I've been giving them. I had no idea it was so dangerous to mess with the Fabric," she said after a long pause.

"And I underestimated your skill," Hashkan replied. "You would have been fine out here without me. It seems like we both learned something tonight."

She nodded. "So it seems."

The next morning found them both up at first light, packing as they forced themselves to eat more of their bland, preserved trail rations. The horses, who had been out on the thick grass of the clearing all night, both boasted small grass bellies and reluctantly allowed themselves to be pulled away from their grazing.

Two days ago, before meeting Li'or, when Hashkan was leaving the forest to make his way back into Breen, he had been exhausted, frustrated, and had moved forward with his eyes fixed on the ground in front of him while the details of the world passed him by unnoticed. Now, his exhaustion was batted aside by a growing sense of accomplishment. He rode with his head high, a satisfied smile fixed across his face.

As far as he knew, he was the only Weaver to use Altering in combat since the Rak-Shai War. During his training in Harthmere, all his instructors had assured him that he would never need to use Altering as a weapon. Foreign armies feared them too much to invade Anagovia and they were too valuable to society to ever come under any harm. They'd spent three weeks on basic self-defense and then moved on.

But there Hashkan was, victor of a battle. Invincible.

He was jarred from his reverie by the twang of a bow string followed by a high-pitched squeak. Li'or trotted her horse off the road a ways and returned holding a rabbit by its back legs.

"This one can be yours," she told him. "I'll show you how to skin it if you need help. Hang it from your saddle."

He cringed but did as he was told, hanging it beside the bags of sparrowthorn. He prayed to the Seamstress the blood wouldn't stain the High Weaver's saddle leathers.

They passed by the Hartwick farm and dusk found them nearing the outskirts of the Millwright farm where they stopped and set up camp well before dark so Li'or could show Hashkan how to properly skin a rabbit. As always, the prospect of learning something new enticed him. He had only ever dealt with chickens on his parents' farm.

Li'or had gotten lucky and scored a second rabbit as they traveled so she sat in front of him, laying her rabbit out on its back. "Now, this is always easier if you can hang what you're skinning by its hind legs, but we'll do this the hard way. If you can learn something the hard way, you'll be more than capable of doing it the easy way later on. Start by cutting here." She demonstrated on her catch and Hashkan followed along best as he could, cutting ragged lines that looked like a child's scrawl when compared to her smooth slices.

He stuck with it, though, and soon had his dinner skinned, gutted, and on a branch roasting over the fire. He leaned back against his saddle and grinned to himself. He might even save the hide. It was small but he could have it sewn into the lining of a hood or the collar of a jacket. It would make a good story. He dug into the meal with fervor when Li'or declared it done. It tasted a hundred times better than the rations.

The next morning they ate what few leftovers they had from the night before and a bit of hardtack before setting off through the Millwright lands. They didn't speak much, but Hashkan found the silence to be comfortable. A true traveler's camaraderie like he'd suggested when he stumbled into her camp.

They cantered up to the gates of the city just as the sun kissed the horizon. The guards at the gate seemed to recognize Li'or and waved them through in a frazzled rush. It certainly was a far cry from the warm welcome Hashkan was accustomed to. A quick glance at Li'or brought little comfort. She rode through the gates with a stiff back, hand clenching the pommel of her sword.

"They were acting strangely, weren't they?" Hashkan said as they rode down the Land-and-Sea.

"Well, it's almost dark," Li'or answered. "They have to be careful."

Still, she seemed tense, even more so than normal. Hashkan watched her for a few moments as she stared straight ahead. Clearly, she wasn't in a sharing mood so he held his tongue.

He'd been around other elves, but never too long, and never quite like this one. They had been scholars with enough knowledge in the shelves of their minds to rival any Gathering library. Li'or- stunning as she was with her bright eyes and exotic features- carried an air of danger with her. She was like the jungle cats he'd read about in Gnür. It was fascinating.

They snaked through the dwindling crowds until they found themselves outside the Tilted Barge once again.

"This is my stop," Li'or announced as she swung from her saddle.

"What a coincidence, the High Weaver keeps all of the Gathering's horses here."

"I thought that mare looked familiar." She took her packs off her saddle and slung them over her shoulder as a stable hand came out to take her horse. She pulled out a coin purse and grimaced at its contents, or lack there of. "I can't spare any coin for your help right now, but after they pay me for those ears tomorrow I can square up with you."

"Completely unnecessary," Hashkan said, shaking his head. "A Weaver has no use for coin. No one would accept any from me anyway."

What had started as a courtesy for the Weavers who ended the war had evolved into a tradition over the years. No decent Anagovian citizen would expect a Weaver to pay for anything. The Weavers, in return, were expected to keep very few personal belongings in order to avoid greed. Most of the things Hashkan considered "his" really belonged to the Gathering; he just used them.

"Alright, then. In that case, I'll owe you a favor. Within reason," she added with a small smile. She extended her hand to shake.

"Within reason," he agreed. He clasped her arm firmly, the way he had seen soldiers do. "I'm sure I'll think of something."

Chapter Six

Eye to Eye

*N*ight had fallen across Breen like a thick blanket by the time Hashkan made it back to the Gathering in the city square; he was moving slowly thanks to the four sacks of sparrowthorn he was lugging with him. Fortunately, the crowds had thinned out significantly as the sun set and he wasn't forced to wade through hordes of people or stick against the walls to safely make it back. The last few dregs of energy he'd been holding on to at the end of his trip finally ran out. By the time he had carried the bags the last couple of miles, he had lost feeling in his arms.

He gritted his teeth, though, and pushed through. He was starting to think of himself as a soldier, like the Weavers who had fought in the war. And they hadn't had the option to quit.

He shuffled down the path to the kitchen and sat one of the bags down so he could open the door. Loud squeaking announced his entry and a group of volunteers and apprentices scurried out to take all of his packs. He followed one of them back to his assigned quarters, feeling like he'd been gone an entire lifetime. He took off his dirty clothes and sank into the mattress, falling asleep before his head was all the way onto the pillow.

When morning came, he called for a bath and scrubbed the dirt of the road off his skin, out of his hair, and out from under his nails. He even had to pull burrs out of his hair as he washed it. The beginnings of a beard had started to invade his cheeks, so he took some extra time to rein it in before going to breakfast.

He looked himself over one last time before leaving his room, meeting his silver eyes in the mirror. He looked like a new man. More worldly, more experienced. He grinned and strutted towards the dining hall.

High Weaver Skaen Liestenin came into the dining hall just as Hashkan was sitting down. The apprentices and other Weavers had all already taken their seats and left Hashkan with the seat directly to the High Weaver's left. Around them, the votaries brought out the last few breakfast options, the selections filling the entire table yet again.

"You were slow," the High Weaver observed as he poured himself a cup of tea, glancing up at Hashkan from under his gnarled brows. "I was starting to worry something had happened to you."

That certainly felt like a veiled insult, and Hashkan's hackles rose. He took a deep breath to calm himself before answering. "I ran into an elf woman on the way back who had been sent out after a band of zhu'dac. I went back out with her to help. And to learn, of course." Hashkan became aware that all the others at the table had paused in their meals and were waiting for the High Weaver's response.

"And what did you learn?" he asked between bites,

apparently oblivious to the tension around them. Their eyes met again, the High Weaver's as hard as silver ingots.

"I learned a bit about tracking," Hashkan met his gaze firmly. "That is a truly impressive talent that takes an eye for detail that even I don't have. I helped kill a band of five zhu'dac. I have new notes on the creatures you may find interesting."

Liestenin stared at him as if waiting for more, his face completely expressionless. "I see." Liestenin then bent back down to his food and all the others who had been silently waiting did as well.

Hashkan waited for the High Weaver to offer him some kind of praise. He'd accomplished more on his short excursion than most Weavers would in their lifetimes. Surely that was worthy of some kind of recognition?

But the silence continued to stretch, every moment grating against Hashkan's nerves. He shifted in his seat as he worked to contain the sardonic remarks forming on the tip of his tongue.

"Even with the delay, I'm happy with the amount of sparrowthorn you brought back. The healing houses are in desperate need, so we'll need to make as much ointment as we can while the sparrowthorn is still fresh. We'll meet in the herb garden once we're all done with breakfast."

Hashkan ate slowly, trying to determine if he would be included in such a menial task. Sure enough, to his frustration, he was. By midmorning he found himself sitting on a bench, solemnly grinding sparrowthorn into a paste with a mortar and pestle along with all the apprentices in the Gathering.

In the afternoon, he found himself mixing the pulped sparrowthorn in with a paste made from willow bark in a careful three-parts to one-part ratio. He had done this countless times before and could almost do the job with his eyes closed. The apprentices, however, were awkward with the measuring utensils and he often lent them a hand, feeling more like a glorified baby sitter than a teacher. The other Weavers met with visitors and led the two afternoon rituals- jobs he would have preferred.

"Clearont," Liestenin said as Hashkan packed the jars of finished salve into a quilted bag. "Since you started this bout of salve making, it's only fitting you should finish it. We need to deliver these jars to the five healing houses in the city tomorrow. If you leave just after breakfast, you should be done before the second afternoon ritual."

His grip on the bag tightened but he forced himself to nod. "I'd be glad to do it."

A dread that he was going to be assigned a long list of apprentice tasks was settling deep in his gut. That combined with a splash of worry about when he would actually be assisting with Liestenin's studies was enough to kill his appetite. He retired directly to his rooms where he tried to document his observations from the trip and failed. He was too preoccupied with feeling sorry for himself.

The next morning, he ate breakfast quickly, eager to be out of the Gathering. A young groom was standing outside of the front gates when he went out, a familiar dappled gray mare in hand. Hashkan forced a thanks from his lips and a smile onto his face as he helped load the heavy salve jars.

The city was just as busy that day as every other and he was once again grateful for the extra height of the horse as he rode through the throngs of people going up and down the Land-and-Sea. He stopped at the nearest healing house first, just on the other side of the square. The others were located to each corner of the city and it would take up the majority for his day just to ride between them. They were all long, single-story buildings that had once been barracks during Breen's more war-like past. They were painted white to match the stone of the rest of the city and the roofs were thatched in a dark wood.

At each stop, he walked into the building and was quickly met by an attendant who took the ointments and passed a handful of coins to him, a "donation" to the Gathering. He was glad they didn't leave him to linger. The insides of the houses were too quiet and there was always sobbing coming from further inside. Healing houses were often dying houses, too.

Unfortunately, the long rides between stops left Hashkan with more than enough time to think about what he was doing and that did nothing for his peace of mind. Between each stop, he found himself growing more bitter towards the High Weaver as he considered how banal this task was. He should have been in the Gathering, studying and making new discoveries, not out here thoughtlessly plodding through the city.

By the time he made it back to the Gathering, his eyes were molten with rage and a tick had started in his jaw from keeping his teeth clenched for so long. He slipped into the Sanctuary in time to catch the end of the second ritual and waited impatiently in the back as the people filtered out of the clearing. He had words to exchange with Liestenin.

The High Weaver noticed Hashkan standing in the back and waved him forward once the last worshiper started to leave. He smiled as Hashkan walked up, seemingly oblivious to the storm clouds that Hashkan was towing in his wake.

"Weaver Clearont, how did go? Did they place any more orders?"

"No, they didn't." He crossed his arms. "I need to talk to you."

Liestenin's brow creased. "Alright, what's bothering you?"

"I want to know when I'll be done with apprentice's chores. I didn't come here to be degraded. I came here to study."

"And you will, but there are other things that demand our attention and all of us share those responsibilities," Liestenin answered, his frown deepening.

"I haven't seen any of the other Weavers doing menial tasks like what you've assigned me," Hashkan said. Heat rose from his collar and he knew his face was getting red, but he didn't care.

"You haven't been here to see what the others were doing, so you're making an assumption. I know you've been taught the danger in that." Liestenin's tone grew cold and his eyes narrowed. "It seems you're speaking from a place of wounded pride. Arrogance has no place within the Seamstress's service. You should have been taught that as well."

Hashkan scoffed.

"Enough!" Liestenin's voice echoed and birds burst out of the tree above them. "You will remember your place as the Seamstress's servant, and you *will* serve. Once you've remembered your humility, you can begin assisting with my studies. You're dismissed."

Hashkan spun on his heel and stormed down the rows of pews, gravel crunching under his boots. He snatched the Threads of a tree branch and bent it out of his way as he cut around a corner.

He had had enough. He hadn't studied for ten years and crossed the entire continent to be patronized. He'd finished his apprenticeship with the highest marks in his age group. His Altering was strong and he was resourceful. Whatever Liestenin may think, these chores and errands *were* beneath him. Allowing him to work on his Altering studies would be the best way to provide service to the Seamstress.

That was the only reason that he'd come here.

Once he made it to his room, Hashkan flung the door open and made straight for the bed where he collapsed. Months of work and research had gone into getting this position. Months that were now a complete waste. He would never get the time back. He heaved a sigh and reached towards one of his discarded notebooks. After flipping through a few pages he found what he was looking for.

During the time he'd spent searching for a Gathering where his skills would be put to the best use, he'd found several good fits before ultimately deciding on the Gathering in Breen. His second choice was in Straeth.

It was time for him to write more application letters. He wouldn't be staying here long.

※ ⁎

LI'OR SHOULDERED through the hundreds of people milling about the marketplace. On her first day back, she'd turned in her bounty and collected the second half of the reward. Since then, she'd been trying, and failing, to relax. It was the busiest time of the year in Breen and no matter where she went, she couldn't get away from the crowds. The night before, while eating in the jam-packed common room at the Tilted Barge, she'd decided it was time to move on.

She'd spent even less time here than in the last city. The crime, the filth, the stink- she couldn't abide it. One more guard job, though, and she'd have the coin to buy enough supplies to disappear for a while. So she dealt with the herds of people and tried to work her way over to where a few traders were packing up their wares. With any luck, she'd be able to score a last-minute job riding back north with them.

As she wove through the square, she kept noticing the same pattern of colors out of the corner of her eye and it struck her as more than just coincidence. With all the people scrambling around, it was unlikely for her to see the same person more than once.

She casually pushed her way up to a vendor and pretended to rifle through an assortment of buttons while actually taking note of who was lingering nearby.

Two men in nondescript brown and tan garb were standing nearby, talking and glancing over at her. It could be a coincidence. Any elf that wandered out of the forests was subject to plenty of stares. She'd grown used to it over the years and barely even noticed it anymore.

She worked her way down a few stalls, even purchased a few odds and ends, all while keeping an eye out for the two men. They trailed after her, pretending to shop and trying to disappear into the crowd. And doing a terrible job at it. Immediately, her mind made the leap back to Aighar. He was the only person she could think of who would hire people to tail her; he was the only person with a reason to.

What she really wanted to know was what, exactly, he was hoping to accomplish by having these idiots follow her around.

Leaving the vendors behind, Li'or made her way back into the crowded streets at a casual walk. She turned a corner and started walking faster. Another corner and she broke into a jog. Turning a third corner, she sprinted to an alley and darted down it. People looked at her with their brows raised but continued on their way. A few strides down the alley, she used a windowsill to boost herself up and swung onto an awning over a door. With a couple of jumps and she was on the roof, just in time for her followers to run panting into the alley.

"Blight, I knew we'd lose her! Damn elves, they're too fast!" one of them said, a pock-marked man with large arms. He looked like any other brawler that could be hired out of a gutter in the slums.

"Fuck her, we've got bigger problems now," the other said. He was wiry like a weasel- probably one of the few cut-purses who survived long enough to get caught up in worse occupations as an adult. "What's that officer gonna say when we don't turn up with her head? He'll have ours, that's what!"

Anger welled up in Li'or and, for a brief moment, she considered jumping down and putting an end to both of the thugs. Before she moved, she was tempered by a different emotion- exhaustion.

It wasn't the first time she'd gotten on the wrong side of a pompous official. She was still waiting on the others to grow old and die before she returned to some of the cities on the western side of the continent. She tried so hard to keep to herself because when she didn't, something like this ended up happening. She still hadn't learned that not everyone agreed with her idea of doing the right thing. Either that or they just didn't care.

And she hated that she was right about this situation, too.

She crept away from the edge of the roof and sat down on the ridge. The black shingles were warm to the touch under the summer sun as she waited. Her would-be assassins hung around a few more minutes as they worked out a half-baked plan to find another unfortunate victim they could pass off for Li'or. She didn't expect them to find much luck. Elves weren't common in this part of the world.

Once they left, she slid off the roof and made her way back to the Tilted Barge. She'd have to leave a little earlier than she'd anticipated. There'd be no waiting for another job. She'd just grab her things and go.

To her surprise, there was a familiar face waiting for her outside of the inn.

Hashkan Clearont sat in one of the rocking chairs arranged on the front porch of the inn, a drink in hand. At first glance, he seemed to be relaxing, but Li'or could tell by his intense focus on the street that he was on edge.

"Looking for someone?" she asked as she climbed the steps up to the porch.

Hashkan jumped to his feet. "Yes, I was. You. I have a job for you."

"I'm not taking on any jobs right now. I'm sure the Gathering will find someone else." She put two fingers to her brow in a mockery of the Weaver's salute and moved towards the door. She didn't have much to pack. She could be saddled and out of the northern gate before two hours passed.

"It's not for the Gathering, it's for me." He reached out and grabbed her by the elbow. She stopped and looked down at his hand and he jerked it away like he'd been scalded. "Please, just listen for a moment?"

"Fine," she sighed. She stepped out from in front of the door and crossed her arms. She'd listen and then she'd leave.

"I need an escort to Straeth. I know it's not customary, but I'm willing to pay you as well. I know it's no small favor, but you did say you owed me one."

Li'or raised her eyebrows. She could hardly believe her good luck that the job she needed would fall into her lap just as she was trying to leave. "But where will that coin come from?" she asked, suddenly skeptical.

"A portion of the coin donated to the Gathering gets turned around and donated to the needy. When we get to Straeth, I'll pay you from that."

"You're sure that High Weaver will let you?"

"I've already sent three carrier pigeons their way letting them know that I'm coming and that you will need a donation."

A wry smile tipped up the corners of Li'or's lips. "Just a bit presumptuous, eh?" Hashkan had the good graces to blush, but he still met her eyes without flinching. He had quite a backbone, Li'or would give him that. "It's five golden faces for that long of a trip."

Hashkan visibly relaxed. "Done. Thank you." He held out his hand and Li'or shook it.

"We'll need to leave here in the next couple hours," Li'or said with a quick glance at the sun.

"Wait, what?" His eyes doubled in size.

"There's a good, easy to defend campsite that I'd like to get to before nightfall, but we've got to get a move on if we're going to make it." She was about to tell him that she'd meet him at the Gathering when another thought occurred to her. "Do you have a horse?"

"Oh, all the horses that Liestenin boards here are technically the property of the Gathering. I'll take one of them."

"Perfect. I'll meet you at the Gathering in an hour." She tossed another small salute at him and turned to go inside. He gaped for just a second then turned and dashed off towards the stables. Li'or couldn't help but laugh.

✦ ✦ ✦

BEFORE AN HOUR HAD PASSED, Li'or was sitting on her horse outside of Breen's Gathering of the Seamstress. As she waited, a small family went in through the open front gates. A few moments later, an elderly Gnürian woman hobbled down the steps on her way home. All manner of people came to worship the Seamstress, but Li'or didn't notice a single elf the entire time she waited. It seemed very telling to her that the race many considered to be so sagacious was also absent from any of the Seamstress' gardens.

A well-built chestnut mare and a sturdy pack mule were tied just to the left of the gates. The horse was saddled and the mule wore her pack saddle, but nothing was loaded on either of them. A part of her hoped Hashkan had picked out such good stock to take with them, but another part of her hoped there was a packed-up pair of animals hiding somewhere. She was getting tired of looking over her shoulder.

Her shadow crept around her and marked the passing of another half hour before Hashkan finally came striding out of the garden gates. He wore his pack and carried two others while two housekeepers followed in his wake carrying similar loads.

"Oh, you're early!" He said with a grin when he noticed her. He walked towards the waiting horse and mule with exaggerated bravado, but he kept a white-knuckled grip on all his luggage.

"No, you're late," Li'or said with a frown. Something had him on edge and she forced down the urge to ask what it was. She had more than her fair share of concerns to deal with at that moment. Her eyes kept scanning the courtyard around them, lingering on passers-by while she waited for the sudden flash of a blade being drawn. What if Aighar hired someone competent and they were waiting just around the corner?

Hashkan glanced down at their shadows and shrugged. "Well, at least I have plenty of supplies to make up for it."

There was a brief scramble while Hashkan and his help loaded all the bags on to the pack mule and then Hashkan swung up onto the chestnut mare. He urged the horse forward without a single glance back towards the Gathering.

"I can't wait to get out of this city," Hashkan commented as they rounded a bend in the street and Breen's black gates came into view. He glanced over at Li'or out of the corner of his eyes, like he was waiting for a response.

Li'or suppressed a sigh but asked, "You haven't enjoyed Breen?"

"Oh, I like the city well enough. High Weaver Liestenin and I just didn't see eye to eye. We would never have worked well together."

They passed under the shadow of the gate and out onto the road that cut through the rocky hills. The Silver Gilt River flashed in the bright sun off to their right.

"Li'or! Do you see that?" Hashkan shouted next to her. He pointed out into the river and his silver eyes were wide.

Li'or looked back out at the water. Melting snow and spring rains had raised the water level until it threatened to overflow its banks, but that was nothing out of the ordinary.

"I guess I don't. I just see the river," she answered.

"That's what I'm talking about. The water was sending off Thread Flares like someone was Altering, but I didn't do it!"

"And you're sure it wasn't just the light reflecting off the water?"

Hashkan threw his hands up. "You think I don't know the difference? After all the studying I've done?"

"Alright, alright," Li'or said. She waved one hand in a pacifying gesture while she loosened her sword from its sheath with the other. "We'll just have to keep a sharp eye out. Tell me if you notice anything else."

With any luck he wouldn't.

Chapter Seven

Another Bodyguard

The rain started pelting Li'or and Hashkan within an hour of leaving Breen's walls. The deluge continued on well into the night, the thunder rolling in around them, loud and heavy. They had their small tents, but the ground everywhere was already wet, even under the trees, and it made for rough, miserable camping. Li'or laid still and listened as Hashkan tossed and turned in his tent. He'd lie still just long enough for her to start going to sleep and then start thrashing again, jarring her wide awake. She eventually sighed and sat up, admitting defeat. She could put her horse on the road in the morning and trust him to stay on course while she slept in the saddle. She settled in and tried to enjoy the steady tapping of the rain against the canvas.

Hashkan kept rolling around for another hour or so before surging out of his tent in an explosion of jostled canvas and guy ropes. She peeked her head out of her own tent, a question forming on her lips.

"That's it! This is miserable, but I've found the perfect solution!" His eyes seemed to lose focus and his jaw tightened before he reached out towards the ground and jerked. All of the water that had pooled on the ground under their tents flicked up in a whip-like motion and flew out to the side before collapsing back onto the ground. Tiny sparks of light danced along the stream of water and died as it splashed down.

Hashkan flashed a grin her way and then reached towards her.

"Oh, no. Absolutely not." Li'or's eyes grew wide and she tried to scoot back into her tent. Whatever experiment he had in mind, she had no intention of being the test subject.

Before she got out of Hashkan's line of sight, the water that had soaked into her clothes sprang out from the fabric and tossed itself aside. He stepped back under his tent and repeated the process on himself. Now dry, he looked over at her, light dancing in his eyes and a broad smile across his face.

"Brilliant, yes?" he asked.

"Very clever," she admitted with a smirk.

"You're welcome."

Li'or rolled her eyes but couldn't keep her smile from growing. "Thank you. I think this just became the easiest trip I've made during this time of year." Her mind was already whirling. She'd had very limited interaction with Weavers and had never considered such practical applications for their abilities. If she could drag them out of their walled gardens for long caravan escorts, she could eliminate the most common complications. Faster trips, more coin.

"And to think you tried to resist," Hashkan said, pulling her out of her thoughts.

"I know, I know. Maybe I'll be the one offering to hire you next time. Sleep well." She ducked back under her tent flap, cringing as she went. She might never hear the end of it.

The rain stopped in the early hours of the morning and the day broke with a clear sky. Li'or tried to find dry wood for a fire, but after the night's rain, everything was too wet to hold a flame.

"Hashkan, do you think you would be able to use your little trick with the wood? Then maybe we'd be able to get it to catch flame and we could have a warm breakfast," Li'or proposed. She had already arranged all the kindling in a small cleared out area. All the leaves were brushed away to keep the fire from spreading, unlikely as it was after all the rain.

"I don't see why not. In theory, it would work the same."

The look of concentration crossed his face again as he looked at the campfire. The water slowly rippled out from the wood in tiny droplets and floated in the air towards Hashkan, glinting in the sunlight. He pulled out an empty water flask, eyes still focused on something Li'or couldn't see, and had all the water pour into the container. A heavy sigh escaped him and his shoulders dropped just a fraction.

"That should all be pure drinking water. I only Altered the Threads for the water so that's all that was affected." He passed the flask over to her.

"How did I not know Weavers were so damn useful?" Li'or muttered as she swished the water around and took a test sip. It was just as perfect as he'd predicted.

Hashkan heard her comment and sat up straighter, a satisfied smirk on his face. "Maybe you shouldn't be so quick to assume we just skulk around in libraries and council rooms."

Li'or snapped her eyes back to him, the crease between her brows deepening. "I never said that." She passed the water back over to him. "So, what else can you do?"

Hashkan's eyes widened. "Well, it's more of a question of what we can't do."

"Alright, what about healing? If we get attacked by wolves and I get mauled, can you Alter me back together before I bleed out?"

All the color left Hashkan's face and he set his breakfast to the side. "Mauled?" He paused and swallowed with difficulty. "No. I'm afraid not. The Threads of sentient creatures resist change. No amount of pushing or pulling has any effect."

That wasn't the answer she'd hoped for. She was glad to know his limitations, but it was still a disappointment.

Despite the small discomforts caused by the rain during breakfast and while they packed, once on the road, they made good time through beautiful country. The road that followed alongside the river was pure mud at this point, but they swung the horses and mule up into the grass and avoided the treacherous footing entirely. The Silver Gilt River was just to the east of them, never out of sight, and the land rose and fell as it changed from rocky hills to the gentle swells of well-maintained fields.

After a week on the road, they made it to Crespwell. A cozy farming town wedged between the Silver Gilt and the Aine, it was the halfway point between Breen and Straeth. Crespwell was more of a collection of homes than a real town, made up of one inn- The Autumn's Gold- a town hall, and a few craftsmen shops all grown up almost at random on either side of the road and mixed in with farm-houses and dab-and-waddle homes. Fields and pastures ran right up to the edge of the road, adding the earthy smells of ripe produce and farm animals to the thick, marshy smell of the river.

Without any discussion, Hashkan led them right up to the inn.

"I can hardly wait to sleep on an actual bed. Sleeping on all those rocks isn't healthy," he complained as they walked through the front doors.

The inn was decorated like a farmhouse, with mismatched tables scattered around the ground floor and yellow and white gingham everywhere. Though the town straddled the main road and was no stranger to travelers, every head still turned as they made their way towards the counter to speak to the innkeeper. A Weaver in his robes and an elf out of her forest was an odd sight anywhere.

The patrons returned to their meals and drinks while Li'or and Hashkan arranged for dinner and two rooms for the night. By the time they found their seats, the room was bustling with activity again, all except in the corner near the bar.

A trio of elf men crowded together at the table, sipping dark red wine. They eyed Li'or from across the room, creases forming between their sharp brows as they glanced back and forth between her and Hashkan. One of them caught her eye and smiled. She glared daggers at him and looked away.

Unfortunately, Hashkan noticed them.

"Li'or, there's elves over in that corner," he said with an enthusiastic nod in their direction.

"I know." Li'or's tone was as dry and flat as the deserts of northern Gnür.

Hashkan hesitated. "Is something wrong?"

She lifted her gaze from her tankard of ale. He was leaning towards her, both hands wrapped around his own drink. The corners of his mouth pulled down in a concerned frown. He looked so genuine. Like it would be easy to expose a dark piece of her past and he would help her drag it into the light.

But no. That's not why she was here. This was just a job.

She slouched back into her chair. "It's a long story. I'm not getting into it tonight."

"Oh." He looked disappointed, but then his eyes darted back over to the elves and he perked up. "Well, one of them is coming over this way."

Li'or hissed a curse under her breath and turned towards them. Sure enough, one of them was sauntering her way, twirling his wine glass confidently as he went.

She stood in a rush that sent her chair screeching across the floor. "Have them send my meal up to my room."

She stalked away from the table, feeling all the eyes in the room boring into her as she left, but she didn't care. Her room would be empty and that's exactly what she needed.

THEY LEFT first thing the next morning. Li'or didn't speak during breakfast or while they were loading the horses. Hashkan practically squirmed the entire time and more than once looked her way and opened his mouth to speak, only to close it again and sigh. She ignored him.

"Li'or, if something is wrong, I can help," he finally said, long after they'd left the town behind. He fixed her with those silver eyes again, candid and full of worry. "Did you know them? Was there some kind of feud I should know about?"

"No. And there's nothing to help with. Everything is fine."

Hashkan was quiet for a moment. "As long as you're sure."

"I am." And the silence settled back around them.

They made camp as the sun started setting behind the trees, dyeing the clouds bright pinks and purples. Hashkan told her goodnight and sulked off into his tent, but Li'or stayed up, tending their fire and thinking.

Hashkan had asked about a feud and he wasn't far off. Her first experience with elven culture hadn't gone well.

Not long after she'd left her home town of Zenick, she was wandering through the Eimear forest when she was ambushed by an elven patrol and imprisoned. They kept her in chains just long enough to figure out who she was. She was the daughter of a famed jeweler and a poetess, and she'd been given to the forest as a sacrifice when she was only a few months old. That was where her real parents had found her, half-starved. How anyone could do that to a child was beyond her.

Elven culture was a foreign, abstruse thing and she wanted no part of it. As soon as the elves freed her, she'd fled their city and the Eimear forest without so much as a glance over her shoulder. And she'd never been back. Knowing how little the elves as a people valued life... Those weren't *her* people.

She was feeding another branch into the fire when she heard a howl off in the distance to the northwest. It was far enough away that she dismissed it until she heard the answering howl to the south, closer, and then another to the west- closer still. She crept over to Hashkan's tent and shook him awake.

"Wake up," she told him. "Wolves."

He shot up with wide eyes and scrambled out of his

tent while Li'or scanned the area, trying to figure out where the wolves would come from. There was crashing through the brush to their south, like the wolves were flanking them. She drew her sword and dagger. Hashkan moved to stand back to back with her, his face as pale as snow. Li'or pressed her lips into a thin line, mind whirling as she tried to come up with a plan.

Before she had even an inkling of an idea, a wolf burst into their camp. It stood waist high at the shoulder and its summer coat was a blend of brown and gray. Li'or tightened her grip on her sword and crouched as she watched the wolf charge towards her. As she raised her sword to strike, the wolf darted to the side and ran past her, leaving the camp.

Li'or lowered her sword and stared after it.

"What in the name of the Seamstress?" Hashkan muttered.

"I don't-" Li'or started.

Two more wolves charged out of the brush, followed shortly by a third. They all sprinted through the camp, claws churning up the ground, and disappeared out the other side. The crashing and snapping of underbrush continued all around them.

"Is that… normal?"

"No," Li'or said. "Keep your guard up. Something's not right."

Lifting her sword, she crept towards the tree line. Just before she took her first step out of the camp, a zhu'dac exploded out of the brush in front of her, howling, muzzle frothing.

Li'or hissed a curse. She was forced back onto her heels as she blocked a wild swing of the zhu'dac's club. She batted it aside with her dagger then slashed down with her sword, catching the creature in its broad neck and dropping it like a stone. As she wrenched her sword free, four more came screaming into the light of the fire.

"Try to distract them!" Li'or yelled and she charged towards the beasts. She bashed a zhu'dac in the face with the cross-guard of her dagger, sending the beast staggering back, then swung her sword around aiming at another's face. The second zhu'dac screeched and jumped back.

Li'or stepped in towards the stunned beast and drew her dagger low across the zhu'dac's knees as it held its snout. It howled then fell on useless legs.

With a high-pitched wail, a third zhu'dac barreled into Li'or, knocking her off her feet and forcing all air from her lungs in a rush. She tucked the flats of her blades against herself and rolled, coming up on one knee with her teeth bared.

The last three zhu'dac fanned out around her. They were all dressed in rags and had no weapons other than their teeth and claws, but they snickered at her and started to close in.

Damnit, what is Hashkan doing?

"Get away from her, ya mangy bleedin' bastards!"

Li'or and all the zhu'dac looked back into the trees. That wasn't Hashkan's voice.

A giant of a man burst into the camp, still yelling obscenities and whirling a heavy war hammer around his head like it weighed as much as a dagger. He ran past a stunned Hashkan and slammed his hammer into the head of the nearest zhu'dac. It went down with a wet crunch.

Before the others could regroup, Li'or went on the offensive. She lunged forward with her sword leading towards the closest zhu'dac's left. It fell for her feint and started to swerve to the right at the last second, right into her dagger. Li'or slipped it between the zhu'dac's ribs and rammed it home up to the hilt.

Abandoning her dagger, she spun back around to face the last of the attackers.

A flash of light stopped her in her tracks.

Hashkan made a throwing motion and fire streaked through the air. It sailed at the last zhu'dac and splashed across its shoulders. Its fur burst into flame. The zhu'dac screamed before dropping to the earth and flailing desperately as it tried to put itself out. A second glob of fire fell on it, this one taking it full in the face. It used its last breath to howl one final time.

With a grunt, the man walked over to the burning corpse.

"A Weaver, eh? That's plowin' perfect! Always preferred havin' one of yeh around," he said, every syllable carrying a strange, harsh accent that sharpened all the consonants.

Li'or's grip on her sword tightened. He was from Anagovia's neighbor, Vaeshek. That southern-most continent was known for its harsh, bitterly cold weather and it's ruthless warriors.

"And an elf! It's me lucky day after all." The man strapped his hammer on his belt and stood there grinning, hands on his hips.

Li'or kept her sword in hand and moved closer to Hashkan. Now that she had a moment to breathe, she was able to get a better look at him. He wore a padded jerkin with a chain mail shirt over the top, worn breeches, and a leather cap. Thin strips of metal were sown into the backs of his gloves and worked into the shins of his boots. In addition to the hammer, he carried a longbow and a full quiver of arrows. There was a dagger on his hip and the hilt of a second one poked out of his left boot.

Dangerous.

"So, we'll be moving on then?" he asked, glancing

between Hashkan and Li'or and gesturing around at the corpses.

Hashkan was pale and his silver eyes were wide with shock. He was staring down at his hands, then up at the dead zhu'dac, and then back at his hands. Pity and irritation welled up in Li'or. Taking your first life was never easy, even if it was something as vulgar as a zhu'dac. And Hashkan wasn't a soldier. The fight could have easily taken a different turn.

Irritation won out. There was still a threat in their camp.

"Who are you?" Li'or spat.

"Emond Galefridus, at yer service," he said, bowing awkwardly and sweeping his leather cap off his head. His hair was so blond it was almost white. "Madam…?"

She ignored the question in his voice. He waited for a response, still smiling. When none came he continued on, unfazed.

"Alright, might I ask for some directions, then? I'm bound for Voronigrad and I'm a bit turned around."

"You're more than turned around. You went past it entirely. You're too far south and you're on the wrong side of the river." Li'or narrowed her eyes, sensing a lie. He didn't seem the sort to become so hopelessly lost. Not to mention how convenient it was for him to show up at just the right time to help them.

"Seamstress's tits!" Emond cursed. Hashkan jerked like he'd been struck and glared at the man, red rising from his collar. "Yeh track one deer just a hair too long and then next thing yeh know, yer up to yer arm pits in bramble and dealin' with blighted zhu'dac…" He continued on, stomping and waving his hands. "Why didn't I buy a blighted map?"

Hashkan's face softened and he shifted his feet

awkwardly. "We're bound for Straeth. It's only a couple days from Voronigrad. You're welcome to travel with us," he volunteered.

Li'or couldn't stop the frustrated hiss that escaped her lips as she whipped her head back towards Hashkan. She narrowed her eyes. "What are you doing?" she asked through gritted teeth.

Hashkan blinked in surprise and he pushed his hair out of his face. "Li'or, the camaraderie of the road, remember? He needs help. Besides, he just saved us. We owe him."

"Aye, I am a bit desperate, truth be told. I won't get in yer way. And I have me own supplies." He took a few steps closer to where Li'or and Hashkan stood.

"There is no fucking camaraderie of the road, and don't take another step." Li'or flicked her sword up to point at Emond's face. Every muscle in her body was coiled tight, ready to spring. "You're going to turn east and keep going until you across the Silver Gilt. I want you out of my camp."

Emond held up his hands and took a small step backward.

"Li'or..." Hashkan chided her. He stepped forward and put a hand on her arm. He tried to push it down but she resisted.

She met his stare, fighting to keep her voice steady despite the fury that was welling up in her. "Take. Your. hand. Off me."

"Li'or, don't you think you're over-reacting? He risked his life to help us." Hashkan pulled his hand back and put his hands on his hips.

"You don't know what you're doing," she whispered. He didn't recognize what a skilled fighter Emond was. He didn't notice how easily the man ended the zhu'dac's lives. There was no hesitation in his swings.

"Yes. I do. I'm hiring another bodyguard." Hashkan's silver eyes were as cold as steel. "Lest we forget who is holding the coin pouch for this trip."

Li'or gritted her teeth so hard she thought they would break. "Fine," she spat. "But if I have to save you from him too, I'm tripling my fee." She sheathed her sword and took a steadying breath. "We need to load the horses and move camp. Both of you get to work."

* * *

THEY BROKE camp and rode out into the dark, Emond jogging between Li'or and Hashkan's horses where she could keep an eye on him. The big man's pack jostled around on the mule along with the rest of their supplies and he easily kept pace. Li'or watched him with narrowed eyes. Not only could he fight, but he had the stamina to fight all blighted day.

They carried on, barely slowing, through the sunrise into midday. Hashkan kept glancing at her with his eyebrows raised, but she ignored him. She was still furious that he'd pulled the authority card and ignored her counsel. He knew she had more experience on the road, knew her job was specifically to keep him safe, but he'd ignored her. It was that kind of blatant arrogance that would get a person killed. Did he not see how contrived Emond's arrival had been?

When she finally called for them to stop for the night, the Vaeshekian collapsed onto the ground with a grunt.

"Ack, what a day! We're close now, yeah? Me feet would like to just plowin' fall off."

Good, Li'or thought. She'd pushed them hard hoping to

leave him behind, but she'd settle for exhaustion.

"I believe we're a few more days out. Right, Li'or?" Hashkan asked as he swung off his horse.

"Three, maybe four more days," she answered. "Of course, that's assuming we don't have any more trouble." She looked pointedly at Emond where he was still sprawled out on the ground.

"Those little blighters, the zhu'dac, we don't have any in Vaeshek. I heard tell they lived in the mountains and snatched ornery tykes away in the night," Emond said.

"Oh, those are just superstitions. There's no evidence that they've ever snuck into someone's home and stolen their children."

"No, but they are a threat," Li'or added. "And they do usually stay in the mountains."

If they said anything else, it didn't register. Li'or had been so distracted by Emond that she hadn't spared a thought for the zhu'dac. First, there was the horde of them outside of Breen, then a band sheltering on the outskirts of an elven forest, now this. She could count on both hands the number of times she'd dealt with the creatures over the course of her life and none of those other times were so far from mountain ranges.

Something isn't right.

It kept nagging at her through their small dinner- during which Emond and Hashkan talked and laughed like old friends- and into the night. Li'or reluctantly took the first watch and sat down in front of their dying fire. Lack of sleep from the night before and their hard push through the day weighed her down. Every movement felt like it was passing through honey. She knew she needed to get up and walk around before she fell asleep. She didn't make it there.

Someone grabbed her shoulder and gave her a rough

shake, snatching her out of the quagmire of sleep. She gasped and jerked her dagger from her side. A massive hand closed on her wrist before she could get it in front of herself.

"Well now, that won't be needed right this instant," Emond said. "I just wanna talk."

Li'or snatched her arm away from him and stood up, putting some safe distance between them. She lowered her blade but kept her feet planted in a fighting stance and her body bladed to the side to present a thinner target. "What do you want?"

"I know yeh don't trust me. I know yeh won't believe me, but I *was* avoidin' those zhu'dac until I heard the two of yeh yellin'. I really was right lost, though it pains to me admit it." He paused and looked a Li'or, studying her expression. She clenched her jaw and raised her chin a fraction. "No, yeh don't believe me. But do believe that if I'd wanted, I could have just slit yer throat, and the lad's, taken yer shit, and none the wiser. Instead we're here, just havin' a chat. I'm not askin' fer yeh to love me, just fer some peace til we get where we're goin'."

He held out his hand to her. She stared at it for a moment.

He was right, damn him. She'd been lax, and if he'd wanted to take advantage of that, she'd given him ample opportunity. She was still hesitant but reached out and clasped his forearm.

"I'll still be watching."

Emond grinned. "I'd be worried if yeh didn't." He plopped down in her seat at the fire. "Time fer a shift change. I got it from here."

Li'or left him to it and slipped into her tent. She'd give Emond a chance to prove himself, but she kept her sword right beside her, just in case.

Chapter Eight

Artisan Work

6 months ago

It took hardly any effort for Ordelieus to organize the zhu'dac, but it soon became apparent he would need humans in his city if he was going to make any real progress. Zhu'dac just weren't made to handle artisan work the way Ordelieus wanted it done- correctly. They would fight when he needed them to and they would carry heavy loads, but that was where their usefulness ended.

So, despite the threat of winter, he left and made the trek through the foothills of the White Stone Mountains, through the swamp, and into the closet city of Pinescar. The city was known for carpentry and logging, but the insistent pulling of some half-remembered story told him there were plenty of skilled masons there too.

Ordelieus wandered through the trade quarter, keeping a close eye out for a mason's shop. The humid air made his worn clothes stick to him as it carried with it the combined smells of the ocean and the swamps surrounding the city. Occasionally, he spotted the odd bit of jewel-toned trim around a door or paper lanterns hanging from awnings-tiny reminders of friendlier times with the Rak-Shai. A young page dashed past him carrying a satchel bigger than his body. He ran to the corner and disappeared into the last shop on the street. Ordelieus looked through the front windows as he passed by and grinned.

Samples of various stone types were on display in the front, most of which was marble and rare colors of granite. A young woman, her dark hair pulled into a knot on top of her head, traded a scroll for a few copper crosses then sent the page back on his way. Ordelieus held the door open for the boy as he walked inside. Sharp hammer strikes echoed from the back of the building.

"How can I help you?" she asked as the door shut behind him.

He glanced at her hands as she toyed with the scroll. No calluses. So she was either a clerk or a new apprentice.

"I need to speak with the master mason," he answered, walking up to the carved counter that separated them.

"I'm afraid he's busy at the moment. I'd be glad to take down your name and where you're staying so we can send a runner for you when he's available." She gave him a tight smile, eyeing his frayed clothing, and pulled out a loose piece of parchment, prepared to take a message.

Ordelieus started to tell her the name of the inn where he was staying, but a headache stabbed into the side of his skull for half a heartbeat. His mouth closed with a snap. He realized he didn't have time for messages.

Quick as a snake, his hand shot across the countertop and grabbed the woman by her hair, dragging her towards him. Her feet kicked against the back of the counter and she opened her mouth to scream. Ordelieus's mind reached across the small distance and he snatched at the Threads of her mind. She froze and her screech died before it ever really got started. She hung, paralyzed, as he rummaged through her thoughts, stretching them different directions, making her more pliable. Once everything was arranged how he wanted, he took a tiny Thread from his own mind and wove it back through, knotting everything into place.

He released her and she slowly slid off the counter then fixed her hair.

"Is there something I can help you with today?" she asked with a smile.

"Take me to the master mason."

"Of course, he's in the back. Right this way." She turned and gestured for him to follow through a door behind the counter. The dinging of the hammer grew louder as she opened it.

A small smile pulled at the corners of Ordelieus' lips as he followed her back.

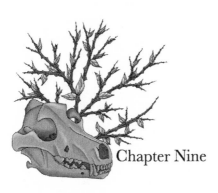

Chapter Nine

Night Crept In

Now

*A*s Li'or had projected, Straeth's walls came into view during the late afternoon three days later. The city closed its gates at nightfall, but if they kept a steady pace, they would slip through just before entry was barred until the following morning.

Straeth was located just to the west of the Silver Gilt River and north of where the Aine River joined its flow towards the Rak-Shai Sea. The rivers joined up in a riot of white water that had a tendency to flood, so the craftsmen of the city had designed a complicated system of moats, channels, and sewers to divert the flood waters. Even though they were dry for part of the year, the labyrinth of ditches doubled as an additional defense for the city. The walls were made of heavy peach-colored stone and the peaks of hundreds of colorful roofs peered out from over the walls. The traffic on the road heading in both directions swelled the closer they got, people rushing to get into the city to their homes or back out to their farms before dark. Storm clouds hung low on the horizon, breathing down everyone's necks and pushing them home faster.

They crossed the outer-most moat and rode up to the southern gate of the city when the sun was just barely a sliver on the western horizon. The line of traffic slowed to a crawl and then stopped. The people ahead of them milled around nervously, complaining under their breaths. Crammed between the outermost moat and the wall as they were, it was like being in a giant winepress.

Li'or stood in her stirrups to peer over the crowd. Guards in navy and gray uniforms wielding halberds were blocking people from entering the city while others pushed the gates shut just in front of the crowd.

Li'or pulled her gelding off to the side and cantered beside the crowd up to the gate. "Wait, it's still light out. These people need to get home," she shouted over the tumult.

The crowd got even louder, feeling brave while they hid behind Li'or.

"Can't see the sun anymore, madam elf. We're shutting the gates." A young guard told her before turning to address the crowd. "You folks can camp in the grass between the walls and the moat, but we're not letting you in tonight."

Li'or urged her horse forward a couple more steps so that she was right in front of the guard. A tiny voice in the back of her head told her not to get involved, but she had never been very good at listening to that voice.

"Are you in charge of this gate?"

"I am," he answered, crossing his arms.

"And you think you can just take it upon yourself to change the city's policy and close the gates whenever you feel like it?" Li'or raised her brows.

"Look, lady, I don't know who you think-"

"Wait, Marth! I think I know who that is." The gate ground to a halt and a guard poked her head around the door. She was of average build and looked to be about Hashkan's age with shockingly red hair sticking out from under her helm.

"Ylinia?" Li'or asked in shock, her eyes widening as the guard approached.

"Li'or! I thought that might be you!"

Ylinia all but skipped up to Li'or, who dismounted and held out her hand. The woman ignored it and clutched Li'or in a brief bear hug before backing up, flushed.

"I was hoping I'd run into you one day! What have you been up to?" she asked.

Li'or took a half-step back, putting a more comfortable distance between them. "I'm still guarding caravans, mostly along the river. And you? You gave up on the mercenary life?"

"This is more steady. Of course it's not perfect," she said, throwing a glare at Marth, "but it beats sleeping in the mud."

"Of course." Li'or glanced over her shoulder to where the crowd was steadily filing in through the half-closed gates. She looked back at Ylinia and smirked.

The woman's eyes flashed conspiratorially. "Plus, I was promoted to sergeant a few months ago, even with the blighted chauvinistic attitude around here."

Li'or nodded. "You were quick to learn the sword. I knew you'd do well."

"I hate to interrupt this heartfelt reunion," Marth sneered from behind Ylinia. "But can you take this chat inside the damned gates? By the time Ylinia finishes talking, it'll be pitch dark."

Li'or looked back towards the gates to see the last of the travelers slipping through. Just as she'd hoped. She winked towards Hashkan and Emond before following Ylinia through to where the city waited for them.

Straeth had started out as one simple inn that an ambitious man had built close to the middle of the long route from Pinescar to Breen. The inn offered the only break for those traveling by land or water for weeks in either direction. It thrived and it wasn't long before others wanted to take advantage of the clientele that the original inn had built. So an entire city had cropped up around the inn, most of which was made with the purpose of entertaining weary travelers and, years later, it had become one of the largest cities in Anagovia.

Inns, taverns, and brothels dominated the city, each trying to attract more people than the last. Bright walls painted with fanciful and glaring designs assaulted the eyes from all different directions. Li'or caught a glimpse out of the corner of her eye of Hashkan openly gaping at a building shaped like an anvil, the dings of metal striking metal ringing out from inside, even this late in the day. Small boats propelled by push poles wound though the channels and passed under the many bridges, each lined with leaded glass lanterns that glowed different colors.

Once they passed through the gate Li'or and Ylinia swung off to the side a short distance to continue their conversation, trailing Hashkan and Emond behind. She'd introduced everyone, but the pair had fallen back and were walking slow and pointing things out to each other, eyes wide and mouths moving nonstop. Li'or shook her head but grinned. She had been the same way when she'd first arrived in the city- and it had only gotten more incredulous as the years went by.

"Thanks for the help, Ylinia." Li'or watched as Marth stormed off in the direction of the seedier parts of town. "I hope you don't end up being reprimanded."

Ylinia followed Li'or's gaze and scoffed. "His shift ends when the gate closes so he's always trying to close up as early as he can. If you follow him, you'll end up at the worst brothels in the city. He likes women too much for the comfort of his purse, I think. Shittiest lieutenant on the walls. But it's good to see you again, Li'or. It's been over five years."

"Has it really been that long?"

A tense silence stretched between them. Ylinia scuffed her boot across the ground.

"Can ye point us to an inn with a good, stout ale?" Emond interrupted. Li'or fought back a sigh of relief. "I've a hankerin' fer a good, *stout* ale."

"I thought we'd go to the Ale Boat. It is still there, isn't it?" Li'or asked, swinging back onto her horse.

"Yes, it is." Ylinia looked a tiny bit deflated. "It's still run by Faraden. He'll be glad to see you, too."

"Perfect. If everything goes as planned, I'll be leaving through this gate again soon. I'll see you then," Li'or said by way of farewell.

"The Ale Boat! Ah-ha! That sounds like my kind of inn!" Emond shouted as they moved off. "First round's on me, eh friends?"

"I won't turn one down," Hashkan told him. Li'or thought that she might even enjoy a couple drinks when they got there. This trip had been entirely too eventful.

The gate they'd passed through opened into an area of the city where a lot of craftsmen made their homes, but as they rode further in, they had to pass through a poorer area of Straeth. As they navigated the first block of ramshackle housing, Li'or was reminded why she didn't like entering through the south gate near dark. Most of the oil lanterns along the road were broken or outright missing and night crept in along with a fog from over the river, obscuring alleyways. Most people had already gone inside for the night, the few stragglers walking quickly and jumping at every sound.

Li'or heard shuffling off to the left and her horse's ear flicked over towards the alley they were passing. She turned just in time to see a man dressed in rags run out from the shadows towards Hashkan's mare. He grabbed the reins and jerked. The mare squealed and threw her head up, ears pinned back, but the man held on.

The musky smell of ale mixed with sweat rolled off the man and he smiled, revealing teeth blacken by rot. He swayed on his bare feet and leaned against the mare's neck, one grime-covered hand twisting into her mane.

"Hey, folks, hey," he said and then started to laugh drunkenly, almost crazed. "This is a fine animal- oh yes, very fine- and those are sure nice clothes you're all wearing, yes, very nice." He fell into another fit of laughter. "And I need some coin. So you should pass some on to a man in need, eh?"

"Let go of the horse, man. Yeh don't want to cross with us tonight," Emond walked up to the man, his hammer already in hand. "Now, go on back to whatever sewer yeh crawled out of."

The beggar let go of the mare, still laughing. "Oh, I don't want to cross you, oh, no! But they do!" He pointed a crooked finger across the road. Li'or wheeled her horse around just in time to see five armed men jump over a board fence holding crude, rusted swords. She snatched her sword from her scabbard and shot Hashkan a pointed look. He nodded and his eyes slid out of focus, jaw clenching as he prepared to Alter.

The men started to charge them as soon as they hit the ground.

"Oh, no yeh don't!" Emond bellowed and he ran to

meet them. Li'or kicked her gelding forward and he lunged, his teeth bared.

Emond dashed off to his left, so Li'or reined her horse to the right. The warhorse reared and struck out with his front legs, taking one of the men in the chest and landing on him on the way down, crushing him.

Another man ran up on Li'or's left side, swinging his blade in an arc aimed at her thigh. She swung her sword across and blocked his blow with a hasty slap across his knuckles. He cursed and snatched his hand back, dropping his sword. The thug was surprisingly determined, though, and as Li'or turned her attention to another, he reached up and grabbed hold of her sword belt.

The would-be thief hauled on her belt and Li'or swayed in her saddle, fighting to stay on her gelding. He swayed under the additional weight, but lurched to the side right as a ball of flame whizzed overhead. The man still clung to her, dragging behind her horse and, straining, Li'or chopped down wildly with her sword.

There was a gasp and a spray of crimson blood, then she was free. Her assailant crumpled to the ground, trying in vain to keep his lifeblood from escaping the yawning wound at the base of his neck. She crawled back into her saddle and pivoted her horse, ready for the next.

But there wasn't anyone else. All five men laid in the road, dying or dead- her two, two more with dents in them like old armor, and the last one burning and still twitching. Li'or wrinkled her nose at the smell. There was no sign of the beggar.

"Hey! Are you alright?" Several guards, including Ylinia, were running up the road towards them.

"It'll take more than a few gutter rats to cause us any real issue, Sergeant!" Emond answered. He rolled over one of the men he'd hit and cringed. "This one won't be doin' much of anythin' anymore."

The guards turned a couple of the men over and made quick work of patting them down, looking for anything to identify them with. They came back empty-handed.

"Did they, by any chance, work with a beggar?" Ylinia asked.

Li'or opened her mouth to answer but Emond cut her off. She glared at him, but he didn't notice.

"Oh, aye, they did. Most rank smellin' blighter I've met in all me years. Lucky if he had two teeth in his whole damn head."

"That describes every beggar," Hashkan muttered.

"He must have taken off when the fight started," Li'or said, cutting Emond off before he could start again. Mercifully, the dolt stayed quiet.

"Damn. I think he may be the one organizing the thefts. He gets a good group together and they harass people in the city. Then they seem to disband and he starts another group of thieves. Been at it for months, but we're so understaffed right now we can't track his movements the way I'd like."

"Understaffed?" Li'or asked.

"Yeah, people are quitting in droves and leaving town. A couple have even abandoned their families."

"Really?"

"Yeah, and nothing's changed. Nothing. Same officers, same shifts." Ylinia put her hands on her hips and sighed. "I'll report this back to a decent lieutenant that will make sure you three get some kind of reward."

"Thank you again, Ylinia. If you need us to give a report, you know where we're staying."

"I'm sure you'll be hearing from someone soon," the guard muttered as she turned back towards the corpses.

✳ ✳

THE ALE BOAT was a huge hulk of a building that stood on the southeastern side of the city, overlooking the rushing waters of the Silver Gilt River. It was four stories high and it took up an entire city block on its own, not including the stables and paddocks. The upper stories were fancifully built to be shaped like a ship, while the first story, as well as the huge stairway leading up to the double doors at the front, were carved into the semblance of waves. All the windows on the first floor were even stained blue to keep up the facade of water. Blue tinged light drifted out towards the street. The stables and paddocks were hidden behind the building so they wouldn't distract from the inn's architecture.

They made their way up to the main stair at the front of the inn where three grooms waited to take the horses and the mule. One ran forward to meet them and took the mule's lead rope from Hashkan.

"Are there any stalls with paddocks still available?" Li'or asked him. She hopped off her horse and started unloading her things from the mule.

"Yes, ma'am. We have five left. Do you want a paddock for the mule too?"

"Yes, please." She tipped the young boy a copper cross and started up the stairs with Hashkan and Emond. Music and the sounds of conversation were drifting out through the closed double doors at top of the stairs and Li'or could already smell the food.

"A vast improvement over a tent," Hashkan said.

Li'or smirked. "Just wait until you see the inside."

She opened both front doors and stood aside so the men could get the full view of the main hall. The walls were painted in bright colors, each depicting a different nautical scene. The entire room was lit as bright as day by hundreds of candles in gilded sconces, but vents around the top of the walls kept the room cool and smoke free. Serving girls in bright, multicolored skirts moved through the tables holding trays over their heads. Directly across from them was a huge polished bar that had five bartenders working behind it, running and scrambling to keep up with orders. There was a large stage on the left side of the room where several musicians played and the stairs to the upper floors were on the right. The room was nearly filled to capacity and laughter competed with the music spilling out through the doors along with the golden light from all the tiny lanterns.

"That's it! I've found me new home!" Emond exclaimed as he all but ran through the front doors. He went straight to the bar and sat on one of the high, brass stools in front of it.

Hashkan laughed and Li'or rolled her eyes as they followed behind him. Li'or picked her way through the crowd looking for the innkeeper.

The owner of the inn was a woman named Eseldra, who also owned several dress shops in Straeth and Voroni-grad, so she left the management of the inn to a man named Faraden and she only checked in every few nights. To Li'or's disappointment, she was here tonight, though.

Eseldra always stood out from the crowd where ever she went thanks to her bright dresses with huge skirts and her tall blond hair that resembled a massive beehive. To go with her strange hair, she wore makeup so thick it looked like it was applied with a mason's trowel and her dresses always had a high collar rising in a frill behind her head, framing her face and hair. And, of course, they always showed off most of her ample chest.

She was standing near the stairs, where a hallway also

opened into the first-floor rooms, checking a list and making sure all the people passing through were paid guests. There was a large man with a club standing next to her.

"Mistress Eseldra, are you taking any more guests this evening?" Li'or asked as they approached.

"Oh! Li'or, you're back! How wonderful! Larg, look!" She grabbed the arm of the big man next to her. "Li'or, I was just telling Larg about the huge fight that you helped break up the last time you came through. It's Larg's first night here." She cast a lascivious gaze up at Larg and scraped her eyes up and down his frame. "He's doing very well so far, though." There was no doubt in Li'or's mind that the man would find himself in Eseldra's bed by the end of the night, or at least he would if he wanted to keep his job. "But to answer your question, we always have a room available for you and any friends that you bring in. How many rooms do you need?"

"Three. One for myself, one for Hashkan," she gestured towards him, "and one for the large man in the leather cap at the bar over there, Emond." Li'or pointed Emond out to Eseldra over the crowd.

"Oh…" she cooed following Li'or's finger. The spark in her that had dimmed a bit as she talked business flared back up. The woman liked big, brutish men. She wrote them down on her list and waved to Larg, never taking her eyes off Emond. She showed him the list and he pulled three skeleton keys off a large ring at his waist. "Here you are, dearie. These are the last three rooms on the second floor, all over in the western wing as you prefer- less traffic past your door. Please enjoy a hot meal on the house… and have your friend over there come and introduce himself," she said, winking at Li'or like they were sharing a secret.

"I will. Thank you," Li'or told her, forcing herself to smile back as she turned away. She couldn't understand Eseldra's taste in men, but she didn't want to lose a good connection so she played along. At the end of the day, it wasn't any of her business.

She motioned for Hashkan to follow and they worked back through the crowd towards Emond. Just as they walked up, the bartender deposited a large stein full of dark ale in front of him.

"Here's your room key, Emond. They're numbered, see? It's on the second floor, west wing. Also, the owner of the inn over there," she pointed out Eseldra to him, "has given us dinner on the house tonight. You might want to go thank her later." Li'or fought to contain her cringe at the end, but Emond was an adult and could make his own choices about where-and if- he slept that night.

Emond looked over to Eseldra and nodded, raising his mug to her in a salute. "I will be sure to thank her after the meal. Where's the food?"

They picked out one of the few empty tables and a serving girl was right behind them with their first course. She had chestnut hair and a smattering of freckles across her nose- pretty, in an innocent kind of way- and Hashkan couldn't take her eyes off of her. Li'or stifled a groan.

Food and drink came in waves and they all ate with the half-starved fervor only people straight off the road could manage. Though they ate so fast Li'or had a hard time believing they were breathing, Emond and Hashkan kept up a steady stream of conversation. She mostly kept quiet, snorting at an occasional joke and scanning the crowd.

Straeth attracted every kind of person, and the Ale Boat was a popular inn. Men and women, humans and elves, Gnürians and Vaeshekians all milled through the common room. Separately, that is. A table of elven men kept looking over at Li'or and smiling in an effort to catch her eye. She ignored them.

"Hashkan," she said, inserting herself into the conversation and trying to block out the elves. "Didn't you need to go to the Gathering?"

"Ack, yes! Supposed to be there, aren't yeh?" Emond asked around a mouth full of food.

"It's fine if I report tomorrow. There wouldn't have been time for me to do anything but eat and go to sleep if I had gone there tonight anyway." As he spoke, his eyes wandered the room until they finally settled back on the pretty serving girl.

Emond noticed immediately and burst into a full-bellied laugh. "Oh, that's what it is, is it? Look at that, Li'or, even the mighty Weaver needs a nice place to put-"

"Emond!" Hashkan exclaimed, a furious blush rising from his collar. "We're in mixed company!" He glanced at Li'or and blushed even brighter.

"I've heard worse," she said, brushing it off.

He must not have been as embarrassed as he'd looked. Not even fifteen minutes later he excused himself and never came back. A quick scan of the room proved that the girl was gone too.

"What about one of those elves, yonder?" Emond asked her, pointing.

"Put your hand down before they notice," Li'or hissed. "I'd rather drown in this ale." She took a hearty swig just to prove her point. "They're nothing like me."

"Oh?" He raised his eyebrows expectantly.

"It's a long story. Not tonight, Emond."

"Alright, alright. I know when I've worn out me welcome. I'm for bed then. Well, after I thank our generous host!" He winked at her and sauntered towards Eseldra.

Li'or sighed and swirled her ale. A new act was coming on to the stage, but before they even got set up, some elves from across the room stood and started prowling towards her. She jumped out of her chair, then stomped off towards the stairs, nodding at Larg as she passed. He was alone too, his boss having passed him over for the night, but he didn't seem to mind the slight at all.

Oddly enough, she minded. When did the loneliness start to feel like a dagger in her gut?

⁎⁎ ⁎

"IT'S BEEN SETTLED, Li'or. I'm stayin'," Emond proclaimed as he collapsed into the chair across from Li'or the next morning. "Eseldra is as generous as she is beautiful. She's offered me a job as a bouncer. The Seamstress got me lost that day so that I could come here! Would have been nice if she had kept me out o' the brambles, but she knows better than me."

Li'or poured herself more tea from the pot on the center of the table and shook her head. "Just don't get too attached."

"What are you trying to say?" he asked, scrunching his face up.

Li'or hesitated, uncertain of how to break the news to him.

"Guards come and go in here damn near every week." The most direct route was usually the best.

Emond looked like he was going to be angry for a moment, but then his expression cleared and he chuckled and waved a hand dismissively. "She's a woman of ferocious appetite, I can't deny it. But we're different. I- it's love, ya see. I'll be here 'til I'm a crooked old geezer!"

"So in five years?" Hashkan asked. He took one of the

empty seats and poured himself a cup of honey with a little tea mixed in. His dark hair was in complete disarray and the faint circles under his eyes that had developed as they'd traveled were still in full effect.

"Oh, I ain't that old yet!" Emond scoffed.

A serving girl with dark blond hair swept up to the table and deposited a plate heaped with scones.

"There's some extras on there. Elline sent them," she whispered.

"Oh-ho! Elline is it?" He leaned over and nudged Hashkan with an elbow.

Hashkan smirked. "A gentleman doesn't share secrets."

"Bah! Don't be such a blighted prude! I'll tell ye all about last night with Eseldra! Why, we start-"

"No!" Li'or and Hashkan yelled together.

Emond just smirked and dug into his breakfast.

"So," Hashkan started, mercifully changing the subject. "I'll be reporting to the Gathering today. If you want to go with me, we'll collect your payment."

Li'or nodded while she chewed. Those five golden faces would be the last chunk of coin she needed. She'd be able to buy enough supplies to disappear into the wilderness until the winter. She felt a small stab of concern over the weird movements of the zhu'dac, but she'd be alone and would be able to avoid them, just like she'd always avoided any humans and elves that wandered the woods around her.

Just as they were wrapping up their meal, a uniformed man walked in through the front doors. He paused at the bar and spoke briefly to the bartender, who pointed him over towards their table. Li'or's eyes narrowed. She cleared her throat to get the other's attention and nodded towards the solider.

His uniform matched the ones that the guards at the

gate wore, but the extra stripes across his chest indicated a higher rank. The sword at his hip was polished to a high shine, but his boots had mud on them. This was a man who valued his weapon. He had his priorities straight.

The guard noticed their attention and took off his helmet, tucking it under an arm as he approached. He gave them a tight smile as he stopped.

"Good morning, sirs, madam. I'm Lieutenant Veltaire. Lord Klevelt has asked that you accompany me back to the capitol building. He would like to speak with you regarding the incident last night."

"Well, well! Word of our heroics have already spread that high, have they?" Emond said, beaming. He stood up from the table with a flourish. "Lead the way, good man! I'm ready fer me reward."

"Is there a reward?" Li'or asked, also standing. Maybe she'd be able to extend her trip even longer, maybe even make her way up north where the winters were milder.

"I wasn't given any specifics," the lieutenant answered curtly.

Li'or looked over to Hashkan. "Can we go to the Gathering after the meeting?"

"Of course. A meeting with the lord is more than enough reason for a short delay."

"Alright then, Lieutenant. Lead the way."

Chapter Ten

Fifty Gold Faces

The people of the city were out in full force as they roved through the streets on their way to the capitol building. Every road they wandered down was a riot of color made up of both the buildings and the brightly-colored clothes of the city's residents.

Even this early in the morning, there were people calling out the merits of their wares, shouting so loudly their lungs might well burst in order to be heard over their competitors. A crowd of limber dancers even put on a show outside of a brothel, dressed in nothing but bright purple chemises. Hashkan stopped and gaped with his mouth wide open, a small part of his brain registering that Emond had stopped beside him. He heard someone clearing their throat nearby, but it didn't process in his addled mind until Li'or jabbed him in the ribs with her elbow. He jumped and followed behind her as she continued on, his face burning as he rubbed his side.

They made their way to the northwestern side of the

city. The more distance they put between themselves and the inn, the richer the town became and the less advertising they saw on the streets. The houses and buildings turned from wood to stone. Hashkan saw gardens with paths and places to sit in the shade and even the occasional fountain. What wealth these people must have to gamble extravagance against barely contained floodwaters.

"So, is it common for women here to…" Hashkan paused as he struggled for the right words, but he couldn't contain his curiosity any longer. "To dress like that in public?"

"I hope it is," Emond said.

Veltaire laughed. "It's not *uncommon*. Most of the brothels aren't that extreme with their advertising, but if you walk the city, you'll see one or two like that. Lord Klevelt tries to keep it from getting out of hand, but we are a city of entertainment." They all paused as a small girl of about eight passed by leading a string of heavy draft horses. Each of their feet was bigger than her head, but they followed docilely behind her. "We don't produce anything here, so it's a fine line between policing the exposure and denying the city its revenue."

Hashkan nodded. He'd studied economics as an apprentice on the off chance he would end up as an adviser to a lord, and he knew how important it was for a city to have an independent source of revenue. Without it, the cost of living would become too high for most people and the lord wouldn't have the funds to keep up the walls or pay the guard.

Hashkan looked over at Li'or, who had been silent during the walk. Her eyes moved constantly as she scanned the crowd while keeping her face carefully blank. She was so focused and alert he wondered if she ever actually slept, or if each time a floorboard in the inn creaked it had her jumping for her sword. They were with an officer of the guard; surely, she could relax just this once.

Still, he couldn't help but notice how bright her eyes were as they scanned the people passing by, or the graceful way that she moved as she navigated through the thick crowds.

He frowned. He couldn't allow himself to go down that road. There were too many conflicts, the very least of which was the impending departure he'd heard her mention to the guard at the gate. He pulled his attention away from her, but it was drawn right back as a man came staggering towards them.

He was dressed in clothes that any commoner would wear and was wavering back and forth like he was drunk. He staggered into Hashkan, who barely got his feet planted under himself in time to avoid falling and taking the man with him. Hashkan grimaced and tried to pull away, but the man held him tight.

"'Scuse me, Weaver. Many… apologies." He pushed himself away from Hashkan and nearly fell again. He began to stumble away, still muttering apologies under his breath.

Before the drunk had made it three steps, Li'or was in front of him. Quick as a snake, she reached and grabbed on to one of his hands. She twisted it, then cranked it back. The drunk yelped as he fell backward onto the hard cobbles. Li'or screwed his wrist around the other way and kicked him, flipping him over so she could pin his arm down behind his back.

"Give it back," she growled. "Now."

"Okay, okay, just don't break my arm!" he pleaded, all of the slurring suddenly gone from his voice. He groped around in his pocket and pulled out Hashkan's alms purse.

Hashkan stood frozen for a moment, shocked, before

he snatched it back from the thief. Like all Weavers, he was required to carry an alms purse with him whenever he traveled. He wasn't allowed to spend any of the coins inside, they were strictly for donating to people the Seamstress pointed out as being in need. He couldn't afford to lose it.

"Stealing from a Weaver is a serious offense," Veltaire said, crossing his arms.

Emond moved up beside the lieutenant and crouched down until he was eye level with the thief.

"And we're all feelin' pretty offended," he growled.

By now a small crowd had gathered around the group. Three more city guards pushed through the press and stumbled into hasty salutes when they saw the lieutenant.

"Men," Veltaire addressed them. "Take this thief to the dungeons. I witnessed him attempt to steal from a Weaver."

The guards saluted again and escorted the cut-purse away, one holding either of his arms and one leading in front to part the crowds.

With all the excitement gone, the people of the city moved on like nothing had ever happened, parting around them like a river around a stone.

"I'm sorry Weaver Hashkan. The thieves have started to notice how short-staffed we are and they're taking advantage of it," Veltaire said. He swept his helmet off and rubbed his short brown hair. "That one was pretty brave. Li'or, thank you again."

Li'or nodded in acknowledgment, but Hashkan adjusted his robes and frowned. Brave was an understatement. Assaulting a Weaver was downright blasphemous. The implicit insult in the gesture grated on his nerves.

"I'm sure you've been very stressed, but if Weavers aren't safe, it must be terrifying for your common citizens to walk the streets. It's unacceptable. Work harder," Hashkan said, barely able to contain his sneer.

Li'or turned to him with her sharp brows knitted together and she crossed her arms. A tiny thorn of regret worked its way under his skin. He should have controlled his temper and kept his mouth shut. But, it was too late to take it back now. He had to hang on to what authority he could.

Veltaire frowned, but did a much better job controlling himself. "I'll discuss increasing our recruitment efforts with my captain. Now, shall we?" He turned on his heel and started back towards the capitol building.

✵ ✳

EVENTUALLY, the road poured them out into an open square where the crowd thinned enough for a large and stately fountain to come into view. It was shaped like three shipping barges going down the river and it dominated the square; nothing competed with it for attention except for the huge building looming behind it.

The capitol building took up the entire western side of the square. It was a colossal structure surrounded by mono-lithic stone pillars, all carved to look like trees. They flared at their bases to give the appearance of roots and flared again at the top where they were carved like branches and leaves. The entire building was made of rose-colored marble. As they got closer, Hashkan could make out the pale red and gold swirls spiraling through the stone. There was a beautiful garden at the front of the building, bordered only by a low wall without any gates, leaving it open for anyone to come and enjoy. Even the pathway through the gardens was made of marble. The building was five stories tall on its wings with a ten-story, shining brass dome in the center. On top of the dome, the Straethian flag whipped in the wind- one half navy and one half gray, divided diagonally from the upper left corner to the lower right corner, with a silver barge in the center.

It was impressive and intimidating in equal measure. Hashkan craned his head back to stare at it as they walked up. This was firm evidence of the wealth in Straeth and the power of its lord. Nerves tumbled in his stomach.

They followed Veltaire up a pathway through the center of the garden to a large stairway that flared wide at the top and bottom, pinching in the center like a woman in a tightly laced corset. At the top of the stairs two guards armed with halberds held the brass doors open for them.

They stepped into the main hall and Hashkan looked up at the underside of the brass dome. It shined with the light of five table-sized chandeliers that hung evenly spaced around the circumference of the dome. The light of their fires refracted off the dome in a hundred different directions and cast disorienting shadows across the entire hall.

Hashkan took a deep breath through his nose and tried to pass it off like he was used to grandeur like this, but even the Gathering in Breen paled in comparison. Emond walked in front of him gaping openly, mouth nearly dangling against his chest.

A wide hallway opened to the left and they followed Veltaire as he turned down it. Two more guards with halberds stood at the entrance and watched as they passed. The heels of their boots clacked against the marble floor as they went.

The hallway stretched on, yard after yard, before finally turning off to the right, through another set of double doors, this time made of shining mahogany. Another pair of guards flanked the doorway. Veltaire pulled the double-doors open and let them into a large sitting room.

A bookcase dominated the wall to the left and an ostentatious desk sat in front of it made of the same mahogany as the doors. To the right was a sitting area with five large, navy sitting chairs that looked as plush as down pillows and a small fire crackled in the fireplace behind them. The fire wasn't putting off much heat, but it made the room warmer than was comfortable.

"Please wait here. Lord Klevelt will arrive shortly," Lieutenant Veltaire told them. "If you will excuse me, I have to return to my duties."

"Thank you, Lieutenant," Hashkan told him as he went back out into the hall, closing the door behind him. Hashkan sank into the closest chair and sighed. It was just as comfortable as it looked.

"A private meetin' with the lord! Blighted fancy! Did yeh ever think we'd be so important so quickly?" Emond asked as he slumped down in the chair beside Hashkan, legs stretched out in front of him.

"It *is* out of the ordinary," Li'or agreed. "Typically, honors are given during the city gatherings in the main hall. I was here for one years ago. This type of reception makes me think something else is going on." She didn't sit down, instead standing next to the back of the chair furthest from the door.

"Yeh worry too much, Li'or! I reckon we're gettin' high, secret honors! Right, Hashkan?"

"I can't be certain," he answered with a smirk. "I have no experience with high, secret honors."

Emond snorted and crossed his legs.

They waited about half an hour- during which Li'or never sat down- before the door opened back up. A guard carrying a spear walked through the door and stopped, slamming the butt of the weapon down.

"All stand for His Excellence, Lord Zivere Klevelt, second of his name, lord of Straeth, defender of the branching, keeper of the river."

Hashkan and Emond stood and Emond snatched his leather cap off his head and bowed. The guard with the spear spun to the side and Lord Klevelt stepped into the room.

He was an aging man, maybe in his mid-sixties with more gray in his shoulder-length hair than black. He wore a goatee similarly striped with gray, but keeping more of its original color. A wicked scar ran from his hairline, across the corner of his eye, and down to his jaw on the left side of his face; it tugged down the corner of his eye but had spared his sight. He stood straight but, as he entered the room, he walked with a pronounced limp in his right leg. He swung the leg out to the side instead of bending it at the knee, but he didn't carry a cane. He was dressed in rich fabrics in grays and blues and carried a longsword at his hip.

"Welcome. Be seated, please," Klevelt told them, taking one of the chairs himself. "Do excuse the warmth. It helps with all my aches."

They all waited until he had settled into his seat before sitting back down themselves. Li'or perched on the edge of her chair, coiled like a cat ready to pounce.

"Now," he began as they all got settled, "I understand the three of you helped to rid us of some nuisance thieves as you came into the city and caught a cut-purse just today. So, I am twice indebted to you all for doing work that my guards should have done. But I cannot place blame on them. This brings me to the reason I summoned you here."

An uncomfortable weight settled into the pit of Hashkan's stomach. Had he come all the way from Breen just to be sent around on more errands? He'd refuse. Technically speaking, the lord didn't have any authority over him. He only had to answer to the Gathering.

"I asked you here to offer you payment for what you have already done and then, regrettably, ask you to do even more. We have recently suffered a wave of desertions in my guard force and are thus grievously undermanned. We've seen a rise in crime and the populace is nervous- understandably so. The streets are getting more dangerous and we're having a hard time training new men quickly enough to get them on the walls and in the streets.

"Add to this, the blight of increased zhu'dac activity near the farms to the north, and I don't have enough men to send out there to properly protect my people." He paused and ran his hand through his beard, scowling so much that great furrows ran across his brow like a plowed field.

"So, I have an offer. There's good coin waiting for the person who can discern why so many of my soldiers have deserted their posts. I can not abide the notion that it's mere coincidence."

Hashkan and the others had listened in silence as the lord spoke and when he finished, the silence dragged on, all waiting for the others to say something. Finally, Li'or spoke up.

"How much?" No title, no honorific, just a blunt demand.

Hashkan and Emond each sucked in a breath and looked at her with wide, horrified eyes. Hashkan darted his eyes back over to Lord Klevelt, silently beseeching the Seamstress that he wouldn't be offended.

Klevelt's face was tight and controlled as he looked

over at Li'or, the silence stretching as he studied her. On the other side of the room, she gazed back at him, her expression just as unyielding.

Hashkan unconsciously wiped his sweating palms on his robe as he looked back and forth. There was a nauseating lurch in his gut as Klevelt sat up a little straighter and studied Li'or.

"I've heard about you. A respectable sell-sword, if ever there was such a thing. I've never had to deal with mercenaries before, and I've heard it's not always a smooth process..." He gave her and Emond pointed looks. "But, I appreciate honesty and brevity in those I employ. To an extent."

A small amount of tension oozed out of Hashkan's muscles. There was a threat in those words, one that the lord could easily make into a reality. But a threat was better than a call for an arrest.

"Now, I'll pay you a silver star for each of the men you have already dispatched, and the information regarding the desertions is worth fifty gold faces."

Emond let out a low whistle. Fifty faces was a small fortune, likely more than Li'or or Emond would make in an entire year. Hashkan was almost jealous, but he hadn't had a use for coin since he started his apprenticeship.

"Well, milord, as it would happen, I was just given a prestigious position at the Ale Boat and I do believe it'll be a good spot to start trackin' down yer information," Emond said. He rubbed his meat slab hands together and grinned.

"Excellent," Klevelt responded, barely sparing Emond a glance. "And you, elf?"

"There's a few people I can ask. I might be able to find a good lead."

"I need more than just a lead. I need a concrete answer

to justify payment," Klevelt said with a casual wave of his hand.

Hashkan's eyes flicked back over to Li'or. Her hands were clenched and her emerald eyes flashed. He didn't understand why she was so tense. Klevelt was being more generous than most nobles he'd met through the Seamstress's service. Really, he was quite humble by comparison.

"Of course. I'll see what I can do, my lord," she answered. Hashkan sagged a little in his chair. Whatever rage she was fighting, she'd beaten it down.

"Perfect. Now, Weaver. I have a request for the High Weaver." He waved over his shoulder and the herald swept forward with a scroll in hand. He handed it to Hashkan before scooting back towards the door. "Please deliver that when you return to the Gathering," Klevelt continued.

Hashkan blinked. "Of course, my lord," he recited by rote before his brain could catch up.

Lords liked to pretend that the Gathering of the Seamstress didn't exist until they needed something; they didn't like to admit how much power it held. They especially avoided thinking about how much it was growing. Was Klevelt's situation so desperate that he was reaching out? Hashkan brushed his thumb against the wax seal, resisting the temptation to open it.

"Perfect. I look forward to the High Weaver's response. And to seeing what information you find." He rose out of the chair an inch at a time with his bad leg held out in front of him. The others stood up with him. "The guards at the door will show you out. Good day." And he was gone, leaving Hashkan speechless in his wake.

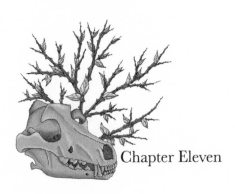

Chapter Eleven

A Calculated Risk

*O*nce Lord Klevelt left the room, Li'or, Hashkan, and Emond were swept out of the meeting room and out of the building with all the enthusiasm of a maid sweeping dust into the street. They stopped in the shade of an oak just to the side of the palace gates. Hashkan turned and scowled at the front doors.

"I've never been so rudely dismissed in my entire life, even before I joined the Gathering!"

"Better get used to it if you're going to hang around with us," Li'or said. She flicked her braid over her shoulder and eyed the handful of people milling about in the square.

Hashkan held a hand to his chest. "You had a Weaver with you."

Li'or looked back at him and shrugged. "Guess they don't care."

"Well, anyway," Emond interrupted, just as Hashkan opened his mouth to continue complaining. Hashkan glared, miffed at the interruption, but Emond plowed through and changed the subject. "We've just been given the jobs of our lives, eh? And I don't even have to leave me new home. Can't get any better than that, can it?"

"I'm not upset about it," Li'or agreed. "The pay is blighted outrageous for how little work it's going to be, but who am I to correct a lord?" She shared a knowing smirk with Emond.

"It must be nice being compensated..." Hashkan sighed. "We just get a thank you and then get pushed off back towards the Gathering." He was beginning to feel like some kind of strange camp follower, or like Li'or and Emond were nobles in service to a lord and he was just their attendant. It was like he was standing in their shadows, doing small chores while they saved the day.

It wasn't right. *He* was the Weaver- blessed by the Seamstress herself. He shouldn't be pushed off to the side like a recalcitrant child.

Li'or crossed her arms. "No one charges you for anything. Are we supposed to feel bad for you?"

The heat in Hashkan's face returned full force. "I didn't always have that privilege you know. I know what it's like to worry about coin, about food."

Emond glanced back and forth between them with a worried tilt to his mouth.

"Do you?" She stalked toward him until they were inches apart. Somehow she managed to look down on him even though he was a couple inches taller. "While everyone has handed you whatever you've wanted since the day you put on those robes? And all just for the scant hope of a *blessing?*"

"I worked hard to earn these robes!"

"Alright, now," Emond said forcing himself between them. "No need to be at each other's throats, right?"

Li'or just sighed and started walking towards the Gathering.

"Come on, the Gathering is this way." She didn't even check to see if they were following.

While he would have preferred an apology, Hashkan just adjusted his robe and followed behind her.

Movement caught his eye. A cat jumped out of a nearby tree and several leaves were knocked loose to float down behind it. The cat scrambled along the ground, claws skittering across the stone as it careened into an alley. Hashkan leaned to the side to get a better look just in time to see one of the leaves float *up* into the tree. It fluttered just as it would have if it had been falling and then nestled itself back into the branches. And it stayed there.

He froze, eyes wide and mind whirling. He hadn't seen any Thread flares to point towards another Weaver. In fact there was no one around the tree at all. Could it have been a sign from the Seamstress?

He refocused his eyes and looked at the Threads of the tree, squinting. Everything looked normal except for one small area where some of the Threads seemed to sag, drooping away from the neat grid of the Fabric.

"What is it?" Emond stopped beside him, looking towards the tree where Hashkan was still staring.

Hashkan blinked a few times and shook his head. When he opened his eyes and looked back up at the tree through normal vision nothing was amiss. A small breeze loosened a leaf and it drifted down to the ground. It hit the ground and didn't move again until another breeze pushed it along the street.

Brows creased, Li'or turned back towards them.

"Well?" she asked after a few moments.

"Nothing. I just thought I saw something. It was just a

cat." He had to have been mistaken. It was a trick of the light and nothing more.

Li'or rolled her eyes. "Alright. Let's get going then."

They left the square and crammed themselves in with the rest of the traffic moving down the streets.

The Gathering of the Seamstress was also on the eastern side of the city, almost centered between the northern and southern walls. It was only a short walk from the capitol building and as they crested the first bridge out of the square they could see the trees looming over the buildings.

The Gathering revealed itself to them in the gaps between shops and homes as they got closer, a forest in truth that somehow hid behind other, lesser man-made constructs. As they walked up, they found themselves in the shadow of the trees that towered over the wall of gray stone. The walls themselves were intricately carved, telling the story of the Gifting, when the Seamstress touched common soldiers and made them something more, and thanks to that, the victory over the Rak-Shai. It was beautiful work, and everywhere the Seamstress appeared in the story she was emphasized by pieces of glass set into the stone that burst from around her in a rainbow of shining color.

"Hashkan!" Li'or called.

With a jerk, Hashkan dragged his focus away from the mural and saw that Li'or and Emond were staring at him, waiting to enter through the open front gates.

He dashed over to meet them and passed from the bright light of the afternoon into the shade of the gardens. They followed the main path as it cut through the trees, bromeliads made of bright explosions of color and tangled vines lining the walkway. The trail took them straight to the Sanctuary, but their path was blocked by a pair of closed gates painted with a miniature likeness of the outer walls. A man in Weaver's robes, his hood pulled up, stood just in front of the entranceway. He bowed, fingers to temple.

"I'm sorry, but the apprentices are currently preparing the Sanctuary for the evening ritual. If you want to view the Sanctuary, you'll have to return in a few hours' time, when these gates will be unlocked."

"Oh, sir, me friend here," Emond gestured to Hashkan, "is a Weaver himself and he's actually here to report to whoever needs reportin' to. Ya know, he's here fer work."

"I see. Your name, Weaver?"

Hashkan stepped forward and introduced himself. "I sent letters ahead a couple weeks ago and I have a message from Lord Klevelt," he added.

"Yes, we've been expecting you. I'm Willeric Larkenspear. There's a tendency for everyone around here to call me Lark, which is fine."

After brief introductions, he waved them over to a smaller path to the left that Hashkan had completely overlooked.

"Since your friends are here, I'm sure the High Weaver will want to ask them about your character before he officially agrees to take you on. Just head straight down the path. I'll be right behind you."

They walked down the narrow track with Emond in the lead and Li'or to the rear, Lark close behind her. Before long, they came to an intersection in the path where they could continue straight or turn to either side.

"Follow the one to your right, please," Lark called ahead.

They walked along as instructed, passing the individual quarters of the resident Weavers- they were smaller and more austere than what Hashkan had seen in Breen or

Hearthmere- and the long single-story building of the dining hall. All the buildings were made from coarse cream-colored stone and had clay shingled roofs. Birds sang in the trees and the scent of freshly chopped mulch permeated the air. Oaks grew alongside the gravel path that led them through ferns and lilies that thrived in the cool shade.

They continued past a row of hedges until they came upon a large gravel clearing ringed in torches. Hashkan pushed a hand through his hair, confused about why they would waste torches in the middle of the day. On the far-side, a gentle fountain bubbled up in the center of a pool about six feet wide. A man stood on either side of the clearing, both in Weaver's garb. They were as still as statues. Only their robes moved as a light breeze swept through the garden.

"Oh, good timing." Lark smiled and crossed his arms. "Charlain and Aoth are about to spar."

※ ＊

LI'OR WATCHED as the Weavers sized each other up from either side of the clearing. The tension stretched the air thin around them as they both waited for the other to make a move.

"The balding man is Aoth. He's been at this Gathering since he was fresh out of his apprenticeship. The other man, with the dark beard, is Charlain. He has only been with us for two years," Lark told them.

The men watched each other for a moment longer and then they suddenly burst into a flurry of motion.

The man named Charlain reached behind him to where a pair of torches burned and with a quick throwing motion, pulled the fire through the air and flung it at Aoth.

It arched up from the torch, over Charlain's head, and launched towards Aoth.

Aoth jumped to the side and rolled, his robes flapping behind him. With a hiss, the glob of fire splashed across the ground just beside him. More fire chased the Weaver as he sprang lightly to his feet and dashed towards the fountain. Each fireball fell closer and closer to his heels.

When Aoth reached the fountain, he slid to a halt and spun back towards Charlain. The other Weaver was still chucking globs of flame at his opponent, torch after torch winking out as he stalked forward. There was a short pause as he took better aim at the now stationary Aoth. Then, with his entire body behind the throw, he lobbed another orb right at the other Weaver's head.

Li'or sucked in a breath and held it, but Aoth just reached forward and, with a jerk of his arm, threw the ball harmlessly to the ground on his right. It scorched a line into the gravel and Aoth looked back at Charlain with a smile.

Charlain didn't return the gesture. He growled and swept his arms around in a full circle. Each torch fire joined with the one next to it until they'd combined into a ball the size of a man's torso. Charlain set his feet and hurtled it at Aoth.

Aoth's eyes grew wider, but he responded by reaching towards the small fountain with both hands. At his command, the water flew from the pool in a glittering stream and met the fire mid-air with a hiss and a burst of steam. Before the cloud dissipated and while Charlain was still fumbling for a response, Aoth widened his stance, reached out, and pulled sharply back towards himself. He strained like he was pulling a rope attached to something heavy.

Charlain was flung backward, the ground just under

his feet heaving forward in response to Aoth's pull. Char-lain landed with a heavy thud, the air knocked out of his lungs. It took a full ten seconds for him to get back to his feet. In battle, it would have been a fatal delay. The match was over.

Li'or realized she'd been holding her breath. She exhaled at the same time as Hashkan, who was staring wide-eyed at the Weavers. Beside them, Emond clapped enthusiastically.

Aoth's posture relaxed and he walked over to clasp arms with the other man who grimaced but smiled.

Li'or watched, impressed with both of the Weavers-Aoth in particular. She hadn't seen Altering used in combat since her first visit to Wraithport over forty years ago when she'd witnessed a group of Weavers turn back an entire Rak-Shai fleet. In fact, until today, she'd assumed the Gatherings had stopped training their Weavers in combat Altering beyond the basics of self-defense. Once the war ended, most people assumed it wasn't needed- wrongly so, in her opinion.

"Well, he lasted a bit longer this time," Lark muttered to himself before turning back towards them. "This way, please." He waved Li'or, Hashkan, and Emond towards a small path to the right.

They followed him along the path as it mirrored the curve of the sparring arena. It passed under the boughs of more ancient oaks before they reached another, smaller clearing under the shade of the interwoven branches. The area was gravel like the path and had several wooden benches set up towards the front, looking out at the arena. Near the back were two long tables with chairs. A handful of men and women in Weavers' robes milled around, discussing the short match. In the very center, a wooden throne sat on a raised dais, all carved with a grid of inter-secting lines.

Lark led them around to the front of the throne where an elderly man in bright blue robes sat, stroking his long white beard. Once he noticed them approaching, he flipped his hands at the other Weavers. They all nodded and walked towards the other end of the small observation area, giving the old man some privacy to receive his guests.

"High Weaver Mengovik. This is Weaver Hashkan Clearont and his friends Li'or Halwyn and Emond Gale-fridus. Hashkan is reporting for service to the Seamstress. I brought his friends to give witness to his character."

The old man rose smoothly from his seat- surprisingly spry for a man of his age- and smiled. He had been lucky enough to keep all his teeth.

"Welcome, welcome to the Straethian Gathering! We're always glad to have new faces around. Please, have a seat, all of you. Lark, if you don't mind going back to the front door. I think you have another hour there before Catrisse takes over." Lark gave a small bow and walked back towards the Sanctuary. "It is a great exercise of patience to do nothing at all," he added to them with a wink once Lark was out of earshot.

"Mistress elf, were you around when we were given the Gift from the Seamstress, like I was? Did you happen to witness it? The First Weaving?"

"I witnessed the attempted invasion at Wraithport and I saw some of the first Weavers turn it back. I wasn't in the army, though. I didn't see the First Weaving."

"I see. I figure it can't hurt to ask anyway, though the elves have always kept mostly to themselves. Not that it's a bad thing, not a bad thing at all. But what a great coinci-dence! I was one of those Weavers in Wraithport!" He smiled and laughed at himself. "I was a much younger man then, wasn't I? Now, to the task at hand. Enrika!"

A woman, perhaps in her mid-thirties with dark brown, almost black, hair that matched her rich skin stood up from one of the benches facing the arena and walked towards them. She moved with long confident strides, more like a warrior than a Weaver, and her silver eyes were sharp as daggers.

"Hello," she greeted them with a nod after bowing to the High Weaver. She had a faint accent from the Gnürian Isles.

"Hashkan, Enrika will test your Altering abilities for us. Just a short test, don't fret. We don't have a recommendation letter so we need to see where you are. We do things a little differently here, as I'm sure you noticed. Mistress Halwyn and Master Galefridus, if you'll stay here with me for a bit longer? I'd like to have a short conversation."

"Before I go, High Weaver, I have this message from Lord Klevelt." Hashkan pulled the parchment from a pocket in his robe and handed it to the High Weaver.

"My thanks," the old man answered. He immediately broke the wax seal and started reading, effectively dismissing Hashkan again.

"This way. We'll go into the arena," Enrika said, leading Hashkan around a bush and along a path towards the gravel arena. Li'or turned back to the arena and noticed a group of people had walked out into the center and were lining up to face another Weaver who stood with his hands clasped behind his back. They were all ages and wore either gray or white robes.

Mengovik folded the letter back up and looked out at the arena. "Ah, that's one of the other classes starting. I always like to watch, when I can," the High Weaver said. "It's a shame that most Gatherings barely touch on combat instruction these days. I'm sure both of you agree. It's a true reflection of the long stretch of peace that we've enjoyed. But it will end eventually. It always does. So here we focus on it just as much as all the other areas of study."

Li'or nodded in agreement, but the High Weaver wasn't looking at her. Out in the arena, some of the students were Altering small clumps of gravel from in front of them to behind them while others pulled small globes of fire from a torch and dashed them into the ground over and over again. One of the students fumbled and nearly caught his robe on fire.

"Ah! See! Altering repeatedly like that teaches them speed and control, they have to find and release the Threads quickly to get the job done."

They watched the drills go on for a while until the instructors pulled out hoops made of thin metal. They set them on the ground and the students Altered their fire or earth to land within the ring. Hashkan and Enrika joined with a group of students standing near the fountain. She gave a command and they all began the same drill, only with water.

Emond scoffed. "They're doin' the same drill. Shouldn't they work on something else?"

Li'or stifled a groan. It was just like Emond to offer his opinion on things he knew nothing about. And be rude while he was at it.

The High Weaver just laughed. "Well, water is very tricky. It's not solid like earth, so you can't get a good grip on it, nor is it light like air and fire where just the lightest touch can cause huge changes. So, you have to do all the exercises with all the elements. Your friend is doing quite well," the High Weaver observed. Hashkan was moving water just as quickly and smoothly as any of the students.

"Lad's great with water, it's true. He pulled all the rainwater out of our clothes on the road here. Kept us all from growin' mushrooms *and* he put it right into our water skins," Emond said. He hooked his thumbs into his belt and grinned out at Hashkan like a proud parent.

"What an interesting and innovative solution! I'll have to have him show that one to the others. I'm sure any army traveling in the rain would be grateful for that technique."

Hashkan's group in the arena changed exercises and were tossing their water and forcing it to change directions in midair. Hashkan was excelling, whipping the water more quickly than the others, giving his Alterings a sharper change of direction.

Enrika started to walk through the small group of students, distracting them. She stood between them and their streams of water or kicked one of their legs out from underneath them. They started to lose track of what they were doing and the water would scatter into shining droplets and fall to the ground.

Enrika walked up to Hashkan from behind, hooked her foot around his left leg, and pulled back. Hashkan stumbled and went down to one knee. His water stalled and started to fall, but he swept it back up at the last second and sent it soaring twice as far as his other attempts.

The High Weaver laughed and clapped. "Excellent! Truly excellent! It's not very often that someone can do that on their first try. Exceptional control and focus. He'll do well."

In the arena, Hashkan's group finished with water and moved on to Altering earth. They ran through the precision drill again, throwing clumps of gravel into the metal hoops. Hashkan struggled. He wasn't as accurate and was making more exaggerated gestures with his arms.

"Now do you see? Every element must be handled in a

different way. It's common for a Weaver to excel when working with one, then struggle with another."

Sure enough, when Enrika went around this time and stood between Hashkan and the gravel he was working with, he lost control and it all tumbled to the ground. Li'or saw him blush all the way from where she was standing.

"What makes earth so difficult for him?" she asked.

"It's heavier, of course," the High Weaver said, turning to face them. "It takes a lot of focus and a strong mental grip to affect a change- just as much mental force as it would take to physically move it. Because of that, it's the most difficult substance to elicit change upon. Forcing a Weaver to continuously Alter earth is one of the fastest ways to wear them down."

Li'or shared a glance with Emond, who shifted on the wooden bench and fidgeted with the belt that held his quiver across his back. While all this was interesting, it was useless to both of them. Emond was probably wondering why the High Weaver was telling them all this. She was too.

"We appreciate the lesson, High Weaver," Li'or began. The old man pulled his pale silver eyes off the training and turned to her. They were nearly white from age and frequent Altering. Li'or fought to keep from shivering, but plowed on. "Do you have any questions for us? About Hashkan? There's also the matter of my payment. He hired me to escort him from Breen."

"Did he now? And promised a 'donation' no doubt?" he answered, a smile crinkling the skin of his face like parchment. "I'll sort that out with him tomorrow. As for questions about his character, I can tell what kind of man he is from the way he trains. He's taking instruction well and fully applying himself. He doesn't seem to enjoy being corrected, but he listens. What I want is for you each to understand the basics of what the Weavers around you are doing.

"When you work hard at something, it's obvious to anyone who looks. You need to know that the Weavers are putting in just as much effort. Every time they grab hold of a Thread, they are taking a calculated risk. Fire could burn their minds; air is so finicky you could easily create a gale that would level a town. Not to mention it is mentally and physically exhausting. Look." He pointed back out towards Hashkan. "He's talented, but he's not used to Altering so much so quickly. He's used to the small, short tasks- likely how he's been trained up until now."

Li'or looked back out towards Hashkan and saw that he was indeed flagging. He was still standing upright, but he was slouching. He didn't look like he'd be able to keep it up much longer at that pace.

"He will need to practice and build his endurance, but after a few years of training, he may be one of the best we've seen. He was very precise before the fatigue started setting in," Mengovik said as Hashkan threw another sloppy cluster of gravel. "Now, this letter from Klevelt..." He fell silent and toyed with his beard again. "Hmm. Maybe he'd do best with some work in the field..."

Li'or glanced over to Emond, who raised his eyebrows at her.

"Now, there's only two more things that I want to tell the two of you," the High Weaver started again with a crooked smile. "If you should find yourself on the field of battle, make sure the Weavers know where you are. The last thing you want is a fireball falling on your heads. And may the Seamstress bless you both."

Chapter Twelve

Close to the Shadows

*A*oth escorted them out of the Gathering once Hashkan's training session was over. They didn't have any open rooms for him, but Li'or didn't see any disappointment on his face when it was suggested he continue to stay at the Ale Boat. The tired-looking Weaver was scheduled to come back the next day, first thing in the morning, for more drills designed to help him build his endurance and to start work for the Gathering.

"I'm starving!" he declared as they walked out into the street. "I don't think I've been this drained since I first started moving little pebbles around. This is like an entirely different skill! They didn't train us for anything like this during our apprenticeship. They teach us parlor tricks compared to this! This... This feels like real military training."

"Ack, if we had Weavers in Lir'daas, it would be like this! Every man is required to serve as a soldier. The

Weavers would be no different, I'm sure," Emond observed.

"Things really are different over there, aren't they?" Hashkan mused.

"Lad, everything is different. Fer one, yeh work with a great deal more elves! They come out o' their forests a lot more."

Li'or carefully looked away and pretended that she didn't notice Emond's encouraging glance. She didn't have anything to add to the conversation. She'd spent less than twenty-four hours in an elven city the first and only time she'd gone to one. She scanned the road around them, looking for something else to discuss.

They were about even to the square in the center of Straeth, where most of the inns and taverns were located, and the crowd was thick with people rushing home for the evening. Her eyes were drawn to a trader's cart, driven by an elderly man.

The wagon was filled with bushels of dried wheat, likely left over from last year's harvest. He must have been passing through or planned on selling his harvest to a trader to take down the river by boat. She scanned the street around him and frowned. He had no guard. Even though he wasn't traveling with incredibly valuable wares, it was likely still an important load. There wasn't a farmer in Anagovia who would have been able to lose a harvest and make it easily through the rest of the year.

Li'or felt a tug on her heartstrings. Her parents weren't farmers, but she'd known many growing up and she understood how hard it could be to live at the mercy of the seasons and the elements.

"I'll meet the two of you back at the Ale Boat. I'm going to make sure that farmer makes it to where he's going tonight," she told the others and, without waiting for an answer, she jogged over to the farmer.

"Sir?" Li'or called out to the man, slowing to a walk beside his cart. "It's getting close to dark and I noticed that you don't have a guard with you. If you'd like an escort, I'd be glad to help. There's been an increase in crime here lately and I don't want you to lose your harvest."

The man eyed her skeptically, glaring down his knife blade of a nose. "I heard things about that as well, but I've no money to pay for a guard. Thank you anyway."

Li'or fought back a frown and forced herself to give a friendly smile. "I don't ask for any payment."

"Aye, and let us help as well!" Emond said as he and Hashkan jogged up behind Li'or. Her brows rose in surprise and the old man narrowed his eyes at Emond. The man couldn't help but look like a brigand, even if he was just an oaf. "What? Me brother's a farmer. Sometimes they need a little help. And besides, none of us would eat without them, eh?"

The old man nodded then noticed Hashkan and grinned. He was missing several of his front teeth. "Oh! A Weaver! Well, I imagine I'll be the best guarded little wagon of wheat this side of the Heart's Blood River, won't I? Thank you all. I'll need all this to feed my cattle this winter. If you can get me to the southern gate, that'll be enough. I'll leave out in the morning."

Emond took point at the front of the wagon while Hashkan and Li'or took their places to either side, carefully watching the dwindling crowd. They only had about two miles to go and they moved briskly, reaching the gate in little over half an hour.

Li'or grew more nervous the closer they got to the southern gate, their fight from the day before still fresh in her mind. They were lucky, however, and even though they passed through the slums they didn't encounter any trouble. When they reached the gates, they left the farmer with the guards and bid him farewell, wishing him luck on his way.

"I'm glad you noticed him, Li'or. And I'm glad you didn't try to charge him," Hashkan said as they made their way back to the inn.

Li'or frowned, uncertain how she should respond. Surely, he knew she wasn't *that* kind of mercenary by now. "Why wouldn't I help him?" She couldn't keep the bite out of her words.

"I didn't mean it like that," he back-tracked. "I was just glad to help. My parents were farmers. Not rich ones either. I spent the first fourteen years of my life struggling with them. Like that man. Then the scouts from the Gathering discovered that I could Alter and they paid my parents handsomely to take me off for training."

A strained silence wrapped around them, Li'or once again at a loss for words. Up until now, she'd just assumed Hashkan had spent his life in comfort. Finding out that they had some common ground shed a different light on the Weaver. They were more alike than she'd allowed herself to consider.

And with that realization came a fresh wave of guilt. She owed him an apology for her comments outside of the capitol building.

It wasn't the time to dawdle, though. Night had fallen around them as they took the farmer to the gate and they were now walking quietly through Straeth's dark, empty streets. Li'or forced herself to focus on the dark alleys where thieves could easily hide. All the strangely shaped buildings cast threatening shadows across the road that would provide even more cover for attackers. There was a loud crash and they all jumped as a stray cat raced across the street in front of them.

"This city is not as friendly at night," Emond commented.

"No, it isn't." The voice came out of an alley near what looked like a butcher shop. "It'll be a lot less friendly unless you hand over your weapons and your coin." A man dressed in leather armor stepped out of the nearest alley, an unsheathed scimitar in his left hand. He had long, blond hair pulled into a tail at the base of his neck.

Gravel shifted behind Li'or and she cursed as she twisted around. Three more men and a woman emerged from the shadows on the other side of the street. Two of the men carried clubs, the third had a longsword, and the woman carried a pair of curved daggers.

Li'or took a step back and glanced over her shoulder towards the others. They were turning their backs to her as well and backing an inch at a time so they would all be back-to-back. Emond pulled out his hammer. The thieves fanned out to form a circle around them. Li'or unsheathed her sword and dagger.

The blond man laughed "You're outnumbered folks, but you're brave, I'll give you that. I'll cut you a deal. Why don't you just come with us and help us out, eh?"

"Go eat shite yeh bastard!" Emond hissed through his teeth.

The man laughed at them. "It wasn't a request."

The air around Li'or warped and refracted the lantern light like water. A splitting pain bloomed behind her eyes and she struggled to avoid collapsing. She staggered and widened her stance, barely staying on her feet. Gravel crunched behind her as Emond and Hashkan fought to stay upright too.

"What kind of Altering…?" Hashkan gasped.

Li'or risked a half turn so she could keep the leader in view. Her knees almost buckled, but she pushed through. Strange Altering or no, she wasn't going to give up easily. She met the blond man's glare with one of her own.

His eyes widened for a half a heartbeat and then his face crumpled and flushed with rage. "If you won't come, then you die!" He leapt towards them with his scimitar held high and the pressure on Li'or's mind vanished within the span of a heartbeat. The crushing pain disappeared completely like it had never existed. It was such a drastic change that she was caught off guard and stumbled backward.

The other thugs joined in on the charge. The woman with the daggers closed on Li'or just as she was getting her feet back underneath herself. Li'or threw up her dagger and blocked the woman's leading arm, then brought her sword around and batted her second dagger to the side as hard she could. Still on her heels and working in too close of quarters, Li'or couldn't put the weight behind the blow that she wanted, but the block had the desired effect. The woman was forced off-balance and slipped past Li'or's left side.

Following right behind her, one of the men with clubs ran in, his weapon held foolishly above his head. Li'or stepped inside his guard and thrust her dagger through his thin leather jerkin and under his ribs. He coughed blood that splattered onto Li'or's arm then fell backwards off her blade.

Li'or spun back towards the woman and felt a flash of heat from behind her. Hashkan was Altering fire. The woman's eye grew wide and Li'or couldn't help but smirk. Daggers clattered against the cobblestones as the woman turned and ran.

She turned to face their other attackers. Hashkan was Altering more fire while Emond swatted at two other thugs with his hammer. Neither of them looked like they were in trouble, so she turned her attention to the leader.

She took one step before something slammed into her from the side, sending her sprawling across the ground. She barely kept her weapons in hand.

The other woman was back and pounced on top of Li'or. She didn't have her daggers, but she slashed at Li'or with her nails like a rabid animal, lips pulled back in a feral grimace.

The blond man was laughing again, voice drawing closer. "See? She actually listens. She won't stop until *I* allow it! If only you three were more like her, we could all leave peacefully!"

Li'or fought to get her arms in front of her face. The woman was clawing at her like a wild cat. Fire ran across her jaw and neck as the woman's nails drew blood. Li'or abandoned blocking and punched at the woman's temple with the crossguard of her dagger. It only brought her a split second of respite, but it was enough time to get her sword in front of her. The woman swung at her again, meeting with the edge of Li'or's blade.

She still didn't stop. Her hands met the blade over and over again, but no sign of pain registered across her face-just the same mad rictus.

Horrified, Li'or scrambled across the ground on her back using her blade as a shield. The woman dashed herself against it like waves on stone over and over again until she couldn't move from the ground.

Li'or sat upright and watched the dying woman as her life's blood seeped into the stone. It was wrong, so wrong. No one in their right mind would do that to themselves.

The thoughts repeated themselves over and over again in Li'or's head as she caught her breath.

More screams pulled Li'or's attention away from the body of the woman. She caught a glimpse of Emond felling the man with the sword with a devastating blow to the back of his head. The other man with the club was a smoldering heap farther back towards the buildings; he'd met with Hashkan before making it up to them.

Hashkan shouted and she watched as another gout of flame sprang out of a lamp post and flew towards the blond man. The man barked a laugh and swept his hand in front of him. The fire changed direction and splashed harmlessly against the road. Hashkan tried again with the same result.

And then the laughter stopped.

Suddenly the world heaved around Li'or like a ship in a terrible storm and the crippling pain returned, her head seeming to crack under the pressure.

"Why can't you just stop fighting it? We could have avoided all this." Li'or's body grew heavy, like it was sinking into molasses. She slowly sank down to one knee. "I'll bring the three of you back or you'll die here!"

Hashkan was on his knees, panting and grabbing his head with both hands. Emond had dropped his hammer and was on all fours, fingers digging into the road, nails ripped and bleeding. How was this possible? What was this man doing?

Li'or drove the point of her sword into the ground and leaned her weight into it, glaring at the man. He smiled wickedly back at her and the weight around her body doubled. She struggled to breathe.

"It's pointless, elf. Stop resisting." The veins were standing out in his neck and his hand was held out towards them, straining like a claw.

Li'or forced herself up off her knee. "I will resist as long as I draw breath," she gasped.

The man stopped smiling. "I'll kill you and take your friends back then. They're about to break." As he spoke, he dropped his arm and put a second hand on the hilt of his sword, stalking up to her. Li'or glanced back towards Hashkan and Emond and saw them sprawled out on the ground. They were tiring. He was right, they didn't have long.

As the man drew closer, the pressure on her mind lessened ever so slightly. She stayed where she was, leaning on her sword. She looked back to the thug as he strolled the last few paces up to her, casual as if he was touring a garden. He glared down at her as he went, his gaze cold and oddly unfocused, even as he stared right at her. Whatever else might be wrong with him, she just prayed he'd get close enough. He stepped right up beside her, less than an arms-length away and raised his sword. He was going to behead her.

She stopped resisting and let that alien pressure force her back down. As she fell, she drove her dagger into the man's foot with all her weight. The pressure lifted from her and the pain in her head stopped instantly. She heard gasps from Emond and Hashkan and the man screamed, falling away from her.

Li'or didn't waste a moment. She ripped her sword up out of the ground, and with both hands thrust it into the man's stomach. He tried to pull away from her, but she grabbed him by the front of his shirt and gave her sword a savage twist. The thug groaned, but still pushed at her with weakening resolve.

Before she could finish the job, the man's face burst into flame. The heat flared in Li'or's face and she flinched back, shielding herself. The man collapsed, bleeding and clawing at his face.

There was a thud behind her and she whirled around. Hashkan was on the ground in an ungainly heap, unconscious. Blood pooled around his head from a wound she hadn't noticed during the fight.

"Gods-damnit," she hissed. She snatched her sword and dagger out of the man's body. "We need to get out of here, there may be more of them," she told Emond.

"Right yeh are." He bent down and, with a grunt, lifted Hashkan up over his shoulder. "Let's go."

Li'or hesitated for just a moment, something on the man's shoulder catching her eye. It was a broach shaped like a wolf's skull. She ripped it off his cloak. It looked like an insignia of some kind, maybe someone would know what it meant.

They left as quickly as they could, moving as silently as possible through the night-cloaked streets. They took an out-of-the-way route to the Ale Boat just in case they were being followed, Emond carrying Hashkan the entire way.

"How did that man fight off the fire our lad threw? He wasn't a Weaver. Eyes weren't silver. Was yer skull splittin' wide open?"

Emond panted a seemingly unending stream of questions at her as they went. She didn't have an answer for any of them. She just tried to stay focused on making sure they didn't run into any more issues, or into any other people at all. They needed to get Hashkan somewhere safe where they could assess his wound and they needed to get there quickly.

The streets were less crowded since night had fallen, most people had either gone home or they'd arrived at their first stop for the evening. Li'or scouted ahead and directed Emond down empty streets and alleys. Her mind raced ahead of her while she navigated the shadowed corridors of the city. All the questions that Emond asked replayed in her head in a loop and she couldn't make them stop no matter how hard she tried to block them out. And at the end of each loop, the worst thoughts of all.

They had all almost died.

She had been essentially powerless against whatever that man had done. And what *had* he done to the woman? What if it happened again? She was lucky that, in his arrogance, he had given her an opening. She couldn't count on getting one again.

She gritted her teeth and tried to focus on listening for other footsteps. It worked for a few moments and then the questions started anew.

It took longer than it should have, but they made it back to the inn before midnight. Light spilled from the common room windows and the sound of music drifted down the sweeping stairwell, ignorant and carefree despite the monster that had lurked in the streets.

"Let's go through the back," Li'or suggested. She wanted to avoid any questions that may follow them and Eseldra was a terrible gossip. They didn't have time to deal with any concerned crowds, serving girls, or any intrusive guests calling the guard. No matter what angle you approached it from, they looked like they were kidnapping a Weaver.

Emond nodded and followed her around the building. As they crossed the city, he'd sagged further and further down under Hashkan's weight. Li'or was thankful that he'd been able to help even though he'd likely been exhausted before he'd even picked Hashkan up. If straining against that man's powers had drained Emond as much as it did her, it was a wonder he'd been able to carry Hashkan at all.

There was no one behind the building and Li'or led the way around back to the server entrance. They shuffled in through the narrow door, staying close to the shadows. Once they got in, they hung a left and dashed up the back stairs as quickly as they could, Li'or creeping forward, peering around corners, and checking the top of the stairs. She waved Emond towards her, indicating for him to be as quiet as possible.

The hall was empty and the carpets muffled their steps as they hurried down to Li'or's room. She opened the door and stepped aside so Emond could get through the door. He laid Hashkan down as gently as he could while Li'or lit a few candles.

"He is goin' to be alright, isn't he? I saw him get hit, but it wasn't a heavy blow," Emond said.

Li'or was parting Hashkan's dark hair to look at the wound and froze. She looked back up at Emond with wide eyes. "Hit?"

"Aye, one of the bastards with a club. But a light tap, like I said. If the lad had worn a helmet, he'd never have felt it."

Li'or shook her head and bent back to her work. If this was Emond's idea of a light tap, what would a heavy blow look like? The big man came over holding more candles so she could get a better look at Hashkan's wound.

"It looks like it just split the skin. Nothing broken," she said. She washed the wound with clean water from her basin and applied a thin coat of sparrowthorn ointment. Satisfied she went over to her packs and pulled out a thread and a curved needle.

"Stitches?" Emond asked, a sickly pallor spreading over his features.

"You can leave if you need to, just put the candle next to me."

"No, I'll stay for Hashkan, I'll just look away."

A brief silence fell over them as Li'or worked. She'd only stitched a handful of wounds, so she went slowly and carefully. Emond shifted next to her several times and cleared his throat.

"Yes?" Li'or asked, frustrated by the interruption.

"He was a warrior tonight."

"He was," she agreed.

"I know yeh've just been working for him, but he considers yeh a friend. And he tries hard to keep up with yeh... Thank yeh for makin' sure he was okay."

Li'or paused as his words sank in, then threw a final knot into the sutures and cut the extra thread with her knife. She didn't want to get into this, not now when she was so exhausted. Besides, she shouldn't have to explain herself to a man she barely knew, even if the guilt over how she'd spoken to the Weaver outside the capitol was still gnawing at the back of her mind. If Hashkan didn't wake up...

"I'm doing what any decent person would. I'm not so heartless that I'd leave him to bleed in the street." Her words came out more clipped than she'd intended and she frowned.

"I understand, but would it kill yeh to-"

"I travel too much to keep friendships."

Emond shrugged and rose to leave. "At least be kind. Tell the lad bye when it's time for yeh to leave."

Li'or nodded and pressed her lips into a thin line. He was twisting the knife into her side. She'd made the choice to keep to herself years ago in order to avoid things like this. She was glad she was leaving.

Wasn't she?

"I'll come get you if anything changes with him, but

I'm sure he'll be fine," she said. She looked back towards Hashkan. He looked thin and pale against the navy blankets. "We've got a lot to discuss tomorrow."

"Aye. That we do," Emond agreed. He gave her a tiny salute and went down a few doors to his room.

Chapter Thirteen

Tied Off

*O*rdelieus walked through the halls of his keep on his way to the kitchens. Everything was cleaned and repaired, but most of the rooms were still empty and his echoing steps reminded him of that fact everywhere he went. He had vague memories of a small home with thick green rugs, a warm hearth, and dried herbs hanging from the ceiling- the opposite of these stark corridors. Try as he might, he couldn't figure out where that house had been or why it kept coming to mind. He had to remind himself he was building an army. Gilderan didn't need to be cozy.

The kitchens were warm and full of activity compared to the rest of the keep. A handful of serving men and women scuttled around the ovens and stoves preparing the evening meal. Some of them cooked, others chopped up slabs of meat for Ordelieus's zhu'dac army.

"Is that enough for all the squadrons?" he asked the butcher in charge of feeding the zhu'dac.

"Yes, for all two hundred and forty... four, my lord,

with some extra that can be dried. All as you ordered, my lord."

Ordelieus shook his head. The beasts ate constantly and they weren't picky when they got hungry. Feeding them had been his biggest struggle. "We lost three more to the usual problem?" Obedient as they were for most things, he couldn't keep them from falling on each other in feeding frenzies.

"Aye, my lord. They were hungry, it seems."

"Thank you."

He'd been meticulous with how he'd arranged the Threads on all the people he'd recruited, and his efforts hadn't gone to waste. The majority of Gilderan's population was still made up of zhu'dac, but his human citizens were efficient and amenable. He couldn't have been more pleased with them. With zhu'dac, though, he couldn't figure out how to Alter their minds. Their Threads were so tight it was almost like they'd already been tied off.

"And all of our meals?" he asked, turning towards the woman who oversaw all the cooking and baking.

"Dinner will be ready in about ten minutes, my lord," she replied with a soft smile. She wiped her hands on her apron. "We're just waiting on the bread."

"Excellent, I'll wait in the dining hall."

He walked out into the adjoining hall and sat in the chair at the head of the table to wait. His mind wandered and he drummed his fingers against the wood. Why did he always feel like he had to check in on his staff? It wasn't possible for them to disobey. Was it because he had such a tentative hold on the zhu'dac?

It was yet another thing that nagged at him. He went to check in on all these people almost by habit, but why would he habitually need to monitor people that were so efficient by his own design?

He flinched as a tiny headache flared in his temple like a thin needle was inserted into his skull. It was gone before he had time to raise his hand to his head. What had he been pondering?

He was interrupted as servers walked into the room bearing his dinner. They laid out the few dishes in front of him as if it was a grand feast, but in reality, it was little better than army rations. He tucked in without hesitation. If it was good enough for his troops, it was good enough for him.

As he lifted his fork for another bite, he was interrupted by a sharp, searing pain in his head. He dropped his silverware to the table with a clatter and fell from his seat. When he hit the floor, he curled up, his hands on the sides of his head. Dimly, he was aware of a serving woman gently touching his shoulder, asking if he was all right. He couldn't answer.

A single Thread, spun tight and thin enough to stretch across hundreds of miles, had snapped. It was under so much tension that, once it was cut, it snapped back against Ordelieus's mind with the force of a war hammer. He hadn't felt such agonizing pain since he'd woken up in Gilderan.

Slowly, the pain faded and he came back to himself. He sorted through his mind, winding through the forest of the tiny Threads he'd tied off on all his human subjects. Degan was missing. He'd sent the man to Straeth to collect more citizens and acquire better weaponry.

And now, Degan was dead, which should have been next to impossible, even though the man was brash and enjoyed causing trouble. When he'd smoothed some of his rebelliousness out, Ordelieus had given Degan enough skill in Altering that none should have been able to stand against him.

Ordelieus sat up, pushing a servant away. "I'm fine, I'm fine. Bring me Toshear and Stach." He looked up. A small crowd of concerned faces surrounded him, but none of them were moving. He snatched at all of their Threads, causing a collective flinch. "Go!"

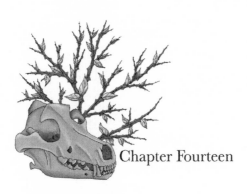

Chapter Fourteen

A Fire Glows on its Own

*H*ashkan woke slowly, as though wading through a mire thick with fog. He opened his eyes and they refused to focus, the world a blur of dark shapes encircling him. He blinked rapidly, fighting down panic, and slowly details of the world around him came into view.

He was in a dark bedroom. Silver and gray curtains revealed a slice of the night sky. It was a room in the Ale Boat, but something was off about it. The furniture in the room had been reversed.

He tried to prop himself up on his elbows, but the effort sent the world to spinning again and he leaned back, covering his eyes. He had a splitting headache, radiating from just above his left ear. He touched the side of his head and panic seized hold of him. There was a three-inch gash, stitched closed, but he had no memory of getting the wound. He forced himself to sit up, squeezing his eyes tight as he fought down a surge of nausea.

When he opened them again Li'or was sleeping against the wall, under the window, her sword on the floor beside her. Her head had lulled forward and her brown hair, normally in such a neat braid, was in complete disarray, thick locks of it hanging down to cover her face.

"Li'or…" he croaked out.

He'd barely made a sound, but she jumped up, her hand shooting toward the hilt of her sword. "Hashkan!" she exhaled. "Thank the gods. I wasn't sure what we were going to do if you didn't wake by morning."

"How long have I been out?"

She stood and swept the curtains to the side, looking out at the night. "Judging by the stars, about four hours." She came over to him and gently took hold of his face and turned his head. She parted his hair with soft fingers. "The sutures still look good, and no more bleeding. You're lucky."

"Is that what you call it?"

She scoffed and tucked her stray hair behind her ears. "It is. And I owe you an apology. I shouldn't have treated you like you don't know how to work. I knew it wasn't true when I said it."

"Don't worry about it, Li'or. I'm not even sure I remember everything that was said."

She chuckled and leaned back, a shaft of moonlight falling across her face. It revealed an ugly gash running from her cheek, down onto her neck, with a smaller one just in front of her pointed ear. The skin around it was inflamed and a bit of dried blood still clung to her collar.

"Seamstress, Li'or," he whispered, reaching towards her face before he knew what he was doing. His hand lingered there, mesmerized by the silken feel of her skin, so at odds with the steel and fire of her personality. He met her eyes and she held his gaze while Hashkan's heart hammered wildly against the cage of his ribs. He saw something- sorrow, perhaps- swirling under the surface of her gaze for just a split second. "Your eyes. I've never noticed they have gray flecks in them."

And just like that, the shutters snapped shut. She closed her eyes and turned away. Hashkan took a steadying breath as he dropped his hand.

"I'm going to get Emond. He wanted to know the minute you woke up. I'll send him this way and then go down to the kitchen and see if I can't find anything to eat."

"Thank you," he replied by rote, all the while cursing himself. He'd lost all his sense along with the blood he'd shed that night.

She unlocked the door and disappeared into the hall, leaving the door cracked. He heard her knock softly on a door a few rooms down. When there wasn't an answer, the knocking turned into pounding. There were muffled voices and then Emond came into the room at a run, flinging the door open so hard it rattled the window.

"Hashkan! Am I ever glad to see yer eyes open again!" he exclaimed and then launched into a tirade of questions that Hashkan could barely keep up with. Thankfully, Li'or returned with a covered platter before Hashkan lost his patience.

"They sent me with some snacks for all of us. I had to wake the cooks, so be glad for what we could get," she told them.

She pulled the napkin away to reveal several rolls of bread, a few hunks of cheese, and three small apples.

"I don't care what it is. After a night like we've had, I'm glad to be the ones eating," Hashkan said, reaching for a roll.

"We got lucky," Li'or muttered.

"Aye, we did. Hashkan, what manner of Weaver was that bastard?"

"None that I've ever seen. He was Altering when he redirected the fire I threw, and when I pulled on the Threads for the ground, he wrested them out of my control. As far as what he did to us... Altering can't directly affect a living thing, and the Threads around him weren't following normal patterns when that started. They were distorted. I have no idea what he was doing to crush us like that. It wasn't the air. There was no wind. And my head..."

"Oh, that bump? Glancin' blow, lad. Yer fine."

"*Glancing?*" Hashkan asked, then just shook his head. He regretted it immediately. "No, I had this splitting pain, like my skull was being squeezed. I thought it would break."

"We all did. And did either of you notice his eyes?" Li'or said.

"His eyes? What about them?" Hashkan asked.

They both looked at her, confused.

"No, but whatever it was, we got 'em so it's done now," Emond said, smiling and popping a bit of cheese into his mouth.

"Maybe not," Li'or said, reaching into her pocket. "I found this broach on the shoulder of the man who batted away Hashkan's fire." She pulled out a silver broach in the shape of a wolf skull. "He may have been part of a guild. I'm going to ask around about it while I'm looking for information on the disappearances. Hopefully, someone has seen it before and knows where it's from. More information usually means more pay."

"Heh, ever the prag- pregme-."

"Pragmatist?" Hashkan asked as he scooted further up on his pillows.

"Aye! That. I will do the same."

"I have to report back to the Gathering. My duties start with the first ritual. And I have training…"

"And you need to have a discussion with Mengovik about my pay." Li'or looked at him in that way that she had that made him feel like she was reading his mind. Her stare made him feel even more self-conscience than normal after the idiotic thing he'd done when he'd woken up. He looked away, but not before the warmth of a blush crept to his cheeks.

"I'll address that first thing."

Emond glanced back and forth between the two of them before he began laughing. "Yeh had better, she looks like she might sell yeh to the Rak-Shai if yeh don't!"

"I know a pirate who'd be good for it," Li'or replied with a perfectly straight face. It held for only a moment before she cracked a half-smile.

Emond laughed even louder, slapping his knee. It was contagious, if only because they were all so tense and exhausted, and soon Li'or joined in. Hashkan watched for a moment, bewildered, before finding himself being sucked in as well.

"Alright," Li'or said, wiping the corner of her eye daintily. "Both of you get out of my room. I want to get some real sleep before the morning comes."

Hashkan stiffly drew himself up out of the bed and stretched. He was glad it was still dark out. He was exhausted and couldn't wait to take his boots off and get some real sleep of his own. He followed Emond's lead and grabbed some more of the food Li'or had brought before following the big man out the door. Li'or held the door open for them as they left, and he heard the lock slide to once she shut it behind them. His room was three doors down on the same side of the hall and he shuffled that way, Emond walking beside him.

"We were worried about yeh, Hashkan. Glad yeh came back around," Emond said in a soft voice, his hand on Hashkan's shoulder.

"Thank you for the concern, but I'm fine. I'd honestly prefer if we didn't discuss it again." Ending up with a gaping head-wound was defiantly not his most gallant moment.

"I know, I know. The gods were throwin' weighted dice against us, but we still came out ahead. Focus on that." He smiled again and patted Hashkan's shoulder before turning into his own room.

The key to Hashkan's room was still in his pocket and he unlocked the door. The room was exactly as he'd left it, somehow unaffected by the night's dramas. His blankets were a snarled mess from the night before, but he shucked his boots and belt and climbed into it without a second thought. Sleep came for him as soon as his eyes closed.

⁂

HASHKAN WOKE up late the next morning as the sun crept through a gap in the curtains and landed across his face. He got up and was preparing to leave when he heard the crunch of paper underfoot. He bent down slowly and carefully, lest he set the room to spinning again, and retrieved it. Saying a quick prayer that his notes hadn't escaped their bindings, he unfolded it.

It was a note, but not his. He scanned to the bottom and saw that it was from Li'or. She wrote in a slanted, cramped hand and he had to squint to decipher it. Thankfully it wasn't long. She wrote that she and Emond had already left for the day, but she'd be back to recheck his stitches that night.

He snorted. Did she think she knew more about healing than the Weavers did? Then it occurred to him that she very well may. She could have hundreds of years of practice by now. How old was she anyway?

He shoved the thought away and walked down to the dining hall. Breakfast had already been cleared, but it wasn't time for lunch yet so only a few patrons lingered at the bar. He scooped up a strawberry scone and a few cold links of sausage before scooting out the door as quickly as he could without looking like a thief. He kept his head low and said his second prayer of the morning. He didn't want to run into Elline. The evening he'd spent with her had been pleasant enough, but something was different this morning. Somehow the extra attention made him feel guilty.

He crossed the city as quickly as he could, and the second he set foot in the Gathering he was put to work. The noon ritual was about to begin and there were candles to light, prayer sheets to pass out, and donations to collect. He sat beside Aoth in the stands while the High Weaver delivered his sermon, squirming and sweating in his robes as he worried over all the different ways the ritual could proceed and all the ways he could ruin it and embarrass himself.

The Seamstress was merciful. Everything they did was familiar and Hashkan lost himself to the comforting patterns of the ritual. There was minimal scolding for his tardiness and the High Weaver gladly gave him the coin he needed to pay Li'or, though he was warned against offering payment for anything again. Weavers were elevated above coin. The donations were supposed to go to the needy.

After that day, Hashkan fell into a comfortable routine.

He had breakfast early, mostly just with Li'or while Emond slept in, then he made his way over to the Gathering in time to help with the first ritual of the day. Duties done, he'd dive headfirst into his training. Once his head healed, he did drills with the apprentices, sparred with other Weavers, and in the afternoon, he buried himself in the library. The Straethian Gathering housed hundreds of books on warfare, many of which were written with Altering in mind.

He devoured them. The more he learned, the more he felt like the High Weaver in Harthmere had done him a disservice. Battlefield tactics was a broad area of study in which Hashkan was completely ignorant due to no fault of his own. And he was determined to correct it. Even in this long stretch of peace, there was no reason to be uneducated. Besides, if a soldier could make battle strategies, so could he. And, as he was more educated, his would probably be better.

After spending nearly two weeks in Straeth, he was leaving the Gathering for the evening when he heard his name echoing through the trees. A young apprentice was running after him, over-sized robes billowing behind her.

"Weaver Clearont? The High Weaver needs to speak with you."

Anxiety fluttered into Hashkan's chest. "Just me?" he asked.

"Yes, sir," the girl answered. She dipped into a small bow.

Hashkan saw Mengovik every day, but he'd only ever been summoned as part of a group. He motioned the apprentice to lead the way and followed her back down the path, all the while reviewing every bit of his work from the day. It had all been exemplary. There was no need to worry. Confidence restored, he followed the young girl across the garden.

The High Weaver was sitting in his usual spot in the shade overlooking the sparring grounds. Some Weavers were moving through drills and the High Weaver watched while dictating notes to another young apprentice. A warm smile spread across his face when he noticed Hashkan walking up.

"Perfect, you didn't quite escape for the day!"

Hashkan smiled back and sank into a bow. "You asked for me, sir?"

"Yes, I did, I did. Please sit." His attention turned back to the sparring as Hashkan lowered himself onto the nearest bench. "Lord Klevelt has asked for a Weaver to accompany a patrol he's sending out to the northwest. He says the farms out that way have been reporting zhu'dac activity and he needs brave souls to hunt them down. I'm sending *you*."

Hashkan's head whipped around to stare at the High Weaver, eyes wide. "I'm… flattered."

Hashkan stood and bowed again, first two fingers pressed to his forehead. Despite his qualifications, it was more typical for tenured Weavers to be chosen for these kinds of missions, not one who was brand new to the Gathering. Pride welled up in him and he was grinning again when he straightened up. This was exactly the type of recognition he'd been hoping for when he'd arrived in Breen. He'd made the correct decision when he chose to leave.

"Oh, none of that. Just start getting ready to go. You leave in two days. I'll send my response to Klevelt and have more details for you tomorrow."

"Yes, High Weaver."

❋ ✲

HASHKAN'S HOURGLASS was running through its sand faster than he could keep up with it. He felt prepared as far as his Altering technique was concerned, but still painfully lacking in his knowledge of military strategy. No matter how many books he picked up, none of them answered his questions. What was his job within a scouting squad? What was he expected to achieve? He even went as far as asking for his normal duties in the rituals and lectures to be put on hold so he'd have as much time to study as possible. The chamberlain grumbled but granted Hashkan's request.

Li'or and Emond were completely useless when he brought his concerns to them. They just congratulated him on being chosen, before giving him half-baked advice and leaving him sitting alone at the table. They still hadn't found any information for Lord Klevelt regarding the rash of desertions, and their frustration was evident in the way they stalked around with short tempers. Li'or had even mentioned leaving on another job before her coin ran out. Hashkan stared at his food and bit his tongue through that entire conversation.

Finally, desperate for answers on the eve of his trip, Hashkan sought out High Weaver Mengovik. He found the old man sitting in a secluded corner of the garden, silver eyes focused on the Fabric. Hashkan bowed, but the High Weaver didn't notice him. Impatient, Hashkan shifted and the gravel crunched under his heels.

"Hello, Hashkan," Mengovik said, humor coloring his voice.

"Good afternoon, High Weaver. I need one last piece of advice-"

"Hush, hush, now. Sit. Look."

Hashkan held back a sigh but did as he was told. Mengovik still hadn't so much as glanced in his direction. He followed the High Weaver's order and let his vision shift to the Fabric.

"Isn't it wonderful? The complexity of the Seamstress's vision? We're fortunate that she revealed it to us in our lifetime."

"Yes, High Weaver, but if I may-"

"You may not," Mengovik cut Hashkan off. The old Weaver's voice fell into the staccato rhythm of the rituals and lectures, likely out of pure habit. "Sit and look. How long has it been since you just *looked* at everything? You young men think everything is urgent, that everything has to be managed and controlled. Sometimes, the wisest thing you can do is just *allow* the Fabric to reveal its pattern to you. A fire glows on its own. Try to squeeze out more light and you'll smother it."

Hashkan furrowed his brows but stayed quiet and focused on the Fabric. The High Weaver was right. Hashkan couldn't remember the last time he'd done this and it was considered an important practice in the service of the Seamstress. It had always seemed like a waste of time. He was familiar with the Fabric and couldn't he better serve the Seamstress by actually doing something?

The minutes stretched by. A breeze blew through the gardens, the Threads for the air rolling in a wave like what normal people saw in water. The billows rolled against the leaves of an oak and the Threads of the branches wobbled slightly as the leaves danced. Deeper in the garden, a dragonfly buzzed around a patch of tufted hair grass. The air bent in tiny ripples around its needle-thin body, the effect barely radiating out from around it.

But the effects were there. The more Hashkan looked, the more he noticed how the different Threads bent and stretched to accommodate for changes made to the Threads around them. Everything was woven together-tightly in some places, loose in others- in a way that allowed for all the different parts to function individually while still being a part of the whole. Of the Fabric.

Maybe this was what The High Weaver wanted him to see. Maybe someone had reported to him about Hashkan's frantic research and he'd been expecting this meeting all along. Either way, the message was clear. All that he and the soldiers needed to do was work together. If they were flexible, like the Threads for air, he'd be able to fit into place wherever he was needed.

Relieved, Hashkan sighed and let his mind grow still as the Fabric danced around him. Eventually, as the shadows stretched out from under the trees, Mengovik groaned and reached his arms overhead.

"Beautiful patterns today, wouldn't you say?"

"Yes, Seamstress be praised," Hashkan answered automatically. He blinked as his eyes focused back into the normal spectrum.

"And now, your question! What wisdom can I impart on you?" Mengovik's eyes crinkled in the corners as he smiled.

Hashkan pushed his hand through his hair. "Actually, High Weaver, the Seamstress answered everything for me already."

"Perfect. Hopefully, it's in your favor."

"I believe it is."

"Excellent. Now, it's almost dinner time. Let's see what they've prepared for us today, shall we?" Hashkan helped the High Weaver stand and walked with him to the dining hall.

Chapter Fifteen

A Little Bit of Reputation

*H*ashkan ate with the Weavers that evening and walked back to the Ale Boat in the dark after bidding everyone farewell. Almost every person in the Gathering wished him good luck, to the point it started to fray his nerves. He had his answer and the Seamstress's favor, what did he need with luck? His nervousness had faded, replaced with a growing excitement, and his mind wandered as he strolled along the dark streets. He imagined his warm welcome when he reported to the barracks in the morning. He saw himself riding at the head of the line, advising the commanding officer on the best routes to take.

Then the rain started. Water fell by the bucket-full and he was drenched in a matter of seconds. He pursed his lips. If it rained like this while they were out, his biggest responsibility would be keeping the guards dry at night.

Heavy rain clouds were still hanging over Straeth when Hashkan got up the next morning, though the rain had finally stopped in the early hours of the morning. He grabbed his pack and went downstairs to where Li'or and Emond were already waiting.

"Emond, you're up early," Hashkan said as he sat down at the table.

"Aye, yeh know I wouldn't miss yer big send-off!"

"He was even here before I was," Li'or added as she sipped her tea.

"Come on now, yeh act like I sleep late every mornin'!"

"Not all, just most," Hashkan said with a smile.

"Ack!" Emond scoffed as he gnawed on a scone. Eseldra still commanded most of Emond's attention.

A stiff silence fell over them as they ate and Hashkan didn't know what to say to break it. Elline waited on a table near theirs, making a point for Hashkan to notice her not noticing him. He sighed. He'd tried to be gentle with his refusals, but they still hadn't gone over well. And Emond and Li'or noticed her scorn, of course. It didn't make conversation any easier and the silence dragged on until they were all standing in front of the inn, preparing to part ways. Hashkan caught himself toying with his reins and frowned.

"You'll be fine, and we'll see you when you get back," Li'or told him. She held out her hand and clasped his forearm. Hashkan smiled, remembering when she'd first done that months ago in Breen. She flashed him a rare, ear-to-ear grin and Hashkan's breath hitched in his chest.

"Show them what you're blighted made of, lad. Yeh aren't some fool with his nose rubbin' on books all day," Emond added, pulling Hashkan's attention from Li'or.

"I'll do my best," Hashkan said, still distracted by Li'or's smile. He couldn't remember her ever smiling at him like that. Normally, her smiles had an edge as sharp as her blades. This smile sparked off a warmth inside him like a shot of Vaeshekian liquor and the same heat tinged his cheeks.

Emond must have noticed. He smirked and winked at Hashkan conspiratorially.

"And yer best is more than enough. Yer as much a fighter as any of them guards yeh'll be ridin' with."

Emond slapped his shoulder, Li'or nodded to him, and then they left him standing outside of the inn with his horse. It wasn't exactly the grand send-off he'd been expecting- better in some ways and lacking in others. He pushed the thought aside and adjusted his stained travel robes before climbing into his saddle.

It was a short ride to the barracks where he was supposed to meet up with the rest of the squadron. A few men and women in navy and gray uniforms were already lined up outside of the building, standing next to their horses and waiting. Hashkan took his place at the end of the line next to a man with a thick beard that covered his face nearly up to his eyes.

"Well, the rumor was true. They did get us a Weaver," the man said as Hashkan dismounted.

Hashkan bristled at his condescending tone but gave a shallow bow. "Yes, Lord Klevelt sent the request to the High Weaver and I was the most suited for the mission."

"Yeah?" The man scratched at the thick pelt springing from the top of his tunic. "Well, I'm glad they're looking out for us. I go by Bearson." He held his hand out for Hashkan to shake. Hashkan took it and introduced himself.

"Is this all of us?" Hashkan asked. He fought back the urge to cradle his hand. Bearson had a grip like a vice.

"Gods, no. You're early is all."

The soldiers trickled in, some alone and some in small groups, and before long Hashkan was standing in the middle of an organized line of thirty men and women and their horses. Every one of them was in uniform and it was easy to see that their jackets had been freshly laundered, their leather vests recently oiled. Hashkan looked down at his robes and was suddenly conscious of every frayed thread. The soldiers weren't in their Solstice best, but they all looked sharper than he did. He felt like a poor representative of the Seamstress and he wished he had time to change. Common soldiers should never outshine a Weaver.

But he didn't have time. The door to the barracks swung open and a man with pure white hair walked out. He wore a light gray tunic and breeches with tall black boots polished to a high shine and a shining silver breastplate. He didn't walk so much as he marched, casting an appraising eye on the soldiers as he went. He paused on Hashkan for a moment, his dark gaze hard, before passing down to the end of the line.

"Who is that?" Hashkan whispered to Bearson.

"That's Major Jaerrek Glisairin, your new commanding officer."

Hashkan cocked an eyebrow. "I answer only to the Gathering."

"Men!"

Hashkan flinched and turned back to the front. The major was standing right in front of him, hands clasped behind his back and eyes narrowed.

"If there's something so gods-damned important you'd better share it with the rest of us," Glisairin said. His voice carried so well that the entire block probably heard him.

Hashkan blushed and stayed silent.

"No sir, the conversation is over. I apologize for interrupting," Bearson said.

Glisairin shook his head. "I'd expect a Weaver not to know how to act, but I thought better of you, soldier."

Hashkan seethed. How dare this man insult him like

that, especially when the Gathering was volunteering his services. They'd been the ones asking for help!

"I'm sorry, sir."

The major turned on his heel and continued back towards the barracks. Hashkan stood frozen, too furious to even form a rebuttal. He gnashed his teeth and sighed heavily through his nose.

"They're all yours," Glisairin said. He patted a tall man with dark hair on the shoulder before disappearing back into the building.

The newcomer stood at the end of the line, inspecting them. His boots hadn't been polished recently, and he didn't have a glistening breastplate, but there was still an undeniable air of authority about him. He followed the major's tracks and stalked down the line before stopping in the center- right in front of Hashkan. The man's eyes were narrow from squinting against the sun.

"All right. You all know why we're here. Any last-minute questions?" All of the soldiers stayed silent. "That's what I like to hear! Mount up, everyone. They've got our supplies at the gate. Weaver, up front with me, please."

Hashkan swung into his saddle and smiled. "Of course." This was the treatment he'd been expecting.

Hashkan rode beside the officer as the soldiers filed down the street in pairs.

"I'm First Captain Ardrick Filan," he said as they passed through streets that were rapidly filling with morning traffic. "We're honored to have you ride with us, Weaver."

"Of course. It's an honor to serve alongside Straeth's best."

Filan laughed. "I don't know about that, but we damn sure aren't her worst. We'll get the job done and have you safely back to the Gathering before too long."

Hashkan glanced over at Filan, unsure how to respond. It almost sounded like the captain considered him more of a burden than a blessing. Either that or the man was implying Hashkan would be uncomfortable on the road and would have to be rushed back behind the Gathering's stone walls.

Before Hashkan could form a response, he was distracted by a small group of people cheering for them as they rode by. He immediately forgot about the backhanded insult Filan had dealt him. To these people, they were heroes. They saw a parade of soldiers on prancing horses, on their way to save friends and family members. Hashkan sat up a little straighter in his saddle. He even forgot about the stains on his robe.

There was a call from up ahead as they neared the gate. Filan kicked his horse forward to meet with another officer and the soldiers started to spread out around the entrance to the gate. There were guards loading supplies into a wagon hitched to a pair of mules while others began distributing camping gear to the soldiers in the squad. Hashkan reined his horse in to wait.

"Don't stop in the middle of the fucking road, blasphemer," a course voice grumbled from behind him.

A guard rode up beside Hashkan, passing by so closely that their legs scraped by each other. Hashkan hissed, twisting in his saddle to avoid his leg being crushed and his horse took a hasty step to the side. The guard kept going, glaring at Hashkan over his soldier. Hashkan's horse fidgeted, still dancing sideways, and he put a steadying hand on her neck.

"Try to ignore him," Bearson said. He rode up beside Hashkan's horse and reined in. "He's a naturalist. And a blighted serious one. Almost dropped out of the mission when he heard you were coming."

"Well then he's a fool!" Hashkan said, almost shouted, before he could stop himself. "How could anyone deny the existence of the Seamstress when her gifts are in plain view?"

"Probably got dropped as a child."

Hashkan snorted but didn't respond. Naturalists infuriated him. They still followed the old gods, but instead of allowing people to choose their deity for themselves, they openly condemned Weavers and the Seamstress's followers. Most would just protest outside of the Gatherings, but the more extreme among them didn't hesitate to commit acts of vandalism or to assault Weavers. He hadn't expected to have to deal with them in a large city like Straeth.

The guards handing out gear finally worked their way over to where Hashkan and Bearson stood and passed each of them a bedroll. Hashkan took his and tied it onto his saddle next to the one he already carried. He'd use whichever one was in better shape.

"Do you tend to get cold, Weaver?" Bearson asked. Hashkan felt several other soldiers turn their attention his way. Their gazes fell on him like physical things, but he set his jaw against the irritation bubbling up inside him.

"Not at all," he answered. "I've just learned that you can never be too prepared. I've spent some time outside of the walls of a city. It's an unforgiving place."

"I'm surprised you know that, Weaver. Have you been on a patrol before?" another soldier chimed in.

"No, this is my first patrol. I've just done some traveling with an elven mercenary and I learned a few things from her along the way."

"Oh, *her*, huh? I see," Bearson drawled with a mischievous look on his face. "You're friendly with an elven woman, are yah?"

"No, no, not like that at all," Hashkan said, but it was

already too late. He was blushing and the men and women around him had burst into conversation and laughter.

Bearson patted Hashkan's back. "There you go friend, a little bit of reputation. There's nothing soldiers and guards like more than a little bit of gossip, especially if it's the kind you wouldn't share with your mother."

Hashkan opened his mouth to respond but was interrupted when the call to move out drifted over from the gate. He moved into line beside Bearson and passed through the gates, leaving the protection of the city behind.

Chapter Sixteen

A Thin String

*E*ven outside the city, the soldiers rode in formation. Hashkan trotted his horse beside Bearson's, the view in front of him blocked by the worst ends of man and horse alike. Captain Filan rode at the head of the line alone. For the first few miles, Hashkan had waited for Filan to call him back to the front, but when no summons came, he'd settled into a sullen silence.

He hadn't anticipated being treated like a common soldier. He'd gleaned from the conversations around him that a handful of the soldiers on this trip were fresh recruits on their first patrol and here he was, a fully trained Weaver in service to the Seamstress, mixed in with boys barely old enough to leave home. His jaw ached from clenching it so tightly for so long.

To make matters worse, all the soldiers did was complain about their work or their women. They were soldiers, but they didn't want to guard the walls. They wanted pretty wives and lots of children, but they didn't want to take care of them. Hashkan couldn't relate. Didn't want to.

"Is something bothering you, Hashkan?" Bearson asked.

"Whoreson thinks he's better than us, while he goes around defiling the earth!"

Hashkan turned around. The soldier that had nearly scraped him off his horse was glaring at him from two rows back. The man had broad soldiers, graying hair, and a cruel twist to his mouth.

Bearson turned around in his saddle. "Really, Shilander? You have to do this shit now?" he said with a sigh.

"Someone has to! It's only a matter of time before those bastard Weavers bring the wrath of all the gods down on us!"

Hashkan groaned. "It was a goddess that gave us this gift!"

Shilander pushed his horse up between the soldiers separating them. "No one knew a thing about your Seamstress until people started taking the gods' work into their own hands. If she even exists, she's a yab'bask!"

A wraith. A hag. An evil spirit. Hashkan yanked his horse to a stop and jabbed a finger towards Shilander.

"You take that back," he said through gritted teeth. "You will not defile the Seamstress's name."

"Or what?" Shilander move his horse closer to Hashkan's. He stared Hashkan square in the eye, mouth twisted in a snarl.

"What in the name of the Seamstress is going on back here?" Filan yelled. Shilander hissed through his teeth but didn't so much as blink.

Hashkan looked away and saw that the entire party had stopped… and Filan was riding towards them, his face like a thunderhead.

"This Weaver shit needs to learn his place!" Shilander yelled. He didn't take his eyes off of Hashkan.

"His place is wherever I say it should be, and that's all you need to concern yourself with," Filan said. He paused for a moment, but Shilander still didn't respond. "Shilander! Are you deaf?"

"No, sir. I hear you," Shilander muttered.

"Good. Shilander, get up front with me so I can watch you. Weaver, in the back, please. I'll deal with this when we get to camp. And this better be the end of it!"

Hashkan waited as the squadron rode past him, flabbergasted. Shilander got to ride in a place of honor while he, the innocent party, was exiled to the back to the line? He stared after them and squeezed his reins until his knuckles were white.

"Come on, Hashkan." He blinked and noticed Bearson waiting next to him. "Filan will keep an eye on him up there. He won't start anything again."

Hashkan sighed and urged his horse forward. "Let's hope not."

The day became even more miserable not an hour later when the clouds that had threatened them all morning finally opened up. Hashkan pulled his hood over his head with a sigh, knowing that his cloak would be soaked through in a matter of minutes. The soldiers around him did the same and all their cheerful conversations tapered off. The rain pounded down around them in a deafening torrent.

The downpour persisted until the sun started to set, before finally giving them a reprieve as they started setting up camp. As soon as all their feet hit the ground, Filan was giving more orders. Hashkan was tasked with caring for the horses with Bearson and two other soldiers while

Shilander- to Hashkan's delight- was punished with twice the normal amount of chores.

Hashkan was tempted to argue against being given any chores at all. He technically wasn't under Filan's command. But Bearson had grabbed him by the shoulder just as he was about to voice his protest. In the end, he was glad he'd followed the man over. Feeding and grooming the horses was relaxing after such a stressful day.

"Weaver!"

Hashkan flinched and spun around. The captain was standing not an arm's length behind him.

"Think it's okay to take it easy because you're the only Weaver in this squadron?" His eyes bored holes into Hashkan's.

"I honestly don't know what you mean... sir." He added the title as an afterthought and it was obvious.

Filan's scowl deepened. "Your tack, Weaver! You've got it all on the ground! That's an easy way to lose things in the grass after dark. Pick everything up and keep them in the pouch. Don't let me see this again." Filan didn't even wait for a response before storming off to harass someone else.

"Yes, of course," Hashkan muttered. He felt his face redden as he knelt to collect the hoof pick and brushes he'd set on the ground. He tried to look nonchalant while he organized everything. Filan was right, but the *nerve* the man had to think he could tear into a Weaver like that...

"Shilander! Do you think that's funny? Did I not give you enough to do?" Filan shouted as he walked back over towards the camp. "That guy rope you just tied is as slack as your mother! Redo it before the tent blows over."

Hashkan smirked. Maybe he was being treated with a little more respect than the others after all. He finished up with the last horse, shouldered his pack, and walked back into the camp with Bearson. He followed the soldier back towards where the tents were being set up in two neat lines, the cook fire at the opposite side of the rows. A few tents down the aisle, a short dark-haired man had just finished pitching a tent.

"Perfect, you did all the hard work for me!" Bearson said, shaking the man's hand and smiling.

"How are the tents distributed?" Hashkan asked, trying to sound unconcerned and failing as worry pulled down the corners of his mouth. It was already fully dark and he didn't savor the idea of setting his tent up that late.

"Three to a tent," the stranger answered.

"Do you already have a third person for this tent?" Hashkan shifted his pack on his shoulder and glanced off to the side.

"Yes," Bearson grunted as he tossed his pack into the tent. "You." He gestured over at the other man. "This is Smithie."

Hashkan shook the man's extended hand. He had a firm grip and arms that were testing the limits of his sleeves. "Smithie? What kind of smith?"

"I ain't a smith at all! Just a soldier. Some lads just decided one day that I looked like one and the name stuck ever since."

"Better than Bray. He looks like an ass." Bearson jerked his thumb towards a lanky man with a long face setting up a cooking stand a couple of tents over. "He's a good cook though, so don't pester him too much."

"Yeah, I can't wait to eat something warm after all that gods-damned rain. And what I'd really like after that," Smithie complained, "would be some dry clothes for the night. Every blighted thing I packed is soaked through."

"I can do something about that. Stay still."

Hashkan let his eyes shift into focus on the Threads

while concentrating on Smithie's clothing. The Threads of water were interwoven with the fabric of the cloth, the two patterns combining like an elaborate tapestry. He reached out with his mind and plucked at the water Threads, then dragged them out of the clothes before letting them spill out onto the ground.

"Well, they finally sent us a useful Weaver!" Bearson clapped Hashkan's shoulder. "Never did like sleeping soggy. Me next."

Before Hashkan knew it, the entire squad, including the captain, was crowded around him, waiting for him to drag the water out of their clothing and packs. He made his way around the group of soldiers, snatching out all the rainwater, and as he went the excitement in the camp swelled.

Hashkan had never slept in wet clothes himself, thanks to his little trick, but it must have been awful to warrant the kind of relief he saw on all of their faces. All of the conversations that had died in the rain sprang back to life and the camp was filled with chatter while they ate dinner. Hashkan grinned until his face hurt and accepted his thanks gracefully. It wasn't until well after sunset that Filan called for the first watch to take their positions and sent the rest of the guards to their bedrolls.

Hashkan put his bowl back with the others on the supply wagon and walked back towards his shared tent. He was still being thanked and he smiled as he nodded to the last of the stragglers heading off to bed. He paused briefly at the entrance to his tent and looked back out towards the dying campfire. He'd been wrong to think poorly of these men and women earlier in the day. Already they were beginning to see the value of having him along.

"I didn't know whoresons had anything to smile about, Weaver."

Hashkan whipped around just in time to see Shilander glare at him as he entered the next tent over. The man's hair and clothing still clung to him, saturated with rainwater. Hashkan drew his brows together. It seemed that the naturalist wasn't finished hounding him after all, and he'd already come close to being violent.

There were threats on all sides now. Zhu'dac on the outside and this halfwit inside the camp. Hashkan cast one more worried glance at the neighboring tent before ducking back into his own. Hopefully, his sleep would be undisturbed.

※ ＊

WHEN MORNING CAME, the sun rose bright and hot, burning through any lingering cloud cover. Hashkan had barely slept. He'd already grown accustomed to soft down mattresses again and he'd tossed and turned the entire night. When he got up, his joints ached like an old farmer's.

The sunrise was beautiful. The light caught on all the dew drops and trimmed the world with gold, but Hashkan barely spared it a glance. He couldn't find it in him to marvel at the Seamstress's creation when he was working with a man who denied her very existence. A muscle feathered in his jaw every time he thought about it.

The squad was quiet while they broke camp, only a few snatches of conversation and the snorting of the horses breaking the early morning peace. As they saddled and mounted their horses, Bray and another man walked through the lines and passed out breakfast. Hashkan fought to hide his disappointment when Bray handed him a sausage link and a hard biscuit. It was only a step above what he'd been surviving on before he ran into Li'or and it tasted much the same.

While Hashkan gnawed on his biscuit, Smithie came up and handed him a rolled-up piece of leather.

"What's this?" Hashkan asked around a mouthful of food.

"Leather vest. Was issued to me a while back, but it's too small. Kept it just in case but I hate wearin' it- rubs my armpits. It'll probably fit you though. You never know when you'll need it," he said with a shrug.

"That's very generous, thank you."

"Oh, he's just tired of carrying it, is all," Bearson said with a laugh as he rode up. "Looks like an oxen and lazy like one too."

"That's not what your wife said before we left," Smithie retorted.

Bearson burst into laughter. "That's a good one. But you know, your mother told me…"

Their banter continued and Hashkan just shook his head as he shrugged the vest on under the outer layer of his robes. They both had entirely too much energy for so early in the morning.

The vest didn't quite fit him either. It was a touch too big, definitely enough to be noticeable. He considered taking it off, but Smithie caught his eye and nodded. Hashkan shrugged and smiled back. He was too polite to refuse a kind gesture, even if it meant feeling a little ridiculous.

"It'll do," Smithie said and continued on to where the others were beginning to line up for the day's march. Hashkan swung up on his horse and started to follow behind him.

As Hashkan approached his place in the group, Shilander pulled away from the line-up and reined his horse in hard, stopping sideways in front of Hashkan's mare so he could glare down at the Weaver. Tension crackled off of the man and set Hashkan's teeth on edge.

It was *entirely* too early for this.

"Look, Weaver," he began, spitting Hashkan's title out as if it were a curse. "You may have the others fooled, but I know what you are. I won't stand by again while you work your damned magics with your whore-goddess on these good people." He coughed and spat on the ground beside their horses.

A challenge.

Hashkan narrowed his eyes. "Is that so?" Already his heart was hammering in his chest, but he crossed his arms. He wouldn't let the man know that he'd gotten under his skin. He refused to give him that satisfaction.

The soldiers that were already gathered grew quiet. All eyes were on Hashkan as he stared Shilander down.

"That's so," Shilander answered with a slash of a smile.

The words just fanned Hashkan's temper even higher. He'd done nothing to this ignorant man, done nothing but help this squad, and his thanks was this backwater hostility? He felt his face warm, but glared back at Shilander, his silver eyes unblinking.

"And what exactly do you intend to do about it? I could have killed you half a hundred times by now if I'd wanted."

"You bastard!" Shilander snatched up his sword and had it half-drawn before Hashkan had time to respond.

"Shilander!" Captain Filan's voice echoed around them, loud enough that a pair of horses jumped and scuttled to the side. A silence wrapped around them so tightly that Hashkan held his breath.

"I *know* this isn't what it looks like. I *know* you aren't starting shit with the Weaver again."

The color drained from Shilander's face for half a heartbeat before it flushed a violent crimson. He rammed his sword back into its sheath. "He's impersonating a soldier in that vest! And he threatened to kill me! We're better off without him. We need to send the bastard back before he brings the wrath of the gods down on all of us!"

Hashkan barely kept himself from rolling his eyes. The man was whining and it was pathetic. Not to mention anyone with half a brain could look at the scene Shilander caused and know exactly what was going on.

Filan slammed his hand down on his saddle. "There's no time for this. Both of you set this aside, we have a job to do. Weaver, to the rear again. Shilander, with me. And you'll be assisting Bray tonight with the dishes."

Hashkan's jaw dropped. Was that it, no further punishment? Shilander turned and glared at Hashkan as he rode away, a nasty smile curling his lips. Hashkan's teeth slammed together with a clack as the pattern slowly started to become visible.

Despite his years of study, despite his gift from the Seamstress, in this group, he was a second-rate citizen. Filan was a soldier and it was clear he wouldn't choose a Weaver over one of his own, no matter how out of line that soldier got. The realization left him cold. He was already a day's ride from any sympathetic party and the distance would only grow. Maybe he should turn around rather than suffer through further indignation.

Someone scoffed beside him and Hashkan turned to see Bearson throw a vulgar gesture towards Shilander.

"Ignore him. He'll get over it eventually. He's never been anything but a blighted arse," Bearson said.

"Who? Shilander or Filan?"

As if to prove that Hashkan's epiphany had been right,

Bearson scowled at him. "Filan isn't to blame here. He's a good man, and fair."

"Fair to who?" Hashkan asked, unable to keep the ire out of his tone.

The line started to move out and Hashkan kicked his horse into a trot to catch up to his place at the end. Bearson trailed behind him and sighed as they pulled their horses back down to a walk.

"You're right. Shilander's a prick and Filan is too distracted to handle it properly. He has family out here you know."

Hashkan grunted in response. Knowing that, he could easily forgive the captain's incompetence- even felt guilty for passing such hasty judgment. It still didn't make it easier to admit out loud.

"We'll deal with Shilander, huh? The rest of us have your back."

Hashkan looked at Bearson. The soldier looked determined and offered the Weaver a tentative smile. Hashkan believed the man was on his side, but none of the other soldiers had moved when Shilander cornered him. Bearson thought more of them than they were really worth.

Hashkan kept it to himself. He just thanked the man and turned his sight back towards the front where all kinds of threats lurked.

※ ⁛ ＊

It was three long days of riding before they found anything. Three more days of enduring Shilander's glares and catching him mumbling insults under his breath. Three more nights of sharing a camp with men that snored like boars and kept him up all hours of the night. Hashkan was exhausted and his temper was hanging on by a thin string. Filan was keeping him and Shilander separated as much as possible and it was a blessing from the Seamstress herself. One more push from that cretin and Hashkan was afraid he'd snap.

They'd passed by several farms along the way, and each stop had been the same. They had seen no zhu'dac, but the one farthest from town - the Loewen farm- had, so the squadron pushed forward.

"This is too far out for a farm," Hashkan commented early the third day. "They're too isolated. Too far from the city."

Bearson, still riding at the end of the line with him, nodded. "Normally I'd agree. But we've been on the Loewen's land since we passed that gnarled tree last night. Their farm is huge. They basically make up their own town."

"Well, then we should have run into someone by now…"

Bearson frowned. "You're probably right."

There was nothing probable about it. Hashkan hadn't forgotten what it was like to live on a farm. An operation this large would have had at least one person working in every field planting, weeding, harvesting, watching livestock. Every day there was something. It was the only way to stay profitable.

Something was very wrong.

In the afternoon, they found the first corpses. The squad rode through the pasture, silence creeping down the line as they all noticed the bodies. They were mangled and mostly eaten, but Hashkan could tell by the skulls that the majority of the bodies were cattle. There at least thirty of them and they had been dead long enough that scavengers had already passed through. His eyes fell on a smaller corpse. Bones of what looked like a hand reached towards him out of shredded muscle and cloth. A chill spider-climbed up Hashkan's back. How many zhu'dac had done this?

"Soldiers!" Filan yelled from the front, shattering the silence. "Let's ride! Swords out, be ready!" He spurred his horse into a gallop and they all followed after him, hooves eating up the ground. Hashkan's heart was in his throat, but he squinted against the dust and leaned low over his mare's neck.

They tore down the narrow road between two fields, up the side of a hill, and as they crested the rise the Loewen farm came into view.

Bearson hadn't exaggerated. It did look like a small country town; several generations and all the extended family must have lived there. There were at least ten homes of different sizes nestled in among barns and silos. The paddocks and pastures were empty. A few gates swung and squeaked in the breeze, and as they got closer there was still not a soul to be seen.

The squad thundered into the courtyard between two barns and the largest house and Filan reined in his horse, holding up a hand for them all to halt behind him. They slowed and fanned out between the buildings. Every soldier's head swiveled back and forth, scanning for some sign of life. Tension settled in Hashkan's shoulders and he and his horse both spooked when the wind slammed a gate shut.

"Everyone wait here," Filan ordered. He dismounted and walked up to the front door of the largest house. Hashkan waited with the others as Filan climbed the stairs and knocked on the door. No answer came. Filan turned and started back towards them with his brows knitted tightly together.

"This is bad," he grumbled when he got back to his

horse. "I want to check in these barns. Split up. Weaver, with me."

Hashkan nodded and dismounted. He left his horse and followed after Filan to a barn on the outskirts of the commune. It looked like it had a full second story and the double doors in the front were easily fifteen feet tall.

Filan knocked on the door of the barn once they reached it. "Hello? I'm First Captain Ardrick Filan, Straethian Guard... Hello?" They waited a few moments and when it became apparent they weren't going to get a response, Filan nodded for Hashkan to open the right door.

As soon as he tugged the door open wide enough, the business end of a pitchfork thrust through, narrowly missing Hashkan's face. He inhaled through his teeth and immediately his sight slipped to focus on the Threads. There was no fire around, but a blast of wind could do plenty of damage.

"Not another step! Back up three steps and be quick about it!" a panicked voice called out from behind the door.

Hashkan and Filan complied, holding their hands up and away from any weapons. Hashkan kept his focus on the Threads and forced himself to take slow, even breaths.

The door swung open further and revealed two men, one holding the pitchfork and the other a spade. They had the wiry but strong build typical of farmers and each had a shock of bright blond hair and freckled skin. They so strongly resembled each other that Hashkan immediately started to think of them as brothers. And they were covered in dirt and blood.

"Well, show us then. Let's see the uniform," the farmer with the spade demanded.

Filan slowly opened his cloak, showing them his arms

with their bands of rank encircling them. "I'm Captain Filan, this is Weaver Clearont." Both men snapped their eyes over to Hashkan. He met each of their gazes in turn, allowing them to see the silver of his eyes. It was more validation than any uniform.

"We're here to help," he told them. It was like soothing a frightened animal.

The farmers lowered their makeshift weapons, but the shadows didn't leave their eyes.

"What happened here?" Filan asked.

The man with the pitchfork pushed the door open wider and motioned them in. "Come see for yourself."

Filan slipped through the door and Hashkan followed behind him, then froze in his tracks. The rotting, metallic scent of old blood punched him in the face as soon as he took the first step into the barn.

Three men laid on blankets on the floor against the wall, rust colored stains all over their clothes. One was missing a leg at the knee and squirmed, sweating through fevered dreams. The other two wore more bandages than clothes but were awake, staring at Hashkan and Filan with hollow, exhausted eyes. Four women milled around a table, preparing bandages and mixing medicine. Farther back a draft horse stood tied in a set of stocks. Thick ropes were wound under his chest and flanks then fastened off to the stakes to hold him upright. He swayed and leaned against the ropes for support, ragged gashes along his shoulders and hips oozing. A teenage boy and girl were trying to clean and bandage the wounds.

Hashkan grimaced. The Threads around the wounds on the horse and the unconscious man were already weakening and fraying. Infection. Neither one had much time left.

"I'm Vidmar Loewen," the man with the pitchfork

volunteered, dragging Hashkan's attention away from the dying. "This is my brother, Evmar. And this is what's left of our family. Zhu'dac ran through here four days ago- over a hundred of them…"

Hashkan drew in a hissing breath. They weren't prepared to deal with that many. He glanced over at Filan.

Filan's eyebrows had disappeared up into his hair. "How many?"

"Well over a hundred," Evmar chimed in. "All the live-stock dead and my wife- " he broke off and turned away from them. Vidmar put a hand on his brother's shoulder and squeezed.

"Excuse us," Vidmar said as he led his brother over to a bench where they sat down together.

Filan sighed and kicked at a clump of dirt. "This is far worse than I was led to believe."

"I recommend turning around. We don't have enough men to deal with that many zhu'dac," Hashkan said.

Filan looked up at Hashkan from beneath a furrowed brow. "Are you asking me to abandon my mission?"

Hashkan gaped at him. Of course that was what he was asking! Sending thirty soldiers against hundreds of zhu'dac was suicide.

"Don't look at me like that, Weaver," Filan said. He took a step closer to Hashkan and lowered his voice. "We keep going until we can confirm the numbers and the direction this horde is traveling, then we'll turn around and report back."

Relief draped itself over Hashkan like a blanket against the cold, but he narrowed his eyes and feigned giving the plan some thought. "If we're cautious… that would be useful information for Lord Klevelt."

Filan gave him a sharp half-smile that Hashkan wasn't sure how to interpret. "Glad you agree." He turned back to the farmers. "What direction did the zhu'dac leave in? Is there anyone else hiding in the other buildings?"

"Northeast," Vidmar answered. "And no, we are all that's left."

It was like Vidmar had to force each word out and they pierced Hashkan like arrows. He looked around the barn again, avoiding eye contact with any of the survivors. He'd never seen a more broken group of people. Even as they fought to keep their injured alive, they went through the motions as if they were all already dead. It is was either that or they were bunched up in the corner with a few young children, all crying together. He wanted to tell them he was sorry for their losses, but what good were his words against such a bleak reality?

"Come on, let's get everyone back together," Filan said as he herded Hashkan towards the door. "And not a word about the zhu'dac numbers, do you hear me? Not. A. Word. I can't afford a panic. This is a scouting mission now, but they don't need to know that just yet."

"Of course," Hashkan said with confidence in his tone that he didn't feel. In his mind, it seemed wiser for the soldiers to know what they were looking for, if only so they would be more cautious.

"Tell Bray I want him in there. He's got some training with healing. Maybe he can do something for that man and the horse," Filan continued as they walked to the small courtyard. "And tell him to give them the spare gold we were sent with."

"Is that all we can do?"

Filan spun back around on him. "What else are we supposed to do? What else *can* we do?" He glared into Hashkan's eyes with an intensity that rocked the Weaver back on his heels.

Hashkan frowned. He didn't have an answer. Instead,

he stubbornly held Filan's stare. He stood in the middle of the ruined farm, with the dead and dying all around him, and glared at the captain. Filan should have had the answers. This was his job.

"Weavers…" Filan said with a sigh. He broke eye contact and walked away.

The comment threw Hashkan off balance and he started to ask what Filan meant, but the captain was already shouting out orders to lingering soldiers. Hashkan just shook his head and went to get Bray.

Chapter Seventeen

Blood Threads

*T*he squad lingered at the farm for several hours trying to help the farmers set things back to rights. They repaired fences and helped round up the scattered surviving livestock while Hashkan assisted Bray with the injured men and the plow horse.

Though both he and the cook were knowledgeable healers, infection had set in and spread far enough that even amputation wouldn't solve anything. They had a painful conversation with the farmers who led the horse around to the back of the barn to humanely put him down, then left them with large doses of pain medication derived from poppy flowers that would bring the dying men some comfort in their passing. They might hallucinate, but they would feel no pain.

It was the hardest afternoon of Hashkan's life. They tried hard to find a way to save all the injured and leaving them to die made his heart ache. By the time he walked back out into the courtyard where the rest of the soldiers waited, he was weary down to his very bones. He pushed through the double doors of the barn and saw about half the squad clustered around Shilander, who was- to Hashkan's annoyance- ranting about the evils of Weavers. Hashkan balled his fists and stalked that way. He'd dealt with too much that day to allow an idiot to drone on like he was some wretched bringer of the apocalypse.

"Don't," a voice beside him commanded and a hand grabbed his shoulder. Hashkan turned to see Filan next to him. "I'll send someone else over to break it up. You'll only make it worse."

Hashkan resisted the urge to slap the captain's hand away. "I didn't expect this kind of treatment when I agreed to take this job."

"No, I suppose not," Filan said with a sigh. "I'll talk to him."

"Like you did before?" Hashkan asked. In the back of his mind a small voice- it sounded a lot like Li'or- chided him for whining like a child. He pushed a hand through his hair and ignored it.

"Today was hard for everyone, not just you, so don't expect me to tolerate your insubordination. I'm still in command of this mission and you'd do well to remember that. Now, I said I'd break it up and I will, so go collect your horse. It's time to go."

Hashkan spun on his heel and stormed back over to where the horses were tucked into an empty corral.

The squad rode out just as darkness was beginning to settle on the horizon. They fell into their usual marching order, but Hashkan felt like they were more of a funeral procession than a group of heroes. In fact, the only one who seemed to want to speak at all was Shilander. Hashkan could hear his every complaint. He tried to ignore it, but it was a constant, nagging thing, like a burr under a horse's saddle. Between that and what he'd seen at the farm, he could barely bring himself to eat that night.

The next day, Hashkan woke to a gray and overcast sky. He dressed as best as he could in the cramped tent and started going about the day the same as the one before. He stomped through the dew and over to where the horses were picketed. The few other men that were up were poking around in last night's campfires and putting on water to boil for tea. He nodded and told them good morning as he walked past, but received nothing but nods and grunts in return.

Immediately he was reminded of all of Shilander's talk from the day before. What if the naturalist's lies had finally started to turn the others against him? He tried to tell himself that they were still half asleep, that he was being irrational, but he couldn't shake the feeling that they all thought he'd done something wrong.

He stood and watched the horses eat while the camp came to life around him. Smithie and Bearson crawled out of their tent, so Hashkan made his way back over to help pack. Everyone began breaking down their tents and loading their things onto their horses while Bray started to prepare their breakfast- from the smell of it, salted pork and grits. Hashkan helped with the tent and got his horse packed just in time to eat. He lined up with the rest of the soldiers, bowl in hand, to wait his turn for the breakfast slop.

"Things are bad, my friends, real bad. And things will only get worse until we start living as the gods originally intended, not putting these blasphemous Weavers and their fake goddess up on a pedestal." Shilander strolled up with a few soldiers in tow. As soon as he saw Hashkan at the tail of the line, his face darkened. "Don't you think it would be best if you just turned around today and rode back to

Straeth and from there, on back to whatever plagued hole you crawled out of?" he sneered. His eyes razed Hashkan from head to toe.

The soldiers in Shilander's tow and those in the meal line spread out around them, forming a loose circle. Hashkan glanced around and saw Filan, who was seated by one of the smoldering campfires, stand up with his bowl in hand and eye them wearily. Hashkan turned back to Shilander and felt the man's hatred rolling towards him like heat off a forge.

"Shilander, who taught you that Altering is evil?"

"It doesn't have to be *taught*. Anyone with any sense can tell it's unnatural."

Hashkan flung his arms in the air and several soldiers flinched away. It was an absurd reaction. He'd never so much as pointed a finger at any of them. It only made him more angry that Shilander's nonsense had worked its way under their skins.

"The Seamstress is a *part* of nature," Hashkan said, trying to reason with him. "She *created-*"

"Your existence is an affront to the gods!" Shilander yelled, taking two steps forward so he could jab Hashkan in the chest with his index finger. "Your *kind* is slowly destroying nature's balance- the thing the true gods charged us with protecting! You've tainted the natural order around us and I'm telling you one last time to get your ass home."

Hashkan heaved a heavy sigh and closed his eyes. He tried to count to ten, all the while reminding himself that he represented the entirety of the Gathering, but he only made it to a rushed five. "I'm here on orders from the lord just like you are. If you won't show me the respect due to my station, you can at least show me the respect you give to your fellow soldiers. This conversation is over." He brushed past Shilander, headed back to where his horse was hobbled. His appetite was long gone.

He didn't make it very far. Shilander grabbed him by his left elbow and jerked him back. "Don't turn your back on me, whoreson. I wasn't done talking to you yet." Hashkan heard the drag of steel against a sheath.

And then something inside him snapped. Anger flared up in him like a wildfire and burned away any conscious thought. Before he even knew what he was doing, Hashkan spun with his free arm and slammed his elbow into Shilander's face. Shilander yowled and immediately let go of Hashkan's arm, covering his face with his hands as blood drained from his nose.

"Why you fucking-"

But Hashkan wasn't done. He shifted his focus to the Threads. For a split second, he watched as the Threads for the air parted to let the blood Threads from Shilander's face fall to the ground, then he reached behind himself and blindly grabbed at the Threads for air.

He flung them at Shilander, unconcerned with how much he may have grabbed and how much might tag along with it. The wind slammed into Shilander's chest, forcing him to lean forward against the wind and shield his face with his arms.

On the tails of the initial gust came the aftermath that all apprentice Weavers were warned against. The vacuum Hashkan created when he dragged the air forward caused more wind to follow behind it and a veritable gale hammered Shilander in the chest and flung the man backwards off his feet. It continued to push at the man, blowing him in a tumble across the ground. The wind blasted past him and ripped up two tents, the stakes narrowly avoiding the heads of the nearby soldiers, and flinging them into a tree. Shilander stopped rolling and

Hashkan reached behind himself again, gathering more air.

"Hashkan, don't!" Bearson wrapped him in a bear hug from behind, pinning his arms to his sides. "That's enough! You've done enough."

Hashkan struggled against Bearson for a moment and then sagged as all the rage drained out of him. His focus on the Threads loosened and they slipped away on a light breeze.

"Are you done?" Bearson asked.

"Yes, I'm finished."

Bearson turned him loose and patted his shoulder.

Hashkan pushed his hair back from his face and turned towards Bearson. "Thank you."

He looked around the rest of the camp. All the other soldiers were staring at him, some with fear in their eyes and others openly disgusted. A few bystanders caught on the edge of the blast were standing up and brushing themselves off, and about thirty feet away, Shilander was struggling back to his feet, favoring his left leg.

"I should have known better than to grab air like that…"

Bearson didn't respond. He just nodded, his face tight, and walked back towards the horses.

"Clearont!" Captain Filan stormed up and then continued past where Hashkan stood. He pointed a finger out towards the edge of camp. "With me. Now!"

Dread grabbed at Hashkan with icy fingers, but he followed Filan out past the tents and out of earshot. The captain stopped so short that Hashkan nearly ran into him, then he whipped around, shoving his face mere inches away from Hashkan's.

"Look, I know that Shilander is a bleeding, arrogant fool but he's also a soldier in this squadron. If something happens, I'll need him. And I'll need him alive and in one piece, just like I'll need every other soldier in this squad. I know he's been trying his best to instigate this little scene, but I expected better from you. Quite frankly, a Weaver is next to useless if the rest of the squad is so scared of him they can't focus on the real enemy in front of them. If anything like this happens again, I swear I don't care who you do or do not answer to or what you may do to me afterward, I *will* kick your ass. Am I clear?"

Hashkan fought to swallow. If he acted out, or just turned around, he knew there would be serious repercussions. He could be kicked out, or worse, stripped of rank and set to work with the apprentices.

"Yes, Captain," he forced out, resigned.

A vein stood out in Filan's forehead and his eyes were so wide that Hashkan had no doubt he would make good on his threat.

"Good." Filan took a step back and sighed, hands on hips. "Go get those tents out of that blighted tree and you pack them away by yourself. I'm going to talk to Shilander."

"Yes, sir." Hashkan turned and shuffled back through the camp, headed towards where the tents were still hanging in the tree like wet laundry. None of the other soldiers so much as looked at him.

✳ ✳

HASHKAN SAT on his horse and waited as pair of scouts crept up the small hill. Since they'd left the camp that morning, Filan had the squad on high alert, which meant no more blindly riding over hills where they would be exposed and no more conversation.

None of the soldiers wanted to talk anyway. There was

enough tension among the group that it would take days to saw through it. For once, Shilander was keeping his mouth shut. The Captain had chewed Shilander up one side and down the other after he'd gotten done with Hashkan, then put the man on a grueling work detail that would continue long after the patrol. Even Bearson was silent. He'd offered Hashkan a tiny smile when they lined up that morning and that was all.

The soldiers crawled up to the crest of the hill on their bellies and peeked over the edge. After a few moments, they stood up and signaled back down the hill to the restless squad and Filan made a gesture back. Hashkan let out a sigh of relief. As much as he wanted this trip to be over with, he didn't know what he'd do if they stumbled upon hundreds of zhu'dac. Even with the drama from that morning, what he'd seen at the farm was still foremost in his mind.

But instead of calling for the squad to ride up and meet them, Filan sat and waited until the guards jogged all the way back down the hill. He rode off to the side and listened to their report where none of the squad could hear. Hashkan shifted nervously in his saddle.

"The zhu'dac aren't there, are they? They would have had to crawl back down, right?" he whispered to Bearson.

One of the soldiers in front of him turned around and shushed him, but Bearson ignored the interruption. "Half right. They didn't find zhu'dac, but they did find something else."

Hashkan had a pretty good idea of what they must have found. Another slaughter. More bodies, more broken survivors with dead eyes- if there were any survivors at all. He found himself homesick for the monotony of life at the Gathering in Harthmere, for the lighthearted companionship he'd found with Li'or and Emond. He'd even go back to Breen and work under the patronizing eyes of High Weaver Liestenin if it meant he didn't have to ride over that hill.

The scouts saluted to Filan before jogging back to their horses and as soon as they swung into their saddles, Filan gave the signal for them all to move out. They started up the hill and Hashkan reluctantly followed, hands slick with sweat. The squad was as tense as a bow string; each soldier seemed to be holding their breath. Hashkan looked at Bearson out of the corner of his eye and the man had gone pale under his beard.

And then Hashkan got to the top of the hill and his breath caught in this throat.

Mangled corpses and bones lay scattered at the base of the hill. They were torn apart and strewn around until it was impossible to tell what they were or how many bodies created such a mess, but it was clearly caused by more than just a few predators. Hashkan rode by the body of what might have been a deer and his stomach roiled. The smell of rotting flesh was overwhelming and flies covered everything.

"Weaver Hashkan!" Filan yelled from the front of the line as they came to a halt. "Bovdan!"

Hashkan and a wiry soldier in an odd triangular hat pulled their horses out of line and rode to meet the captain at the front.

"Bovdan, what does this look like to you?" Filan asked, gesturing at the massacre.

"Zhu'dac camp, sir. Lots of 'em. There's places where the grass has been pressed down where they slept, but no cooking fires. Corpses look like their handiwork."

"Weaver," Filan turned towards Hashkan. "Do you agree?"

"I do," Hashkan answered. Why had he been called

out? Anyone could have drawn the parallels between this scene and the one they'd found at the farm.

"How old do you think these bodies are?" Filan continued.

Hashkan glanced around, unsure what to look for to be able to tell, but Bovdan answered first.

"They're all different. Some look like they were carried here, pretty rotten. That one over there," he said, nodding towards an unidentifiable animal with its entrails snatched out and draped into the branches of an oak tree. "That one was killed here, and recently. The blood hasn't dried yet."

Hashkan cringed.

"So they haven't been gone long..." Filan chewed on his cheek for a moment then nodded to Bovdan. "Head back to the line-up. We're turning back. Try to get me an estimate of how many zhu'dac passed through here." When he was far enough away, Filan turned back to Hashkan. He hesitated, then looked back up at the hill. "Has the Seamstress shown you anything?"

Hashkan's eyes widened and stared at Filan for a moment. The captain hadn't shown any signs of being a religious man. It took Hashkan a moment to find an answer.

"No, I haven't seen anything in the Fabric since we left."

"I was afraid of that." He rubbed a hand across his face and looked back at Hashkan with haunted eyes. "You better pray that these monsters keep heading north."

Hashkan nodded. "I will."

A heavy weight settled into the pit of his stomach. He hated that he was right about what they would find, and it wasn't often that he hated being right.

THE TROOP PUSHED HARD until well past nightfall before setting up camp alongside the Silver Gilt River. No one complained about the extended hike. Every last one of them was eager to put as much distance between them and the killing field as possible. The guard was doubled and no one dared light a cooking fire. Cold meals were a small price to pay for a little extra security.

Despite all their precautions, in the early hours of the morning, everything started to unravel.

Someone grabbed Hashkan by both shoulders and violently shook him awake. Hashkan's eyes snapped open and he shoved the hands away. Tense whispers filtered through the tent along with scuffling noises like the camp was being packed up.

"Captain wants you," a soldier said before slipping out of the tent before Hashkan's eyes even came into focus.

He stumbled through the flaps of the tent and into pandemonium. It seemed like all thirty soldiers were running random paths through the camp like ants- some in full sets of armor, others still in their bedclothes, and every-thing in between. Men were pulling down their tents and as he watched another was leading all the horses through the camp in a line, their halters all tied together.

"Weaver!" Filan called from the outskirts of the camp. "Get your ass over here!"

Hashkan trotted to him. "Yes, sir?"

"What can you do about that from here?" he asked, pointing north.

A seething dark mass rolled on the horizon. The moon gave just enough light for it to glint off the bare steel of weapons and Hashkan could barely hear the odd yipping of the zhu'dac language echoing over the plain. He couldn't see well enough to count them, but there were easily more than twice as many creatures as there were soldiers.

"Have they seen us?" Hashkan asked, his voice barely more than a whisper.

"Well, they're moving right this way so I'd say yes," Filan bit off each word. "Now answer my gods-damned question."

Hashkan cringed and focused on the Fabric. He peered through the layers and layers of loose air Threads and tried to distinguish the individual Threads of the zhu'dac or their armor, while he fought to keep his breath even and calm. It was no use. They were too far away and all the Threads just blurred together.

"I can't do anything. I can't see the Threads from this far away." He barely got the words out over the bile rising in this throat. He forced himself to take a long steadying breath.

"Shit!" Filan hissed. "That's what I was afraid you were going to say. Well, help get the horses ready and grab everything you can carry. We need to ride. Now!"

Hashkan turned back to the camp and the yelling around him grew louder, the clang of steel shattering the night.

Another pack of zhu'dac, their brindled hides caked with old blood, slammed into the camp from the west. Hashkan spun around, his heart slamming against his ribs, just in time to see about fifteen of the beasts dash through the tents. The soldiers could easily handle such a small group, but it would cost them precious time.

"Get rid of them and be quick about it. We have to leave!" Filan shouted over the bedlam. "Weaver, for love of the Seamstress, *do* something!" Filan drew his sword and charged into the fray.

Hashkan watched, fear rooting his feet to the earth, as Filan gutted one of the zhu'dac then ran to where the squad was gathered. They'd formed a loose ring around some of the other soldiers who were frantically trying to get horses saddled. One of the soldiers took a step back while he blocked a wild slash from a zhu'dac. The man's foot landed on a stray tent stake and his ankle rolled, sending the guard to the ground and putting him at the mercy of the monster.

Hashkan shook himself; he had to be quick and he had to be efficient. He grabbed hold of the ground under the zhu'dac and snatched the dirt out from under it as quick as he could. He was only able to grab a thin layer, but the beast stumbled and it was just enough time for the soldier on the ground to lunge forward and drive his sword between the beast's ribs. Its scream was lost in the havoc engulfing the squad.

Hashkan cast his eyes around the camp. Everything was happening so fast and he had no idea what to do or where to help. The yells and grunts from the soldiers and the screeches from the zhu'dac pierced through his thoughts like hundreds of arrows. He covered his ears and fought for the calm he needed to focus.

His eyes landed on a discarded pack and an idea flared to life. Hashkan turned and ran back to his tent. He had a small pouch with a piece of flint and some tinder. If he could get a fire going, he might be able to buy them time to escape. *If.* He'd never successfully lit a fire on his own. It was time to finally figure it out.

He scrambled through his bags and found his tinder kit. Half the soldiers were still guarding the horses while the others worked frantically to get them all saddled. About ten more zhu'dac crowded around them while the horde drew ever closer.

Hashkan cursed loudly and threw the ground out from underneath the closest beasts, giving the soldiers an opening to move out and press the advantage. His head ached from the effort of moving so much earth, but he dashed through their lines and into the protection of the circle before he dropped to the ground to work.

He piled up a few discarded tent stakes and put a fluff of tinder in the center. A man screamed and he fumbled and dropped his flint. The dark stone blended into the ground in the night, and he lost precious time scrambling for it before he finally scooped it up to try again. Once. Twice. Thrice. Nothing. Hashkan gritted his teeth to try again, but a hand grabbed his shoulder.

"Give me that, I'll do it," Bearson yelled.

Hashkan looked around wildly. The soldiers had the small group of zhu'dac surrounded and they were picking them off one by one. In the distance, the host of monsters drew closer still. "Just hurry!" Hashkan said in a rush as he passed the flint over.

Bearson had a fire going in a matter of seconds. As the flames crackled to life, a small spark of hope flared up in Hashkan as well. He might be able to turn the tide. As soon as the fire grew enough, Hashkan grabbed the Threads and started chucking them out towards the horde. They were still too far out, but the zhu'dac in the front lines hesitated and Bearson smiled and clapped his shoulder. Hashkan dared to think that they might get away.

"Keep it up, Weaver! Scare them off!" Bearson shouted.

Meanwhile, the soldiers had finished off the zhu'dac in the camp and turned all their attention to getting the rest of the horses saddled. Hashkan lobbed flame after flame towards the zhu'dac army, and though they were going slower, they were still moving in. His flames were hitting the front lines and ear-piercing shrieks carried over the noise in the camp.

"Everybody mount up, we're out of time! Let's ride!" Filan called.

Hashkan glanced over his shoulder but kept throwing fire. He could buy more time if he kept at it just a little longer. His head was splitting, but he gritted his teeth and Altered again. The zhu'dac kept moving forward, but they were apprehensive as their pack-mates turned into living torches in front of them.

"Weaver, that's enough! Come on!"

Hashkan couldn't tell who'd given the order, but he released the Fabric and ran to his horse. The squad turned their horses to the south and raced out of the camp. Hashkan grabbed a handful of mane and struggled to stay on as his mare stretched out underneath him. The troop flew through the night, the cries of the zhu'dac falling away behind them.

A surge of relief washed over Hashkan and a smile bloomed across his face. He'd done it. He'd held off the horde long enough to save the squadron. Leftover adrenaline coursed through his veins. It was almost like being drunk.

Then he heard the howling coming from ahead of them and to the right, closing as they raced over the plain.

No...

More zhu'dac burst out of the darkness, running on all fours like the feral animals they were, easily keeping pace with the horses. Hashkan tried to knock them off balance by dragging more earth, grabbing at the scraps of their clothing, at anything. But the Threads flew past too quickly and it was all he could do to stay on his horse. He couldn't make it work. A horse screamed behind him and he turned just in time to watch the animal and a tall, thin soldier fall under a pile of zhu'dac.

"Keep going!" Filan shouted from ahead of him.

Hashkan reached farther up his horse's neck and leaned low, urging just another ounce of desperate speed out of her. Two more horses went down, kicking out and screaming, their riders' cries cut short. A soldier in front of Hashkan was ripped off his horse. The terrified animal continued to run wildly without him.

Then everything unraveled further.

As a horse and rider went down at the front of the line, a riderless horse swerved to the left to try to avoid the thrashing, bleeding pile in front of him. He swerved right into another horse. Bearson's horse. They both tumbled, a tangle of legs at the front of the stampede. More horses tripped over their herd mates, launching their riders off their backs into the waiting mobs of zhu'dac. Others veered off, completely out of their riders' control and in a blind panic. They ran right into the jaws of the monsters.

Hashkan watched the cacophony from between his mare's ears as his world narrowed into that tiny space. His grip tightened on her mane, but his mind was filled with the Threads, trying desperately to find something he could do to save his friend. To save any of them. He would have to stop, but he couldn't. If he stopped, he would die along with them. His mare's back bunched up beneath him and she jumped, Hashkan's legs locking onto her sides like a vice and still barely staying a-horse. She cleared the writhing mound of horse and man flesh but landed hard, slinging Hashkan onto her neck and off to the side. He dangled there, arms clamped around her as she staggered and tried to keep upright. She veered right, countering his displaced weight and inadvertently slammed them both into a pack of waiting zhu'dac.

The monsters clawed at Hashkan's back and at the mare's side, trying to drag them down. Hashkan's shirt ripped and a chunk of his skin went with it; the pain burned through his back like fire. His scream mixed with his horse's as she ducked back to the left, away from the zhu'dac. He used her sideways momentum to swing himself upright onto her back. His arms screamed in protest, already exhausted from clinging to the mare, but he made it up.

He looked back in front of them and saw nothing but the dimly lit plain. None of the others were charging ahead.

It wasn't until the noise of the zhu'dac faded away that he noticed the pounding of more hooves beside him. He lifted his face from where he'd buried it in the mare's mane and looked to his left. A gray horse galloped next to him, its saddle empty and reins dangling around its neck. A large smear of blood ran along its flank.

And there, clinging to his own horse, was Shilander, eyes focused forward in grim determination.

There were no others.

Chapter Eighteen

Trading in Secrets

 $\mathcal{L}$ i'or swept down the stairs of the Ale Boat six days after Hashkan's departure, already wearing a frown despite the early hour. She was eating into her savings and didn't have a thing to show for it. Even with both her and Emond's efforts, they hadn't found a scrap of information about the disappearances and nothing about the gang that had almost killed them. Li'or had sifted through almost every section of the city at this point- including the area where the attack happened- and still she returned to the Ale Boat empty-handed every night. She was almost ready to call it quits and take another job.

She was running out of ideas, so she headed to one of the richer areas of the city in the northwest quarter, nearly against the walls themselves and further from the river to avoid flooding. She'd made the assumption thus far that she'd find her answers in the slums and markets, but that wasn't working so it was time for a new plan.

As she walked, her thoughts kept spiraling back to their mysterious attackers. To the terrifying power that blond man had wielded and the desperate way the woman had thrown herself onto Li'or's blade. Her frown deepened and she tried to rein herself in and focus on the people around her. If she couldn't find any clues, there wasn't a point for all her worrying.

But the power that man had displayed had been terrifying, and the more she thought about it, the more anxious she became. She started thinking about the havoc that he- or others like him- could cause if they were left unchecked. Anything was a weapon in the hands of a Weaver and that was dangerous enough, but the thug surpassed that and affected them directly somehow. The strange pressure he'd used against them could have easily become fatal. If she ran into anyone else like him, she'd have to approach the fight from a different angle.

Hopefully, there weren't any others like him.

She passed by barracks and the capitol building again before turning down a cobbled street that led into a largely residential part of the city. She wasn't sure what she hoped to find up here. Nearly everyone on this side of town had guards of their own, crime was rarely heard of, and even foot traffic was a rarity. Her chances of running into anyone involved with gangs in this area- at least at the street level- were slim, but she was getting desperate.

So she kept her eyes peeled anyway, looking for loiterers in the alleys or bold pickpockets. The occasional filigree and lace covered carriage rolled past her, complete with glaring nobles that she scoffed at. They were probably off to blackmail some poor sap or another. Leave them to it, as long as it wasn't her.

A scrap of shadow caught her eye near the doorway of a manor house on the other side of the street. Keeping her gait casual, but rolling across the balls of her feet to silence her steps, she drew even with the door.

Nothing.

Li'or paused and stared at the entranceway, puzzled. She knew she'd seen something there. Her eyes lingered on the front of the house as she reluctantly turned to continue down the road.

Another snatch of black cut across her peripheral vision, this time slipping around a corner into a narrow alley ahead of her. Heedless of what the uptight aristocrats might think, she sprinted up to the corner of the alley and charged in.

No one was there. No assassin in a black cloak, no villain with mysterious powers- and the alley dead-ended fifteen feet in. Li'or scanned the walls and the rooftops, but it remained empty.

"Am I that desperate?" she muttered to herself.

She shook her head and continued down the street. Two blocks later, she saw just the kind of person she'd been looking for, real and in the flesh. A predatory grin snuck its way across her face and she forgot all about her wandering imagination.

A little over a year ago, she'd taken on a bounty for a clever cut-purse who disguised himself as a crippled beggar. When people came up to give him a few copper crosses, he staggered into them, feigning a bad leg, and swiped the rest of their coin purse. He was also a known snitch. If there was anyone in the city who would know about the desertions or the thugs, it would be River.

And here he was again. He was wearing what looked like a worn grain sack and didn't have on any shoes. If you looked at him closely, though, the dirt and grime smeared all over him started to look intentional and he never smelled like a man who lived in the streets.

She pushed her braid over her shoulder and walked over towards him, trying to remain hidden in the thin crowd so he wouldn't bolt. She was nearly on top of him before he turned and caught sight of her.

"L- Li- Li'or! I wasn't thieving. I swear it! Honest begging, I was! Honest!" He held up his hands and started to back further into the alley.

"I didn't see you doing anything, River. I'm honestly just curious about how you got out of jail already. I know they didn't just let you go." She walked a few steps closer.

"Well, um... Ya see, I can explain that."

"I'd love to hear it." She crossed her arms, making it obvious that she was keeping her hands near her weapons. His eyes landed on her blades and he swallowed audibly.

"One of the guards is me friend! And I, uh, bought me way out."

"You bought your way out?" she asked, flatly.

"Aye! And just been honest begging for me since! Honest!" he said, forcing a laugh.

"So you aren't trading in secrets anymore, then?"

"Oh! Well, now everything's for sale for the right price. If ya catch me meaning." He adjusted his makeshift tunic and glanced around nervously.

"I do, but I'm not here to play your games." She reached into her pouch and pulled out the wolf skull broach. She held it up in front of River's face. "Have you seen this before?"

The silver of the broach flashed in River's eyes, which grew very round as he looked at the jewelry. "Oh, now that... I may have seen that afore. Seamstress, but it's hard to remember-"

"I said I'm not playing this game," Li'or ground out through gritted teeth. "You know I won't pay you a single copper cross."

"Oh, Li'or! You dishonor me and me family suggesting such a thing!" He grabbed the front of his feed sack like he was having chest pains. "It's a shame though. I think three gold faces would really jar me memory."

"Your Threads are tangled. Tell me what you know and I'll agree not to break all your fingers. A thief with maimed hands wouldn't last long."

River paled under his carefully applied dirt. "Oh, all the dishonor on River's good name! Fine, fine. I saw a man wearing a broach just like that last week at the Curving Path." He drew his hands in the air, mimicking the outline of a curvaceous woman. "You'll want to ask for Relford."

"The brothel? In the middle of the city?"

"The same. Now, can we be done here? You're scaring off all me clientele."

"Alright." She turned to leave but not before throwing one last threat over her shoulder. "I better not hear about anything being stolen over here today. I don't care if you did it or not, I'll be looking for you."

"Only honest begging! Honest!" He shouted after her as she left the alley before breaking off abruptly in a fit of fake coughing. Li'or rolled her eyes and started her trek back across Straeth.

※ ＊

THE CROWDS GREW THICKER the closer Li'or got to the middle of the city. The most popular and extravagant inns, brothels, and shops were crammed together around the intersection of four major roadways and canals, right where all the tourists would eventually end up. Li'or worked her way through the press, ignoring calls from merchants in their sporadically placed booths and lewd catcalls from male and female prostitutes alike. Clouds of perfume floated through the streets and on all sides were oddly shaped buildings painted bright outrageous colors, each one trying to out-do their neighbors.

Even among all the blinding colors around it, The Curved Path stood out and demanded attention. The brothel was a tall pillar of stone, easily eight stories tall and narrow like a tower. Instead of being square or cylindrical in shape, however, the tower curved just like the gesture that River had made with his hands, like the curves of a woman. The roof, the door, and all the shutters were painted a glaring red.

It was nearly noon when Li'or made it to the brothel and a brisk wind was blowing, threatening to bring rain later in the day. She stood across the street from The Curved Path and toyed with the pommel on her sword. Two voluptuous women were standing to either side of the tower's doors, hawking their wares.

Li'or pressed her lips into a thin line. She hated the thought of going into the brothel. Everyone inside would automatically think she was a customer and that kind of attention made her skin crawl. Not to mention she didn't expect the midday crowd in *any* brothel to be a good one.

She gritted her teeth and stomped across the street towards the doors. She didn't even pause to speak to the women outside, she just swung the doors open and plunged headfirst into the tower.

It was like walking into a wall of smoke. Incense burners were sitting on nearly every flat surface in the room and filled the air with musk and nag champa. The bottom floor seemed to operate as something like a tavern, with a large white marble bar directly across from the doors. Low tables were strewn about the floor with jewel-toned cushions next to them and a staircase spiraled up the wall to the left. Opposite the stairs, a man in a double-breasted coat and dress breeches played a relaxing tune on a piano. Prostitutes floated around the room in various states of undress, giggling and flirting with the few patrons they had this early in the day. There was a tall, broad-shouldered man behind the bar, pouring drinks for a balding, round man and a prostitute with golden hair so long it grazed her stool.

Li'or started towards the bar. She'd never met a bartender who didn't know everything that went on in their tavern and there was no better place to start asking around.

"Oh, hold on, Mistress Elf," a sultry voice cooed at her and a soft hand slipped into hers. "Why are you in such a hurry?"

Li'or froze, every muscle in her body going rigid. How could she let someone sneak up on her like that? She was so focused on her goal that she'd completely dropped her guard. It was such an amateur mistake.

She looked to her right and a beautiful woman with sleek black hair and porcelain skin gazed back at her through eyes so dark they were almost black themselves.

"We don't get a lot of women in here, but I'm always happy when we do," she purred, running her free hand up and down Li'or's arm.

"Oh, no." Li'or untangled herself from the woman. "I'm only here for business. I'm looking for someone."

"Someone like me?"

"No."

The woman pouted prettily, pursing bright red lips that almost matched the doors. "Well, if you change your mind, I'll be near the stairs…" She sashayed away, glancing back at Li'or and winking.

Li'or shook herself and squared her shoulders before crossing the rest of the room and taking a seat on one of the gold-trimmed stools that lined the bar. She sat a few seats over from where the round man and the blond woman were sitting with their heads close together, talking in hushed tones.

The bartender came up to her immediately. "What can I get for you, madam?"

"Just an ale, please."

He nodded and went to get her drink. "That's two stars," he said as he placed a pale northern ale down in front of her.

Li'or clamped her teeth together so hard they hurt. She'd never paid so much for an ale in her life. She slid the coins over the counter in an act of sheer will. Her coin pouch literally couldn't afford to stay in this place for long. She would have to take a direct approach. "What's your name?"

"Tragner, madam."

"Well, Tragner," Li'or started, placing another silver star down on the table but keeping her finger firmly on top of it. She lowered her voice. "I have a question. I understand a man named Relford frequents this place. Where can I find him?"

Almost as soon as the question left her lips, a stool clattered to the floor and all conversation stopped in the room. The music ended on a sour note as the pianist whirled around on his bench. The round man had leapt off his stool so quickly that it had fallen over and he stood stockstill, staring at Li'or with frightened eyes.

"Relford! Run!" he shouted.

A man in dark clothing jumped up from a pile of cushions near the piano and made a dash for the door, leaping over the low tables.

"Blight," Li'or hissed and she darted off after him.

She didn't make it two steps. The man at the bar

shoved his fallen stool through her legs and she stumbled, barely keeping herself upright. He made a grab for her arm, but she backhanded him with everything she had, sending him to the floor in a heap. She kicked him once just to ensure he'd stay down then flew towards the door.

She burst out into the street, startling the women standing to either side of the door, and squinted against the light. Off towards her right, a merchant was cursing and picking up a basket full of spilled cabbages. The people near him were all looking in the same direction so she sprinted that way, leaping over the merchant's basket and barreling into the crowd. She shoved past a soldier, dodged a woman with her children, and then a gap opened up and she charged ahead.

She caught sight of Relford just as he ducked into an alley. She skidded around the corner and plunged in after him, catching sight of his heels disappearing around a corner to the left. She jumped, kicking off the opposite wall and rounding the bend after him, barely losing any of her momentum.

Li'or was the faster runner and she steadily caught up to him. She was close enough to see his light brown hair and make out his pinched features when he turned to check if he'd lost her. She made a grab for him just as they burst out into the crowded street again and missed. Relford charged out into the street and was nearly run over by a carriage as it careened by. Li'or skidded to a stop just in time, then cursed when she lost sight of her quarry.

The carriage zipped by and she found him again, off to her left. She raced after him, streaking down the street before disappearing into another alley. Relford was tired and Li'or drew right up to his heels, so close she could hear him panting.

She reached out and caught him by the shirt collar,

yanking him backward. He gagged and reached for the knife at his hip, but Li'or grabbed his left arm at the wrist and twisted it around behind his back. She drew her dagger and laid it against his throat. This close to him, she could smell the tang of body odor and liquor rolling off him.

She blew a loose tendril of hair out of her face. "Now, as fun as that was, all I wanted was to have a nice quiet conversation. It shouldn't take long. What do you say?"

He didn't say anything, so she applied a little extra pressure to his arm. "Relford..." she scolded. "Let's just do this the easy way, shall we?"

"Okay, Okay!" he gasped and the movement of his neck pressed the blade more firmly against his throat. He recoiled, trying to back up, which in turn only put more pressure against his trapped arm. He groaned dramatically. "What do you want to know?"

"Did you see a man last week at The Curving Path wearing a broach of a wolf's skull?"

Relford was silent for a moment. "Look lady, I don't remember anything. Well, I mean I might remember..."

Li'or shook her head and changed the angle that she was holding the dagger against him, causing it to nick the man's throat. A small trickle of blood rolled down his neck and vanished in his shirt collar. "This isn't a negotiation, *friend*. You better tell me what you know and quick."

Sweat ran down the man's face and landed in fat drops on Li'or's hand.

"Oh, it's the funniest thing, I remember now! You're right! There was someone in there last week wearing something like that," he prattled out in a rush. "Blond man. Was meeting a lotta others in there and when they left, they said they were headed to the mountains in the northeast. The White Stones or whatever they're called. Said anyone looking for a fresh start was welcome to tag along. Said he could help people pack and be on their way right then and there. Seemed like some kind of fanatic or something. But that's all I know, lady, I swear! Let me go!"

Li'or scowled and took her knife off the man's throat. She shoved him away and he stumbled before scurrying off like a scalded dog. Li'or watched him leave, absently wiping the small bit of blood off her blade, waiting until his footsteps faded away before she turned and made her way back to the street.

She looped a wrist over the hilt of her sword as she retraced her steps back to the Ale Boat. If Emond was there, she'd fill him in. If not she'd leave him a note and head to the capitol building. It was time for her to finally take Klevelt the information he'd asked for and get her reward.

She turned onto Cross Current Street and cursed under her breath. Since there was no permanent marketplace in Straeth, they tended to pop up all over the city in places that were convenient or fashionable at the moment. Li'or had stumbled upon one that hadn't existed the week before, or perhaps not even the day before. People swarmed around the stands in a bewildering vortex of brightly colored clothes. Shoppers bartered at the top of their lungs, others argued, and vendors cried out their prices, desperately trying to be heard over the crowd.

It pained her, but she drew herself up and plowed into the crowd anyway. A rare few people saw the look on her face and moved out of the way, but she had to resort to squeezing and forcing her way between the rest as she navigated the crowd.

As she squeezed through a gap between shoppers, a stray elbow caught her in the ribs. She spun around and searched for a guilty face, but the people were moving around like river rapids and it was next to impossible to keep track of a single person in the mob.

Li'or grumbled and gave herself a quick pat-down to make sure nothing was missing as she walked away. All this society was starting to chafe. She would leave as soon as she got her pay and said her goodbyes.

⁕ ⁕

SHE ARRIVED at the Ale Boat in the mid-afternoon, just as the last of the lunchtime stragglers were beginning to clear out. Emond was leaning against the bar, arms crossed as he watched all the patrons. He perked up when she walked through the door and waved her over. Li'or waved back as she crossed the room but couldn't bring herself to smile back. He probably wouldn't take the news well. He'd taken to calling her and Hashkan his adopted family.

"Li'or, Li'or! I missed yeh at breakfast again!"

"That's what happens when you don't get out of bed."

"Yeh wouldn't leave either if yeh had company as excellent as I keep!" he said, waggling his eyebrows. "So tell me, how was yer luck today?" He waved a bartender over as he asked and ordered an ale for each of them.

Li'or took a long swig of her drink and sighed before she answered. "I had better luck today, actually." She told him about what she'd discovered from her talk with Relford.

"White Stone Mountains? There ain't any towns in there, though."

"Not since the war. But I can't think of a better place to hide something than-"

"Someplace no one has any reason to go!"

She arched an eyebrow at his interruption. "Exactly what I was going to say."

"Those of great minds, share great thoughts, Li'or. Those of great minds."

She blinked at him for a moment then shook her head. "Right. So, I was stopping in to collect my things before I reported to Klevelt, then I'll be on my way."

Emond stared at her blankly and rubbed at his flat nose. "On yer way where?"

"No place in particular. Just away from cities for a while."

"What about Hashkan? Yer not even gonna stay to tell the lad bye?"

Li'or paused midway through bringing her drink up to her lips as an unexpected stab of guilt hit her in the chest. "I was going to leave a note." She sounded despicable even to her own ears.

"A note? By the Seamstress, Li'or, he considers yeh a friend and yer just gonna vanish on him like that? With a blighted *note*?"

That was exactly what she'd planned on doing. This was supposed to have been just another job, and she'd completed it. It was time for her to move on. Li'or stalled by taking another gulp of her drink. What was she supposed to tell Emond? People never understood that she was doing them a favor. It wasn't easy saying goodbye and she knew they would hate her for it. But it wasn't easy growing feeble next to a friend that shrugged off all of time's advances, either. It created a distance that stretched relationships as thin as a spider's silk. It was easier just to break it before anyone became too entangled.

And she wouldn't be able to stand staying close to them and watching them grow old and die, either. She'd done it in Zenick and she would never do it again.

Thankfully, she was spared from having to respond when the front doors swung open. She shifted just a few degrees to the side to look over Emond's shoulder and her jaw dropped open.

Hashkan was standing in the doorway, scanning the room for them with his pack swung over one shoulder. He caught sight of them and his eyes locked with Li'or's as his mouth curved into a relieved smile. Somehow, despite the cool silver color of his eyes, they always managed to look warm and inviting.

Hashkan started towards them, but Emond met him halfway across the room. "There he is! We were just talking about yeh, wonderin' when yeh was gonna make it home!" He dropped an arm like a tree trunk across Hashkan's shoulders.

The Weaver's knees buckled and he grimaced in pain. Li'or was out of her seat and across the room in the span of a heartbeat. "You're injured? Were you attacked? Followed?"

"What? No, it's fine. I'm fine. This happened outside of the city and a healer has already seen to it," he answered through gritted teeth as he sank into a nearby chair.

"What happened?" Emond asked. He collapsed into the chair across from Hashkan and leaned forward onto the table, concern written in every line of his face.

"We found the zhu'dac. Hundreds of them. Or rather, they found us."

"What?" Li'or narrowed her eyes. He had to be exaggerating. Things like that just didn't happen. She'd traveled around Anagovia for years and the only time she'd ever even heard of more than ten zhu'dac traveling together had been back in Breen.

Hashkan ran a hand through his hair, leaving it disheveled. "I know how it sounds, but I swear on the Fabric it's true." He took a deep breath and told them how he and one other soldier were the only survivors of the patrol, the rest cut down by a flanking maneuver too complex for the beasts to have planned on their own.

Emond let out a low whistle. "Lord Klevelt isn't going to like this."

"I already gave a full report to be taken back to him. They're moving towards the northeast though. He shouldn't have to worry about them for long."

"True, if it weren't for the information I got today," Li'or said. "It looks like all the missing people are headed to the northeast too."

Li'or watched Hashkan's eyes widen as he reached the same conclusion she had already drawn.

"Do you think they're related?" Emond asked.

"They must be. That man that jumped us... He wanted our weapons and then tried to abduct us, most likely to go back up into the White Stones where he's sending all these other people. And now these unnatural numbers of zhu'dac are headed the same direction and they're more organized than they've ever been. Someone is building an army."

"That's very grave news. It will cost a lot of lives for Straeth to go to war," Hashkan said quietly. He traced a finger along the wood grain in the table and clenched his jaw. Li'or watched him through narrowed eyes. He had left something out of his retelling, something that was gnawing at him. She started to ask what else had happened when Emond interrupted.

"Good thing it won't be us, eh? I'll be here with the queen of me heart, you'll be studyin' at the Gatherin', and Li'or will be..." he waved vaguely, "wherever it is that she's going."

Hashkan's eyes softened and he frowned. "You're leaving?"

"As soon as I give my report and collect my coin, yes." If her guilt were a knife, his expression was twisting it into her side.

Hashkan glanced at the windows where the light was slowly bleeding out of the sky. "It'll be dark by the time you finish at the capitol and they won't open the gates for you. You should wait until the morning. At least have dinner with us."

Li'or followed his gaze to the window and sighed at the deepening red sky and shadows that stretched out across the floor. She would probably be denied an audience with the lord this late in the day as it was- especially since he was likely already busy with the troubles Hashkan brought back. She looked back at the others and they were watching her with hopeful faces.

"Fine, order another round," she conceded.

"Haha! Wonderful!" Emond roared. "Tonight we party, and in the mornin' we'll both go with you to the capitol!"

Li'or shook her head and reached for her drink. There *was* a tiny part of her that was relieved. As much as she was ready to leave this city behind her, she would miss both of these men. She leaned back in her chair and allowed herself a small smile. She'd enjoy their company while she was here, however painful it might make it when she left them tomorrow.

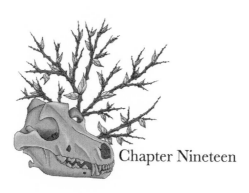

Chapter Nineteen

Adamant

a violent pounding on his door jarred Hashkan from his sleep. Groaning, he rolled over and buried his head under a pillow.

"Let us in!" Emond yelled. His voice came from lower down on the door, like he was crouched down to yell through the keyhole.

"Just a moment," Hashkan grumbled as he staggered out of bed. He still wore the guard uniform he'd been given at the medic's the day before- right down to his boots- and his bandages itched across his shoulders. He'd been so exhausted the night before that he'd barely had time to lock his door and stumble into bed before sleep took him.

He undid the lock and held the door for Emond and Li'or to come in. Before he could even close the door behind them, Emond walked straight to the curtains and flung them open with a flourish.

Hashkan flinched and covered his eyes. "For the sake of the Fabric, Emond!"

The big man just laughed. "Eh, yeh've slept long enough! It's time to go!" Hashkan dropped his hands and glared.

"How's your back?" Li'or asked.

"Stiff. Itchy."

"Let's take a look," she said, gesturing with a finger for him to turn around. "Did the healers give you any directions for the next few days? Specific medicines?"

Hashkan shook his head as he turned where he sat on the bed and reluctantly shrugged out of the ill-fitting shirt before he shifted his vision to the Threads. The healers had scraped and scrubbed his wounds the day before until he felt like they might have even made them worse. He'd sat, cringing and slowly plucking at the Threads of the stone floor, and only his focus on the Threads had kept him seated. They actually had left him with very precise instructions, but he'd been so exhausted, so ragged, that he hadn't listened. Another short-coming to add to his growing list.

Li'or didn't give him time to brace himself before she started to work on the bandages. The loosely woven gauze stuck to his back where it was raw, and though Li'or worked gently and carefully, it felt like she was ripping each wound open anew.

"It could be worse," Emond said. The way his voice rose at the end of the comment was the opposite of comforting.

The bed sagged as Li'or sat down behind him. "The healers did a good job on it. I've got some sparrowthorn ointment and then we'll wrap it back up. You shouldn't have to wear a bandage for long."

Hashkan nodded and balled his fists in his lap.

He expected the ice-cold sting of the ointment, but he didn't expect Li'or's free hand to rest on his uninjured shoulder. He knew it was a careless gesture- maybe she wanted to make sure he stayed still- but every Thread of his existence thrummed under that casual touch.

And then, as quickly as she began, the ointment was applied and fresh bandages wound back around him and she patted his shoulder like he'd seen her pat her horse's neck. He sighed. Exhaustion, that had to be the reason he'd reacted that way. Exhaustion from the patrol where he'd failed and cost so many good soldier's their lives. He wouldn't be able to look her in the eye if she knew how useless he'd been.

"Yeh might end up with some good scars!" Emond said with a smile while Hashkan pulled on a proper set of Weaver's robes. "Real women, like me Eseldra, they *love* scars." He winked at Hashkan like he'd shared a grand secret. Hashkan smiled as they followed Li'or out the door, but his heart wasn't in it. Why would he want to carry a reminder of his inadequacies with him for the rest of his life?

They made it across town and to the capital building where they were treated with cold efficiency, like they were normal petitioners, here to complain about an argument with their neighbors. Instead of waiting in a plush sitting room, they were left in the entranceway to sit on hard marble benches while Klevelt held audience under the gleaming brass dome in the main hall. The guard assured them that they would be called for when the lord was available.

Messengers came and went with scrolls and letters for nearly two hours while they waited. Li'or fidgeted in her seat like a caged animal while Emond was starting to doze off where he sat on the floor slumped against the wall. It seemed like they weren't going to get to speak with Klevelt today, even though they'd relayed the urgency of their message. None of them spoke, and it only made their wait seem longer.

Suddenly the doors to the main hall swung open, causing Emond and Hashkan both to jump. A group of disgruntled looking nobles and diplomats filed out of the hall, mumbling to each other as they went. A guard followed on the nobles' heels and cut across the entryway towards where Hashkan and the others waited.

"Hurry. Lord Klevelt has a few moments that he can spare for you on the way to his next engagement." He waved for them to follow him.

They fell in behind the guard as he all but ran back into the main hall. Klevelt stood at the head of the hall next to an attendant holding a tablet out for him. The lord signed his name to a document with a flourish before waving for them to follow him down a side hall. They trotted to catch up as he strode away as fast as his locked knee would allow.

He hardly spared them a glance. "I hope you have better news for me today. I've already been rushing around all morning dealing with the news Weaver Hashkan apprised me of yesterday. So please, enlighten me." His face was drawn, his mouth pressed into a thin line, and his shoulders pulling forward so that he looked like a huge bird of prey.

Hashkan opened his mouth to explain, but snapped it shut again when Li'or beat him to it. She was hired to gather the information. He shouldn't begrudge her wanting to deliver it, but there were some details he hoped she would leave out. Like how ineffective he'd been during each encounter.

She explained the attack, their search, and her theory

that all the missing people and the zhu'dac were going to the same place, mercifully leaving out any humiliating details. All the while they stormed down halls, trailed by guards with their armor rattling with every step.

Li'or's tale ended and they walked down a long hall in silence as Klevelt seemed to process everything she'd told him. They eventually stopped outside of a set of double doors. The lord turned to face them for the first time, meeting each of their eyes before speaking.

"I know what you're thinking. You're wondering when I'll be sending an army out to cut those beasts out of the Fabric. Let me curtail those thoughts. I'm not. I cannot. We barely have enough men to manage our walls as it is. I've sent word about the zhu'dac to every city and town north of here and warned them about the disappearances, though I'm sure they're dealing with that too. But I won't send my men away. Not unless the king himself orders it and even then, I'd argue against it. I've gotten even more reports of zhu'dac attacking my farmers since you were gone, Weaver Hashkan. I *am* sorry, but those other cities will have to handle this for themselves."

Hashkan stared blankly at the lord, his eyes wide. Was it really that easy to disregard all those other cites, all those other people? The zhu'dac were probably carving their way through someone's family while they stood safe within Straeth's walls. Something was brewing that was bigger than just this city. Now wasn't the time for them to hide behind their walls and keep their resources to themselves. The entire Silver Gilt River basin, maybe all of Anagovia, would need to band together.

Hashkan looked to Li'or and Emond. Li'or's face was completely blank as she met the lord's gaze, but Hashkan had seen her staring down armed assailants with the same expression. It wasn't as neutral as it appeared. Emond stared at the floor, his hands curled into fists and propped on his hips while a muscle in his jaw ticked from being clenched so hard.

"I know this wasn't what the three of you wanted to hear, but I have a duty to my people. I'm grateful for your services and I'll honor my end of the bargain and make sure you get paid for the information." A thought must have occurred to him then, because his brows shot up towards his hairline. "There is something that might help. I'll pay you to scout into the mountains and report back to me." He snapped his fingers at his attendant who jumped to ready a quill and started taking notes. "It would be wise to get a better idea of the goings-on up there. I'll pay double what I offered for the original job."

"Deal," Li'or answered without hesitation, her green eyes as bright as the pile of coins she'd be making.

"And you?" the lord asked Emond.

Emond hesitated for just a moment before shrugging. "Eseldra will have to forgive me. Yeh can't argue with that kind of coin."

Hashkan felt the familiar twinge at being left out. A Weaver couldn't be hired like a mercenary could.

"And you, Weaver Hashkan? Will you be available to help guide them?"

"I'll speak with the High Weaver. It would be advantageous for a Weaver to go as well," he offered. He was still seething over the lord's excuses, but he couldn't let his friends go out there alone, not when he'd seen what they might come up against. And not when he needed to atone for the loss of an entire scouting party.

"I agree," Klevelt said. "Let me know what he decides. Now, I have more to do today than I have hours to do it in. Forgive my rudeness."

And just like that, Lord Klevelt opened the door and

slipped away, the guards following him like they were being led on leashes.

Hashkan and the others were once again escorted out through the expansive main hall and into the street, Hashkan's hands in tight fists at his sides the entire time. They trudged through the midday crowds, a thick and awkward silence stretching between them.

They'd only made it five minutes down the road when Hashkan couldn't take it anymore. "How could he just dismiss all the other cities like that? Handle it for themselves? All of Anagovia will suffer if there really is an army brewing up there!" He stopped in the middle of the street and crossed his arms.

"Lad, the man wasn't wrong. I've been a guard for a long time and I can tell this place is barely keepin' it together. If he sent only fifty men out there, some nasty blighter would be runnin' this city in a matter of days." Emond held up his hands in a gesture of supplication. "He's warnin' the other cities and he sent us to scout. That's all he can do."

"No, it isn't! And you two! Don't tell me you're fine with it just because you're making so much gods-damned gold! People are going to be killed!" A small crowd was starting to gather around them, but Hashkan dismissed them. Li'or and Emond had to still be furious. They couldn't possibly be that greedy.

"We aren't fine." Li'or interrupted before Hashkan's lecture could continue. She looked up at him, that same tightly controlled expression on her face. He clamped his teeth together and dropped his eyes, unable to meet her gaze. "You know we aren't, but what else do you expect us to do? We're helping the only way we know how."

Hashkan cringed. He knew there was nothing they would be able to do against an army of zhu'dac. He remembered how their howls had echoed through the night, how broken the farmers had been. He would always remember. Embarrassed, he looked at the people who'd stopped to stare and whisper to each other.

"Come on," Li'or said. She glared at the crowd and, to his relief, they started to disperse. Then she looked back at him and he could have sworn there was warmth showing through the layers of armor she wore.

Emond's arm dropped across his shoulders and he flinched away with a hiss, shattering the moment. "Ack! Yer back, I'm sorry. Get to walkin', though. Yer holdin' up traffic."

Hashkan looked back at Li'or, but whatever tenderness he'd seen was gone, replaced with a countenance of stone as she walked.

"Alright," Hashkan said as he fell into step beside her. "So when do we leave?"

※ ⁎

AFTER A HEATED DEBATE OVER DINNER, a plan was finally agreed upon. They would cross the Silver Gilt at Voroni-grad, where they would have one last chance to stock up on supplies before cutting through the wilderness towards the White Stone mountains. Hashkan pushed to leave immediately, as every moment they delayed could be crucial, but Li'or and Emond were adamant that traveling with his wounds still in bandages was too much of a gamble. He'd reluctantly admitted that they might be right, and they decided to leave in five days.

The small wait actually worked in Hashkan's favor in more ways than one. As much as he'd hated his brief stay with High Weaver Liestenin, his abrupt departure from the Gathering in Breen was a stain on his conscience that he'd rather not repeat. If he was going to take leave for personal reasons yet again, he wanted to do it properly and go through the expected procedures. He'd enjoyed his stay in Straeth and wanted those doors open to him again when he made it back.

It took Hashkan until the very eve of their departure to gather the courage to bring up the subject with High Weaver Mengovik. Hashkan found the old man in a secluded corner of the garden, tucked between the drooping branches of a willow tree on the bank of a small pool. An apprentice announced Hashkan's arrival and he bowed, right fingers to his forehead, when Mengovik turned his way.

"Well, well, Weaver Hashkan," he said turning to glance at the sun's position. "Normally you're neck-deep in books right now. What's brought you out here?"

"I have something I need to discuss with you, if you have the time, sir."

Mengovik nodded solemnly and turned his attention back towards the sky. "Did you know that in Rak-Shai, they have men and women who are able to read the Fabric of time itself in the stars as they spin through the night? It's fascinating."

Hashkan gave the High Weaver a rueful look before he could stop himself. How was that wives' tale relevant? "I've heard the stories, yes."

"Oh, but they're much more than stories- so much more! There are days I can't help but think they must have known something we didn't, and it led us to war all those years ago." He paused for a moment before continuing in a softer tone. "I heard your first patrol trip was the wrong kind of exciting. Lots of zhu'dac I understand."

Hashkan shifted his weight from one foot to the other. "Yes, unfortunately."

"Hmm," the old man hummed to himself, still staring up at the cloudless sky. "Now, I don't claim to be able to predict the future like the Rak-Shai, but I'd place a good bet that you're here today to ask for permission to leave again. Aren't you?"

"Yes, actually."

Hashkan knitted his brows together. How could he have possibly known? To Hashkan's knowledge, the lord and the High Weaver interacted only when necessary and he didn't think the zhu'dac army- or Klevelt's refusal to act- was public information. It would only incite panic. Not to mention, he hadn't told anyone about his plans except Li'or and Emond.

"Will you be going alone or with more of Klevelt's soldiers?"

"Alone. Well, with my friends. The ones you met when I arrived. The city of Straeth is not involved."

"I see... Well, good! Klevelt has turned soft in his old age. Twenty years ago he would have sent an army after those beasts, even if it meant he had to stand guard at the walls himself." He finally turned to face Hashkan, a large smile deepening and multiplying the wrinkles in his face. "You're going to see and do amazing things, Weaver Hashkan. Amazing."

"Sir, what do you-"

"I'll see you again. Some day." He stood with a groan and patted Hashkan on the shoulder, then bowed with his fingers pressed to his temple. Stunned, Hashkan went through the motions to bow back. "I can't wait to hear all about it. Just don't keep me waiting too long. I am old, you know." Then he turned away, shuffling down the path towards the Sanctuary, leaving a confused Hashkan behind.

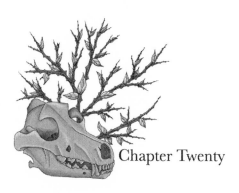

Chapter Twenty

According to Plan

*D*awn was still hours away from warming the walls of Gilderan and Ordelieus thrashed in his sleep, trapped in lucid dreams that wouldn't release him.

He stood on top of a wooden wall looking out over a marsh full of ancient oaks and cypress heavy with moss. Cicadas trilled as night settled in around him. The familiar weight of a sword belt pulled at his waist and unconsciously he reached down to grab the hilt of the sword. The leather-wrapped handle fit his grip better than any glove.

"Corporal!" a voice called out behind him and he found himself turning to respond without a second thought.

The dream changed. He was in a small, dark room, lit only by the light seeping in through the shuttered window. He laid over a woman with dark hair, her face beautiful in a simple way, and somehow indescribably familiar and precious to him.

"Ordelieus," she whispered as her eyes closed and she drew him in closer.

Again the dream shifted. He was in a cluttered room, sitting at a worn and dinged-up table near a hearth. A cast-iron pot hung over an open flame and the same woman stood over it, stirring something that smelled delicious. To the side, a young boy and a tiny little girl argued over a carved wooden horse. The older boy snatched it away from the girl and she immediately burst into tears.

"Daddy!" she bawled as she ran across the room and jumped into his lap.

Ordelieus jerked awake just as he was reaching out to catch the little girl, his hands closing on thin air.

Throwing the covers off, he strode across his room to the window overlooking the southern half of his city. His hands shook as he ran them over his face, so he pressed them against the cool stone of the windowsill and tried to steady himself.

None of the places he'd seen were in Gilderan and he'd never met any of those people, never taken a lover, never been called corporal or *daddy*. But somehow, it had all seemed so familiar, like a line from a song he knew but was just on the tip of his tongue. Had something like those dreams happened in Pinescar?

As soon as the thought came to mind, the now-familiar stab of pain drove into his temple and he gasped. He let the dream and his worries about it fade from his mind. It was easier that way. Anytime he realized how many gaps he had in his memory, the pain would return. A healer he'd recruited hadn't been able to find any sign of a head injury, and her only suggestion was for him to do his best to stay calm. For him, calm meant working, so that's exactly what he focused on.

He stretched his mind out along his web of Threads to

where each one was tethered to his recruits in the field. He checked each one off his mental list after verifying that things were still going according to plan until he got to Stach. Ordelieus sent the man out a few weeks ago to investigate a Gilderian death in Straeth, but the man had turned around.

Ordelieus poured more of himself through the Thread connecting him to Stach and started sifting through his thrall's recent memories.

Stach had made it to Voronigrad before he'd changed his route. His original plan was to spend the night at an inn before pressing on to Straeth, but he'd never even found a place to stay. On the way into the city, a scrap of conversation stopped him in his tracks. He'd heard the words "in the White Stone Mountains." The only thing in the White Stones was Gilderan.

The outskirts of Voronigrad was an over-grown shanty town that circled around the city's walls and though the streets were narrow, it wasn't crowded. It was easy to pair the booming voice with a large blond man moving in the opposite direction as Stach, headed to the north. A willowy elf woman with brown hair and another man in robes were walking with him, but there was no recruiter. Not a Gilderian in sight to have told them that there was something worth looking for in an otherwise uninhabited mountain range.

It was then that Stach had turned and started following the small group, Ordelieus's command to always protect Gilderan overruling his order to investigate in Straeth. He'd trailed behind them at a careful distance until they set up camp for the night, outside of the city and off the road far enough to avoid casual notice.

Along the way, there had been plenty of idle chat, but

Stach had also heard plenty of discussion about missing people.

Ordelieus's recruiting campaigns. He hadn't expected it to go unnoticed, but he didn't think anyone would have put together where they were going until he'd had a bit more time.

"Shit…" he hissed.

He released the Threads to Stach's mind and pulled himself back into his room in Gilderan. He was still at the window, the ever-present chill of the mountain night creeping in around the edges of the glass. Outside, his city slept with the only light coming from the torches of his guards that patrolled the walls and streets. There were still gaps in those walls and buildings on the outskirts were still empty and crumbling in on themselves.

He pushed off the windowsill and started pacing. Only half of the barracks were manned. If the people Stach found were scouts and led an army into Gilderan, he wouldn't be able to hold them off. His army would be demolished before they ever went into the field, he wouldn't gain any more followers, his influence wouldn't spread.

Followers.

Ordelieus slowed his pacing, then stopped, as an idea solidified in his mind. When he'd made the decision to send Stach out, he'd based it solely on the man's ability to blend in. Ordelieus hadn't given him any Altering abilities and no ability to recruit, he was just a common man that was good at getting people to talk.

Ordelieus grabbed Stach's Thread and stretched back out to the man's mind. Focusing, he plucked at the minuscule Threads of the mans mind, moving them less than a hair's breadth one way or the other before tying them off so they would hold. It wasn't as efficient as relaying orders in person- there were details he might have missed, questions Stach might have asked- but when his spy woke up he'd have an entirely new focus for his trip and some new abilities to get the job done.

Bring those three to me. In chains or in pieces.

Chapter Twenty-One

Cause for Concern

They made it to Voronigrad without incident and spent a quiet night in an inn on the outskirts of the city.

After a quick trip to the market for last-minute supplies, they waved farewell to civilization, hopefully not for the last time. Li'or steered them off the road half a day out from the city and into the scattered pines of the White Stone foothills. She said she'd take them on a direct course to Shimmer Falls Lake and they'd be able to follow its bank into the White Stone Mountains.

Hashkan had no reason to doubt her, but not having a road to follow still made him anxious. The feeling only doubled when she rode ahead to look for game, dwindling into a tiny speck on the horizon just barely able to be seen.

Emond and Hashkan watched her go.

"I hope she finds somethin' worth eatin' up there. Now, it's not that I mind the jerky- I've lived off the blighted stuff most me life- but a man needs…"

Hashkan listened to Emond trail off, not paying him any mind. As long as you nodded and agreed occasionally, Emond would be happy to ramble until you interrupted him with food or a drink. Instead, he focused on the tiny speck that was Li'or and worried.

He worried about what would happen if they did find the zhu'dac, and what they would do if they ran into another army of them. He hadn't been able to save his squad. It was only with the Seamstress's blessing that he'd survived at all, and he couldn't expect the same favor twice. He'd failed Bearson, Smithie, and Filan. He couldn't stand the thought of failing Li'or and Emond as well.

"How long do you think we'll be out here, Emond?" Hashkan asked, trying to distract himself.

"Oh, I don't rightly know. I know it takes about a month to get up to the coast, so hopefully not any longer than that." Emond shifted in his saddle. "Hopefully I'm more used to this seat by then. It's killin' me tail bone…"

A rumble of horse hooves announced Li'or riding back, a dead pheasant dangling from her hand. A small smile tipped up the corners of her lips and her hair gleamed in the sun. Hashkan forced himself to look at a point over her shoulder before she caught him staring. From what he could tell, her feelings towards him hadn't changed, but he found himself watching her more and more. She was too observant not to have noticed.

"So we'll be havin' a fire tonight, then?" Emond asked as he eyed the bird and licked his lips.

"As long as it's a small one," she said. "The farms nearby are still more interesting targets than us if there are any zhu'dac around. We should be safe."

They set up camp as the shadows deepened around them and the nocturnal animals started to stir. As Li'or cleaned the pheasant and Emond set up their tent,

Hashkan gathered firewood and sat down to start their cook fire. The further north they went, the more humid it became, and dry kindling had started to become a rarity. It was lucky for Emond and Li'or that they had a Weaver with them. Hashkan shifted his eyes to the Fabric to pull the water from the wood and gasped.

Normally, the Threads for earth and stone appeared stationary, but to the careful observer, all the Threads flowed and vibrated in their own way. When Hashkan looked at the Fabric he expected to see air or water flowing, but he didn't expect the Threads for earth to roll like waves in his peripheral vision.

His pulse hammered in his veins as he braced himself for the earth to shatter. The Threads undulated, tilting the Threads of the trees into awkward angles and buffeting the air with enough force to leave Hashkan's ears ringing.

"What is it?" Li'or asked. She walked up with their dinner cleaned and ready to cook, completely unperturbed.

Hashkan shook himself, he was looking at her through the normal spectrum. He'd been so shaken that he hadn't even been able to hold his focus. He scanned around them, but the landscape was unchanged. The ground was steady and unmoving where he knelt by his makeshift fire pit.

"Did you just notice anything strange?"

Her shoulders tensed and she glanced around them. "No. What am I looking for?"

"The Fabric. It's behaving unusually." Nervous, he switched his focus again. The ground wasn't heaving like before, but it still wavered like heat coming off a forge. "It's… unsteady. I've never seen it like this before. I've never even heard of it being like this."

"What's it doing?"

"Moving…" Hashkan said as he watched the Threads

warble. "It's almost like someone's Altering, but there are no Thread flares."

Li'or lowered her voice to where Emond wouldn't be able to overhear her. "Are we in danger?"

"I don't think so, no. That's the other odd thing, though. They're moving but everything else is still normal. The way things were moving just a moment ago should have ripped this place apart."

Li'or knelt down and thrust the pheasant onto a spit. "Just keep an eye on it and let us know if we need to be concerned."

Hashkan nodded, but he was only half paying attention, his focus still on the Fabric as the vibrations of the Threads gradually slowed to their normal rhythm. This was already a huge cause for concern, but he didn't correct her. If the Seamstress chose to cast them bodily from the Fabric, there was nothing they'd be able to do to stop it.

He turned his attention back to his task and reached his mind towards the water entwined with the Threads of the firewood. As he closed his focus around the water, the Threads warped again and slipped through his grasp.

A cold sweat coated his brow. He glanced around in a barely contained panic, but all the Threads around him were completely normal. No tidal wave of earth loomed over him. Hashkan sighed with relief. They were safe... in theory. Li'or caught his eye from where she was caring for the horses and lifted an eyebrow. Hashkan waved her off with a forced smile. Things were still definitely not right.

It took him another three tries to get a handle on the water. The Threads were difficult to grab like air, but with all the weight of water, so it felt like he was trying to hold on to sand in a gale. He managed to drag enough Threads out to be able to light a fire just as Emond finished with the tents.

"It's still not right," he confessed to Li'or when she took over the watch early the next morning.

He hadn't been able to think of anything else and most of his shift was spent plucking at clumps of dirt. Everything *seemed* normal again, but the Fabric didn't just change. There was an order to it, patterns that it kept. The things he'd seen that day contradicted the sequence he'd known for most of his life.

Li'or sat down on the ground beside him with a sigh. "What is it doing now?"

"It's not that, it seems like it's gone back to normal. I just don't understand what happened… and I'm worried it will happen again, but worse," he confided.

"You'll figure it out. There's plenty of time to think between here and the White Stones."

His heart clenched. Would she still be so confident in him if she knew how useless he'd been just a couple of weeks ago?

Despite his worry, three more days passed without Hashkan noticing any other abnormalities. He was just starting to feel comfortable again when another problem made itself known.

They were eating away the miles at a ground-covering jog when Emond jerked on his reins and dragged his horse into a panicked sliding stop. "Li'or, look!" he shouted and jumped out of his saddle.

Li'or swung off her horse and knelt down next to where Emond was on all fours, face close to the ground. They poked around in the dirt and spoke quietly enough that Hashkan could only make out the odd word here and there.

Hashkan crossed his arms and took a deep breath. His pride rankled at being excluded, but he knew he was no tracker. He'd have to be patient and leave them to their work.

Patience had never been one of his strong points.

"So, what is it?" he asked, unable to keep the edge from his voice.

"Zhu'dac tracks. We're definitely going in the right direction." Li'or glanced back at Hashkan. "Not the army that you came across. This was less than a dozen. The tracks lead off in the direction we're headed." She stood and wiped her hands on her pants, leaving smears of orange. "We should go slow and quiet until we find them, just in case. They're about two days ahead of us, maybe closer. The clay makes it hard to tell."

Hashkan gave a grim nod. "So, now if we find them, we can follow them to the source."

Li'or and Emond shared a knowing look as they climbed back into their saddles.

"No, lad. When we find them, we kill them," Emond said. His accent coming out more clipped than usual.

"Exactly." Li'or agreed. "It's too risky to follow them. We run the chance that they'll notice us and sneak up on us at night. They could meet up with a larger force and then turn around on us, or pin us between the two groups. I would have never given the beasts credit to think that far ahead... but they've also never formed an army before either."

Phantom fingers crawled up Hashkan's spine as the specters of rabid zhu'dac chased him across his mind's eye. He shoved the memory down as hard as he could.

✳ ✳

AT LI'OR'S INSISTENCE, they didn't make a fire that night. Hashkan tried not to draw too many comparisons to his last night with Filan's soldiers, but the mood in their camp was just as tense. They gnawed on their hardtack and stale cheese, just waiting for monsters to burst out of the darkness. When it was Hashkan's turn to keep watch, he was more alert than any other time in the past, poised on the tip of a needle. Sleep eluded him when it was the others' turns. He woke up haggard and disheveled. They all did.

"I'm going to ride ahead," Li'or announced as they finished their cold breakfast. "Check everything out and make sure we don't run up on the zhu'dac by accident."

Hashkan froze as he was packing away his utensils. "That's too dangerous. You can't go alone."

"Dangerous or not, it has to be done," she answered.

"There has to be a better option! What would we do if you got hurt?"

"Hashkan..." Emond drawled in warning.

"And what if we all run up on an army? We'll all die. I'm not trying to be noble here. I'm trying to get done and get paid and I'm trying to be efficient about it. I'm quieter alone and I know how to work the landscape to stay hidden. I'll come back in half-hour shifts. It'll be fine. Just stay headed to the northeast."

Before Hashkan could form another argument against it, she jumped into her saddle and rode off up a small rise and disappeared into a thicket of trees.

"No need for yeh to fret," Emond said. "No different than her goin' huntin'."

Hashkan knew he was right, but she hadn't been hunting with zhu'dac so close by before. Between the Fabric's odd behavior and now this, Hashkan felt like he was being worn thin. If things kept pulling on him like this, he'd rip before long.

Thankfully, Li'or was good to her word and the Seamstress was merciful. They caught up to Li'or every half hour and she didn't see the first zhu'dac. Then, later in the afternoon, it took them nearly an hour to find her again. Hashkan fought against his panic and was insisting that they start their own search when they finally saw her, dismounted and standing just below the crest of a small hill. She turned towards them before they could call to her and made two sharp gestures.

"Stay quiet and go slow," Emond translated.

Hashkan shoved a shaking hand through his hair and followed him forward.

"Jump down and walk with me," Li'or whispered when they reached her.

Hashkan glanced nervously at Emond and then swung down from his mare.

"The tracks started to look really fresh, so I slowed down and kept following them while I waited for you two to catch up. Look what we've found." She gestured over the rise of the hill.

Hashkan took a couple steps forward. Rolling hills spread out before him, scattered with trees to the west and rising slowly to meet with the foothills of the White Stone Mountains. But what drew his attention wasn't the beautiful scenery, it the small band of zhu'dac slowly making its way to the northeast. Hashkan's eyes slipped instinctually over to the Fabric as he counted them.

Eleven. Thank the Seamstress, only eleven.

"Yeh weren't far off on the number or distance, Li'or. That's some fine trackin'," Emond whispered.

"Thank you," she said. "Now, we're going to have an advantage here. They shouldn't be out during the day. They'll be nearly blind from the sunlight."

She looked back out at the zhu'dac and her lips pressed into a thin line, the only sign of any reaction to the pack. She seemed confused, but not worried. Hashkan wished he had that kind of confidence. She waved them down the hill to the horses.

"Here's the plan," she said.

Li'or traced a rough sketch in the dirt as she explained three different paths their encounter could take. Their first option was simple- brutal, but simple. Thanks to his studies in Straeth, Hashkan could tell the backups were redundant. It would be a slaughter.

Hashkan switched his focus to the Threads while the others readied their weapons. To his relief, everything looked normal. He reached out with his mind and tugged on a single Thread of air and it flowed as easily as a thought, dragging a few others along as they were wont to do. Satisfied, he looked back towards Li'or just in time to see her spur her horse forward.

Her gelding lunged into a gallop with Emond following close behind, the horses' necks stretching low as they churned up the ground beneath their hooves. Li'or's sleek warhorse easily outpaced Emond's heavier mount, and she pulled ahead to cut off any escape through the trees. Hashkan rode in a sweeping arc towards the mob's eastern side, standing in his stirrups and pushing his mare hard. The scabs across his shoulders strained, but he gritted his teeth and asked his horse for even more speed.

The zhu'dac noticed them within seconds. At first, they just squinted and stared but then, like a spark catching, they dissolved into vehement barking and howling. They turned and charged- no organization, just a mad rush to draw blood. It was exactly what Li'or had hoped for. Whatever ties had held them together this long snapped and they crawled over one another in their desperate attempts to get to prey. It was chaos.

But there were no other monsters lying in wait to lend them aid. And this time, Hashkan had the flank.

Li'or and Emond ran the zhu'dac down, sword and hammer flashing in the sun. Two of the beasts had pulled ahead of the pack and Li'or and Emond fell on them without mercy. Li'or leaned to the side of her horse and swung her sword in a graceful arc as she charged past. Blood trailed behind her blade as the zhu'dac fell. Emond swung his hammer into the back of the next beast. There was a reverberating thud that even Hashkan could hear and the zhu'dac went down beside its pack-mate.

Hashkan leaned low over his horse's neck and drew even with the zhu'dac's flank. Grabbing as much air as he could, he whipped the Threads towards the back of the pack where a handful of the beasts were lagging behind. The Threads rolled across the clearing and took all the air Threads nearby with them, setting off hundreds of friction flares. Five zhu'dac were ripped off the ground and hurtled towards the trees like they were nothing more than dead leaves. They slammed into the trunks and through branches in a cacophony of breaking wood. If they survived, they didn't come back out from the protection of the trees' shadows.

The four remaining zhu'dac stopped, shocked, and Li'or and Emond charged straight in.

Li'or reached them first yet again. The warhorse reared as soon as they were close and slammed down on the nearest zhu'dac with his front hooves. The beast screamed, but its cry was cut short as Li'or's gelding reared a second time and crushed it as he fell.

Emond galloped into the fray with his war hammer held high. The last three zhu'dac howled and swarmed towards him and Li'or before Hashkan could grab any Threads to help. Then they were all too close together—anything he did would affect Emond and Li'or as well as the creatures. Cursing under his breath, Hashkan rode closer. If he wanted to help, he had to find an opening.

Emond didn't pull his horse up at all when the zhu'dac started to charge, recklessly urging his horse on to meet them. He dealt one an underhand blow to the snout. The power in Emond's arm, doubled by his horse's momentum, obliterated the zhu'dac's skull. Hashkan was close enough now to see bones and teeth fly into the air. Emond's charge carried him past the creatures and he wheeled his horse around for a final pass.

Li'or was faster.

She reined her horse in and slashed down at the zhu'dac beside her. It pulled its rusty sword up just in time to deflect her blow at an awkward angle that forced the beast to take a small step backward. Li'or's sword slid down its blade and wedged itself into the battered cross guard. With her teeth barred, she snatched the sword towards herself and dragged the zhu'dac further off balance. Her horse side-stepped and snapped his teeth at the beast's throat. The zhu'dac yelped and released its sword, stumbling backward to avoid the gelding's bite.

Hashkan felt his breath catch in his throat. The other zhu'dac circled around where Li'or wasn't watching and leapt at her with a ragged scream. Li'or's attention turned to the new threat and she batted it away as it tried to claw up her gelding's side. But the other zhu'dac was getting up from the ground and readying for another attack. Hashkan reached out and tugged at the ground under it, sending it tumbling back to the dirt, but he was still too afraid of hitting Li'or to send any air towards the one that was almost in her saddle with her. It was too imprecise. The wind that would follow his blast could hurt her just as easily as it would hurt her foe.

Her warhorse saved her. The gelding jumped to the

opposite side and the zhu'dac lost his balance and fell from the horse before he was able to latch his claws into Li'or. But as it fell, it flailed. One of its front paws scraped down Li'or's leg and shot sparks up from her armor.

Li'or cursed and switched her sword to her other hand. She chopped down and buried her sword into the beast's shoulder where it joined with its neck. Blood splashed up her arm, but she didn't even flinch. She turned to face the last one just as Emond rode back in. He delivered another accurate blow to the head and the battle was finished.

Hashkan reached them mere moments later and reined his horse in. Adrenaline still thrummed through him; he could feel his heart pounding somewhere in his throat. He kept his eyes focused on the Fabric as he swung his gaze around him, double-checking that they had gotten them all. He knew there weren't anymore nearby; Li'or had checked before they'd even decided to ride into this fight. But a small, paranoid part of his brain still expected another mob to appear on the horizon and charge in, blades whirling and teeth bared.

But they were alone and the countryside was quiet again.

"Thank the Seamstress," he sighed. He brought his hand to his heart and closed his eyes for a moment.

"Alright then! Let's see what these blighters had on 'em, eh?" Emond yelled, jarring Hashkan out of his prayer. The big man slid out of his saddle and squatted down near one of the bodies.

"What are you doing?" Hashkan curled his lip as Emond shifted a corpse over and its intestines rolled out from a vicious cut across its gut.

"Lootin' the bodies!" Emond proclaimed.

Hashkan had to look away. Part of him looked at the violence and the death and was revolted. He looked at his companions calmly cleaning the blood off their weapons and hesitated to keep company with such comfortable killers. He longed for the quiet of the Gathering where he had been trained and the peace of scholarly pursuits. But it was only a small part. Its voice was slowly being overpowered by the part of him that looked at the dead zhu'dac and grinned knowing that those beasts would never terrify farmers or drag down men and horses as they screamed.

He would be sure of it.

"So, what exactly are you expecting to find?" he asked Emond.

"Oh, yeh never know. Might be nothin', but trust me, yeh always loot the bodies."

Hashkan grimaced but was thankfully distracted as Li'or climbed off her horse. Or he was thankful until he saw her sit down and start examining her leg where the zhu'dac clawed her.

"Li'or, what's wrong?" He jumped out of his saddle and rushed to her. In the heat of battle, it looked like her armor had stopped the zhu'dac's claws.

Li'or glanced up at him then back at her leg. The leather of her breaches was cut clean through just above the knee and a thin gash showed through the slice. It didn't look like it was deep and the blood had already clotted.

"Just a flesh wound," Li'or answered, sarcastic. "One that could still be full of the gods only know what and rot my leg off. I've got to boil some water."

She moved to stand, but Hashkan stopped her with a gentle hand on her shoulder.

"I'll do it, just wait here."

Hashkan rushed to build a small fire, all the while with something niggling in the back of his mind. Something wasn't adding up, or there was some detail that he was missing. The feeling stayed with him until he was watching

Li'or reopen and clean her wound. He'd offered to help and she'd just snorted at him.

"Wait, didn't you have metal protecting your legs during the fight?" he asked.

"No, never. Cuisses are heavier than what I like to wear. Why?"

"I thought I saw sparks when the zhu'dac fell off you…"

Li'or paused and looked up at him, concerned.

"Was it the Fabric again? What's it doing?"

"Nothing at all, everything is perfectly normal."

"Lingering flares from the Altering you did, then," she turned back to her work, satisfied with her explanation.

It did seem like a perfectly logical interpretation. The only problem was that friction flares didn't normally linger for more than a few seconds. But then again, Threads didn't normally take on the characteristics of different matter either.

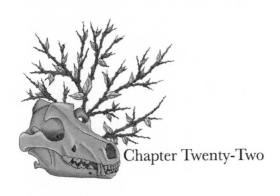

Chapter Twenty-Two

The Original and the Poor Copy

*L*i'or planted her foot on the zhu'dac's chest and kicked, pushing it off her sword. She felt her blade grate against its ribs before sliding free, and the zhu'dac fell back in a heap to join the others.

Six this time, and the fourth pack they had found over the last two weeks. The route they were taking was rife with so many zhu'dac tracks that even Hashkan could have followed them without getting lost. Their pace had slowed for the sake of caution, but fortunately, they'd only found small groups like this one that were easily dealt with.

More worrisome was their food situation. All the zhu'dac passing through the area had either scared off all the game or the bastards had killed and eaten everything on their way through. They had a remarkably clear trail to follow, but Li'or would have felt better if she'd been able to find more food or at least know how much further they had to go. She was starting to think they'd packed too light.

"I've seen more zhu'dac in the last few days than I've

seen in the rest of me life combined!" Emond groaned as he crouched down next to one of the bodies and started riffling through the burlap pack strapped to its hip.

"Be grateful they haven't all been in one place," Hashkan said. He pinched a thread-bare piece of zhu'dac clothing between his thumb and forefinger and cringed as he searched its pockets.

"If one of them had a map, I might be willing to risk it," Li'or commented under her breath.

Hashkan perked up and asked, "Are they smart enough to read a map? Is that even a possibility?"

"I doubt it. Just wishful thinking."

"No, bunch o' stupid blighters, ain't they? Oh, but what is this, now?" Emond said. He walked over to Li'or and Hashkan and held out his hand.

Hashkan tilted his head to the side. "It looks like a lump of wood," he drawled.

Emond just brushed him off with a wave of his hand. "Ack, no. Look harder."

He passed it over to Li'or and she turned it over in her palm. It was true that it looked like a knot of wood, but the more she looked at it, the more it started to take on some shape. It was crudely carved, but if she squinted just right it looked like a skull.

"A wolf skull," Li'or whispered.

"What? Where do you see that?" Hashkan took the carving and studied it. "Huh. So it is."

"And yeh thought it was a lump o' wood. What do yeh take me fer, eh?"

"Well, to be fair, it's not a very good likeness."

Li'or pushed a few loose strands of hair out of her face and sighed. If she didn't stop them, they'd end up having a whole conversation on wood carving technique.

"More importantly," she interrupted, "this proves we're on the right track."

She reached into her own pack and pulled out the wolf skull broach she'd taken off the thug in Straeth.

"The original and the poor copy," she said with a half-smile.

"This confirms our theories," Hashkan said in a soft voice. "Everything is related. There's more armies of zhu'dac."

The Weaver stared down at the baubles in her hands with an odd, unreadable expression. Li'or watched him then looked over at Emond who just shrugged. Hashkan hadn't been quite the same since he'd come back from the patrol. He was more anxious and wore dark circles under his eyes. Li'or understood the feeling- had felt it herself- but coddling him wouldn't help him through it. He didn't need to feel so guilty for surviving, but he'd have to over-come it on his own.

"Alright," Li'or said, closing her hands around the broach and the carving. "Let's ride before these blighters start to stink."

Without another word they mounted and moved out.

Over the course of the next three days, the landscape slowly started to change around them. The rolling plains and scattered trees gave way to the oak and pine forests more commonly found in the north. The air became thicker, more humid, and the only thing keeping them all from sweating through their clothes every day was the cool breeze blowing in from the northeast. They were getting ever closer to the White Stones and to Shimmerfalls Lake.

They followed the zhu'dac trail as it weaved through the trees until, finally, on the fourth day, they spotted Shim-merfalls Lake on the horizon.

It was like a sea. The lake draped over the horizon to

the north and to the west, the wind off the mountains stirring up waves that reflected the sun in a million places and beat against the muddy shores. Even when they reached its banks at dusk, Li'or still couldn't see to the other side.

They made camp in the trees away from the shore as dark, threatening clouds rolled in from across the lake. It turned the water from deep blue to steel gray as the waves churned into a frothy chop. They all squeezed uncomfortably into the tent as the rain started and they begrudgingly broke back into their rations.

The next morning, they crawled out of the tent to be greeted by a bright sapphire sky reflected onto a lake as flat as glass. Emond and Hashkan poked around in the debris that had blown onto the shore while Li'or started setting everything up for a small breakfast.

As she shuffled through their packs, she couldn't help but start to worry again. She'd made sure to pack as much as she could onto their poor mule, but it was by no means an unlimited supply and they were down to about half of what they'd left with. The thought of being this far out with no food- and even less game- made her head feel like it was under a blacksmith's hammer.

"Li'or, look!"

"Across the lake!"

She was jarred from her thoughts and glanced up to where the men were pointing. The last of the clouds had finally cleared and across the water, the peaks of mountains jutted up from the belly of the lake and into the sky. The trees had hidden them from view thus far, but now they stood proudly for all to see.

A sigh blew out from Li'or's lips and a tightness she hadn't even noticed eased out of her shoulders. They were getting closer after all. She stood up from where she was sorting through supplies and walked over to join them.

"If only me love were here to see this view…"

Hashkan sighed. "We know you miss her. We'd all like to be done with this and be back."

"Ah, yeh don't really understand, though. Yeh won't until yeh meet a woman that can…"

Whatever new thing Emond had to say about Eseldra's charms went right over Li'or's head. She looked down as she stepped over a piece of driftwood and gasped.

Animal tracks were pressed into the soft mud near the shore of the lake, large enough and deep enough that last night's rain hadn't washed them away. They were shaped like bear tracks, but no bear had ever grown large enough to leave these, and there were no marks from any claws. No, this animal retracted its claws like a cat and kept them razor sharp. And those claws would be twice as long as Li'or's index finger.

"Li'or? Is everything alright?" Hashkan asked.

"Did you two see these tracks?"

"Yeah, of course! Bear, right? Big blighter."

"This is *not* a bear. You should have told me about these. Damnit… I should have seen them last night. I never would have camped here."

Emond opened his mouth to speak, then closed it again.

"If they aren't from a bear, what are they from?" the Weaver asked.

"These are from a bul'arc."

Hashkan froze and looked at her like a deer catching sight of a wolf. He, at least, understood the danger they were in. Emond just scrunched up his face.

"Those are like bears, ain't they? We don't have them in Vaeshek."

"Bigger, nastier, more aggressive bears," Li'or told him.

"Breakfast is going to be on the road. We need to get out of this thing's territory."

She stormed back to their pile of supplies and started bundling everything back together to load onto the pack mule.

"I guess it's serious, if we have to be in such a blighted rush…" Emond mumbled to Hashkan. Unfortunately for him, Li'or's elven ears heard him and she whirled around.

"Very serious. If we run into a bul'arc, you'll wish we'd met up with thirty zhu'dac instead. A caravan I guarded years ago got attacked by a bul'arc. We had fifteen guards and only six of us lived. Six."

"Oh." Emond looked down at the tracks with either a thoughtful or a confused expression. It was hard for Li'or to tell.

"Yeah. Now, let's go!"

Chapter Twenty-Three

The Welcoming Committee

For three days, they skimmed along the shore of the lake as quickly as they dared.

While they saw no other signs of a bul'arc, the threat still weighed heavy in the back of Li'or's mind- a feeling she wished the others shared. Time and time again, Li'or had to remind the others not to shout or shake them awake when they dozed off in their saddles or during their watches. This wasn't a leisure trip. They were tracking an army, pieces of which could be hiding behind every tree. And they were tracking it through the territory of a ferocious predator. Vigilance would keep them alive. She repeated it to herself and the others like it was an incantation. If she said it enough, it would come true.

And it was by being vigilant that she noticed him just as they were coming out of a section of forest that reached out close to the lake.

A man was walking along the bank ahead of them,

moving in their direction. He was alone and wasn't carrying any weapons. At least none that she could see. He was wearing plain clothes like what any villager in the north would wear and carried only a small pack strapped across his shoulders.

When they got close enough that the others would be able to see him, Li'or pointed the traveler out.

"Now what do yeh suppose he's doing all the way out here, alone, and not a blighted weapon to be seen?" Emond asked as they watched the man.

"There's no way he doesn't have a weapon. It's probably just something small and easy to tuck away, so we'll have to be careful as we get closer." Li'or frowned. "He could also be bait. There may be others in the trees."

Hashkan looked from the man, to her, then back again. "Should I take the flank again?"

"No. You two ride up like normal. I'll flank him through the forest, try to flush out any friends he has hiding in there." She swung off her horse and started to string her bow.

"Maybe he'll know where all these zhu'dac are going. He's following the trail too, just not in the same direction. We should ask." Hashkan held out his hand for her reins and she flicked them over to him.

"He probably does know. Whether he'll tell us or not is the better question."

Hashkan fixed her with a quizzical look that made her pity him and pissed her off in equal measure. How could he still be so naive?

"Zhu'dac aren't the only dark spots in the world, Hashkan, and those thugs in Straeth weren't that unique. I've seen people be just as monstrous and even more cruel. Just expect the worst, and you won't be surprised."

She left a grim-faced Emond and a pale-faced Hashkan behind her and jogged off into the tree line bordering the trail, bow strung and an arrow nocked and ready. The thick canopy choked out the sunlight and gave her plenty of shadows to hide in, and she searched past where the man was walking, just to err on the side of caution.

The forest was empty.

It was so silent that it made the hairs on the back of her neck stand on end. There were no birds chirping, no rustle in the brush as small animals looked for food. The only time a forest was silent was when something was wrong, or a large predator was lurking about. And she didn't qualify as a large predator.

She backtracked until she was even with the stranger and stalked beside him, keeping one eye on the forest around her while trying to infer something from the man's body language. She watched him like a hawk, but she couldn't find anything telling about the way he moved. He was casual, careless even, and didn't seem like a threat at all. In fact, if it hadn't been for the silence around them, she might have been able to dismiss him. But it just wasn't *right*. She could feel it.

When Emond and Hashkan came into view, the stranger perked up and called out, "Helloooooo!"

"Hello, sir. How's the road treating you?" Hashkan asked when they'd rode up a little closer. Li'or rolled her eyes. What made him think people talked like that?

"Oh, just the same as ever. It's so good to see some other people out here!" He propped a hand on his hip and shielded his eyes against the sun with his other hand, squinting so hard his eyes were reduced to slits.

He was average height and build with the dark,

leathery complexion often found in sailors. His hair flopped around his ears in complete disarray like a shaggy dog. His face was round with the barest whisper of a mustache trying to gain ground on his lip.

And he didn't move like a fighter. Li'or still hadn't found even a suggestion that he might be armed.

Emond and Hashkan reined up and dismounted.

"So are you folks bound for Gilderan? We might end up being neighbors! I'm Stach Larzohn."

Hashkan took the lead again and made their introductions while Emond watched Stach much like Li'or was doing.

"Bound to where, you asked?" Hashkan said.

"Gilderan." He looked at them all for a beat then his narrowed eyes widened a fraction and he swung his hands out the sides. "Surely you've heard of the rebuilding and restoration? It's the most exciting thing of our time, friends! All of the best artisans and builders are there. We're bringing the city back to life!"

Emond opened his mouth to speak, but Li'or walked out of the forest and interrupted him.

"We heard rumors that something exciting was happening in the mountains so we decided to come see for ourselves. Is it much further?"

Li'or looked more closely at him. He was still squinting against the sun but as Li'or studied him, something just seemed off about his expression. On top of that, he didn't act surprised when she came out of the trees at all. Her fingers tightened on her bow.

Stach rolled his hand around in a vague gesture. "Oh, a couple of weeks, give or take a few days. Not a short jaunt, no. Going around a lake this size takes up a lot of time, doesn't it?"

"It does," Li'or answered. She took her reins back from Hashkan and flipped them over her horse's neck. "Well, we'll let you get back on the road. Seems we have a long way to go ourselves."

"Oh, no, no! What kind of possible future neighbor would I be if I didn't show you the way?"

"It'll be fine, we're just wantin' to see what all the fuss was about, yeh know? Not tryin' to move in or anythin'. No need to worry with us," Emond told him with a chuckle.

"No one just visits Gilderan."

Li'or's muscles tensed and she moved her lead foot in front of her without thinking. The way Stach delivered that comment made it sound almost like a threat. But still, he wore the same doltish smile on his face. He walked up a little closer and a painfully important detail hit Li'or like a wave of ice water.

His eyes. They had the same flat, unfocused look that the blond man in Straeth had. Of course he wasn't armed. If he was like that thug, he was a weapon in and of himself.

"Well, we'll see how we like it. But we really should get going." It took a monumental effort for her to keep her words calm and steady as she hovered on the edge of action. She flexed her bowstring and the wood of her bow creaked ever so slightly. If he felt threatened by it then the feeling would be mutual. Out of the corner of her eye, she saw Emond put a hand on his hammer.

If Stach noticed the shift their conversation had taken he didn't show it. He said, "I'll help guide you. I insist. It'll be an honor to bring new citizens into the city."

"Li'or," Hashkan whispered. "The Threads again."

"What about them?" she hissed back at him. She kept

her eyes trained on Stach, who watched them with his head tilted to the side.

"I don't know, but it's around *him*."

"What do you- " And then she heard it.

Just on the edge of her hearing, there was a rumbling growl and the cracking of underbrush as something large pushed through the forest.

"What is that?" she demanded.

"What is what?" Stach answered.

"You know damn well. Don't play dumb with me. What's in the woods?"

The source of the sounds got close enough for the others to hear. Hashkan took a small step backward and Emond unslung his hammer.

"Oh! That!" he chuckled. "That's just my favorite part of the welcoming committee."

With a deafening crash, a massive creature broke through the trees and barreled straight towards them like a bull.

Tree branches rolled off its back as it ran towards them, a huge fang-filled mouth roaring. The horses and the mule screamed and bolted as the ground shook under the thing's massive paws. At the last moment, Emond jumped to the side and rolled, landing in a crouch and jumping back up to start a charge of his own. Li'or shoved Hashkan to her right and then jumped left, barely keeping them both out of harm's way. Off to the side, Stach was shrieking and laughing.

The creature reared up on two hind legs, putting its height easily above fifteen feet tall. It was covered in a course grayish fur mottled in places with darker grays and browns, and near its joints and along the ridges of its eye sockets bony scale-like protrusions jutted out from the hair.

Its face was similar to a bear's, only shorter and wider, and curling ram's horns thrust from it's skull.

Li'or's fist clenched tight around her bow. "Bul'arc," she hissed.

It opened its jaws impossibly wide and loosed a roar that vibrated inside of Li'or's chest. Then it charged again.

Muscle memory alone guided Li'or's hands as she drew back her arrow, aimed, and shot it straight for the bul'arc's head. The arrow hit one of the bone ridges on the monster's snout and skimmed off to the side, useless.

Li'or gritted her teeth and reached back to grab another arrow, but before she could even set it in place on the string, Emond barreled past her, yelling at the top of his lungs, his hammer ready. He met the bul'arc's charge head-on with all his weight behind a swing that ended in a solid connection at the hollow between the beast's neck and shoulder.

The bul'arc roared in pain, but it didn't stop its charge. It heaved a heavily muscled shoulder into Emond's chest. He braced, but was still spun by the force and left staggering. Somehow, he managed to stay on his feet.

Li'or loosed her arrow as the bul'arc flew past her at point-blank range. The arrow buried itself into the beast's flank as it passed, eliciting another roar of pain, but it didn't slow or falter. It swept past them again, turning to make another charge.

Out of the corner of her eye, Li'or saw Stach scramble off into the trees. She cursed through her teeth and shoved him from her mind. Let the bastard run. If they died, the bul'arc would hunt him down next. Hopefully. She readied another arrow as Hashkan reached towards a hastily built fire. A ball of flame streaked through the air and burst apart just below the bul'arc's face as it turned back to face them. It just bellowed and shook its head while it careened towards them.

"Shit." She shot another arrow, aiming for the soft area at the creature's arm pit and scored another hit. "Shit!" The bul'arc barely flinched. Her arrow was simply stuck in the skin and the fat, hitting nothing vital.

Emond squared himself back off in the path of the bul'arc, a two-handed grip on his hammer.

"Hashkan! More fire!" Li'or yelled. Emond was doing a great job keeping the monster busy, but he was playing a dangerous game.

The Weaver grabbed two balls of flame and hurled them at the bul'arc; Li'or chased them with arrows as quickly as she could. It drew the animal up short as it shook the fire from its hide, wiggling her arrows loose. Her heart sank into her stomach when she saw the arrows fall, but the distraction served its purpose. Emond planted his feet and swung his hammer from behind his hip in blow that connected with the side of the bul'arc's jaw.

The beast's head jolted to the side and, finally, it stumbled. But there was no time for the three of them to breathe a sigh of relief. It righted itself almost immediately and roared loud enough to shake the mountains.

"Bollocks!" Emond shouted back at it.

The bul'arc inhaled into lungs like a bellows and let loose another roar before lashing out at Emond with a paw. The Vaeshekian barely got his hammer up in time to catch the blow against its haft and he was forced back onto his heels. It swung with the other paw and Emond was forced to yield even more ground.

Li'or launched another arrow. It struck the bul'arc in the cheek and it turned towards her for a split second before fire hit its face on the other side. It shook itself, snarling, and looked towards Hashkan just as Emond pulled his hammer through a mighty underhand swing that connected with its chin.

The bul'arc reared back and howled in pain. Li'or and Hashkan rained arrows and fire towards its stomach and Emond followed them with three quick blows with his hammer, but it wasn't enough. It staggered back a single step then swept forward. Its paw swung down and its claws sliced into the meat of Emond's thigh as he tried to back-step out of range.

Emond's gasp was stifled. The bul'arc lunged at him with an open mouth as soon as its foot landed. Li'or and Hashkan both shot at its face, connected, but the jaws snapped shut so close to Emond's arm that Li'or couldn't tell if it had him or not.

She reached for another arrow and grabbed empty air, so she flung her bow off to the side and unsheathed her sword and dagger. As she readied herself to lunge, an all-too-familiar howling rang through the trees and she froze. The others hadn't heard it yet, and Emond kept struggling against the bul'arc. It had a hold on the sleeve of his chain mail shirt and was dragging him down to batter him more.

Li'or didn't allow herself time to think twice and ran to help Emond. Hashkan continued to chuck fire at the bul'arc, but now the thing's face wasn't an option with Emond trapped there and his attacks sputtered out, ineffective against its neck and shoulders.

"To your right, Hashkan! Cut them off!" Li'or yelled as she dashed to Emond's aide.

The Weaver looked confused but turned just in time to see about ten zhu'dac burst screaming from the trees. Stach and another weathered-looking man brought up the rear.

Li'or made it to the bul'arc and threw every bit of her weight into a blow across the beast's leg. The wild swing left her guard open, but she was counting on dealing enough damage to finally get a big reaction and buy herself enough time to get her guard back up.

She was wrong.

Her blow finally drew blood, but the bul'arc snatched its head away from Emond quicker than something that big should have been able to move. In the same heartbeat, it slammed Li'or across the torso with a paw the size of a dinner plate. The force of the blow flung her backward several feet and her sword flew out of her grasp. She landed in an ungainly sprawl that knocked all the air from her lungs and slammed her head into the hard ground. She tasted blood in her mouth and sparks danced in front of her eyes. She thought they were friction flares, but Hashkan was busy lobbing fire at the zhu'dac to hold them off. Despite his efforts they were moving in to encircle them.

She gasped for breath and struggled to her knees as a wave of nausea rolled over her. Muffled, as if it was coming towards her through layers and layers of blankets, she heard the bul'arc drawing closer. She managed to get one foot under her and was straining to draw the next up when it batted her aside again. Li'or rolled with the blow and was sent tumbling across the clearing. Stars exploded across her vision when she finally came to a stop, flat on her back.

The bul'arc's pounding strides followed after her, the smack of its jaws opened above her, and she knew she was done. She had to think of something to at least give the others a fighting chance. The thing had already laid her down. Her ribs felt broken and the blow to the back of her head had done enough damage that her thoughts seemed to swim up to her through heavy syrup.

The bul'arc's hot, wet breath blasted down on her face

and she raised her arm, ready. It lunged down to her, almost in slow motion, its lips curling back from teeth like daggers and it sank them down, down towards her face.

She swung, burying her dagger in its eye. It roared and jerked away from her and the blade went with it. The bul'arc back peddled, roared in pain and rage, and shook its head in an attempt to dislodge Li'or's dagger, but the blade was deep and it didn't budge. Li'or struggled to her feet and watched as Emond slammed his hammer into the hilt of her dagger and drove it deep into the bul'arc's skull.

The creature stopped moving, stopped roaring, and slouched into a heap with one last exhale.

And then the zhu'dac got around Hashkan's fire and ran straight towards Li'or.

She barely had time to brace herself before the first one was within striking distance. It carried a club and brought it around to deliver a blow to the side of her head. At the last moment, Li'or stepped in and reached for its shoulder, taking a hit from its arm on her ribs instead. Its breath smelled like carrion and she grimaced as she kicked the zhu'dac in the side of its knee. There was a crunch as it screamed and went down, loosening its grip on the club as it went. Li'or snatched the crude weapon away from it and turned on unsteady feet to face the next one.

Emond slammed into it and flung it backward.

"Buyin' yeh bit of time, there, eh?" he yelled and then charged past the fire into the mob.

Heat washed over her. Turning she watched as Hashkan flung more fire around them. He fanned it higher and higher into a blazing tempest as he went and created a wall of flame easily ten feet high to hold the zhu'dac back. They were almost completely encircled. She took an awkward step forward towards where Emond was desperately fighting, then another.

"Look out!" Hashkan yelled behind her. She stopped just in time for another ball of fire to burst in front of her and complete the circle.

Li'or threw her arms up to protect her face from the sparks and ash. "Hashkan, tear it down! Emond's out there alone!"

The Weaver's eyes shot wide and his face, flushed from the heat of the flames, grew pale.

"I don't know if I can!"

Frantic, he grabbed at the fire and threw it back behind them. Li'or found her sword and then waited, gnashing her teeth as the clamor of fighting continued just outside of her reach. If she ran through the wall, she would surely catch flame. She kicked sand onto the flames to smother them, but it was still taking too long.

"Enough, enough! Just take him!" an unfamiliar voice called out.

"Alright!" Stach this time.

"Hashkan..." Li'or growled

"I'm trying!" Sweat ran down his face and cut little trails through the ash and dirt smeared onto his skin.

Emond, who had been yelling the entire time, suddenly grew silent and the battle died immediately. Li'or's jaw dropped. She turned towards Hashkan. He was frozen, a shocked expression on his face that matched her own. Tears pricked the corners of his eyes.

"No! Not again!" he screamed and redoubled his efforts.

Li'or scrambled alongside him as they fought against the prison of their own making and as the world went still beyond their wall.

Finally, they made a gap and Li'or rushed through with her stolen club held high to meet...

Nothing.

The bul'arc corpse laid to her left along with a few scattered zhu'dac corpses, but no Emond.

Hashkan skidded to a stop behind her as she dropped her sword, defeated.

"They took him."

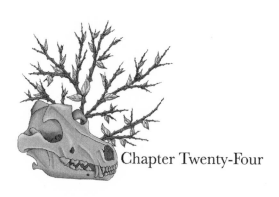

Chapter Twenty-Four

Direct Altering

*H*ashkan slumped to the ground as the last of his damning fire sputtered out.

"I can't believe they took him. Why would they take him? And how? He fights like a beast..." he turned to face Li'or.

She was systematically pilfering through the belongings of the fallen zhu'dac, but she paused and sighed. "I don't know."

She tossed something palm-sized over to him. He caught it and knew before he even looked at it that it was another crudely carved wolf skull.

"They *are* some kind of strange fanatical cult," he muttered. "And there was something very wrong with that Stach."

Li'or eased herself down in front of him, her face tight with pain. Shame made his chest constrict and he threw the skull trinket into the trees. If he had been stronger, she wouldn't have gotten hurt. He was less like the warrior Weavers of the past than he'd once thought.

"Something was very seriously wrong with him," Li'or prodded him back to the present.

"Yes, with his Threads. In his mind specifically." Li'or lifted an elegant brow- skeptical no doubt- so he continued. "Everyone has their own patterns, but we're all built around a very similar design. His pattern was… tangled."

"And to think, he looked so normal."

"Yes, his appearance was perfectly normal. It was his mind. When he started behaving strangely, I shifted over to the Fabric and that's when I noticed the odd fluctuations again. It was all centered around him. So I looked closer and his Threads were all bunched up in odd places where normally they would be evenly spaced. And I don't think it was natural. It looked Altered."

"I thought Weavers couldn't affect people like that," Li'or said as she shrugged off her leather vest, flinching as she did.

"We can't! Or at least that's what I've always been taught. I tried to Alter a barn cat as a child and was completely unsuccessful."

Li'or tossed her vest to the ground with a muttered curse. "He was just like that bastard in Straeth."

"Yes."

Li'or fell silent while she gingerly felt her ribs. Hashkan watched as the fabric of her sweat-soaked shirt clung to the gentle curves of her body and a violent blush heated his face. He should hate himself for looking at her like that when she was obviously in pain. Pain that he could have prevented.

"Are you alright?" he asked softly

She grunted. "I haven't found a break anywhere. Some

bruises, yes, and I'm lightheaded still, but it seems like that's it."

"I wish we could say the same for Emond. It's my fault, Li'or. I'm so, so sorry."

He drew his knees up to his chest and hid his face in his hands. The joy he'd felt at coming out here, doing the right thing, redeeming himself, it was all sliding through his fingers as if it was the Threads for water. High Weaver Liestenin had warned him all those months ago about his arrogance and he'd dismissed it. Now his shortcomings had cost an entire squadron their lives. Even now his friend was likely suffering, if he was even still alive. He hadn't considered the possibility of Emond's death until that moment and he squeezed his eyes tight.

Leaves rustled beside him and the scent of cinnamon mixed with horses and the road wafted over him. A weight leaned against his shoulder and he jumped and picked his head up. Li'or leaned against him, shoulder to shoulder, with her eyes trained to the north and her jaw set. Hashkan's stomach fluttered as he studied her profile. Dirty and scuffed up as she was, she was still lovely.

"We'll go get him," she said in a tone that left no room for debate.

"Do you think he's still…" he couldn't bring himself to finish the sentence.

She turned her bright green eyes back to focus on him. "If not, we'll avenge him."

Her hand found his and she clasped it tightly for just a heartbeat before climbing back to her feet.

"I'll find the horses and the mule. You work on figuring out how to do this direct Altering stuff. We might need it."

Hashkan grinned up at her. What a good name for it. *Direct Altering.*

AFTER LI'OR WALKED AWAY, Hashkan pulled his attention away from thoughts of her and focused on the task at hand.

He'd always been taught that any kind of direct Altering was impossible. During his training, he'd learned about all the powerful and seasoned Weavers that had tried for years to find a way to make it work and failed at every turn. The discovery of Altering had already changed the face of warfare, but to be able to grab and control the enemy completely... it would change everything again. Entire armies could be stopped, controlled. Foreign leaders manipulated so there would not even *be* wars.

It would be incredibly dangerous. If the wrong person had those abilities, it would be all too easy for them to accomplish whatever twisted things they set their minds to. And all signs pointed to that very thing happening in Gilderan.

Armed with a blank notebook to record his findings, Hashkan sat and meditated on the Fabric while he waited for Li'or to return. He studied the Threads in his hand and compared them to the Threads of the world around him, looking for any similarities between the two. His Threads were nearly motionless, like the ground and stone, but flexed almost like water when he moved. Altering stone required mental strength and a firm grip just like physically lifting it would. Altering water required the same firm grip, but also fluidity and speed. It almost had to be scooped up.

Maybe if he combined the techniques...

Excited, he looked around for something to test his theory on. Unfortunately, all the animals in the forest nearby had been scared away during the fight and still hadn't returned. The bul'arc and fallen zhu'dac wouldn't help. Only living things could resist Altering, so he was left with only one other option. Frowning, he looked at his little finger and grabbed the Threads, scooping and straining with his mind. Nothing.

He tried repeating the process a few more times, just to be sure, and still didn't see or even feel anything. He battered his mind against his own Threads in frustration but still couldn't elicit a change even though he was willing to let himself be Altered. The Threads had their own idea of where they needed to be and they wouldn't budge.

He'd have to study the Fabric more. Surely the answer was hiding there somewhere and if some crazed zealot in Gilderan could discover it, then so could he. He was just finishing scribbling about his failures when he heard a rustling in the trees.

Li'or rode out of the tree line with the other two horses and the mule in a train behind her.

"Anything?" she asked.

"Not yet," Hashkan said with a sigh before adding sarcastically, "nothing like pressure for motivation, though." He regretted the bitterness in his voice immediately.

Li'or just nodded and tossed him his reins. She either didn't notice his tone or, more likely, didn't care enough to respond. Discomfort didn't matter out here. He could almost hear her saying it. Only results mattered. That's what would keep them alive. Hashkan swung up into his saddle and followed behind her as she led the way down the trail left by the zhu'dac and, hopefully, Emond.

As they traveled, Hashkan tried to grab hold of the Threads of every small animal he saw. They resisted him one and all, even though he could have broken their bodies with one hand. He stared at the Fabric, willing it to yield, pulling them towards himself, until he felt like his eyes were crossing. He hadn't managed to coerce even a hair of movement. He helped set up camp, going about the routine that had become a habit for him by now, but he was frustrated and distracted. The Threads wouldn't budge, no matter how hard he grabbed or how hard he pulled- except that they had to. There was a way to make it work, he just wasn't seeing it.

As he sat beside Li'or and chewed on stale jerky that night, Hashkan moved his focus so the details of the world blurred and the intricacies of the Fabric came into focus. He watched everything ripple as the horses moved and grazed. The Threads bent and shifted, pulled tight and loosened to allow things to pass by and around each other. He analyzed the horses' Threads against his own, compared those to Li'or's, even compared them all to a tree, but there was nothing new to discover. The tree's Threads were just as static, almost earth-like, as any he'd ever seen. His and Li'or's Threads were still the same odd mixture of all the elements that all sentient life shared, though hers were somehow more fluid than his own. During his lookout shift, he risked a quick snatch at Li'or's foot, attempting another new method, and she didn't so much as flinch.

He couldn't allow himself the luxury of being discouraged, so the next day Hashkan threw himself back into his efforts against the Threads of small animals. He stared at the Threads and strained against them for the entire day to no avail.

By the time they made camp that night, Hashkan's head felt like it was splitting and he had spent so long staring at the Threads that he had a hard time getting his eyes to focus back into normal vision. He slouched next to the fire, ate dinner, and barely made it through his watch.

He had to stand and walk around the whole time to keep from dozing off.

His days started to blur together. They luckily didn't run into anymore zhu'dac and Hashkan's studies and failed experiments were uninterrupted as the days stretched on. Li'or barely spoke, and when she did it was just to comment on how they should have caught up to Emond by now. She didn't say it, but Hashkan could tell that she was starting to worry.

The thin forest and gentle foothills rolled into the base of the White Stone Mountains, the ground becoming more rocky and the trail they followed becoming less distinct. Several times they passed over rocky areas where they completely lost the trail, and Li'or would have to dismount and search for great lengths of time before finding it again. The great, drooping oaks of the forest yielded to more pines and evergreens as they went, slowly gaining elevation, and the air became less muggy, more crisp. The lake fell away as they climbed, craggy ground rising up like the rim of a bowl around the shining water.

And through it all, Hashkan pushed and strained against the Threads of everything he could find.

It took four more days of almost continuous effort before something happened. By that point, Hashkan was only trying out of habit, he had stopped thinking he was capable of making this experiment work two days ago and had quit recording any of his attempts. He tried grabbing just a few Threads in the finches that flitted through the trees overhead, he tried grabbing only one Thread, he tried grabbing all of them at once, but nothing ever changed. The birds never even gave any indication that they felt him.

So, he continued lackadaisically reaching towards the birds and their Threads, and they continued to shrug him off. They didn't so much as blink at him as they hopped from branch to branch, oblivious to the Weaver's efforts. All of his attempts were proving fruitless. Someone could do this with such skill as to manipulate the human mind and he couldn't even draw a finch into his hand. He was wasting his time.

Contemptuously, he flung his mind out towards a robin, its russet breast flashing through the pine needles, and grabbed hold of a single Thread and pulled as hard as he could. Nothing happened, of course, and the robin continued on with its own pursuits. Hashkan reached and grabbed another Thread, then another and another. To his amazement, the Fabric started to yield. The bird let out a confused chirp and started to angle towards him. Hashkan continued grabbing Threads in a sequence, like a harper playing scales, until he was straining against every Thread that made up the Fabric of the bird. The bird came closer and Hashkan held his breath, not even daring to hope, as sweat broke out on his brow from the effort. The bird swung through the air, fighting against him the entire time, but flew towards Hashkan where it all but fell into his waiting hands.

He closed his hands around the bird gently and let go of the Threads, forcing his eyes to focus back on the world as a whole. The bird promptly started to struggle against his grip and cried out in a tiny squeak of fear.

Li'or stopped her horse and turned around at the sound. When she noticed the bird in his hand she fixed him with an incredulous look.

"I did it," Hashkan panted. He opened his hands and the robin blasted away in a flurry of feathers. "I grabbed its Threads. I pulled it to me. It is possible! It's so difficult that it seems impossible, but it isn't! That proves it! That's what was done to Stach and what they tried to do to us!

The Threads fight against you so hard, they seem to resist on their own- probably the pain we experienced- but they can be moved. They can!" He realized he was rambling and took a deep steadying breath.

Li'or simply nodded and smiled. Somehow the smile meant more than any applause. "I knew it was only a matter of time before you worked it out."

Hashkan smiled so hard his cheeks ached.

"It's good to know for sure what we're up against," she added.

Hashkan paused and the smile fell from his face. He'd been so excited about his discovery that he'd forgotten what they were attempting to do. At the end of this road waited Weavers whose abilities outclassed his own exponentially. The things that Hashkan struggled to do, they excelled at. How would they fight against that?

Chapter Twenty-Five

The Rift

*E*ven though it had been over a week since Emond was taken, Li'or still felt like she had been thrown from a horse and then trampled by five others. When she'd shrugged off her leather vest and her tunic during her first moment alone, she'd been shocked by the deep blue and black bruising that wrapped around her like a shroud. The bruises had faded into a sickly greenish-yellow, but they were deep and her ribs still ached if she inhaled too deeply.

Now that he didn't have his studies to distract him, only practice instead, Hashkan trailed after her like an anxious wet-nurse. She'd failed to hide how sore she still was when she dismounted one evening and from then on, he refused to let her do anything alone. On one hand, she was touched, but on the other his constant hovering was fraying her last nerve.

The air was crisp as they winded their way through the tall pines and traversed the rocky rises that led them further and further into the White Stone Mountains. For days now, Li'or had been hoping for some sign that they were gaining on the Gilderians, but they still seemed to be a full day behind them. And, somehow, they were losing ground despite the fact that Li'or and Hashkan were on horseback.

A shout rang out through the trees and set a small flock of birds airborne. They both froze, reining in their horses and searching the woods around them. Hashkan's eyes took on that strange half-focused look as he searched the Fabric and more voices joined in. They didn't have time for his slow and methodical scrutiny. Li'or waved at him to get his attention and motioned for him to follow her to a group of large boulders about twenty feet from where they were.

They barely managed to cram themselves and all the horses behind the boulder. Once she was sure they were all hidden, Li'or nudged her gelding up close to the rock and stood in her saddle so she could peer over the top. Hashkan moved like he was going to join her, but she glared daggers at him and motioned for him to stay. Try as he might, he wasn't very quiet. He needed to stay still.

Tense, she waited for the owners of the voices to come into view. The forest slowly started to reveal them in bits and pieces as she spotted them through the trees.

Six soldiers, wearing uniforms of tan and green, came into view following the same trail that Li'or and Hashkan had been on for weeks now. Each one had a long sword swinging on the side of their saddle and a shield strapped across their back. Even though they were laughing and joking like old friends, they rode in a tight and disciplined formation. No, these were not novices on patrol. These were blighted veterans.

Before they could notice her peeking over the rock,

Li'or lowered herself back into her saddle slowly and soundlessly. She caught Hashkan's eyes and mouthed, "Patrol," to him. The muscles in the Weaver's jaw tightened and his hands flexed on his reins.

The clopping of horse's hooves on the stone and gravel started to accompany the voices of the soldiers as they drew ever nearer. Hashkan was staring at the boulders like he was trying to see through them and, knowing Weavers, he probably could. Hampered by her own normal vision, she focused all her attention on her hearing, hoping none of the horses would decide they needed to snort.

Hashkan's eyes flashed over to her, panic written across his features. He opened his mouth to speak.

Before he could finish drawing breath, Li'or leaned across the distance between their horses and pressed her hand firmly across his lips. The leather of her saddle squeaked and she cringed. Hopefully, the soldiers were too busy with their conversation to hear it. The echoes around the stones would give them away in a heartbeat. She pushed tighter against his mouth. His breath caught and his head rocked back, but he froze. She shook her head.

"Not a word," she mouthed slowly.

Hashkan sighed through his nose and his breath tickled her hand, but he nodded his understanding. Li'or swallowed hard, pushing her heart back down into her chest where it belonged.

The soldiers were right on top of them by then, the echoing diminished enough that their words rang clear over the boulders.

"So then he says to me, 'We need you to change patrols after today.'"

"Bastard."

"I know. So I told him I wanted to keep my shift. It's always been my shift. I have seniority."

"You do. You shouldn't have to yield it up to some scamp fresh to the city."

"That's right. You were one of the first ones here!"

"Yes… but then he tells me it's for the good of Gilderan," the soldier said, voice cracking when he mentioned the city.

"Oh. Oh, well then you better switch."

"I am, starting tomorrow…"

Li'or blinked. She hadn't expected the conversation to take such a strange and sudden shift. They'd all just rolled over and forfeited the point like a knife was being held to their necks as soon as Gilderan was mentioned. There was no doubt in her mind that if she was able to see their Threads they would look like a tangled mess, not unlike Hashkan's description of Stach.

They continued discussing patrol shifts as they rode past Li'or and Hashkan's hiding spot. They started reviewing changes that had been made in the watch schedules- specifically when the guards swapped shifts- and Li'or perked up. She committed each time to memory for when they got to the city. Clearly, these soldiers weren't as seasoned as she thought. Even in the woods a spy could be hiding, just waiting for information like this. Idiots. They must have been so close to home that they were feeling over-confident. It seemed too good to be true.

Fortunately, Hashkan and the horses stayed quiet, all barely moving until the soldiers were long gone. Li'or shook her head at Hashkan when he looked at her with a question in his eyes. She made him wait another five minutes after *she* could no longer hear the soldiers before she spoke to the Weaver again.

"Wait here and stay hidden," she said as she slipped out of her saddle. "I'll tail them for a few miles. If they keep blabbing, I might even figure out where they're keeping Emond." She grabbed her spare arrows out of the pack on the mule.

She'd meant the comment to be light-hearted, but the way Hashkan's face fell told her she'd missed her mark.

"Are you sure you should be going alone? What if there's another one of those… things?"

"A bul'arc? That one getting the jump on us was an extenuating circumstance. Usually, I can smell them long before they know I'm there." She smirked back at him and was relieved that he smiled back, even if it was clearly an effort for him.

"Please be careful. I can't lose you, too."

There was a note of anguish in his tone that stopped her in her tracks. She turned back towards him and met his pale silver eyes, so at odds with his dark hair. And so young. She only hoped that he didn't expect more than she could give.

"I'm always careful."

She squeezed his shoulder and turned away.

The trail was made even more obvious by the passing of the guard's mounts and she followed it with ease, able to focus the majority of her attention into becoming just another shadow under the trees. She didn't want even a squirrel to notice her. Despite her confidence when she'd talked to Hashkan, there were formidable threats in the mountains- even if you didn't consider the zhu'dac, bul'arc, and raging madmen. The bul'arcs were the worst of them, though, and they were native to Anagovia's mountainous regions. And they did frighten her.

Going as slow as she was, she didn't expect to catch up to the soldiers if they kept a normal pace. Hopefully, they would stop for a meal and she'd be able to eavesdrop, but if not, she would at least be able to ensure that their way was clear. She eased herself over a downed pine and nearly tripped when motion exploded through the trees in front of her. She looked up in time to see the tail of a red deer bounding away from her.

"Damn..." she breathed. How had she been that distracted? That deer could have added another week to their supplies- or alerted someone to her presence. She felt like a fool.

She trudged on. Under the trees, a thick carpet of pine needles cushioned her steps and she flitted between the trees' shadows like a wraith. The trail dipped into a gulley and, rather than putting herself in such a vulnerable spot with nowhere to hide, she scrambled up the incline on the side and followed along the edge. The rise was steep and she found herself on her hands and knees as she half walked, half crawled up the slope.

Li'or's heart leapt into her throat and her shoulders flinched towards her ears as the brush in front of her exploded in a riot of broken branches and crushed leaves. Her hands went to her dagger and sword and she shuffled sideways to hide behind a small bush. She peered through the branches, carefully keeping her breath level, soft, and slow.

She expected to see another bul'arc lumbering toward her but instead she saw...nothing. The only movement was the shaking of branches as a small gust of wind blew through.

Li'or edged her way out from behind the bush one inch at a time, eyes darting in every direction as she searched for the source of the noise. She set her feet down slowly, feeling the ground before putting weight on it, and not even the dried needles cracked under her tread.

And then she saw it.

At first, it was just a thin dark crack in the ground, deep if the dirt and detritus falling into it was any indication. There was an ear-splitting screech, like ripping metal and she flinched as the crack widened. Tiny motes of light that looked like friction flares danced along the ragged boundary of the rift, but their light couldn't penetrate the darkness. Phantom fingers traced down Li'or's spine. It wasn't just darkness- it was blackness, deeper than the night or even the space between the stars, and so thick that no amount of light would force it to yield. It sucked all the warmth from the air around her and her breath misted before her.

There was another screech, this time more guttural, carnal. Li'or took a step back and slowly drew her bow and an arrow.

Clawed hands, themselves the color of pitch, reached out of the gap and clutched at the edges. They dug into the ground and left furrows in the rocky soil. The maddening screech rang out again, louder this time. Whatever it was, it was trying to claw its way out.

Li'or's stomach flipped somersaults and her heart slammed against her ribs. Fear like she'd never known grabbed her by the neck and squeezed until she could hardly breathe. The hands stretched out again and raked through the earth as whatever it was screamed a third time.

Li'or shrank away from the sound, but she fought for a gulp of air and snapped her bow up. There was barely a creak as she pulled it back and took aim with the tip of the arrowhead. Moving on instinct and habit while her rational mind wrestled against what she was seeing, she lined her shot up and turned the string loose with a *thwack*.

The arrow sliced through the air and found its mark. Right in the center of the thing's hand.

The shriek that broke free from the rift was ungodly. The sound rammed into Li'or with enough force that she flinched back and crumpled, squeezing her hands over her ears as tight as she could. The wail dragged on, fury and pain lending it power, until Li'or felt blood running down between her fingers.

Light flares swarmed around her. They were bright enough that she saw their light even with her eyes clamped shut. She took a deep breath through clenched teeth and forced herself to look up at the invader. She would meet whatever it was head-on. And she would find a way to make it bleed.

But it was gone. Stray flares of light danced in the area where the crack had been, but there was no sign that the thing had ever been there. The deep gouges made by its claws had vanished and so had her arrow.

Li'or lowered her hands from her ears and looked down at her palms. They were painted red with her blood and a couple tiny motes of light danced around them. She hadn't imagined it. She clambered over to where the darkness used to be and touched the ground with a trembling hand. Not a speck of dirt was disturbed except for a spray of what looked like black ink. Blood. She touched it and it stuck to her like tar.

Strange frantic desperation seized her then and she dug into the earth with her fingers and nails like an animal. The soil this far into the mountains was thin and hard and she broke her nails against random stones, but she didn't care. There had to be an explanation. Things didn't just appear and disappear.

But there was nothing there. Just more dirt and rocks.

She took a trembling breath before standing back up. Her pulse was returning to normal, but her mind was running its own race. It didn't make sense. She'd seen strange winds, then strange shadows, and now this. There were rules in nature and these things broke all of them.

Hashkan.

She had to get back to Hashkan. If there were more, she couldn't let him face whatever it was alone. She took two hesitant steps backward, then turned and sprinted back to where she hoped he was still waiting for her.

* * *

Li'or rushed around the boulders and into the hiding spot, bow still in hand, panting.

"Hashkan," she breathed with relief.

He was shuffling through papers from his satchel and jumped when he heard her.

"Is everything alright?" he asked, concern coloring his voice. He glanced behind her like he expected a herd of zhu'dac to come charging up through the trees. He crammed his paper back in his bag and moved towards her. "You're bleeding."

What she was doing was losing her mind, and she couldn't handle tenderness. She held up a hand and shook her head. Hashkan frowned but honored her request and stopped.

"I'm fine. Have you seen anything?"

"Seen anything? Like what?"

"Blackness. Or heard a terrible screeching."

"Li'or... no. Nothing has happened. What are you talking about?" He spoke to her like he was talking to a spooked horse.

She tucked a few loose pieces of hair behind her ear, then scoffed when she remembered the blood. "I saw something in the forest just now. You won't believe me when I tell you."

Hashkan gave her a comforting smile. "We've seen lots of strange things lately. It can't be that bad."

"Oh, but it is." She rubbed at her forehead where her

brows were drawn tightly together and exhaled until she was out of breath. Then she told him.

He listened with rapt attention. She appreciated it, but she couldn't help but notice the way his face changed during her tale. At the start, he was open-minded, but his face closed off the further she got into the telling. Apprehension and skepticism. He didn't believe her, just like she'd expected.

"You're not kidding, are you?"

"I'm not."

"Li'or... how's your head? You hit it on the ground pretty hard when the bul'arc ran through. Are you still having headaches?"

"There's nothing wrong with my head!" She gnashed her teeth. She should have known he'd act like this. "Look, I wouldn't believe me either. It's ridiculous, but I know what I saw. It's not the first time I've seen something like this either. When you were on the patrol, I saw snatches of black darting around the streets in Straeth. I saw the wind shift outside of Breen like a Weaver had grabbed ahold of it. I thought I was seeing things then, but I wasn't. Weird things are happening. Why is this so hard to believe after what you've seen with the Fabric?"

Hashkan crossed his arms and stared at the ground. Li'or gave him time to process everything she'd told him and, finally, he sighed and shoved a hand through his dark hair.

"I believe you," he said.

"You do?"

"I do. When we were in Straeth, I thought I saw a leaf float upwards. It fluttered like it was falling, but it went up, back into the tree. I wasn't looking right at it so I just assumed I was mistaken, but I wasn't. I know that now."

Relief swept through Li'or. She wasn't alone. She wasn't hallucinating.

"I think it's all related to whatever they're doing in Gilderan."

The idea hit Li'or like two flints sparking. It made perfect sense. Whoever was gathering the army had discovered direct Altering and could control zhu'dac and bul'arc. Why wouldn't they be able to affect nature hundreds of miles away?

But what was that rift and the dark creature? Had they created it or- worse yet- were they summoning it from somewhere?

"I'm afraid you're right," she told Hashkan.

"They're building an army, they use direct Altering unethically, and now this," he waved his hand like he was clearing away smoke, "darkness. We can't let this go on."

He looked back at her with eyes like steel.

"No. We can't. And we won't. Emond is our top priority. We free him and we take out whoever is in charge afterwards if an opening presents itself."

"What about all the people like Stach?"

Li'or paused for just a moment. He wasn't going to like her answer.

"Ideally, we'll sneak in and they won't notice us, but we can't afford to hesitate. If they get in the way, we go through them."

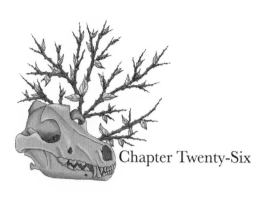

Chapter Twenty-Six

The Teeth of Some Giant Beast

Fear had found a new home in Hashkan's chest and it was settling in for a long stay.

When Li'or had burst out of the trees, she'd been closer to panic than he'd ever seen her, but after working out something of a plan, she'd settled back into her stalwart calm, leaving Hashkan the only one who was unbalanced.

He worried at his cuticles while they slowly made their way along the trail until they reached one of the rare clearings found this far into the mountains. Li'or slipped gracefully from her saddle and starting untacking her gelding.

"We should leave them here. There's some steep ground we'll have to climb and some compromised areas ahead and we'll be better off on foot."

Hashkan dismounted hesitantly. "Will we be able to find them again? After…" After they faced down the creator of nightmares.

"They shouldn't go far, but maybe not." She pulled the

bridle off over her horse's ears with a bitter smile. "I hope we do. This is the nicest horse I've had in decades."

Decades. It struck him that he still didn't know her age.

"Li'or, I apologize if this is rude, but how old are you?"

She stroked the horse's neck one more time before turning to face him. A familiar sad smile tugged at her full lips. "I stopped counting after one hundred. Didn't see the point anymore."

For the second time that day, he was at a loss for words. She could have easily passed for twenty-something, but she'd seen over a century pass by. She probably thought of him as such a young fool. And she'd be right.

"Come on," she said, shaking him out of his thoughts. "Help me with the mule and Emond's horse. Grab whatever food you can carry."

They made short work of distributing their dwindling food stores and set back out on foot. Li'or led him off the path and up a steep hill beside a hollow. Loose rocks sent his feet slipping out from underneath him and he cursed under his breath. No matter how hard he tried, he couldn't move with half of Li'or's grace. He tried to force the thoughts down and focus, but the nagging voice in the back of his mind just wouldn't go away. He was a liability again.

They trailed behind Emond's captors until late in the afternoon. The path changed from just a scattering of footprints into a proper road beaten down by hundreds of feet and it was finally leading them out of the mountains. They wound steadily downwards through the forest, with the sun dipping ever lower to their left and casting long shadows off the trees and scattered boulders. There were more places where the trail passed through gullies and Li'or, fearful of an ambush, led him up onto the rocky ledges hanging over the path.

By the third or fourth rise, Hashkan was panting and

sweating through his Weaver's robes. He wasn't made for this. The travel itself was manageable, and he'd adjusted to it, in his opinion, fairly well. Rock climbing was a different beast. He clawed his way over the ridge with his head down and his focus on hand and footholds. Efficient. He just needed to be efficient.

He looked up just before he ran into the back of Li'or's legs.

The elf took a half step forward to keep her balance and froze again, her gaze focused on the horizon in front of them. Hashkan stood and dusted off his knees.

"What is-" he started and then cut himself off, shocked.

A city lay spread out in front of them across a picturesque green field.

It was blinding. Every structure, even the thick wall encircling the city, was made of bright white stone that caught the fading afternoon light, sharpened it, and threw it back towards them like thousands of friction flares. Even the roofs on the buildings were white. The entire city looked like it had been carved from the same massive hunk of stone, it was so uniform. Hashkan couldn't find any words for how beautiful it was, the way it shined with all the colors of the sky. He realized he'd been standing there with his mouth hanging open and he closed it with a snap.

"Looks like the teeth of some giant beast, doesn't it? All white like that." Li'or's face and eyes were hard. It was the same look she would get before they charged a zhu'dac pack. Dread and determination.

Hashkan wrinkled his brow, struck by the difference in their observations. She noticed his hesitation and didn't give him time to ponder over it, or even respond.

"Look closer. Look at the details behind the grandeur."

Following her directions, he looked back at the city and

started to notice flaws that ate at it like a cancer. The wall was broken in several places, the stones blasted inward. Here and there more stones were piled up near the outskirts, waiting for masons. Buildings scattered around the city were dilapidated and falling into themselves, though it was obvious that people had been through and attempted to organize all the debris, likely in preparation for repairs to come. Further in, the size of the buildings grew, damage became less common, and the buildings had brand new roofs. In the center of it all, a hulking square keep rose up over all the other buildings, the towers on its corners stretching towards the clouds.

People- tiny specks from this distance- milled around and guards were walking along the walls. Hashkan suspected there were plenty of zhu'dac mixed in with the human guards, and all the humans were probably as tangled and warped as Stach. As they watched, a bul'arc lumbered past a gap in the wall, loaded down like a pack mule and being led by either a small human or a zhu'dac, Hashkan couldn't tell.

"What in the name of the Seamstress..." Hashkan breathed.

"Exactly."

"The strength it must take to control all those people, all those creatures. Whoever is doing this is a monster!"

"And they have Emond," Li'or said, her voice as sharp as her blades.

"I think he's probably in the keep somewhere. It doesn't look like they have a jailhouse set up so the dungeon is most likely in there." The word dungeon felt all wrong when he said it. He couldn't imagine his huge friend contained in a cage like that. "What do you think of our chances of sneaking in?"

"Not good."

She dragged her eyes away from the city to face him again. The light that reflected from it bounced off the multiple colors in her hair, making them glow and highlighting her high cheekbones.

"You move loud. The whole city will hear you." Her lips tipped into a smirk.

Hashkan crossed his arms but gave her his most confident grin. He didn't feel it, but he would fake it until he did.

"Then we just have to hit them hard and fast. So, how do we get in?"

*   *   *

HASHKAN PROTESTED, but Li'or insisted that they bide their time for the afternoon and start towards the city in the dark of the night after they'd had a chance to rest and plan. She settled down against a tree and racked her brain as she watched the people and beasts of the city mill around below her. She hadn't expected it to be quite so organized. It looked a lot like what she would have set up if she'd been in charge of a city. Originally, she'd expected to be able to slip quietly into Gilderan once night had fallen, but there were too many guards on the shattered walls to be able to simply walk in. Where the walls were weak, they'd been reinforced with extra manpower and the intact areas were too tall to scale without ropes and stakes. Their only ally would be the darkness, but they'd need perfect timing and no small amount of luck to get inside unnoticed.

When the answer to how they would get inside the walls didn't make itself immediately obvious, Hashkan started pacing like a caged animal, back and forth and back again along the edge of the rise. If he *had* been an animal, Li'or imagined that his hackles would be raised and he'd be snarling.

"I don't think they can see us up here, but if you keep marching back and forth like that, the movement is bound to catch someone's eye," she told him.

Hashkan stopped and forced both hands through his hair with a heavy sigh. The gesture left a few dark locks sticking up at odd angles.

"I can't figure out how to get in there! This is basic strategy and I can't figure it out!"

He stomped over to the tree she was leaning on and sat down next to her with a grunt.

"There's no such thing as basic strategy," Li'or said.

"Tell that to the authors of all the manuscripts on warfare in Straeth."

"I'd be willing to bet that not a single one of them ever did any of the actual blighted fighting or they wouldn't dismiss any part of this as 'simple'."

Hashkan just snorted at her and started methodically plucking blades of grass from the paper-thin soil.

"I think I have a plan that will work."

That got his attention and he dropped the shredded grass and turned to face her.

"Do you remember those soldiers talking about the shift changes for the watch?"

Hashkan crossed his arms and gave her an indignant look. "It wasn't that long ago, Li'or."

"Don't be an ass or this isn't going to work."

He drew in a long breath and uncrossed his arms. "I'm sorry, you didn't deserve that."

She nodded, glad he was willing to cooperate so easily. "Thank you. Now, just listen for a second and tell me what you think. It's simple, but it should work. First though, how's the Fabric been acting?"

"It's still not normal. I haven't seen another big upheaval, but the closer we get to Gilderan the more the Threads seem… distorted."

"Will you be able to Alter?"

"I have been. I don't see any reason that it would change."

She didn't like the ambiguity in his answer. A large part of her plan relied on him being able to Alter with precision. It was still going to be their best option, though, so Li'or cleared a small bit of ground and drew in the sand while she explained her plan. They would have to move fast and they would have to time their approach perfectly, but most of all they would have to be silent.

When she mentioned how important stealth was to her idea, the muscles in Hashkan's jaws clenched and she knew he was doubting himself again. That look had crossed his face too often since he'd returned to Straeth, and Li'or hated it. When she'd first met the young Weaver, he'd needed a good dose of humility, but not like this. Not coupled with so much self-loathing.

"You'll be fine. If the plan works, it'll just be men that we're sneaking past and nothing that can *actually* hear worth a damn," she reassured him.

"Of course," he murmured. He stood back up and started his pacing again, further away from the ridge.

Li'or lounged by the trees, resting and waiting, as the sun became just a sliver of crimson on the horizon. Neither of them had much of an appetite, but Hashkan finally stopped pacing and joined her by the tree to force down a few mouthfuls of dinner while they waited. They'd need the strength, and there was no way of knowing when their next meal would be, if there would be a next meal at all.

Night settled in and the moon rose, whisper-thin and

casting hardly any light. As they waited for the lights in the city to dwindle, a thick fog drifted down over the world. It limited their vision and gave every sound a strange muffled, echo-like quality, but it would help. The guards' sight would be just as limited, if not more so. They would likely be night-blind from their torch light.

"Well, this isn't ominous at all, is it?" Hashkan asked, a wry smile on his face and a veil of water droplets clinging to his hair. Li'or studied him. The tension in his back and shoulders exposed the lie in his attempt at humor. He was on edge.

So Li'or smirked and stamped her own fears down with an iron heel. He didn't need to know how afraid she was that the city would be filled with whatever had tried to claw its way out of the rift. He didn't need to worry about how they'd hide their scent from all the bul'arcs down there. She shouldered it all and let him see the confidence that she didn't feel.

"We'll slip into their city like wraiths on the wind."

With night draped around them, they left their vantage point and crept out of the foothills towards the empty plain surrounding the city. They passed through one last cluster of trees and then they were out in the open, keeping close to the road that wound towards the eastern gate. A chill crawled up Li'or's spine like it was a ladder. This was a killing field, meant to leave incoming armies exposed, and it did its job well. She felt defenseless, but what other choice did she have?

They dashed across the field in spurts. Li'or led Hashkan from one dip in the ground to the next, sticking to the deeper shadows. Their dark cloaks helped hide them, and Li'or kept their movements sporadic. If a guard on the wall were to notice their advance, she made sure they stayed still long enough between sprints that they would lose interest. It made for a slow and tedious crossing, but it was the best way to move when there was a Weaver in tow. He tried his best, but he still made too much noise and didn't crouch as low as she would have preferred. It would do, though. It would have to.

Halfway across, Li'or veered them further away from the road and angled them towards a large gap in the northeastern wall. The hole would easily allow five bul'arcs to pass through abreast with some room to spare. Thankfully, Li'or didn't see any of the beasts nearby, just six ordinary-looking soldiers. They wore the same tan and green uniforms as the men in the mountains, but each one was armed with a spear and a shield. Torches burned in tall stands set evenly in the gap and the guards paced between them in time with the men on the walls. Li'or squinted up at them and scowled. Crossbows. Perfect.

Lying down on her belly in a shallow ditch, Li'or watched the guards a little longer, studying their cadences and habits. She wanted to know as much as possible about them before they made their move. Hashkan shuffled up and dropped down beside her.

"Do you two see what these walls are made out of?" he whispered to her. "They're solid marble, even the insides. Look, you can see where they're broken."

She'd noticed the walls some time ago, but dismissed it. She didn't need to know what they were made of, just how to get past them.

"There was wealth here, no doubt about it."

"And all that rubble, even that's worth a fortune. What could have possibly blown such huge holes through walls that thick?" Hashkan mused.

"Rak-Shai."

Hashkan nodded thoughtfully. "No wonder it took the Gifting for us to put an end to them."

"They aren't *ended*, we just sent them back home. Now shut up and watch," she said with enough bite that he didn't offer any argument.

The guards continued their monotonous marching for hours. They were surprisingly- and disappointingly- vigilant. Li'or lay in the shallow trench with her muscles cramping and Hashkan fidgeted like a child after eating too many sweets. Half of Li'or's energy was spent watching the guards, the other half on making sure Hashkan didn't attract any attention. Finally, when she thought her frayed patience was about to snap, the new shift arrived.

Li'or had kept them waiting for this specific moment. Their best chance at sneaking in would be right after the swap was done and the earlier shift was gone. She'd watched long enough to know that no other guards passed through the area surrounding this gap in the wall. The only ones they'd have to distract would be the ones on this shift, with no other guards due to arrive for hours to come.

The shift changed with hardly a word exchanged between the soldiers. The earlier shift stalked off into the city and the new shift picked up where they left off. Exactly where they left off. They were too far away to tell for certain, but Li'or could have sworn they were even walking in the same footprints. A chill pricked at her skin. She shoved it aside with the rest of her worries and reached for her bow.

"Are you ready?" she asked Hashkan.

"Yes." And he sounded it. His voice was firm and resolute.

She slowly strung her bow, careful to avoid any creaking, and readied an arrow. "Alright then. Let's move."

Li'or rose to her knees and aimed her arrow to hit the ground just outside of the ring of light made by the guards' torches. She turned it loose and it impaled the ground with a muffled thud. The closest guard gave a start and turned towards the sound.

"Did you hear that?" he called out to the others.

Li'or nocked and shot another arrow, this one still aimed outside of the light but closer to the wall.

This time all the guards heard it and turned towards the sound. Li'or got silently to her feet with another arrow ready to go. Behind the guards, the torch flame closest to Li'or was starting to flicker and shrink. Tiny flecks of light almost like sparks danced around it.

Hashkan followed behind her, and as they started to creep closer Li'or shot another arrow into the wall. The metal arrowhead skidded across the smooth marble with a hiss.

"Whoever you are, get away from there!" another guard ordered and they all started to move in the direction of the sound with shuffling, unsure steps. Behind them, the flame shrank even more. They were too busy blinking into the dark to notice the light fading.

Li'or broke into a trot and fired off two more shots in rapid succession, one hitting the wall and the other thunking into the dirt farther off. With threats on their lips, the guards jumped out of their protective ring of light and into the night, spears held in loose defensive positions that could easily be turned into attacks.

At the same time, Li'or sprinted forward and Hashkan dashed along behind her. The dying torch in front of them finally gave up the last of its light with a puff of smoke and they plunged into the shadows it created. Li'or kept her footsteps as light as she could, but the Weaver's were heavy behind her and her blood rushed through her veins with a spike of anxiety. Hopefully, the guards were far enough away and there was enough yelling that they wouldn't hear.

They drew even with the wall and Li'or had to force herself to breathe. Halfway past the thick barricade, she dared to hope. Then they were inside the walls and still running with no sign of pursuit behind them.

She didn't slow even a hair's breadth and led Hashkan across a wide unpaved street before disappearing into a narrow alley between two abandoned and collapsing buildings. The echoes of their steps bounced off the crumbling walls and she finally slowed them down, her sharp eyes picking out their path through the dark. With a quick glance over her shoulder, she saw that Hashkan's eyes were wide as he kept his focus on the Fabric. She was glad he was still alert.

The alley spilled out into an unlit cobblestoned street. Li'or waved Hashkan back and crept up to the edge to peer around the corner. By her estimation, it was past midnight, but the empty street that greeted her still raised half a dozen warning flags. There were no beggars huddled on the corners, no drunks staggering home, not even a guard. Unnatural in any city.

But at least there weren't any bul'arcs.

She waved Hashkan forward. He stepped in close with a wide, almost feral grin across his face.

"Did you see how much control I had with the air and the flame? By the Seamstress, Li'or that was-"

"Hush!" she hissed at him. "We aren't safe yet."

His face fell. "But we made it through."

"That's part of the problem. We're in enemy territory now and I want to get out as quick as we can. Preferably while it's still dark."

"Okay. So to the keep?"

Li'or nodded and glanced out into the empty street

again. Another pitch-black alley opened up across the road and to the right of the one they were in. "If we're lucky, we can stay off the streets most of the way there. Stay close behind me."

Just before she took her first step out, a voice carried around the corner and echoed down the road.

"Everyone look alive! We've had suspicious activity at the walls! Be wary of an archer!"

Li'or's breath caught in her throat. She hadn't expected such a quick and coordinated response.

A trio of soldiers carrying halberds came around the corner. One stayed at the end of the street and the other two continued on. The second one stopped right in front of the alley she and Hashkan were hiding in, leaving the third to go down and stand guard at the end of the street.

A string of curses formed on the end of Li'or's tongue and she bit them back. There would probably be guards stationed here for the rest of the night. She'd inadvertently ruined her own plan.

She hated the thought of what she'd have to do, but they were short on options and running shorter on time. She caught Hashkan's eye. The Weaver was wide-eyed and tense as she mimed her plan to him. When she was done, he looked even more confused, but that couldn't be helped either. He'd just have to follow her lead.

She inched as close as she dared to the edge of the alley and, in one sharp motion, she grabbed the guard by the mouth, jerked him back, and kicked an ankle out from under him. He fell hard, and Li'or helped him along the way, cramming his head into the ground and knocking him out cold. At the last second, she caught his halberd just under the blade to keep it from clanging on the stones. She passed the polearm to a stunned Hashkan and grabbed the unconscious man under the arms. In no time, she had dragged him into the shadows.

Hashkan bent down and started going through the soldier's pockets while she crept back towards the street. She had worked fast, and with any luck, the other two soldiers wouldn't have noticed anything. She and Hashkan could time it right and dash across to the next alley once he was done checking the guard for anything useful.

But it wasn't meant to be. While she peeked out into the street, one of the other guards glanced back in her direction. His eyes widened and his jaw went slack, but then he put his fingers to his lips and gave an ear-piercing whistle.

"Hey! You there!"

"Shit," Li'or hissed. She grabbed Hashkan by his robes and sprinted out into the street.

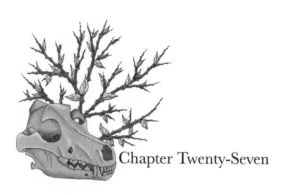

Chapter Twenty-Seven

Guests of Honor

*M*ore yelling came ringing down the alleyway after them, accompanied by the pounding footsteps of the two guards from the street. Li'or clenched her fist as tightly as she could around the fabric of Hashkan's robe and dragged him along behind her. The Weaver cursed while his collar tugged against his throat and he struggled to keep up with her.

The alley came to a junction where the buildings backed up to each other and Li'or hung a hard right, Hashkan staggering around the corner behind her. His shoulder clipped the stone and he yelped. Li'or gave him another hard tug. He had to shut up if they were ever going to lose them. And he had to move faster.

They swung wide around a pile of stones and passed under some flimsy scaffolding that spanned the width of the passage.

"Rip it down," Li'or ordered as soon as they were

safely out from under the planks. They needed to buy a little time- just a few extra seconds- so she could think.

"I don't know if I-"

"Just do it, gods-damnit!"

Hashkan stumbled again as he pulled, but then the satisfying crash of timber resounded around them.

Li'or let go of Hashkan's robes and they took another corner that pointed them back towards the north and towards the street. They shot out into the open air of a broader boulevard.

And right out in front of another trio of soldiers. Hashkan's steps slowed and she glanced back to see him hesitating, surprise painted across his face.

Li'or muttered another curse and reached for Hashkan's arm. If they stopped to fight these guards, it would only give the others more time to find them *and* they'd probably bring more help. She pointed them to the right again, down the street a ways and towards another alley. With any luck, they'd be able to shrug this group off more quietly than the last.

Hashkan jerked to a stop so suddenly that Li'or was pulled back onto her heels. She spun around, braid flying like a whip. His hesitation had cost them. A soldier clung to his arm wearing a startled look that was quickly melting into dangerous resolve.

Without a second thought, Li'or ripped her sword free and dropped the blade on the guard's wrist. Blood sprayed and stained Hashkan's robe and the guard reared back with a wail. Li'or didn't allow herself to look back at the guard as he sank to the ground, didn't let herself think about how young he was. They had to keep their momentum.

If they get in the way, we go through them. She'd hated the words even as she'd spoken them what seemed like ages ago, but she wasn't surprised that they'd come true.

They raced through the city, enthralled guards trailing behind them like hounds.

"One more street," she huffed. Hashkan didn't respond, but lowered his head and pushed for more speed. The soldiers were near enough that Li'or could make out individual footsteps, not just a cacophony of noise.

They ran out into the road and Li'or veered them to the west this time. It would steer them further away from their goal, but hopefully, also help shake off the hunters they raced in front of. They'd turn back to the north at the end of this street, disappear down another alley, and try to find a place to regroup from there. They sprinted down the street and around the corner.

And froze.

A living barricade of dozens of zhu'dac and three bul'arc blocked the way. They all turned towards Li'or and Hashkan in one eerie movement that was so *wrong* it made Li'or sick to her stomach. The zhu'dac yipped and growled as they started to creep forward, weapons and claws just darker pieces of black in the night. One of the bul'arc bellowed and it seemed to shake the very cobbles of the street beneath them. There were too many for them to face alone. Their death strolled casually down the street while the guards kept gaining on them from behind.

Hashkan moved forward to shield her and when he brushed against her, Li'or started from her shock like she'd been slapped. Her mind jumped forward at a gallop and she grabbed at Hashkan again, dragging him down a small side street to the right, back toward the north and the center to the city.

Hashkan snatched his arm free as they fled down the street.

"I can run faster without your help!"

"Well, do it then!"

Guards started to spill into the street behind and there wasn't an alley or connecting street to be seen. Winded as they were, they'd be easy to catch.

"Hashkan, do something!" Li'or yelled at him.

"What can I do?" He sounded frantic.

"Anything! Just buy us some time!"

He slowed and looked over his shoulder. Behind them, the soldier in the front and closest to the edge of the street gasped as his leather vest pulled away from him, then lurched sideways as it snatched him along. He teetered into the soldier beside him and they tripped over each other's feet, making their bodies into obstacles for the guards behind them.

A few of the rearmost guards managed to jump or dodge their way around their falling companions and kept coming, their weapons drawn.

"Keep moving! And do that again!"

Hashkan obeyed and more of the guards tumbled. They slowly pulled away from the pursuit and turned down another street on the right side of the road. They stayed on it only long enough to find another alley to disappear down.

"I don't know how much longer I can keep running," Hashkan panted behind her.

"You don't have any choice."

Guards ran into the alley behind them.

"I've got them," Hashkan said.

Li'or didn't even turn to see what he did. The panicked yelling was reassurance enough and she continued on her desperate race.

They crossed over two more streets, picking up and shaking off more pursuits as they went, before Li'or changed their course and turned them back towards the west and towards the walls. They'd no sooner made that turn before they were faced with another cadre of monsters blocking their way.

"You've got to be kidding me," Li'or muttered as they slid to a halt.

Hashkan was gulping air beside her, his face and lips pale with exertion, and she wasn't in much better shape herself. Her legs felt unsteady and sweat ran into her eyes.

A bul'arc shoved its way out from behind the zhu'dac and reared to its full height, drool running off its fangs as it roared.

Li'or whirled around, ready to drag Hashkan back the way they'd come, but she drew up short again.

Another mixed group of men and monsters ran around the corner behind them and spread out across the road, closing off their retreat. Li'or blindly groped behind her until she caught Hashkan's robes and pulled him against her. They stood back to back while Li'or's eyes darted up and down the street looking for any possible way to escape. Another alley, another street, scaffolding leading to a rooftop- anything that would give them a way out from between the closing ranks of soldiers.

There was nothing. There were no alleys and repairs had reached this street, shoring up the walls and doing away with any wooden supports.

A squeak of hinges grated against her ears and Li'or turned to see a man walk out of a house she'd assumed was empty. He was dressed in nothing but nightclothes and a grim expression, but he was carrying a sword. More doors opened and more people stepped out of dark and empty houses looking like they'd stood straight up out of bed, grabbed their weapons, and walked out to line up for a charge.

"What is this place?" Hashkan asked, panic and disgust blending together in his words.

Li'or's sword and dagger hissed as she drew them from their sheaths. She was afraid- it was impossible not to be. She forced herself to shove it down and put it from her mind. She had been prepared for this the entire trip north and she wouldn't let Hashkan or their opponents see how much she was fraying at the edges.

"This is where we make it all count."

Hashkan shuffled his feet behind her. "I don't know how much more I can do…"

There was more vulnerability in his voice than Li'or had ever heard.

"You don't have a choice *but* to do more, Weaver. You can give more, or you can give up. I'm going to take out as much of this bastard's army as I can, so if you're going to lay down, stay out of my gods-damned way," she told him in a voice like iron.

He took a trembling breath but straightened behind her, even as the Gilderians closed in. "I'm with you, Li'or. Until there's nothing left."

The men from the houses were almost upon them. Li'or shifted her left foot back and lifted her blades.

"Then let's make sure Emond hears us," she said.

The closest soldier stepped within her reach and she lashed out with her sword while a battle cry ripped its way free from her chest. Hashkan yelled behind her and fires from a torch on the end of the street jumped free and soared into the face of another soldier.

Li'or turned herself loose. She didn't expect for herself or Hashkan to see the other side of this fight, so there was no need for caution, no need to keep an eye on the Weaver as she fought. She just needed to make this blighted city bleed.

She spun like a whirlwind into the next guard. Sword and dagger flashed in the light of the torches and spun away, already setting up her attack for the next guard foolish enough to come close. Flares of light danced around her while Hashkan hurled more flames and the screams of men and zhu'dac alike rebounded off the marble walls of the city.

Thought and reason left her as she pirouetted from soldier, to zhu'dac, to soldier again, losing herself to the rhythm of the fight. Battles always seemed like elaborate board games, with rules and consequences to every action, but when she fought like this, she could understand why people called it a dance. She had no plan, no goal other than havoc, and she moved with the flow of the attacks, slipping through gaps in her enemy's guard and leaving a trail of blood as she went.

Light and heat rolled to her left so she pivoted to the right, picking a new target. Panicked screams were cut short where the fire landed, and nothing but silence came from before her when she drew her dagger across a soldier's throat.

She rolled on, never staying in one place any longer than it took to attack once, then spiraling off to the next opponent to keep them all on their toes. It wasn't long before her movements were hindered by the need to avoid bodies lying on the ground, both bleeding and burning. But still, she moved forward. Her arms ached and her lungs burned, but still Gilderians kept coming, so she kept freeing them from whatever enthrallment was holding them hostage.

More came, with even more behind them. Li'or's sword and even her light dagger felt like lead in her hands. She kept darting between attackers, but she was slowing. Her dodges and near misses turned into slashes in her armor and shallow cuts that blended her blood with that of the Gilderians. Friction flares flashed around her almost constantly, but Hashkan's fire came less and less often. A tiny voice in the back of her mind told her that her exhaustion was making her hallucinate, that the tiny motes of light weren't really there, but a zhu'dac's blade bit into her arm and the voice vanished.

She gritted her teeth and lurched backward out of the zhu'dac's reach. She was turning to seek out another target when a blow to the head sent her world reeling. Her vision blurred and tilted as pain exploded just above the base of her neck. She stumbled. Everything slowed to a crawl. A body lying in the road caught her feet and she slammed hard onto the ground. She tasted blood and more friction flares danced around her, but whatever Hashkan was doing it didn't help.

A foot stomped down on her sword hand and the world narrowed down to that singular point as pain crackled through her fingers. She bit back a cry and rolled to slash at the bastard's ankle, but another set of hands grabbed her wrist. They bent it and twisted and a sharp pain flashed up her arm. She gasped as her dagger clanged down onto the stones. Rough hands grabbed her by the arms and hauled her back up to her feet.

But she wasn't done fighting yet.

A growl rumbled in her chest and she flung herself towards the man holding her left arm. The one on her right clenched down on her injured wrist, twisting it again. The pain made her knees buckle.

Li'or swallowed the scream and the tears that threatened just below the surface, instead coiling her legs underneath her to try again, but then she saw a flash of dark hair and froze.

Hashkan was draped between two more guards.

Unconscious or dead, they dragged him by the arms towards the center of the city. Li'or's heart squeezed so tightly it seemed to stop beating entirely. She'd been ready for them both to lay down their lives, but she wasn't planning on ever having to actually see him do it. She thought she would go first.

The guard behind her grabbed a fistful of her hair and wrenched her head back to face forward. When she still didn't move, he kicked the backs of her knees, sending her back to the ground. The others dragged her a few steps before she stumbled back upright.

"That's right, heathen, move along," he spat. "You're the guests of honor."

Li'or ignored him, focusing on Hashkan's body as it trailed behind the soldiers in front of her.

There wasn't a part of her that didn't hurt when they finally made it to the square in front of the keep. Her shoulders ached from trying to break free and the more time that passed, the more it seemed like her right wrist was broken. In front of her, Hashkan's head lolled side to side as he struggled to regain consciousness. Li'or's relief when she first noticed his movement had nearly brought her to tears.

Without a word, they were both unceremoniously dumped back onto the ground. One of the guards jutted a leg out at the last second and tripped Li'or so that she cracked her knees against the cobbles. This new pain shuttered up her spine, but she bit her lip and held in her reaction. The bastards wouldn't get any more satisfaction from her.

"Finally. I was starting to think I wouldn't get to meet you tonight," a deep voice carried across the courtyard.

Li'or looked up and at the owner of the voice. He was tall, broad-shouldered, with dark hair and eyes and short stubble shadowing his jaw. A thin scar ran over the edge of his chin where no hair grew. He strode towards them with the confidence and grace of a seasoned fighter. Even if he hadn't been in uniform, there would have been no mistaking the danger he presented- even a child couldn't have missed it.

It was his eyes, though, that made the hair on Li'or's arms stand on end. They had the same unnatural lack of focus that she'd seen over and over again since coming to this city.

Then a second man drew up beside him and her breath stopped, locked in by the tightening of her chest.

Emond.

His eyes looked straight at her, but they didn't focus either.

Chapter Twenty-Eight

A Real Friend

*T*he world was a blur that rose and fell around Hashkan.

How much longer before they landed in Breen? The blighted rocking of the ship made him more nauseous than any night of drinking ever had and it never stopped. The cot he'd been given was as hard as stone.

He rolled over, the world heaving underneath him, and a woman with long light brown hair came into view. Hashkan squinted and slowly she came into focus. Sprays of blood colored her face and body, ran down her arms to drip on the ground. Her ears rose to delicate points that poked through her hair.

She was on one knee beside him, her teeth bared. In front of them, a blond behemoth of a man and a smaller darker haired soldier stared down at them. And they weren't on a ship, they were in a courtyard. Not in Breen, but in Gilderan.

A cold sweat beaded across his forehead. That was

Li'or covered in blood beside him. Then his pulse jumped and his stomach roiled again. That blond monster of a man was Emond, and he glared down at Li'or and Hashkan without a shred of recognition.

The dark-haired man took a few strides towards them and crouched down until his face was level with Li'or's. He reached out and grabbed her by the chin, turning her head to one side, then the other. As he studied her, the Threads around him seemed to all lean away from him, creating odd gaps in the Fabric where darkness peeked through. Hashkan gasped and his breath caught in his throat. The dark man didn't notice him, but Emond turned his attention to where Hashkan still laid.

"What I'd really like to know… is how you resisted the efforts of my recruiter," the stranger drawled. "I can't afford any mistakes like that in the future."

Li'or's face wrinkled in distaste and she spat. Red flecked across the man's cheek and jaw and he recoiled. Emond lunged forward and planted a kick directly in her stomach. The air left her with enough force that even Hashkan could hear it as she doubled over. Shock showed across her features as the pain crumpled her.

"Yeh will treat Lord Ordelieus with respect, elf bitch!"

"It's alright, it's alright, Emond," the man named Ordelieus said. He calmly pulled a handkerchief from his pocket and wiped the blood and spit from his face. "I'm sure your old friends just didn't know who they were talking to."

Hashkan struggled to his knees against the bile rising in his gut. He instantly regretted it when it attracted the lord's attention. The man casually tucked his handkerchief away as he studied Hashkan with his head cocked to the side. The Threads around him strained to get away.

"Ah, Hashkan. A fellow Weaver. Let's do this the easy way. Tell me why you didn't return here with Degan."

His voice was firm and commanding, with no room for negotiation. This was a man used to getting his way without a second thought.

Hashkan swallowed the lump in his throat and opened his mouth to answer.

"Shut up, Hashkan," Li'or croaked. She was struggling to her feet with an arm holding her stomach. "Emond, I'll get you for that when this is over."

"Over?" Ordelieus lifted a brow and swung his attention back towards her. "You don't expect to get out of here alive, do you? I control this entire city, this entire corner of Anagovia. You're very brave, going on this scouting mission for Klevelt- even more so for trying to sneak in for your friend- but you never had a chance. It was only a matter of time before I found you. And no one leaves here of their own free will. They go only if I send them. Now, one more time. How did you resist Degan?"

"I don't have a rutting clue who Degan is, but I hope he's rotting," Li'or said through clenched teeth.

"You met him in Straeth."

A man with long blond hair and cruel twist to his mouth came to mind and Hashkan paused on one knee.

Ordelieus pointed towards him. "This one remembers. So, will you be civilized, then, and answer me? How did you resist?"

Hashkan staggered onto unsteady feet and looked to Li'or. She focused on Ordelieus, almost without blinking, but he knew from the set of her face that her mind was whirling, desperately trying to come up with a plan. Hashkan looked to the sides and dared a quick glance behind them. To his horror, while they'd talked to Ordelieus, a loose ring of men and monsters had formed around them. Trapped again. He balled his fists to keep his hands from shaking.

"Maybe he just wasn't very convincing." Li'or's voice dripped loathing.

Ordelieus scoffed. "Hardly. He was one of my best. He was difficult to replace."

Those words broke through the last thin layer of dignity that Hashkan had been clinging to. Emond would be impossible to replace. *Li'or...* there would never be someone like her, anywhere, ever again.

"What did you even need us for? Why do you need any of these people?" He sounded pathetic and desperate, even to his own ears. Li'or gave him a sidelong, reproachful look out of the corner of her eye before turning her attention back on their captors.

Ordelieus strolled back over to stand next to Emond. He stood surveying the small army around them for so long that it seemed like he was going to ignore the questions entirely.

"I've worked with lots of soldiers over the years, both good and bad," he said softly. "You three would have been very good, valuable soldiers. If I'm going to capture and hold the Silver Gilt River basin, I'll need lots of good, valuable soldiers."

Hashkan took half a step back and his eyes went wide. Capturing and holding the basin? It would be a long and bloody war, especially with Weavers on both sides. The number of lives that would be lost... He looked back over at Li'or, but if the admission surprised her, she didn't let it show. She stood as steady and still as a statue, her face set in a grimace that did little to hide her disgust.

"You can't have us," she finally said. "We'd rather die."

Her words hit Hashkan in the gut like physical blows, but he knew they were true. A life enthralled the way these people were- the way Emond was- would be a twisted, pitiful excuse for a life.

"After all the casualties the two of you have caused, that's exactly what I was thinking. Emond, let's see how good you are. Deal with them."

＊＊＊

LI'OR WAS RUNNING before Ordelieus was even finished speaking. She grabbed the smaller hidden dagger out of the top of her boot and charged the man, her focus on his throat. This ended now. She'd kill this tyrant, free the city, and this nightmare would be over.

She made it halfway to her goal when Emond stepped in front of her, his hammer swinging in an arc that would end at her head.

Li'or dropped into a slide, skidding across the stone of the courtyard as the hammer whizzed over her head with a gust of air. The rough cobblestones ate through the worn leather of her pants and into her skin. It left a trail of blood as she slid past Emond's armored legs. Friction flares scattered around her as Hashkan pulled Emond off balance. Instinct had her reaching out to hack through the thick tendons on the back of Emond's knees, but she pulled her dagger in at the last second. She wanted to free him, not maim him.

Once she was out of range, she leapt back onto unsteady feet and lurched towards Ordelieus again. All she needed was one solid blow. Even if the bastard took his time bleeding out, she could stall Emond long enough for him to come back to his senses.

Emond was powerful, but he was slower than she was, even in her state of exhaustion. No one stopped her from closing the last remaining feet to her target. She twisted and threw all her weight behind her slash.

And froze in mid-swing. Every muscle in her body strained but she couldn't move even a hair's breadth.

"Impressive," Ordelieus said coolly. He studied her with raised brows. "It really is such a shame for all that talent to go to waste. I hate that I only caught one of you in the mountains." He casually flicked his gaze off to the side.

The result was anything but casual for Li'or. What felt like thousands of minute, clawed hands grabbed at her clothes and at the scruff of her neck and lifted her bodily from the ground. With the ease that she would toss away an apple core, Ordelieus flung her across the courtyard. She tried to tuck into a roll to break her fall, but he snagged her again and held her body rigid.

She landed on her right shoulder with an audible crunch. Her vision went black around the edges as the pain broke over her like a tidal wave and she bit back a cry.

"Li'or!" Hashkan yelled.

She heard his footsteps before she saw him as she struggled back to her feet. He reached back and grabbed an orb of fire from a Gilderian's torch and hurled it at Ordelieus. The other Weaver just batted it aside with a lazy sweep of his hand. To the east, the faint glow of dawn peeked over the roofs. The torches would be extinguished soon and Hashkan would have nothing else to throw. And Emond was barreling towards them. Hashkan strained and jerked Emond's leg out to the side. Their friend fell to one knee.

"Are you alright?" Hashkan asked. Hysteria tinted his words.

Li'or was far from alright. Her wrist was broken, maybe her shoulder too. She was bleeding from dozens of small wounds. All she had to fight with was the dagger she used to cut meat. "Never better, Weaver," she said with a groan as she finally found her feet. "Try to keep Emond distracted."

She didn't give him a chance to respond before she peeled off again. Every step sent a fissure of pain from her shoulder to her wrist, but she pushed it down to where her fear and despair tried desperately to free themselves. They could still win as long as she kept her focus. They had to.

Hashkan's cry split the air behind her.

Li'or staggered to a stop and spun around in time to see Hashkan hit the ground. He barely managed to roll out of the way of Emond's hammer as it fell in a savage overhand swing. The momentum of the hammer dragged Emond forward with it and, when it slammed into the cobbles of the square, dust exploded around them.

"Hashkan, grab him, gods-damnit!" Li'or yelled as she rushed back towards the Weaver. He didn't have a chance sprawled out like he was.

"I'm trying!" he shouted back. "The Threads are squirming like snakes. I can't grab them!" He scrambled backward away from Emond as their friend readied another killing blow.

"Just deal with Ordelieus!" she roared and she rammed her good shoulder into Emond.

He was easily twice her weight, but her momentum was enough to make the warrior stumble. It wasn't enough to make him drop his hammer, however. Gouts of flame exploded around her as she struggled to regain her own balance. Emond, fresh and unimpaired as he was, had an easier time and turned towards her, his entire weight behind the blow as he swept the hammer towards her ribs.

Years of habit, of muscle memory taking over during a fight, made Li'or step inside Emond's reach and drive her dagger into the gap under the arm of Emond's chain shirt.

She gasped and retracted her blade when the warmth of his blood hit her skin, but it was too late. She could have easily hit a lung.

She retreated as he chased her, shouts coming from Hashkan as he flung everything he had at Ordelieus who just shrugged it all off and watched their desperate fight like he was judging a training match. Emond's chest heaved as she dodged his attacks and Li'or prayed he wouldn't start coughing blood. Her right side had gone numb and her dodges were dangerously slow, but she couldn't bring herself to press any opening that Emond gave her.

Claws dug back into her skin and she was lobbed through the air. This time she flew past the gathered crowd and slammed against a marble wall. She slid down to land on her hip and injured shoulder. Stars exploded behind her eyes. The urge to curl up against the pain was almost over-powering and she nearly gave in until Hashkan careened into the wall beside her.

He grimaced as he rolled away from the wall. Blood stained his teeth. His silver eyes found her- lighter from so much Altering- and he struggled to smile as he fought his way to his feet.

"Li'or," he breathed, "I'll do better this round."

Her heart clenched painfully in her chest. She wanted to tell him that he'd already done well, that he'd done better than any Weaver could have hoped to do, but Emond was running towards them with his hammer ready. She dragged her broken body off the ground and fell into a weak defensive stance- for all the good it would do her, wielding what amounted to a table knife against Emond's war hammer.

Ordelieus's voice cut across the square. "Hold!"

Emond froze in place, not even blinking as Ordelieus

sauntered up next to him. Emond kept his eyes on Li'or and Hashkan, but with a small gesture from Ordelieus he lifted his arm. Blood ran down his side from the small but deep wound Li'or had made, small air bubbles peppering the red swath. She *had* hit a lung.

"If the two of you would just stay there a moment. I'll fix this and we can continue testing out the new recruit."

A *test?* Were they so pathetic in his eyes that all this amounted to was an assessment of a new underling?

The now familiar claws of Ordelieus's Altering grabbed hold of her, locking her in place down to the very marrow of her bones. Hashkan fought against it next to her, but she leaned into it. If he was going to hold her in place, he could hold her up too, and she'd rest her weary muscles for as long as she could. She was so spent she doubted it would help much.

Then Ordelieus worked a miracle.

Li'or held her breath. Slowly, like ice forming over a lake, Emond's wound began to close.

"Impossible," Hashkan whispered.

"Evidently not."

"He'd have to place everything back exactly as it was. All of the thousands of Threads. The precision... it's inhuman."

The phenomenon overwhelmed him, and he stood in his invisible bonds with wide, shining eyes. Li'or wished she could share in the wonder with him. Her mind went down a much darker path, one with dire consequences for herself and her friends.

"We can't win," she murmured.

"What?" Hashkan turned his rapt gaze to her.

"He'll just keep healing him while we keep being worn down. And we're fighting with handicaps. Serious ones."

Her arm and shoulder throbbed in time with her heartbeat. "We can't beat him."

"Li'or, surely-"

"Look at me, Hashkan!" she hissed through bared teeth.

He looked at her, really looked at her, then. His eyes focused the way normal human eyes did- on flesh and bone instead of on Threads. On the blood covering her like a cloak and the way her arm hung limply at her side. Worry lines creased the skin between his brows.

He hesitated and Li'or watched a herd of emotions pass across his face in the blink of an eye. Then he said, "We can't lose. He'll be trapped here. We can't leave him like this. He's a slave!"

Li'or swallowed as she fought against the despair that freed itself at his words. It slammed against the cage of her ribs and tried to rise up her throat. She thought of Emond when they'd first run into him in the forest. He'd fought like a monster, true, but the real man was the one that showed when he laughed at his own cheesy jokes, when he fell unabashedly in love with a woman he'd just met... when he told her to wait for Hashkan in Straeth. A real friend.

"No, we can't," she finally croaked out.

"We'll have to..." Hashkan closed his eyes and looked away from her, back to Emond, who looked at them without seeing.

"We have to end it for him and take him with us."

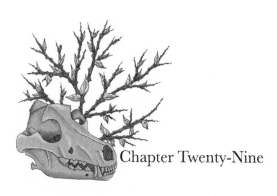

Chapter Twenty-Nine

Fractured

*L*i'or wished she had been more prepared. If she had been well-rested and better armed, things might have turned out differently. With one usable arm and barely a weapon to speak of... she couldn't have hoped for much else. She watched as Ordelieus slowly knitted Emond back up and felt every one of her muscles getting stiff as the exertion of the night finally caught up with her.

And they had to kill Emond.

She'd pictured this ending so differently.

Ordelieus stepped back and studied the pale patch of skin that had replaced the puncture wound she'd put there. Emond's chest expanded and relaxed with ease, the damage repaired from the inside out. Satisfied, Ordelieus nodded to himself, then turned his attention to Li'or and Hashkan. His eyes narrowed.

The claws that were supporting Li'or suddenly

vanished. Her weary muscles couldn't respond in time for her to catch herself and she toppled to the side. Hashkan threw his hand out in the blink of an eye and a softer Altering braced against her, holding her upright until she was able to regain her balance.

Ordelieus scoffed. "Quick learner. What a waste." He turned his back on them and started to walk away. A dismissal. And a sign they'd been judged and found to be utterly unthreatening.

Hashkan looked at her, questions forming on his lips, but there was no time. Emond launched into a renewed assault, uninjured and strong and fast.

Li'or shrugged out of Hashkan's Altering and half limped, half ran the few steps it took to meet Emond's charge. She wasn't going to hold back this time, wouldn't be impeded by worry over hurting him, but she wasn't sure it would make much of a difference. Her body screamed in pain and she was slow, so damned slow. Hopefully, Hashkan would be able to wrestle some more cooperation from the misbehaving Threads or this fight would end before they'd be able to end it for Emond.

The Vaeshekian bellowed and swung his hammer towards Li'or's wounded shoulder. She ducked at the last second but tripped on blighted flat ground and barely caught herself with her good hand. The stone scraped through the skin of her palm and added blood to one of the few clean places left on her.

Friction flares sprang to life around her, but she couldn't wait to see what Hashkan was working. Emond tossed his hammer towards the crowd of soldiers that still circled them and was handed a lighter and- gods, help her- faster arming sword. Before she could pick herself up, he was already sending the blade on an executioner's path to her neck. She coiled her legs underneath her and dove forward, landing in a roll that jarred her arm and shoulder again and brought tears to her eyes. She followed through and was up just in time to jump backward and avoid being eviscerated by a nasty backhand swing.

The fabric of Emond's pants flared out from his calf and then jerked to the side. A small smile tipped the corners of Li'or's mouth as she gasped for breath. Hashkan had found a way to help. Emond staggered to the side, then backwards as Hashkan jerked on his gear and threw him off balance. Li'or's smile vanished as she lunged forward again to press the advantage Hashkan was giving her.

But they'd forgotten Emond wasn't alone. Before she could reach him, a blast of wind broke against her. She dug in and braced against it, gritting her teeth and leaning into the gale while her hair and cloak snapped behind her. Emond, of course, was completely unaffected. He jabbed his blade back towards her and she stumbled away.

Too slow, she was too slow again. The sword point skimmed across her leathers then hit skin as she twirled, tracing a line of fire-bright pain across her ribs.

Hashkan yelled her name, but it was background noise, drowned out by the roaring of her blood in her veins. The wind let up, but it was the briefest of respites before Emond attacked her again. He came at her one precise slash after another and she dodged again and again, trying in vain to hit his wrist with her knife. She felt her body growing heavier as the strength in her muscles dwindled. A swarm of friction flares orbited around them, whether from Hashkan or Ordelieus she couldn't tell.

Ordelieus's voice cut across the square. "Son of a bitch!"

Li'or looked over just in time to see a glob of flame burst against the stones at Ordelieus's feet. The man's uniform was singed on one shoulder.

The distraction cost her. She saw the sword at the last second, but it wasn't soon enough. The blade sheared across her forehead, around her scalp, finally taking the tip of her ear and a chunk of hair with it. As with any head wound, the blood ran freely. More red. In her hair, in her eye. It was already coating the handle of her knife so that it was slick in her hand. She took a shuddering breath, her entire body feeling like it would shake apart, and squared herself back up with Emond. She had to tilt her head awkwardly so she could study him out of her only remaining clear eye.

She called over her shoulder, "Hashkan, I need your help here." If he didn't focus on the fight with Emond, they would be killed and their friend would be trapped and twisted into a tool. Nothing of the man's soul would be left. She could only hope that he didn't realize what he was doing.

"He was open, Li'or, I had to try," Hashkan apologized and the flares around Emond increased. The warrior rocked back, but he was strong and broke loose to attack Li'or again. She felt the wind off the blade as it hissed by, she so narrowly avoided it.

"I'd forgotten how difficult it can be to deal with insubordination." Ordelieus brushed ash off his coat. He shivered and screwed his eyes up tight, then squared his shoulders and turned to Hashkan. "Luckily, I don't have to be so patient anymore."

Emond took another broad swing at Li'or. She stepped into it again, past the blade. An arm like a tree branch slammed into her sliced ribs, bruising her already ravaged skin, but creating another opportunity for her to attack.

Or so she thought.

Emond hooked a booted foot around her ankle and ripped it out from under her, at the same time the arm she'd grabbed drove her into the cobbles. She reached to catch herself- to roll, to do anything to help the fall- but she used the wrong hand. Her wrist gave out, bent at an unnatural angle, and she collapsed. She heard herself scream, but it was like it was coming from somewhere else, the pain was so consuming. She dropped her knife and cradled her wrist against her chest.

Emond turned away from her and ran towards Hashkan. Black spots clouded her vision and mixed in with the friction flares that still swarmed her.

"Shit... Hashkan, forget about me..." she muttered through the pain. Her words barely came out. He didn't hear her. Emond launched his first attack, a vicious thrust that Hashkan barely avoided. "I hope your Seamstress protects you."

She was met with Ordelieus's laughter.

"Your Seamstress is a lie!" Ordelieus said, laughing even louder. "She's not real! Mankind had no idea what they were getting into when they meddled with the Fabric, but it certainly wasn't a gift from some," he waved his hand in a dismissive gesture, "*mysterious* new goddess." His voice and the cadence of his words had changed, like he was used to speaking in another language. It reminded Li'or of the lectures in the Seamstress' Gatherings.

"What did you say?" Hashkan was frozen, his eyes wide.

Emond clobbered him.

Even if he hadn't been distracted, he wouldn't have had a chance in the world to avoid the blow. Emond's fist swung around in a backhand that was almost too fast to follow. It took Hashkan in the side of the neck and he crumpled like a child's discarded toy.

"You bastard!" Li'or cried across the square. She struggled to get back to her feet, but her own blood was slick on the stones of the square and her feet slid uselessly across the ground. "He's just a kid."

"He knew what he was getting into when he decided to come here." Ordelieus's voice had returned to its normal baritone. He looked to Emond.

The Vaeshekian raised his sword. It hovered in the air over Hashkan's bared neck.

"Don't you dare, you whoreson!" Li'or's scream ripped out of her throat. Tears mixed with the blood streaming down her cheeks.

The sword began to fall. Li'or watched it cut the air, all her attention on the flash of the blade like it was the only thing left in the world.

Another scream tore out of her and she screwed her eyes shut tight. She couldn't watch him die. She couldn't go to her own grave with the image of Hashkan's death in her mind. But the image of the Weaver lying there wouldn't go away. It was engraved in her mind's eye, fractured into thousands- *millions*- of infinitesimally thin pieces. She wished she had more arrows, more knives to throw.

Blasts of wind swept back through the courtyard from every direction, pummeling into Li'or. She was buffeted from all sides, trapped in a column of air that lifted her hair into a wild cyclone around her.

And lifted the blood.

Friction flares exploded into existence around her, brighter and more plentiful than she'd ever seen them. Droplets of her blood rose up with them, darting around like sparks from a campfire. The drops collided, forming larger bubbles that floated around her, then folded in on themselves, condensing into something else entirely.

The wind died as suddenly as it had come and Li'or sat in the middle of a cloud of a dozen blood-slicked arrow-heads. She was still as stone, shock locking her joints in place like a statue.

"What...?" Ordelieus whispered, his eyes wide. Emond froze, his blade inches from Hashkan's throat.

The world fractured around Li'or again, and suddenly she realized what she was seeing. It wasn't her mind break-ing. She was seeing the Fabric.

And she knew what she needed to do.

How the arrowheads had gotten there- whether from her or from something Hashkan had done in his subcon-sciousness- she'd make good use for them. She grabbed the Threads to each and every one and whipped them towards Ordelieus.

The bolts rocketed through the air faster than even Li'or could have shot an arrow. Ordelieus, his eyes still wide with shock, threw his hands up. The Threads writhed like snakes around him and a few of the projectiles were knocked off course. They crashed against the ground and shattered like glass.

But Li'or's aim was true, and the ones he didn't deflect met their mark. In his arrogance, Ordelieus wasn't wearing any armor under his coat. The arrowheads drilled into his chest. Bright red stains blossomed against the dark green and tan fabric.

Ordelieus stumbled back. He looked across the court-yard at Li'or and met her eyes. She stared, stunned, as the strange flatness left his dark gaze and his eyes slowly focused on her. His brow creased and he looked down at himself, at the red splotches that continued to spread. He pressed a hand over his heart and when he pulled it away, blood stained it as well. He coughed and a gout of crimson spurted from his lips.

"Milla," he choked out. "Pinescar…"

Lord Ordelieus staggered and he collapsed to the ground into a growing pool of red.

Chapter Thirty

To Pinescar

*T*he world seemed to hold its breath when the man fell and the last of the friction flares faded around him.

For one agonizingly long moment, Li'or thought the city was still enthralled. Emond stood, frozen, his sword still poised to strike at Hashkan's throat. Li'or gathered her strength to try to stand, then Emond released a long trembling breath.

"Hashkan, lad!" He tossed the sword aside and fell to his knees next to the Weaver. Li'or watched as he felt for a pulse, her heart in her throat.

"Thank the Seamstress," Emond said. He sagged with relief but jerked upright and whirled around a heartbeat later. "Li'or? Li'or!"

She knew she must have looked rough, but if Emond's face was any indication she looked like death. He rushed over to her.

"I'm fine," she said, trying to wave him off. Her flinch gave away her lie. "Mostly fine. Help me up."

He gingerly looped an arm around her and helped her get to her feet.

A shriek split the air.

The rest of Ordelieus's captives were shrugging out of their bonds, just as the sun crested the horizon, huge and blood red. Zhu'dac and bul'arc roars echoed through the streets. Li'or wasn't surprised when a small group of men ran over to them while the rest of the gathered soldiers took off to deal with the creatures.

A young, heavyset man came forward.

"Are you folks alright? We're not sure what's going on, but if you need help getting somewhere safe…" He stumbled over his words and trailed off, uncertain.

"Alright? Do yah think she looks blighted-"

"I'll be okay. You've got bigger problems to deal with." A bul'arc roar reverberated behind them as if to prove her point.

The soldiers hesitated, then nodded and turned back in the direction the others had gone. Li'or watched them jog off until she couldn't see them anymore, then she extricated herself from Emond's supporting arm. She thought about going to help with the monsters. They had more than enough soldiers, but from what she'd seen, not nearly enough officers to keep them organized. Then her eyes drifted back over to Hashkan and she knew she couldn't.

So, she limped over to the Weaver and slumped down beside him. Using her good arm, she reached over and shifted him into a more comfortable position. Her hand left blood on his robes and she scowled.

Emond ran to the other side of the courtyard and returned with some fabric and stiff leather from what looked like an armory and rigged up a brace and sling for

Li'or's ruined right arm. They made a piece of his shirt into a bandage for her head. She looked and felt like she'd escaped a war zone.

"Thank you."

"Not to worry, Li'or. Now, if only our Weaver would come 'round." He sat down with her to wait.

"Li'or?" Hashkan's silver eyes finally cracked open a half-hour later and he tried to sit up. Li'or gently pushed him back down.

"Give it a second." The way his eyes didn't seem to focus meant he either couldn't shift his gaze yet, or he had a head injury. "You've got to quit passing out on me."

He started to laugh but cringed and put a hand to his head. There was her answer. A head injury.

"Li'or," Emond interrupted. "Since Hashkan's up now, I have a few questions on me mind. What was I doin' before? When... yah know."

"What's the last thing you remember?"

"Hashkan did his trick with the fire- right smart, by the way. I ran around and then... nothin'."

Li'or closed her eyes gave a tiny relieved sigh. Emond never would have forgiven himself if he knew he'd hurt them. It was better if he never found out.

Hashkan slowly drew himself up. "A lot has happened since then."

Between the two of them, they were able to give Emond a detailed account of what they'd been through since he was taken. When Hashkan started to explain the confrontation with Ordelieus, Li'or glared at him and took over. She glossed over Emond's involvement and treated the whole fight like it had been a stroll through a garden. She hated to lie, but the truth would have been more harmful. It was better than breaking their friend's spirit. If he questioned anything, he didn't voice it.

Finally, Li'or got to the point in the story they'd both missed- and the part she'd been avoiding addressing herself. She told them about the strange arrowheads and what she'd done with them.

"How did you do that?" Hashkan breathed. He stared at her with open wonder.

She looked down at her blood-covered hands. "I was hoping you would know."

"Obviously, yah missed yer callin' as a Weaver, Li'or," Emond piped in.

"Weavers can't make things out of thin air, though, Emond. We would have never ended up in this situation if I could have," Hashkan explained. He looked away and his eyes took on that haunted look she'd seen too often lately. Li'or knew he was blaming himself. Again.

"Stop," she ordered.

His shoulders curved in for just a second, but he pulled himself up straight and nodded. Then he looked back over at her and gasped.

"Li'or! Your eyes!"

"What about her eyes?" Emond crawled around to get a better look. "Well?"

"The gray in them has turned silver."

Li'or's head rocked back. "That's impossible."

"No, it isn't. When an apprentice works their first Altering, their eyes start to change just like that. A little at a time."

Li'or shook her head, "Hashkan, I'm too old-"

"Older than a normal human apprentice, yes," he interrupted. "But what if it's different for elves? You haven't spent much time with them, you wouldn't neces-sarily know. Maybe the materializing arrowheads had something to do with that."

"He's got a point," Emond added.

"When we get back to a city, we can have you assessed," Hashkan offered. "And if you want to start training, I'm sure you'd be welcome anywhere."

The thought of spending years at a Gathering, packed in tight with visitors and children studying, made her stomach turn somersaults. She changed the subject.

"What about the Fabric? Is it back to normal?"

Hashkan blinked and glanced around. "Yes, thank the Seamstress. Nothing out of the ordinary."

Li'or nodded, no more dark tears in the world, no more monsters reaching through. "Good."

Did Hashkan remember what Ordelieus had said about the Seamstress? If not, she wouldn't be the one to remind him. She'd carry another secret without complaint if it made his life easier. Besides, the man wasn't in control of himself, the way his eyes had changed proved as much. But who was controlling *him*?

His last words came back to mind, the way he'd almost pleaded for her to hear those final four syllables.

"There was one more thing that happened, right when Ordelieus died," she said over the lingering howls and roars of the creatures being chased from the city. They listened, looking more concerned as she went.

"We need to figure out who was using him or this entire nightmare will just repeat itself for someone else," Hashkan said once she'd finished.

"What we need to do is go back to Straeth and get the other half of our payment," Li'or said.

"Now Li'or, yah know yah can't just shove this all into the cupboard and forget about it. If I can bear to stay away from the love of me life, yah can bear to stay away from yer money. This Milla in Pinescar might have some answers."

"Excuse me?"

A thin, graying man walked up, flanked by another pair of the former Gilderians. His darker skin hinted at some distant Gnürian isle relatives.

"My name is Resken Breag. I was told you three were also refugees." He paused for a scant heartbeat before continuing on. "We found a map and we're getting everyone together to start towards the closest city. To Pinescar. If you want to go, we're gathering at the western gates."

"Well! Look at that, Li'or. Pinescar!" Emond grinned as he stood up and brushed off the seat of his pants. "We'd love to go."

Li'or scowled and hobbled to her feet, not dignifying his comment with a response. If it was the closest city, it made sense that it should be their next stop. And they were her friends. If they felt like they needed to do something, she would help. They would do the same for her. They *had* done the same for her.

"How many people are making the trip?" Li'or asked. She'd start planning out the watch schedules and how they could best move through the bogs that separated Shimmer Falls Lake and Pinescar.

"All of us." He walked a pace ahead of them, back straight and hands clasped behind him.

Emond gave a low whistle.

"Exactly. And we'd all very much like to know what happened here, if you have any ideas. None of us seem to remember."

"This will be a lot to take in," Hashkan began, "but it's all the truth, I swear it by the Seamstress…"

ACKNOWLEDGMENTS

Thank you to Candace, Bill, and my wonderful editor Kristin for steering me back to the plot every time the goblins tried to drag me off course.

Thank you to Krystal for being the most awesome, supportive friend anyone could ever ask for. Saranghae!

A very special thank you to Jaime, who didn't sign up to date an author, but has put up with me all this time anyway. Also, an apology, because it's only going to continue. I love you!

ABOUT THE AUTHOR

Sam Parrish was born and raised in the woods of central Florida. When she isn't working or writing, she enjoys horseback riding, camping, and fly fishing. She still lives in Florida (despite her escape efforts) with her boyfriend and their menagerie of animals. When the World Starts to Fray is her debut novel.